I0819276

Praise for
Where We Belong

"*Where We Belong* is a heartwarming, faith-filled historical novel that captured me from the first page. The theme of caring for orphans and children in need is dear to my heart, and that made the story even more meaningful. The small-town feeling and unique characters added depth and warmth. This book is well written, and I highly recommend it!"

—CARRIE TURANSKY, author of
A Token of Love and *The Legacy of Longdale Manor*

Praise for
Hope's Enduring Echo

"Honor, love, and duty collide with a young man's passion to pursue God's unique calling on his life. Love and sacrifice conflict with a young woman's desire for friendship and normalcy. Kim Vogel Sawyer paints a vivid picture of the struggle between chasing the dreams God plants in our hearts and our desire to please and honor those we love. She reveals the beauty of God's prevenient grace and provision in ways we could never orchestrate—and the ultimate weaving of exquisite tapestries in surrendered lives. *Hope's Enduring Echo* is a novel rich in friendship, faith, love, and the resiliency of hope. It's a story to lift your heart and warm your soul."

—CATHY GOHLKE, Christy Award Hall of Fame and author of
Ladies of the Lake and *This Promised Land*

"*Hope's Enduring Echo* is a beautifully written story about finding hope in a dark and shattered place. As a former Coloradoan, I loved reading the unique history that Kim Vogel Sawyer discovered in Cañon City and her poignant reminder about the miraculous ways God rescues and restores His children."

—MELANIE DOBSON, award-winning author of *Catching the Wind* and the Legacy of Love series

Praise for *The Songbird of Hope Hill*

"In *The Songbird of Hope Hill,* Kim Sawyer has penned an unforgettable story of God's grace and redemption. Birdie and Ephraim's love story is a parable for the love God has for us. You'll be thinking of these characters long after you've turned the last page. I know I still am."

—KATHLEEN Y'BARBO, *Publishers Weekly* bestselling author of *The Black Midnight* and *The Bayou Nouvelle Brides*

"Kim Vogel Sawyer blends affecting atmosphere, complex circumstances, challenging conflicts, and rewarding resolution in her latest historical novel, *The Songbird of Hope Hill.* In Birdie Clarkson, Sawyer has created that character we all yearn to comfort—the sinner who desperately craves love for her broken, humbled heart. One can't help but cheer for Birdie in her brave willingness to step forward into peace and freedom. This book satisfies our longing to experience again the kind of forgiveness and divine justice that only Jesus can grant."

—TRISH PERRY, author of *The Guy I'm Not Dating*

"What a precious story of God's grace and redemption! Kim Vogel Sawyer writes with poignant precision, weaving stories with depth that draw in her readers. *The Songbird of Hope Hill* had my full attention from its absorbing start to its tender finish, leaving me teary-eyed and longing for a sequel. Splendid!"

—SHARLENE MACLAREN,
author of twenty-three novels

"*The Songbird of Hope Hill* held my heart from the first page. Set in Texas in 1895, this touching story is about Birdie Clarkson, a good girl who was forced to make bad decisions, and Ephraim Overly, the son of a minister and his wife who want to save fallen women. That task proves to be a tough one, and secrets from the past haunt these characters like an ever-blowing prairie wind. Fans of Francine Rivers's *Redeeming Love* should enjoy this story of redemption and one young woman's need to find grace and forgiveness."

—LENORA WORTH, author of *Disappearance in Pinecraft*

"Kim Vogel Sawyer's *Songbird of Hope Hill* illustrates that no matter how often or how far we fall, God is always there to help us back up. Truly nothing—nothing—can separate us from the love of God."

—JULIANNA DEERING, author of the Drew Farthering Mystery series

Other Novels by Kim Vogel Sawyer

Beneath a Prairie Moon
Bringing Maggie Home
Echoes of Mercy
Freedom's Song
Grace and the Preacher
The Grace That Leads Us Home
Guide Me Home
Hope's Enduring Echo
Just as I Am
The Librarian of Boone's Hollow
Return to Boone's Hollow
Room for Hope
Still My Forever
The Songbird of Hope Hill
The Tapestry of Grace
Through the Deep Waters
Unveiling the Past
What Once Was Lost
When Grace Sings
When Love Returns
When Mercy Rains

Where We Belong

Where We Belong

An Orphan Train Novel

Kim Vogel Sawyer

WaterBrook

WaterBrook

An imprint of the Penguin Random House Christian Publishing Group,
a division of Penguin Random House LLC

1745 Broadway, New York, NY 10019

waterbrookmultnomah.com
penguinrandomhouse.com

All Scripture quotations are taken from the King James Version.

A WaterBrook Trade Paperback Original

Library of Congress Cataloging-in-Publication Data
Names: Sawyer, Kim Vogel author
Title: Where we belong / Kim Vogel Sawyer.
Description: New York, NY : WaterBrook, 2026.
Identifiers: LCCN 2025040297 (print) | LCCN 2025040298 (ebook) |
ISBN 9780593600856 paperback acid-free paper | ISBN 9780593600863 ebook
Subjects: LCGFT: Christian fiction | Romance fiction
Classification: LCC PS3619.A97 W455 2026 (print) | LCC PS3619.A97 (ebook)
LC record available at https://lccn.loc.gov/2025040297
LC ebook record available at https://lccn.loc.gov/2025040298

Printed in the United States of America

1st Printing

The authorized representative in the EU for product safety and compliance is
Penguin Random House Ireland, Morrison Chambers, 32 Nassau Street,
Dublin D02 YH68, Ireland. https://eu-contact.penguin.ie

Title page: Jon Ritchie / Adobe Stock

BOOKMAKING TEAM: Production editor: Laura Wright • Managing editor: Julia Wallace • Production manager: Richard Elman • Copy editor: Cara Iverson • Proofreaders: Tracey Moore, JoLeigh Buchanan

Book design by Diane Hobbing

In memory of Helen Haak Vogel, who unconditionally loved so many children—including my dad and me—as her own. She will always be the grandmother of my heart.

If God so loved us, we ought also to love one another.

—1 John 4:11

Where We Belong

Chapter One

New York City
March 1931
Callum Holbrook

The subway car hissed to a stop, and Callum found himself jostled to and fro by those hurrying to exit while others hurried to board. Such a crushing mass of people. More crowded, even, than the shift change at the factory because the subway tunnel was a narrower space. For a moment, he worried he'd be pushed back inside for another ride, but he took a sideways step and stayed on the platform. The doors closed, a bell clanged, and the car clattered into motion.

He blew out a breath of relief and joined the throng milling in the direction of the staircase that led to the city sidewalk above. He didn't use the underground railway much. No need to most days. But today wasn't like most days. A smile tugged at the corners of his lips, and he let it grow. Today was special—the start of being a family again.

A chill wind whooshed down the cement-walled staircase, carrying the mingled odors of garbage and fish. "'Tis the perfume of the Bronx," his Freida used to say with a laugh. He was so used to the smell he didn't even crinkle his nose. But the well-dressed lady moving along beside him, her heels click-clicking against the painted concrete floor, muttered something about a vile stench and wrapped a flowered scarf around the bottom half of her face. Her elbow bumped his shoulder, and she shot him a glare. He was tempted to glare back. After all, he wasn't the one at fault. But no snooty lady could take the shine off this day. He offered a polite "Excuse me," then bounded up the remaining steps two at a time and entered the flow of foot traffic on the wide sidewalk.

A shiver rattled through him, and he pulled up the collar of his tattered jacket. Not for the first time, he wished he owned a slicker to wear on damp spring days. Wool was fine for warmth, but it sucked up moisture—even misty drizzle—like a sponge. By the time he reached the block with the three-story, brown brick structure, the wet wool stank like a creek-dunked dog. Not that the jacket smelled any worse than he did after a week of work.

His feet slowed as he took in the Mission Church Home for Orphaned and Destitute Children, standing like a proud giant between humble single-family dwellings. Maybe he should've waited until he'd had his Saturday bath before coming to see his girls. Thirteen months had slipped by since his last visit to the orphan asylum. Would one more day matter? Then he shook his head. No, he'd made the trek across the city to give Evvie and Winnie his good news today. He opened the creaky iron gate and strode up the short pathway dividing two patches of sparse still-brown grass. He leaped onto the cracked concrete stoop outside the pair of tall wood-paneled doors and reached for the doorbell key. But something brought to mind the subway woman's sour look, and he paused and glanced down his length.

Ugh.

Tiny metal pieces scattered by the grinder peppered his clothes. Those little bits were sharper than glass shards. His hands bore tiny recent cuts and dozens of old scars from the flying fragments that wiggled their way under the leather gloves he always wore when he worked. The bits could get into a child's socks or shoes just as easily. He wouldn't risk the children being hurt. Even though eagerness to see his girls tugged at him, he stopped to yank off his newsboy cap and smack away as many of the shiny flecks of steel clinging to his work trousers as possible.

Satisfied the remaining shavings were too embedded in the rough fabric to fall free on the floor, he tucked his cap under his elbow, finger combed his hair into place, and finally rang the bell. Several seconds ticked by before the right-hand door swung wide.

A young woman wearing a plain brown dress and carrying a feather duster stood framed in the doorway. "Yes, sir? Are you here to see the property?"

See the property? She must've been expecting someone else. Callum cleared his throat. "No. I've come to see my girls."

A frown marred her narrow face. "Your girls?"

He remembered the woman. One of the asylum's housekeepers. But he didn't recall her name, and she didn't remember him at all. Shame hunched his shoulders. He'd gone too long between visits. "I'm Callum Holbrook. My girls are Evelyn and Edwina Holbrook." He leaned sideways slightly and peered beyond her into the shadowy foyer. By this hour of the day, the children would have finished their supper. They should be playing in the hallways or out here in the yard, but those areas were empty. The whole place was quiet. Too quiet.

A sense of foreboding fell over him. He jerked upright. "Miss, where are the children?"

She whirled on her heel and scurried toward the opposite end of the foyer. "Miss Armstrong! Miss Armstrong!" Her shrill voice echoed against the tin ceiling tiles.

Callum charged after the housekeeper. His heart pounded with such force he could hardly draw a breath. The girl disappeared beyond a doorway ahead, still calling for the asylum's matron. If Callum's memory served correctly, she'd gone into the matron's office. A gentleman would stop outside the door and knock before entering, but at that moment, Callum didn't much care about being gentlemanly. He rounded the corner so fast the damp soles of his old boots slid and he bounced his shoulder off the doorframe on his way in.

Wincing, he pointed at the stern-looking tall woman on the opposite side of a massive desk. "Ma'am, I'm here to see Evvie and Winnie Holbrook. Fetch them quick." Imagining how Freida would feel about his forcefulness, he added, "Please."

Miss Armstrong turned to the housekeeper. "Mildred, return to your cleaning." The younger woman scuttled past Callum, clutching the feather duster like a shield in front of her. Her footsteps faded away. The matron gestured to a ladder-back chair in front of her desk. "Please have a seat, Mr. Holbrook."

"I don't wanna sit, ma'am. I wanna see my girls." He crushed his cap in his fist. "I have a surprise for 'em. I've got a real good job now at the Remington Metalworks Factory. Been there a full three months. At the end of last month, I signed papers on an apartment with two bedrooms." Evvie was so big already she'd probably rather have her own room. But after sharing a room with a dozen other girls here at the asylum, sharing with only Winnie would still be mighty nice. "I've been rounding up furnishings and such, getting it ready, and now it's all set." None of the things were fancy. None of them were even new. But new and fancy didn't matter. Being together again was all that mattered. "So I'm gonna pull the girls from here today, and they—"

"Mr. Holbrook."

Callum went silent, but his mouth still hung open. He clacked his jaw closed.

The woman settled in her seat and held her hand toward the chair she'd pointed out earlier. "Sit down, please. We need to talk."

He could tell by her sad face this would be bad news. He'd rather take it on his feet. He'd stayed standing when the doctor told him his wife hadn't survived Winnie's birthing. He stood straight when the boss at the docks told him he didn't have a job there anymore. He stood through countless other bosses turning him away. Callum might not be educated or wealthy or powerful, but he was strong. He'd stand, no matter what Miss Armstrong said. He shook his head.

Miss Armstrong huffed out a sigh that let Callum know she wasn't pleased. "Very well, then." She linked her hands and looked directly into his face. "Your girls aren't here. Nor, as you've likely already discerned, are any of the other children. They've all been sent away."

"To another asylum in New York?"

"No, sir. They've been sent west."

His knees wobbled. Maybe he should have sat. He braced himself against the doorjamb. "Ma'am, you aren't making any sense. What does that even mean, 'west'?" Realization struck with as much force as a two-by-four against his skull. He staggered forward a few feet and gaped at her. "You don't mean *west,* do you?"

She sighed again, this time sounding more regretful than aggravated. "Mr. Holbrook, when you placed Evelyn and Edwina with us, you were informed of our involvement in home finding. Our mission has always been to see our children placed with families rather than forever residing in an institution."

He took another shaky step in her direction. "An' I told you the girls' being here was only for a while. Until Winnie was big enough to go to school." Winnie wasn't quite school-age yet, but Evvie was in her seventh year. That was plenty of book learning for a girl—two years more than either he or Freida got. She could take care of Winnie and the apartment.

Miss Armstrong stood and rested her fingertips on the desktop. "Mr. Holbrook, you must be aware that our country is in a difficult period."

He swallowed a snort. Of course he knew. He'd spent nearly two years moving from borough to borough, doing odd jobs for a meal while seeking employment that would let him earn enough to take care of his girls. He gave a brusque nod.

"The funds upon which we've relied to keep our doors open have dried up. We could no longer care for the children here. Families all across the nation are struggling. The successful home placing of children of the past decades has all but disappeared. If we were to find good homes for the children, we had to act quickly."

Why hadn't he come sooner? Remorse formed a knot in his throat, but a wave of anger pushed it down. "How could you send my girls away without talking to me first?"

"We tried." The woman lifted her chin. "Six months ago, when it became clear the asylum would be closing, we sent a missive to your last known residence. We sent a second notice three months after that, then a third six weeks ago. We received no response from you."

Callum looked at the floor, too ashamed to meet Miss Armstrong's gaze. When was the last time he'd gotten any piece of mail? Not since he lost the dock job almost three years ago and had to move out of the apartment he'd shared with a couple other fellows. How could he keep a mailbox when he slept in alleys or the stockrooms of stores? He had a little cubby for letters now at the tenement, but what good would it do him?

"We could only presume that something had befallen you and left the girls truly orphaned or that you'd changed your mind about wanting them."

Agony twisted through his gut. How could he make this lady understand? It had nearly killed him to leave after his last visit here. Evvie begged him to take her with him, and little Winnie clung to his leg like a monkey to a tree and sobbed even though she hardly knew him. Even remembering it nearly tore his heart in two. He hadn't wanted to put them through such an ordeal again, so he'd promised Evvie that the next time he came, he'd walk out the door with them. And now it was too late. Unless . . .

He raised his head so fast his neck popped. "Ma'am, you said the girls went west. On a train?"

"Yes. We put the girls on our very last transport."

"When?"

"It departed February 27."

Exactly three weeks ago. How far could a train get in three weeks? He inched closer to the desk. "Where was it headed?"

"There were planned stops along the railway in several small towns in Illinois, Missouri, and Kansas."

So many states. And all so far away. His mouth went dry. He licked his lips. "Where did my girls get off?"

Her forehead puckered, and she pressed her fingers to the furrows. "I won't know until the assigned guardians, Miss Harms and Miss Davis, return with the placement paperwork."

Callum tamped back a growl of frustration. "When'll that be?"

"To be perfectly frank, I do not know." She held out her hands in a gesture of defeat. "Evelyn and Edwina went with the last of our children—forty-two in all. In the beginning days of home placing, that many children could be chosen at the very first stop. These days? It might take more stops than children in need of homes to find suitable placements for all of them. However, for the benefit of our guardians, we chose Marion, Kansas, as the last stop for this final trip, and we prayed fervently that each child would be received into a loving home."

She settled in her chair again, like she was too weary to remain upright. "I realize this is a vexing situation for you, Mr. Holbrook, but I assure you the girls were not sent out of malice or indifference. We had only their best interests at heart when they were added to the list of potential adoptees. And what other choice did we have? We didn't know where you were, and the asylum was closing. In fact, the only reason Mildred and I are still here is to ready the property for sale while I await the paperwork that will allow me to complete my responsibilities as the matron of the Mission Church Home."

Callum cringed. He wasn't the only one who was losing something. "I'm sorry about you not having a job or a place to live anymore, ma'am. I truly am. I know what it's like to be let go and not have someplace safe and warm to lay my head. But I've lost something even more dear than a job. My girls are gone, and I've gotta get 'em back." He crossed the remaining distance in two big steps and stopped at the edge of the desk. Pressing his hat against his thrumming chest, he stared into her unsmiling eyes. "Will you please help me get 'em back?"

Chapter Two

Millersberg, Kansas
Hester Weber Haak

Hester gave her reflection in the vanity's oval mirror a slow perusal. Was she presentable? More important, did she look motherly? Presentable, yes, in her church hat with its cluster of wax cherries pinned securely to her tightly twisted chignon and with her tweed coat over her only dress with lace trim. Even her old pumps looked close to new with the fresh polish and shine. But motherly? Well, what did motherly look like, anyway? Presentable would do.

She turned away from her image and tugged on her best church gloves. The black kidskin didn't match well with her brown tweed coat, something that had never bothered her until today. Would something as simple as wearing black gloves with a brown coat make the child-placement people see her as slovenly and therefore unfit to guide an orphaned girl into womanhood? She closed her eyes.

Lord, I know I'm acceptable in Your sight, such as I am, but please let me be acceptable in their *sight. Grant me the desire of my heart.*

The prayer bolstered her, as prayer always seemed to do, and she hummed her favorite hymn, "Abide with Me," as she tucked a fresh handkerchief, some coins, and her small comb into her handbag. She reached for her lipstick, but her hand stilled before she picked up the silver tube. It would be foolish to apply it. She'd probably chew it off in nervousness before she reached Marion, and then her teeth would be red. Completely unpresentable and as far from motherly as a woman could get. No, the pale pink blush she'd brushed onto her cheekbones after doing her hair would suffice.

She gave her reflected image a quick nod of satisfaction, hooked her purse on her wrist, and headed out the back door. She took a step toward her vehicle and then drew up short. Her Ford Model T wasn't parked behind the house, where she'd left it after church last Sunday. She looked up and down the alley, confusion making her pulse skitter.

"Miz Hester?"

At her hired man's voice, she hurried in the direction of the call. "Scotty, my car isn't—"

There it was, waiting near the gas pump in front of the Corner Store. Scotty stood beside it, beaming proudly. He patted the shiny tan hood with his arthritic hand. "Tank's full to the top, an' windshield got a scrubbin'. Everything's ready for your drive to Marion." As she neared, he opened the driver's door. "Figured you'd be all gussied up to meet them children an' wouldn't want gasoline drips on your shoes, so I saw to it."

Dear Scotty . . . What would she do without him? He'd wandered into town only two months after Dale's sudden death. Some folks thought she'd lost her senses when she not only hired Scotty but also invited him to take up residence in the small storage area in the rear of the store. But she hadn't cared what others thought. In her grief-stricken state, she could barely function. She needed help, and Scotty was available. Over the past three years, she'd come to depend on his steady, always willing assistance in whatever she asked for. She relied on him, and she believed he relied on her.

She patted his wrist with her gloved hand. "That's so thoughtful. Thank you." She glanced beyond the automobile to the store, and worry nibbled the corner of her mind. It was early yet—not quite seven-thirty—but when the doors opened at eight, shoppers would come. She'd never left Scotty to see to customers all by himself. She shifted her attention to the wiry gray-haired man. "Are you sure you'll be all right? I hate leaving you to handle things alone when Saturdays are typically so hectic."

He chuckled and rubbed a gnarled finger across his whisker-dotted upper lip. "I reckon I can stack cans in crates an' measure out flour an' sugar good as you. Now, the tallyin' and collectin'—that can be troublesome. But your customers are trustworthy folks. They'll gimme the right amount o' money or write what they owe in the book. Don't fret none about what's happenin' here. Just git yourself to the train station an' pick out a little gal, like you been prayin' to do."

In her mind's eye, she envisioned the child she longed to call her own. A girl nine, ten, or eleven years old—old enough to be somewhat independent yet young enough to still need a mother's tender care. She'd be flaxen-haired, like Hester's dear Dale had been, with expressive hazel eyes and a cherubic face, and she would hold out her arms to Hester and embrace her as her new mother. Tears distorted her vision, and she blinked them away as she gave Scotty's wrist another quick pat. "I trust you implicitly. And I shall return as quickly as possible with the newest member of our family."

"Awww . . ." Scotty brushed his boot toe in the dust. "Git on with you, now."

Hester laughed. "Yes, sir." She slid in behind the steering wheel, and Scotty ambled to the front of the car and turned the crank. She fiddled with the throttle and choke, holding her breath as she always did until the engine revved to life. She loved this vehicle, Dale's last extravagant gift to her before the illness stole him away. But she often wished he were still here to drive it for her.

At the vehicle's first buck, Scotty backed up. Hester gave him a wave as she rolled past the store. She made a jolting U-turn at the corner, drove to Main Street, and took a bouncy right-hand turn south. Gripping the steering wheel with both hands, she squinted out the front windshield and chewed her lower lip. Behind her, Millersberg slipped from view. Ahead, Marion—and the culmination of her dream—awaited. If all went as she hoped, by lunchtime she'd be a mother.

Oh, Lord, please . . .

Marion, Kansas
Evelyn Holbrook

The sun beat down and scorched the top of Evelyn's head. Wind tried to tear the ribbon from her hair. There was plenty of shade on the depot porch in this little Kansas town. It was a good-sized porch, with more than enough room for the last of the kids from the Mission Church Home to fit, and the wind would be blocked some by the building. Why couldn't they stand there instead of out here on the grass in front of the smelly train that kept belching smoke? Nothing the asylum's guardians did made any sense, starting with putting her and Winnie on the train in the first place. She and her sister were not orphans!

While the younger of the two guardians, Miss Davis, stood in the row with the children, keeping an eye on them, the gray-haired one, Miss Harms, paced back and forth in front of the row of kids from New York and talked to the folks who'd come to gawk at them. She gave the same speech she'd given at every single stop since the group of children and their pair of guardians left the train station in New York almost a month ago. By now, Evelyn had heard it so many times she had it memorized. She recited the words in her head and held tight to Winnie's hand. She wouldn't let go of her sister. Anybody in that crowd looking at them had better know they were together.

"As you can see, these are beautiful, healthy children. They are well behaved and . . ." Miss Harms blathered on in a sweet voice.

Evelyn snorted under her breath. What would these fine people think if they'd heard how the guardian talked to her before shooing the group into the depot yard? Her ear still throbbed from Miss Harms's pinching fingers when she'd tried—again!—to convince the woman that she and Winnie needed to go back to New York. Miss Harms's harsh statements rang in Evelyn's memory in place of the speech being delivered to the audience.

"For the last time, Evelyn Holbrook, you cannot return to New York. You're a ward of the Mission Church Home, placed under my supervision. Therefore, you will do as you are told and get off this train." She'd grabbed Evelyn's ear and twisted it. *"You need a home, but no one wants to adopt an incorrigible child. You and your little sister will mind your manners this time or there will be dire consequences. Do you understand me?"*

Evelyn had muttered that she understood. But not what Miss Harms thought she understood. She understood that no one would help her and Winnie go back to New York to Daddy. Somehow she'd have to figure it out for herself. But first she had to make sure nobody took Winnie. At every stop so far, couples showed interest in her. Evelyn couldn't blame them. Winnie was adorable with Daddy's blue eyes and Mama's brown-gold wavy hair. She was small for a four-year-old, making her seem even younger. Folks had grabbed up the littlest kids first because they were so cute and the oldest boys second, probably because they'd be good farmworkers. Winnie was the only one younger than six still waiting for a family to take her in, and Evelyn was the oldest of the few kids left.

Evelyn scanned the crowd. Some couples whispered to each other, pointing at certain kids. Her gaze locked with a lady wearing a little felt hat with cherries wilting under the sun. Did the lady smile at Evelyn? What a silly thought. She inwardly laughed at herself and sent her attention elsewhere in the crowd. Sure enough, at least two couples were giving Winnie those dreamy-eyed looks that said, *Aren't you a cute little girl?* Miss Harms was getting close to the part in her speech when she invited folks to come up and meet the children. There wasn't much time left for Winnie to turn into the uncutest little girl ever.

Crouching down, Evelyn pretended to adjust the bow in Winnie's hair. She whispered, "Remember what you gotta do if somebody comes up to talk to you?"

"I gotta frow a really big fit."

"That's right." Winnie was amazingly good at becoming a little wildcat. When a couple at their first stop in Indiana tried to take her, she'd fought so hard to get to Evelyn the couple had changed their minds. Since then, Evelyn told her to do the same thing, and she'd scared off a dozen would-be parents. For someone so small, she was mighty. At least Evelyn didn't have to worry about someone wanting *her.* She was too big to be cute and too scrawny to be a good worker.

Winnie's lower lip trembled. "Miss Harms said she'd gimme a whippin' if I did it again. I'm a-scared, Evvie."

So was Evelyn. She wouldn't be able to stand it if Miss Harms hit Winnie. But it would be much worse if someone adopted her. How could she ever face Daddy if she let strangers take Winnie away? They'd have to risk Miss Harms carrying through on the threat.

Evelyn gave her little sister's hand a squeeze. "I'll take the whippin' for you. I promise."

Miss Davis leaned forward a bit and caught Evelyn's eye. She scowled and mouthed, *Straighten up.* Evelyn stood and faced the crowd again, keeping her grip on Winnie's small hand.

"If you decide you'd like to bring one of the children into your family, please see Miss Audrey Davis." Miss Harms gestured Miss Davis forward. "She will assist you in completing the paperwork to make the placement official. And now," Miss Harms said, throwing her arms wide, "come meet the wonderful children from the Mission Church Home. I know they are eager to make your acquaintance."

Evelyn rolled her eyes. Eager? Not her. She squinted and scanned the group. A few couples must have decided they didn't want any of the remaining kids, because they walked away. The rest moved toward various kids. Evelyn searched out the two couples who'd been admiring Winnie. Sure enough, both were heading in the girls' direction. Winnie must've figured they were coming for her, because she dove behind Evelyn and let out an ear-piercing screech. Several people jumped, looking their way, and both couples stopped.

Miss Harms marched over and caught Winnie by the arm. She yanked her from behind Evelyn and shook her finger at her. "Young lady, I warned you."

Winnie's chin crumpled, her eyes flooded with tears, and she burst into shrill wails. And she wasn't putting on a show. This distress was real. Evelyn reached for her, but the husband of one of the couples who'd eyed Winnie trotted over. He scooped Winnie into his arms.

She flailed her arms and legs and sobbed out, "Evvie! Evvie!"

Evelyn tried to catch hold of her, but the man turned away, giving Winnie a little shake. "Here now, settle down. There's no cause to take on so." He didn't talk mean, the way Miss Harms had, but Winnie was in a full-blown panic. Evelyn had never seen her so worked up. She skirted past Miss Harms, ignoring the guardian's dark scowl, and grabbed the man's jacket sleeve.

"Mister, lemme hold her. I can calm her down." But did she want Winnie to calm down? They wanted to scare folks away from adopting her. Confused, Evelyn dropped her hand and backed up a step. The man carried Winnie to his wife. The two of them patted her and talked soft and sweet, but Winnie craned her head around, her wide eyes seeking, and kept screeching for Evvie.

Torn between wanting to comfort her sister and wanting Winnie to scare off the couple, Evelyn stared at the scene with her fist pressed against her lips. Someone tapped her shoulder, and she jumped. The lady with the cherries hat stood close by, the smile Evelyn'd seen earlier still on her face.

"Hello. My name is Hester Haak. What's yours?"

Evelyn watched her sister buck in the man's arms. Her chest ached worse than her belly had when she stole an apple pie from the home's cook and ate the whole thing in one sitting. "Evelyn. Evelyn Holbrook."

Hester Haak held out her hand. "Evelyn Holbrook, it's very nice to meet you."

Miss Harms bumped Evelyn's arm, and Evelyn gave the lady's hand a quick shake. "Thank you, ma'am."

"How old are you, Evelyn?"

Evelyn didn't look away from Winnie as she answered. "I'll be fourteen in June."

"My, you're practically a young lady." Did the woman sound disappointed? If so, that suited Evelyn fine.

Miss Harms must have decided Evelyn would behave, because she excused herself and joined the couple who'd snagged Winnie. Evelyn sent a side-eye look at Hester Haak. She seemed nice enough. Lots of lines around her eyes, like she smiled a lot. She was the only lady all by herself. Maybe her husband hadn't been able to come. Evelyn blurted, "Where's your husband?"

The woman's smile faded a bit. "He's in heaven."

Evelyn hadn't expected that answer. What should she say? "So's my mama." She pointed at Winnie, who had stopped kicking but was still crying and pushing at the man who held her. "She died when my sister was born."

Sympathy pursed Hester Haak's face. She turned her head and seemed to stare at Winnie. Or maybe past her. She looked kind of dreamy and lost. "So you're almost fourteen, and you have a sister . . ."

"Yes. She turned four last August, in case you were wondering. And we have a daddy."

The woman jerked and faced Evelyn again. "You do?"

"'Course we do. We ain't orphans." Evelyn's throat went tight, making her voice growly. "Me an' Winnie shouldn't even be here. Her an' me are going back to New York. Those folks over there who've got hold of her can—"

Miss Davis suddenly had hold of Evelyn's arm. Why wasn't she helping people with paperwork? Evelyn glanced across the yard and blinked in surprise. Was everyone gone already? Of course, there'd only been seven kids left of the whole bunch who'd boarded the train in New York. Now she, Winnie, and a little boy named Guy—who sat on the edge of the depot porch, poking in the dirt with a stick—were the only kids left.

"Evelyn, go talk to your sister." Miss Davis spoke in a pleasant tone, but her eyes snapped.

She didn't say what Evelyn was supposed to tell Winnie, but Evelyn knew anyway. She was supposed to convince Winnie to behave herself and go with those people. She clenched her jaw so tight it made her teeth hurt. Well, she'd talk to Winnie, but she'd say what she wanted to, not what Miss Davis and Miss Harms wanted. "Yes, ma'am." She marched toward the man holding her sister.

Chapter Three

Hester

Hester watched Evelyn Holbrook stomp toward the little group surrounding the distraught child. When Hester had seen her in the yard holding the little one's hand, she'd presumed she was only helping with the younger child. She'd also presumed, given her slight frame, Evelyn was younger than nearly fourteen. Now the girl—young woman, really—walked with swinging arms and a stubborn jut to her chin. She certainly didn't match the image Hester had created in her heart concerning the child she hoped to adopt, yet something about the girl tugged at Hester.

The young woman who'd been introduced as Miss Davis gave Hester an apologetic smile. "You must be wondering why Evelyn and Edwina are with our group if they have a living parent."

Hester gave a start. "It's true their father is alive? The girl wasn't making up a wishful story?" How often had she entertained a similar fanciful tale throughout her growing-up years?

Miss Davis shook her head. "To be honest, we don't know what's become of the girls' father. He signed them into our keeping when Edwina was only a few days old. The mother died."

"In childbirth," Hester filled in, her heart rolling over in sympathy.

"Yes." Miss Davis sighed. "Mr. Holbrook simply couldn't care for a newborn and a young child on his own. His intention was to retrieve the girls when the baby was old enough to attend school, but his last visit to the home was over a year ago. That day, the girls made a terrible row, much as the one we witnessed today."

Hester glanced at the little group with the younger girl in its center. Apparently, whatever Evelyn said had dried up most of the little one's tears, but no one looked happy. As a matter of fact, the woman in charge of the children seemed ready to explode with anger.

"We don't know if their behavior made him decide he'd rather not take responsibility for them," Miss Davis went on, "or if something, perhaps an accident or illness, befell him and prevented him from returning."

The girls' story touched Hester for reasons she would never divulge. Her frame broke out with perspiration, and she released the buttons on her coat. "Has Evelyn been told about her father's lack of response? She seems to hold the belief that he's waiting for her and Edwina in New York."

The woman released a soft *humph.* "She's been told. But she refuses to accept it. It's clear to me she's schooled little Edwina to behave badly and dissuade anyone from taking her in. Ordinarily, Edwina is a delightful child. But Evelyn's ploy is doomed to failure. The girls cannot return to New York. The Mission Church Home for Orphaned and Destitute Children has become destitute. Its doors are now closed."

Hester frowned. "There won't be any other children in need of homes coming this way again?"

"I'm afraid not." Miss Davis lifted her gaze to the clear sky, as if seeking to draw strength from the cloudless expanse or perhaps the One residing beyond their view. "All other orphan asylums in New York stopped sending children shortly after the stock market crashed and it became evident that our country was entering an economic depression. If families struggled to feed their own, why would they welcome additional mouths around their tables? Our organization continued to attempt placing out children because we found it difficult to meet the many needs and had no other option for seeing that our charges were properly cared for."

She abruptly faced Hester. "The children here today are the very last in our care. When Miss Harms and I were sent on this final train of orphans, we were instructed to make a total of twenty stops, ending with this one. If these children are not placed with families today, they will be delivered to the poor farm here in Marion."

Hester's flesh prickled with another outbreak of perspiration. An idle, somewhat comforting thought trailed through her brain and left her lips. "If the couple decides not to take Edwina, at least the girls will still be together."

Miss Davis *tsk-tsk*ed. "I doubt that. Young people Evelyn's age are generally apprenticed out to families for a small fee, which helps finance the poor farm. Evelyn will see Edwina once a week if the people who employ her allow Sundays off. Otherwise"—she folded her arms—"Evelyn needs to let Edwina go with that nice couple. Unfortunately, Evelyn is too selfish to do what's best for her little sister."

Hester understood Miss Davis's point of view concerning Evelyn's stubborn determination to keep her sister with her. Being part of a loving family was preferable to living in a poor farm or an orphans' asylum. But there was another viewpoint the woman apparently couldn't see. All the girls had was each other. Little Edwina might very well forget over time that she had an older sister, but Evelyn would never forget being a big sister. She would wonder forever how her little sister was, where she was, whether she was happy. She would carry those memories like a millstone around her neck, always weighed down by what-might-have-beens.

The idea forming in Hester's mind now was ridiculous. She was widowed. She had a limited source of income. And her house was small. But maybe it wasn't so ridiculous. Two children wouldn't take up much more room than one. She'd prayed for a child. Might God have decided two were better? Would keeping these sisters together bring healing to the wound that had festered in her heart for more than thirty years?

A sigh, laced half with long-held regret and half with freshly inspired hope, escaped from Hester's throat. "I am quite interested in adopting Evelyn and"—she gulped—"Edwina. Is there paperwork I need to complete?"

Miss Davis's brows rose. "Truly? Well, that's an interesting turn of events." She curled her hand around Hester's elbow and guided her toward the depot porch. "Of course, if Miss Harms has already verbally approved Edwina's placement with the other couple, we'll have to honor that. But having the girls grow up in the same community would likely be a comfort to them."

"I don't live in Marion. I'm from Millersberg, a little town roughly eight miles north of here." Remorse struck. Would it be kind for her to take Evelyn out of Marion if Edwina lived here? If Evelyn resided at the poor farm, the girls' paths could still cross. But Millersberg wasn't far. Maybe Hester could drive Evelyn over on Sunday afternoons to visit her little sister. It wouldn't be the same as growing up together in one household, but it would be better than what Hester had experienced.

Miss Davis was speaking, pulling Hester from her inner thoughts. "It's customary for both the husband and wife to sign placement paperwork. Will your husband meet us here and finalize the arrangement?"

The familiar ache of loss filled the center of her chest. "I'm a widow."

Miss Davis stopped, drawing Hester to a halt. "A widow?" Furrows formed across her forehead.

"A childless widow." Hester wanted to add she had boundless love to offer a child, love she'd been storing up for years, but her throat closed and the words refused to budge.

Miss Davis snapped her fingers at the little blond-haired boy on the depot porch. "Guy, fetch Miss Harms for me."

The child lifted his head and blinked a couple of times, then tossed the stick aside and galloped in a clumsy gait toward the group several yards away.

Miss Davis escorted Hester to the porch, a worried frown marring her face. "I'm sorry, I didn't get your name."

Hester swallowed and used the name she still claimed as the most precious. "Mrs. Dale Haak. But please call me Hester."

"Hester . . ." The other woman's expression softened. "I suspect my tale about our intentions to deliver the children to the poor farm has stirred your compassion. You seem a very kind-hearted person. But taking in two children—"

"Three." Hester surprised herself more than she did the home representative when the word popped out of her mouth.

The woman gaped at her. "Three?"

"Yes, three." This time she spoke with conviction, absolutely certain she was doing the right thing. "That little boy—Guy—needs a home as well." No child should languish at a poor farm. Her house might be small, but she had more than enough room in her heart to love him.

Miss Davis closed her eyes for a moment, as if gathering strength. Then she pinned Hester with a serious frown. "Hester, taking in three children when you've previously raised none would be undertaking enough if you had a husband's support. The Mission Church Home has never placed multiple children with an unmarried individual. In fact, I can't recall a time they've placed even a single child with an unmarried nonrelative."

Hester wove her gloved fingers together and held tight to hope. "These are desperate times, though, are they not? Perhaps the Mission Church Home should reconsider its standards for placement."

The woman held out her hands in a gesture of helplessness. "How can that be done when the home is closing? We can't convene a meeting with a board that's all but dissolved."

"It seems to me the most important thing is to find the children appropriate homes." Hester spoke calmly although her pulse pounded like a bass drum. "I'm a business owner." Only a humble market, but it provided for her needs. "I own my home." A one-bedroom shotgun house, but it was clean and warm and had a good roof. "At thirty-eight years of age, it's unlikely I'll bear children of my own." How it pained her to admit her motherless state. Why her womb refused to carry a child, she would never know. She and Dale had longed for a family. "If you place Evelyn, Edwina, and Guy with me, they won't be raised in luxury, but I can assure you their needs will be met. They will receive a good education, and they will be lavished with affection."

Miss Davis leaned in slightly. "I'm not averse to placing the children with you. I'd much prefer it to taking them to the poor farm. But my superior, Miss Lucille Harms, is quite set on rule following. If there's any chance of convincing her to bend the Mission Church Home's policy, you need to choose one child. Since I'm certain that young couple will take Edwina, that leaves either Evelyn or Guy. Were it me, I would take—" Her gaze skipped beyond Hester's shoulder, and she drew back. "Oh!"

The indistinguishable utterance raised Hester's curiosity. She turned around and spotted Miss Harms storming in their direction. Guy trotted alongside her. Evelyn, holding Edwina by the hand, ambled behind. The couple wasn't with them anymore. Even from the distance of several yards, Hester glimpsed triumph in Evelyn's eyes. But fury pulsated from the older woman.

Miss Harms huffed to a halt in front of Miss Davis and waved her arm at Evelyn. "This . . . this unreasonable, stubborn, foolish child just destroyed the last opportunity for Edwina to be placed with a family." She glowered at Evelyn, who smoothed her little sister's breeze-tossed hair, seemingly unconcerned. "I had so hoped we wouldn't have to resort to taking the children to the poor farm, but . . ." Tears winked, but the woman blinked them away. "This is now our lot. And theirs." Her gaze connected with Hester's, and her cheeks mottled red. "Oh, please forgive me. I shouldn't have shared my frustration in your presence. I'm just so . . . so . . ."

"Overwrought?" Hester touched Miss Harms's jacket sleeve. "There's no need to apologize. It's clear you care deeply for the children." Evelyn released a little snort, but Hester chose not to acknowledge it. "You want what's best for them, yes?"

Miss Harms adjusted the lapels of her jacket and sniffed, lifting her chin. "Yes."

Hester nodded, smiling. "I want the same."

Miss Davis held her hand toward Hester. "Miss Harms, have you met Mrs. Haak?"

Hester shot her a startled look. Why use the formal title when she'd previously called her Hester? Then understanding dawned. She swallowed a chortle.

"Mrs. Haak has just informed me that she would like to provide a home for Evelyn, Edwina, and Guy."

Miss Harms's eyebrows shot high. "All three children? That is a great deal of responsibility." She glanced around. "But if your husband approves the plan, then—"

Miss Davis cleared her throat. "Mrs. Haak is a widow."

"A widow?" Miss Harms took a backward step, shaking her head. "Oh, I'm so sorry, but the Mission Church Home has never placed children in homes without both a mother and father in residence unless the individual was a direct relative."

Miss Davis wrung her hands. "But Mrs. Haak is a business owner as well as a homeowner. This seems to prove she has the financial resources to provide for the children. Why must she be penalized because her husband passed away?"

Miss Harms gawked at the younger woman. "Audrey, we aren't authorized to change the rules. We've been sanctioned by the

Mission Church Home's directors to abide by their policies for placement."

Evelyn released Edwina's hand and stepped between the pair of guardians. "Wait a minute. Me an' Winnie ain't up for adoption. This lady can take Guy, but I'm going back to New York, an' Winnie's going with me."

Miss Harms pinched Evelyn's ear and leaned forward until her face was only inches from the girl's. "You have no say in any of this, Evelyn Holbrook. Your blathering has caused enough trouble today. You will be silent and respectful or—"

"All right!" Evelyn wrenched loose and returned to Edwina, rubbing her ear.

Miss Harms glared at Evelyn for several seconds, as if daring her to speak again. When the girl ignored her, the elder guardian finally faced Hester again. "I'm sorry to disappoint you, Mrs. Haak, but once we return to the home, we'll submit the paperwork indicating where the children have been placed. If the directors see that we've allowed an unmarried woman to take in three children, we'll face disciplinary action ourselves."

Miss Davis raised her eyebrows and cocked her head. "Will we?"

Miss Harms frowned. "What do you mean?"

Miss Davis shrugged. "The home is closing. When we return the paperwork to Miss Armstrong, our work is done. What kind of action could the directors take?" She slid her arm across the older woman's shoulders. "Is delivering the children to the poor farm more compassionate than placing them in a home with a loving mother?"

Hester held her breath, inwardly praying for God's favor to shine on her.

Miss Harms must have been holding her breath as well, because she heaved a mighty sigh. "All right."

Miss Davis beamed. "Wonderful!"

Hester clasped her hands beneath her chin and allowed her lungs to empty in a whoosh of mingled relief and happiness.

Miss Harms shook her finger at the younger guardian. "But we'll make it a provisional placement." She turned a determined look on Hester. "If, when the paperwork is submitted, the directors do not approve our decision, you must be willing to relinquish the children to the poor farm as per their original instructions."

Hester chewed the inside of her lip. Should she subject herself to a provisional term? It could lead to heartbreak. Maybe she should go home and return to her childless state. She looked at Guy. His bowed head and slumped shoulders spoke of dejection, raising a wave of sympathy. This sad-looking little boy deserved to be loved. She shifted her focus to Edwina. The innocence shining in the little girl's blue eyes stirred the embers of love in Hester's heart. Then she looked into Evelyn's sullen scowl. Surprisingly, empathy washed through her, and she knew what she must do. God had prepared Hester to understand and unconditionally love this girl. If she could love Evelyn, loving Guy and Edwina would come easily. Even if she had the children for only a brief period of time, she would love them and nurture them and give them good memories to carry away with them.

She turned to Miss Harms. "I agree."

Chapter Four

Hester

Hester's certainty that she was meant to take all three children wavered during the drive from Marion back to Millersberg. She had no doubt that she would love them. Guy perched on the edge of the seat beside her with his fingers on the dashboard, smiling out the front window. The eight-year-old had already endeared himself to her with his uninhibited joy. Winnie, as Evelyn insisted she call Edwina, sat in the middle of the back seat, humming and flipping the hem of her pinafore, completely content. Only the most hardened person wouldn't feel drawn to precious little Winnie. And then there was Evelyn. The girl's crossed arms and perpetual scowl aimed out the side window proved she had gone too long without mothering. Hester could fix that.

No, she held no worries about her affection for them growing into motherly love. Her concerns were practical. She had a store to manage. How would she care for Winnie while Evelyn and Guy were in school? Where would the children sleep? There was only one bed in her house, not to mention only one bedroom. Her home was woefully empty of things necessary for raising children. At least they'd each been sent with a drawstring bag of clothing, but what about books and toys and school supplies? She stocked pencils and tablets on one of the shelves in the Corner Store, but she carried mostly foodstuffs and only a few basic household items. How much would it cost to purchase what the children needed for school?

Suddenly Guy pointed ahead and turned a hopeful grin on Hester. "There's a town. Is that'n ours?"

He'd asked the same question when they approached Quarry a quarter hour ago. Then, Hester had responded no. This time she nodded. "It certainly is, Guy. That's Millersberg, your new home."

Guy bounced on the seat, his happy anticipation making Hester smile. A glance in the rearview mirror caught Evelyn craning sideways and peering out the front. Her sour expression didn't change, but the action indicated a hint of interest. Hester's smile grew. "Would you children like to go straight to our house?" Oh, such joy in using the word *our*! "Or would you like to take a drive around town and see where you'll go to school and church?"

"Town!" The word exploded from Guy with as much force as a firecracker.

"The house," Evelyn said at the same time, her tone dripping with boredom.

Hester sent another peek to the back seat. "What about you, Winnie? Do you want to go home or see the town?" A front tire bounced in a pothole, rocking the vehicle and jouncing everyone. Hester gripped the steering wheel and waited for the little girl to answer.

"Winnie wants what I want." Evelyn spoke smugly.

Guy flopped against the seat.

Although Hester was eager to get home, settle the children in, and see how Scotty was doing at the store, she believed Guy needed a victory. She tossed a wink at the little boy. "I need to stop in Ebright's General Merchandise Store and pick up a few things, so we'll see the town first."

"Hurray!" Guy crowed.

At half past eleven, there was still a number of vehicles and a few wagons lining Millersberg's Main Street. Townsfolk traipsed up and down the dirt walkways fronting the stores, some of them carrying packages. The children pressed their noses to the windows and stared as Hester drove to the northwest edge of town. She stopped in front of the two-story red-brick building where the children living in and around town received their education. "This is your new school, children."

Guy seemed entranced by the swings, merry-go-round, and teeter-totters. "You gonna drive us to school? I like drivin'. Never been in a car before you brung us here."

Hester hadn't considered how different the children's lives must have been in the big city. They would have some adjustments to make. She hated to disappoint him, but she couldn't waste gasoline for such a short distance. "All the children walk to school unless the weather is exceedingly foul. Our house is only a couple blocks away. On Monday, I'll walk with you and get you enrolled. After that, you and Evelyn—and Winnie when she's old enough—will walk here on your own."

Guy turned sideways and grinned at Evelyn. "Hear that? We get to walk here every day."

Evelyn huffed.

Hester turned the car east and drove to the white-painted clapboard church where she and Dale had exchanged wedding vows and his funeral service had been held. While the car idled in place, she said, "Tomorrow morning, we'll come here for worship. There's also Sunday school classes." She hadn't attended Sunday school since Dale's death, but the children should go. "Did you go to Sunday school in New York?"

Guy shook his head, his eyes wide with wonder.

Evelyn leaned forward and flopped one arm over the front seat. "We did all our schooling at the home. Book learnin' an' Bible learnin'. There ain't much more I need to know. I'm gonna get a job instead so I can earn money for train tickets."

Guy looked at her, his mouth slightly open. "What do you need train tickets for?"

She rolled her eyes. "To take me an' Winnie back to New York."

Guy angled an uncertain frown at Hester. "Is she goin' to New York, ma'am?"

At some point, Hester would address Evelyn's intention to return to New York, but the girl had very little to call her own. It wouldn't hurt to let her hold on to the dream for now. "Maybe someday, but not by tomorrow or Monday. Tomorrow we're all going to Sunday school, and Monday you and she are going to school."

Evelyn released a grunt. "I told you I don't need no more schooling."

Hester met Evelyn's stubborn scowl with a smile. "'Give instruction to a wise man, and he will be yet wiser.' That's from Proverbs in the Bible. The wise person never stops learning. There's always something more to know."

The girl rolled her eyes and sat back.

Hester adjusted the clutch and put the Model T in gear again. She drove slowly down Main Street, pointing out the various businesses. "There's the barbershop where you'll get your hair cut, Guy. And, Evelyn, when you outgrow your dresses, I'll take you to Miss Sally's Dress Shop for new ones. If you get sick, we'll visit Dr. Ash there on the corner." Evelyn's comment about getting a job stirred an idea in Hester's mind. "Guy, do you see the sign that says Post Office?"

Guy pointed to the narrow wood-framed building with a large glass window. "That one there?"

Hester nodded. "It will be your job to fetch our mail every day." Scotty would appreciate the reprieve, and the responsibility would make the boy feel helpful and needed.

His face lit.

From the back seat, Evelyn humphed. "You gonna pay him to do that? You get paid for jobs."

Hester chuckled. "Perhaps I should have said it will be his

chore." She pulled the vehicle into an open space in front of the general merchandise store and turned off the engine. Shifting sideways in the seat, she scanned each of the children's faces as she spoke. "We're a family now, and in a family, everyone has chores. Since I work every day except Sunday at my store, each of you will help at the house."

Guy tipped his head. "Winnie's too little, though, right?"

By the time Hester was only a little older than Winnie, she was already minding her baby sister while her parents worked at the shoemaking factory, a responsibility far beyond her years. "Winnie will help set the table for meals and keep her belongings picked up." Eventually, she would have belongings—dozens of toys and books—for which to care.

Guy gave a slow nod.

"Evelyn will wash dishes and clothes and help with housecleaning. Guy, you will collect the mail, see to the garbage, and keep the front porch swept."

Evelyn's gaze narrowed. "Who did it all before we came?"

As Hester remembered the lonely years after Dale's passing, her chest went tight. "I did. But there wasn't as much to do since I was by myself. Now there are four of us." Five, counting Scotty. What would he say when she arrived with three children in tow? "You won't have to do everything. I will do my share. We'll all work together."

She imagined conversations over the washtub, in the garden, and at the kitchen sink. When evening fell and the supper dishes were washed and put away, the four of them could play croquet in the side yard or gather around the table for a game of Go Fish or build with Tinkertoys on the living room floor. She would read to them before bed from the Bible and from storybooks. The lovely images filled her head, and she released a happy sigh. "And we'll play together. There will be time for play if everyone helps with chores."

Guy wriggled in place. "Can I help at the store?"

Hester smoothed a lock of his straw-colored hair away from his eyes, savoring this first true motherly act. "Yes, you can help after school and on Saturdays. And someday the store might be yours to run all by yourself."

The child broke into the brightest smile Hester had ever seen. The little boy's cheerful attitude made her want to surprise him with a treat. She swung her door open. "Let's pick out your lunch boxes, and then we'll go to the drugstore for lunch."

Scotty

Scotty turned the charge book so it faced Miz Noone and gave the gray-haired lady a pencil. He scratched his cheek and watched her make marks on the page below the ones made by other folks who'd come in that morning. Numbers and letters—he hadn't learned 'em when he was young. Not the writing down part nor the reading. Wouldn't it be nice to understand what them marks meant? But they had meaning for Miz Hester, and that's all that mattered.

Miz Noone finished and gave him back the pencil. "Thank you, Scotty."

He dropped the pencil into the tin cup next to the register, slid the charge book under the counter, then tipped his old homburg. "No problem at all, ma'am. Have a good day, now."

"I will. You do the same." She scooped up her full basket and waddled out the door. Poor lady's ankles were so swoll' up they oozed over the tops of her oxford shoes. It must pain her something fierce to walk. And she walked everywhere she went. *Dear Lord, wouldja fix that swellin' so Miz Noone's feet don't hurt her? Thank You.* Putting Miz Noone's problem in the good Lord's keeping let Scotty put his attention on work again.

While he worked, he kept his ear tuned for the sound of Miz Hester's Model T. She ought to be back anytime now with her new little girl. Eagerness shimmied through him. He'd already decided what he'd be called—Uncle Scotty. Somewhere out there, he likely had real nieces and nephews, but he'd never know 'em. He'd know this little girl, though. It'd sure be fine to be Uncle Scotty to somebody.

Noontime slid by, and Scotty's tummy was rumbling. But he couldn't leave the store to fetch lunch, so he ate a few crackers from the barrel and fished a fat pickle from the jar on a shelf behind the counter. It'd hold him until suppertime. Would Miz Hester be back by suppertime? No more had he thought the question when the back door of the store popped open and Miz Hester herself came in.

Scotty's heart gave a leap. He looked, but nobody followed her. His spirits fell faster than a knocked-out prizefighter. "Where's the little girl you went to get?"

She smiled real big while she chose an apron from a peg and slipped it on. "In the house, becoming familiar with what is now *home.*"

He danced a quick jig and punched the air. "That's dandy!"

Miz Hester laughed her sweet laugh that sounded like music. "It's dandier than you can imagine." She glanced around. "I'm sorry I was gone so long. Since it was close to lunchtime when I returned to town, we went to the drugstore for bologna sandwiches and sodas to celebrate. But I'm here now and can take over. Why don't you go to the house and introduce yourself? I left a sandwich on the table for you. Egg salad—your favorite."

Scotty's mouth watered. "Thank you, ma'am. I reckon I'll do as you said. Lookin' real forward to meetin' your little girl."

An impish look glinted in her eyes. What was that all about? She shooed him with her fingers and headed for a customer. He shouldn't pester her with questions when she was working. Besides, he had an egg salad sandwich and a new niece waiting.

He shot out the back door, crossed the grass in three eager strides, and stepped up onto the front porch. He whipped off his hat and ran his hand over his hair. Wasn't much covering his head no more, but it wouldn't do to have the strands standing straight up. With his hat clamped in the bend of his arm, he opened the door and stepped inside.

"Howdy!" He searched the neat living room. "Your new mama sent me over to meet you, so come on out." Seconds later, a yellow-haired child wearing brown knickers, striped suspenders, and a tan shirt showed up in the doorway between the living room and Miz Hester's bedroom.

Scotty drew back. "You're a boy."

The boy blinked. "Yes, sir. I'm Marion Guy Sadler. But folks call me Guy." He came closer, the heels of his lace-up shoes scuffing the carpet. "Are you Mr. Scotty?"

"Uncle Scotty." Scotty looked the boy up and down. Kinda scrawny, and kinda clumsy like a puppy that'd not yet grown into its feet. But he was a handsome little fellow. Scotty hadn't expected to find a boy, though. "Weren't there no girls on the train?"

The boy cranked his head and called over his shoulder, "Evelyn! Winnie!"

Almost at once, a pair of girls popped into the doorway, the bigger one holding on to the little one's hand. Scotty's hat dropped to the floor. *Two* girls? *And* a boy? Miz Hester sure was one for surprises.

"Come meet Mr.—" Guy sent Scotty a sheepish look. "I mean, Uncle Scotty."

The older girl pulled the little one into the room, but they eyed him from afar. The little one sucked on her fingers, and the big one sent an unsmiling look from Scotty's head to his toes and up again. He squinted and gave her a good gander back. Was that white bit stuck on her chin from chopped-up egg? Yep, it sure looked to be. So much for enjoying his sandwich.

"Well, I'll be hornswoggled." Yep, Miz Hester had sure surprised him. Some surprises were good, and some surprises were bad. He'd wait to decide which way this surprise leaned.

Chapter Five

Evelyn

The scruffy-looking old man kept staring right at her mouth. Evelyn gave it a swipe with the back of her hand. A little chunk of the filling from the sandwich the lady left on the table ended up on her middle knuckle. She licked off the bit, then said, "What're you lookin' at?"

"The person who most likely ate my lunch." He raised one gray eyebrow. "Am I right?"

Guy nodded. "Yep, she did. She gived a bite to Winnie, but she didn't give any to me."

The old man put his bony hand on Guy's shoulder. "Well, then, since you kids're still hungry, let's find somethin' in the cupboard. Do you like peanut butter?"

Guy licked his lips. "Yes, sir, Uncle Scotty!"

"Then we'll have us some." The man herded Guy past Evelyn and Winnie, grinning like he didn't have a care in the world.

Evelyn followed him through the lady's bedroom and into the kitchen. What a strange setup. One room led into another, all in a line. First the living room, then a big bedroom, then the kitchen with a table and chairs on one side and built-in cupboards on the other. Behind the cupboards side of the kitchen, there was a good-sized bathroom with a claw-foot tub, sink, and pull-cord toilet. On the table-and-chairs half of the kitchen, a narrow room with more cabinets on both sides led to a door. Beyond the door was a backyard. There had to be more to the house than she was seeing.

She put her hands on her hips. "That lady told us you'd be

comin' in and if we had questions about anything, we could ask you 'cause you know where everything's at."

He opened a floor-to-ceiling cabinet next to the icebox and pawed around inside it. "Who're you talkin' about, 'that lady'?"

Evelyn huffed. "The one who brung us here."

He gave her a confused look. "Are you meanin' Miz Hester? She ain't 'that lady.' She's your new mama."

Evelyn rolled her eyes. "No, she ain't. She's just somebody who's letting us stay here awhile until I can get enough money to go back to New York. Was she right?"

He pulled a tin of peanut butter from the shelf and snapped the door closed. "Guy, get the bread out o' the icebox there, would you?" Scotty screeched open a drawer and pulled out a knife, sending a sideways glance at Evelyn. "Right about what?"

Guy was looking around the room like he'd never seen a kitchen before. Well, maybe he hadn't. The kids weren't allowed in the kitchen at the home. There hadn't been a refrigerator in their apartment in New York, but she knew what one was from looking at catalog pictures. She marched past Guy and yanked the icebox door open. "There's the bread."

The boy scrambled over and grabbed out the loaf. He trailed the old man to the table and laid out slices of bread. Evelyn went to the opposite side, plopped into a chair, and pulled Winnie onto her lap. "Right about you knowing the answers to things we wanna know."

The man slathered peanut butter on a slice of bread. "Depends on what you wanna know." He folded the slice in half and gave it to Guy.

Evelyn blew out a huge huff of breath. "Mister, you're aggravatin' me."

He arched that one eyebrow again. "That so?" He spread peanut butter on another slice of bread, folded it real careful, and offered it to Winnie.

To Evelyn's surprise, she took it. They'd been fed peanut butter sandwiches every day on the train. A peanut butter sandwich and an apple for breakfast, lunch, and dinner. She didn't care if she ate either one ever again. "Yeah. An' I think you're doing it on purpose 'cause I ate your egg salad sandwich." She hadn't known it was for him. She was a little embarrassed about it now.

"Truth be told, I was lookin' forward to that sandwich. But I reckon peanut butter'll fill me just as well." He offered her a piece of peanut butter–smeared bread, but she shook her head. He shrugged and set the knife aside. He rolled the slice into a tube and pointed at her with it. "I gotta say, though, you shouldn't be callin' Miz Hester 'that lady,' like she's nobody special." He yanked out a chair and sat, keeping his gray-blue eyes set on her face. "She's real special. Time'll let you see it for yourself." He chomped down on the tube, chewed, and swallowed. "Now, what'd you wanna ask about?"

The man's praise for Mrs. Haak made Evelyn want to squirm for some reason. She was happy to set aside talk about the lady. "Where are Winnie, Guy, an' me supposed to sleep? I could only find one bed."

"Been snoopin', have you?"

She bristled. "No. That la—Mrs. Haak said we could look around 'cause it's where we're living now."

He pushed the last of the roll of bread into his mouth and then swished his palms together. "There's just the one bed. An' just the one bedroom." His fuzzy eyebrows tipped together and made a single long caterpillar over his eyes. "I figure Miz Hester'll have some ideas about where you all's gonna sleep for the long run, but she'll be busy at the store 'til close to suppertime. So we'll help her by layin' out some beds for tonight."

Evelyn pretended to search right and left, exaggerating the motions. "Where?"

He pushed himself from the chair. "The livin' room. Plenty o' floor space in there."

She let out a little *uh!* "The floor? At the home, we each had our own bed. With soft sheets and down pillows and quilts laid out on top."

"That so?"

"Uh-huh. And we had our own rooms. Nobody had to share."

Guy opened his mouth like he was going to say something, and she shot him a glare. He pinched his lips tight. This man didn't need to know the children slept on cots with thin straw mattresses covered by scratchy wool blankets or that the cots were lined up in a row in the sleeping rooms, as many as twelve in each room. So what? Maybe they didn't have fancy beds and their very own rooms at the home. But that's what she'd have when she lived with Daddy again. He'd never make her sleep on the floor.

"It ain't for always." The man talked slow, like he had to think about each word before he spoke it. "Just 'til Miz Hester has time to get things arranged for you all." He turned away and shook his head. "Three of 'em? What was she thinkin' to bring three of 'em?"

He'd muttered, but Evelyn heard him anyway. She said, "Huh?" hoping he'd say more. But he headed for the back door like she hadn't made a sound.

"You all come with me. We'll get what we need to make up some sleepin' spots for you."

Evelyn pushed Winnie from her lap and took her hand, but Winnie pulled loose. "I tired, Evvie."

Mr. Scotty came back, moving as slow as he talked. He bent down and put his hands on his knees. He looked real tenderly at Winnie, the way Daddy'd looked at the two of them the day he left her and Winnie at the home. "You needin' a nap, little one?"

Winnie yawned and rubbed her eyes.

He chuckled. "Well, Miz Hester won't mind you curlin' up in her bed an' sleepin' a bit. Come on." He held out his arms.

Winnie scooted halfway behind Evelyn and stared up at the man, her fingers in her mouth.

He chuckled again and put his hands back on his knees. "Bein' shy, are you? Well, that don't bother me none. Might take a while to get used to things around here. But I reckon you won't be scared o' me for long. Uncle Scotty won't never hurt you, little one. I promise you that." He straightened and looked at Evelyn. "Go ahead an' put her in the big bed, then come out. Me an' Guy'll be in the store." He ambled toward the back door. "C'mon, Guy."

Guy followed him like a faithful puppy.

Evelyn took her time tucking Winnie into the bed in the bedroom. While she did it, she pretended she was Mama and Winnie was her, play-acting what she remembered from when she was a little one, as Mr. Scotty had called Winnie. A knot filled her throat. Would she ever stop missing Mama? Nope. And she'd never stop being mad at God for taking Mama away. If Mama hadn't died, Daddy wouldn't have left her and Winnie at the home. They wouldn't have been put on the train and brought to this itty-bitty house in an itty-bitty town far, far away from New York and Daddy.

She smoothed her little sister's hair, whispering, "Shhh, shhh," the way Mama used to do to help her fall asleep. Winnie dropped off real quick, but Evelyn stayed put. Kept stroking. Kept shushing. She wanted to pretend a while longer.

Hester

Hester waved goodbye to old Mr. Turner, then sent a glance around the store. No one else was there. With things quiet, she could check the morning's receipts and get an idea of how sales had gone. Lunch at the drugstore was an extravagance. She'd need to pay closer attention than ever before to what she spent now that she had three children to raise. Just as she opened the charge book, Scotty and Guy came in. She set the book aside as they crossed the store's planked floor, side by side. The boy had his hands shoved in his pockets, the same way Scotty did, and matched his gait to the man's. It appeared the two had already become friends, and her heart warmed. She'd done the right thing by bringing Guy home with her.

They stopped on the opposite side of the counter, and she bounced a smile over both of them. "Have you had a chance to become acquainted?"

Scotty rubbed his finger across his upper lip, his eyebrows high. "I reckon so. You sure surprised me with how many of 'em there are."

Guy hooked his fingers on the edge of the counter and grinned up at Hester. "Uncle Scotty showed me all over the yard. I even got to stick my hand in your minnow tank. Them little fish're funny. They nibbled at my fingers, an' it didn't hurt a bit. Uncle Scotty says folks buy 'em to use as bait for fishin'. He said we can take some out for free if we want to an' he'll take me fishin' at Cottonwood Crick." Happiness shone on the child's thin face.

Hester exchanged a smile with Scotty before winking at Guy. "Be sure and catch some bluegill when you go. They're my favorite."

"I will!"

Scotty gave Guy's narrow shoulders a few pats. "I reckon Guy an' me are gonna get along like cornbread an' bean soup. But that one . . ."

"Ah." Hester nodded knowingly. "Evelyn is still complaining?" How long might it take for the girl to settle in the way Guy seemed to be doing?

Scotty hooted. He stacked his forearms on the countertop and shook his head. "Miz Hester, what was you thinkin' to take on three children at once? Now, Guy here, I see why you took a shine to him. He's a fine fellow. An' the little one . . . she's cute as a button an' seems to be sweet as sugar. But the other girl is all sass." Worry glimmered in his eyes. "I'm afraid she's gonna give you trouble."

Hester gently cleared her throat. "Little pitchers have big ears."

Scotty jolted upright. His gaze landed on Guy. He ruffled the boy's hair. "Guy, there's a storeroom right next to where we come in the back door—can't miss it. There's a cot laid out for sleepin' in the middle an' lots o' shelves all around. Scrounge around in there an' look for a stack o' tater sacks, would you?"

"Sure, Uncle Scotty!" Guy darted off.

Scotty watched until the boy disappeared around the corner, and then he resumed leaning on the counter and gave Hester an apologetic look. "Wasn't thinkin'. I shouldn't talk ill of Evelyn in front o' the boy." He chuckled. "Even though he's likely thinkin' the same as me. But, Miz Hester . . ." Humor left his expression, and uncertainty crept in. "Weren't there no other girls to choose from?"

"No. They were the very last children on the very last orphan train from New York. But even if there had been . . ." She paused, reliving the wave of peace she'd experienced when she decided to adopt the children. "You know how much I prayed about adopting a child."

"Yes, ma'am. I been prayin' right along with you for as long as I've been here."

She put her hand over his and squeezed. "I know you have. Well, I believe God chose Evelyn, Winnie, and Guy for me."

Scotty shook his head. "I ain't one to argue with the good Lord, as you know, but did He give you any idea what to do with 'em once you got 'em? You all are gonna be stacked up like cordwood in there."

She laughed. "To be honest, at the time, I didn't think. I simply acted." She shot him a hopeful look. "You've been so helpful in building shelves and organizing spaces here in the store. Do you have any suggestions?"

He slowly straightened and pinched his chin between his thumb and finger. "Hmm, lemme think on it." She waited, observing his pensive pose. Dale had been a thinker, but he wasn't necessarily a builder. Had they not inherited the Corner Store from his parents, who expected him to continue the business after their passing, he might have been a lawyer or politician. As much as she loved and missed her dear husband, Scotty had provided more practical help in the store in the past three years than Dale had during their fifteen years of operating it together.

Suddenly Scotty snapped his fingers. "Now, this ain't gonna be a permanent fix, but we could split up your bedroom by hangin' sheets from the ceilin'. The doorways are right in the middle o' the room, so we'll make them doorways the ends of a hallway from front to back. One half o' the room'll be yours, an' we'll slice the other half into two parts an' put beds in there for the kids. Are you followin' what I'm sayin'?"

Hester envisioned her bedroom with its doorways centering the north and south walls. "I am."

He grinned. "None o' the spaces'll be big by anybody's thinkin', but they'll do until you can build on. Summer's comin'. Seems like summer'd be a good time for buildin'."

"Yes. Hopefully by then I'll hear back from the New York orphan asylum's directors and know for sure if—" She clapped her hand over her mouth. She hadn't intended to share the stipulation concerning the children's placement. What if knowing about it prevented Scotty from truly bonding with the children? No matter how long they'd be with her, she wanted them to experience unconditional, unrestrained affection from both her and Scotty. They needed it. But he was staring at her with such concern that she couldn't keep the information to herself.

With her hand over his wrist, she divulged her agreement to deliver the children to the poor farm in Marion if the directors of the home deemed her an inappropriate guardian.

He reared back and gave the counter a solid slap. "Why, just let 'em try an' take them kids from you, Miz Hester! I'll tell 'em there's no finer woman in all of Marion County to mother Guy, Evelyn, an' little Winnie."

She laughed, both embarrassed and pleased by his stalwart defense. "Scotty, I appreciate your friendship so much. You are a true gift in my life."

He lowered his head and chuckled. "Aw, now, you gave me a home when nobody else gave me as much as a kind word." He lifted his face, warmth glimmering in his pale eyes. "An' now I know why you took in all them kids—doin' what the Bible tells us in lovin' the way He does. You just can't help yourself, can you?"

Hester's cheeks warmed at his praise. She wanted his words to be true. She'd been an unwanted, unloved orphan alone in the world. But the almighty God, the maker of heaven and earth, loved her. If He loved her so much, who was she to deny love to others?

The back screen door slammed into its frame, and Evelyn stomped around the corner. "There you are." She plunked her fists on her skinny hips. "I thought you were looking for things to make up beds for us. I can't put 'em together if you don't bring me sheets and such."

Hester shook her head slightly, her lips twitching into a half smile. "We're working on it, Evelyn. Have patience, please."

The girl huffed and flounced off.

Scotty poked his thumb in Evelyn's direction, a grin tugging at his cheeks. "That one could try the patience o' Job. I'll be prayin' for you."

Chapter Six

Hester

Hester had never been late to church—or for any other responsibility—in her life. She'd been schooled on the importance of punctuality from an early age. But she'd never had to ready three children in addition to herself before. Preparing breakfast for five rather than two took longer. Ironing the wrinkles from the children's clothes seemed to take hours. She inwardly berated herself for not seeing to the task Saturday evening. But by the time she'd served dinner, cleaned up the mess, and shuffled the children through a brand-new bath and bedtime routine, she'd barely had the energy left for her own bath. So here it was, nine o'clock already, right when Sunday school was to begin. She hurried them out the door, chewing her lip in worry. How would she get the children to school on time tomorrow? School started a full hour earlier than Sunday school. Her head spun.

Ordinarily, she walked to church, but today she bundled the children into the back seat of her Model T. Scotty turned the crank, then hopped into the passenger seat. Hester aimed her car for the alley's exit, her gloved hands tight on the steering wheel.

"Why do I have to go to Sunday school?" Evelyn's tone held belligerence.

"Nearly all the children in Millersberg attend Sunday school." Hester spoke kindly yet firmly. "This will give you a chance to meet some young people your age."

"Thought you was making me go to school." Now she sounded sarcastic. "I can get to know 'em there."

Scotty sent Hester a dubious look, but he didn't say anything.

"That's true." Hester shifted into a higher gear and increased the speed. Dirt billowed behind the car. "But you won't hear the same lessons in school as you will in Sunday school."

The girl huffed. Where had she developed the skill for releasing such a derisive breath? "I'm too old for all them stories an' such."

Hester stifled the temptation to expel a huff of her own. "We're never too old to learn from the Bible, Evelyn." To her relief, the girl hushed. Hester slowed for the turn onto Maple Street, seeking an open spot between the few cars and wagons already parked near the church. She found a slice of space in front of the cemetery beside the church. She angled the vehicle in, cringing as it bucked and sputtered with the abrupt application of the brake, and then she turned off the engine.

She popped her door open. "Come on, everyone. Let's go."

Evelyn released another of her practiced huffs, but she threw the door open and stepped out. Winnie followed. Guy scrambled out the opposite side and took hold of Scotty's hand. Hester wanted to hold Winnie's hand, but Evelyn kept a grip on the little girl and trudged ahead across the path of flattened grass leading to the church.

The pair of front doors stood open, held in place by sandstone blocks. They all entered the foyer. The deep mumble of a man's voice from behind the closed sanctuary doors let Hester know class for the adults had already started. Today she'd sit on one of the benches in the foyer during Sunday school rather than interrupt. But whether the children created an interruption or not, they needed to go to their class.

The children's Sunday school was held in the basement. Hester ushered the trio of children to the enclosed staircase at the far end of the foyer and down the steps. Childish voices joining in song to the accompaniment of a slightly tinny piano serenaded them as they reached the single large room. Children sat in rows on metal folding chairs facing the piano, where the preacher's daughter, Lillian, sat playing and leading the singing. Elizabeth Stafford, the preacher's wife, was standing to the side. Her gaze met Hester's.

She hurried over. "Why, Mrs. Haak, who have we here?" Her welcoming smile swept across Evelyn's scowl, Guy's big grin, and Winnie's wide-eyed stare.

Hester's chest swelled with pride as she introduced each child by name. "They're living with me." She wanted to call them her adopted children, because in her heart they already were. But legally it was an untruth. She'd have to wait to claim the official title as the children's mother.

The woman squeezed Hester's elbow. "How wonderful!"

Warmth flooded Hester's frame. She hadn't realized how much she worried about the community's reaction until Elizabeth offered such a kind endorsement. "Thank you. I think so, too."

Elizabeth turned her smile on the children again. "We'll start this morning's lesson soon. Let's find chairs for each of you." She slid her arm across Guy's shoulders, placed her hand on Evelyn's back, and urged them toward the group.

Hester considered remaining in case Guy or Winnie had trouble sitting still. But Elizabeth had taught the children's Sunday school ever since her husband took over the pulpit more than a dozen years ago. She had children of her own, now mostly grown. Evelyn, Guy, and Winnie were in competent hands. Besides, no other mothers hovered on the fringes, so she shouldn't, either. Still, her feet plodded up the stairs.

To her surprise, Scotty still stood in the middle of the foyer, holding his old homburg against his chest. She crossed to him. "Did you not want to go in for Sunday school?"

He scratched his cheek. He saved shaving for go-to-meetin'

day, as he called Sunday, and his skin was ruddy from the razor's scrape. "I never been before. Durin' the sermonizin', nobody asks questions an' such. But I might have to say somethin' if I go in there, the way schoolteachers ask questions an' then get mad when you ain't got the right answer."

Although Scotty had lived in the store for years now, Hester knew very little about his history. The man was as close-lipped as anyone she'd ever met when it came to speaking about his life before arriving in Millersberg that snowy January morning. But she sensed he'd suffered countless hurts. She wouldn't force him to divulge anything he didn't want to. She understood the desire to leave the past behind. Maybe that was why they got along so well.

She patted his arm. "I had decided to stay out here until the service starts so I wouldn't interrupt the lesson. We can wait together."

They sat side by side on a long bench tucked beneath a row of coat pegs. Scotty placed his hat on his knee, sat back, and linked his fingers together over his stomach. He released a sigh that spoke of contentment. Hester nodded, smiling to herself. After their hectic morning, it felt amazingly good to simply sit and relax. She enjoyed a few minutes of breathing in the earthy scents of the early spring breeze wafting through the doorway and listening to the soft rumble of voices from behind closed doors and drifting from the basement stairwell. But then she gave a little start.

Scotty swung his gaze in her direction. "Somebody walk over your grave?"

She laughed softly. "No. I just realized I shouldn't sit here doing nothing when I could be thinking. I have much to plan."

He shifted sideways a bit. "Such as . . ."

"Such as establishing a routine for readiness in the mornings." She cringed, recalling the frenzy of their first Sunday together. "I've become lazy since Dale died, only seeing to my own needs."

He raised one eyebrow. "You see to me, don't you?"

She smiled. "You see to yourself, Scotty. I fix meals for you, but beyond that, you get yourself up and dressed each day without any help." She pulled in a big breath. "It's quite different having children underfoot. I've always longed for children, imagined the joy of their company and the privilege of raising them, but I never considered their effect on my daily happenings."

Scotty scratched his cheek again. "Well, most mothers ease into it. They start with a baby that grows up day by day, so the mamas learn the motherin' bit by bit. Becomin' a mother kind o' got"—he grinned—"dumped on you."

Indeed it had. But she held up one finger. "By my own invitation. No one forced it on me."

"'Course not. And . . ." His grin faded. "It could be took away."

His statement revealed worry. She wished she'd kept secret the possibility of having to deliver the children to the poor farm. "It could." Pain stabbed with the acknowledgment. "But whether it happens or not, for now the children are in my care and I need to create a secure, stable environment for them. This morning's rushing around was stressful for all of us. That's no way to begin a day."

"So what're you gonna do?"

"I don't know." After years of ordering stock, arranging the shelves, and keeping the books, she managed the store well. Years of cleaning, cooking, and doing wash in the Webers' grand home had prepared her to see to her own humble home. She'd learned storekeeping from Dale's parents and homemaking from the Webers' house manager. Logically, girls learned mothering from their own mothers' examples, but Hester's upbringing wasn't like most girls'. Could she, at this age, learn to raise children? Perhaps she should have asked herself that question before she brought Guy, Evelyn, and Winnie home.

The question tormented Hester all through Reverend Stafford's sermon, stealing her focus. It rose again as she hurriedly threw together their Sunday dinner of canned pork 'n' beans, fried slices of bologna, and home-canned applesauce. She hated putting such simple fare on the table on the Lord's day. But numerous church members, whether out of curiosity or desire to meet the children, had stopped her in the churchyard. By the time they got home, the children were so hungry the younger two were whiny to the point of tears. Wasn't it more important to fill their tummies than make them wait for something more elaborate?

As she ate, she promised herself that by next Sunday, she'd be organized enough to put a pot roast, pork loin, or whole chicken with potatoes and carrots in her oven before leaving for church, the way she'd done every other Sunday since her and Dale's wedding. They'd have a fine dinner next Sunday.

After lunch, Evelyn lay down with Winnie on their pallets in the corner of the bedroom for a nap, and Guy trailed Scotty outside. While Hester washed the breakfast and lunch dishes, through the kitchen window she watched the man and little boy explore the side yard. Her heart smiled. Guy had taken to Scotty like a duckling to water. Then worry niggled. Should she, a single woman, be raising a boy? There were rough-and-tumble things a boy should know.

She didn't doubt that Scotty would be a good influence on Guy, but the man was a drifter. He never stayed in one spot long. That's what he'd told her when, at the height of her sorrow over Dale's unexpected departure for heaven, she'd offered him a job in exchange for room and board plus a small stipend. He'd stayed for three years already, becoming more a trusted friend than an employee. But what if the arrival of the children proved too unwieldy for him in his longtime bachelor state? He was exceedingly patient, but Evelyn's behavior ruffled his feathers. Would he decide he didn't need such aggravation in his life and move on?

She placed the last plate on the shelf and closed the cupboard door, annoyed with herself. From where was all this worry coming? It wasn't like her. Dale would be so disappointed. He'd been a man of strong faith, whose favorite verse came from the book of Joshua. She whispered it to the quiet kitchen. "'Have I not commanded thee? Be strong and of a good courage; be not afraid, neither be thou dismayed: for the LORD thy God is with thee whithersoever thou goest.'"

Saying the words bolstered her. Or maybe thinking about Dale did. Maybe all these questions flooding her mind was only tiredness talking. After all, the past two days had been physically and emotionally taxing.

She glanced out the window again. Guy and Scotty were crouched down, examining something in the grass. They seemed fine. The girls were fine. There was much Hester could do in preparation for their supper and tomorrow's activities, but Sundays were meant for rest. She would follow Winnie's and Evelyn's examples and take a short nap.

Scotty

Scotty gently peeled back the layer of dried grass and tufts of fur Guy had nearly stepped on. "See there? Glad we was watchin' where we walked. We could've tramped the nest."

Guy bent over until his nose was only a few inches above the tangle of baby bunnies sleeping soundly. He reared back, his eyes wide. "Them are rabbits! But I thought nests were in trees. With birds in 'em. Never seen a nest full o' rabbits." He grinned. "I like it!"

Scotty chuckled. He liked seeing the world through this boy's eyes. "Here now, scooch back so I can cover 'em again. Their mama'll be here close to sundown to feed 'em. We don't want her to know we been snoopin' on her babies."

Guy scooted backward and watched Scotty's hands pat everything back into place. "Uncle Scotty, you reckon I could keep one for a pet?"

Scotty peeked at the boy. "A pet?"

"Uh-huh. The folks who live next door to the home have a dog—a big hairy yellow dog. But we weren't allowed to go over there an' see it. I sure wanted to, though. Always dreamed of having a pet of my own."

The longing in the boy's voice tugged at Scotty's heartstrings. He clamped his hands over his knees and sighed. "Bunnies are wild animals, not like that dog next door to the home. Wild animals ain't meant to be pets. They're meant to scrounge for their food an' live in the outdoors. If a person takes a wild critter an' cages it an' feeds it an' so on, the poor thing can't never be happy. Because it ain't bein' what God designed it to be—free." He placed one hand on Guy's shoulder. "Them baby bunnies are right where they're s'posed to be, an' we need to leave 'em there. I'm gonna trust you not to pester 'em now that you know about 'em. Do you promise?"

The boy sighed real big, his lips making a deep frown, but he nodded.

Scotty patted his shoulder. "Good boy."

"But do you think my new ma'll let me get a pet sometime?"

Scotty looked into Guy's hopeful face. If the boy turned those big eyes on Miz Hester, she'd say yes just because she wanted these kids to be happy. But she had more'n enough to take care of with the store, the three kids, and even him. Adding a pet to the mix might be too much. At least right now. And if the kids ended up being took to the poor farm, Guy wouldn't be able to keep a pet there. It was best to say no, but he couldn't do it. "You know how you promised to leave them baby bunnies alone?"

Guy nodded.

"I want you to promise not to ask your new mama about gettin' a dog. She needs some time to git used to havin' children. But

I know her real good. When I can see she's ready, I'll ask her." Scotty squinted one eye, giving Guy a serious look. "Do we got a deal?"

Guy bolted to his feet. "Yes, sir!"

"Good." Scotty stood up. "I got a tin o' shortbread cookies in my room. Want one?"

"Sure!"

They headed for the back door of the store, Guy taking two steps to Scotty's one. Scotty sure hoped the boy'd be with Miz Hester long enough to have the chance for a dog. A boy like him deserved to have all his dreams come true. The same way Miz Hester did.

All at once, an idea fell down on him like manna from the sky. It hit so hard he stumbled. He turned a quick half circle, aiming his feet for the house so he could tell Miz Hester. Then quick as the happy rose up, worry brought him up short. He wasn't a smart man. Lord knew he'd been told that more'n a few times in his life. It'd squash her hopes flatter'n a soda cracker if he told her his idea and it turned out wrong.

Guy looked up at him. "Uncle Scotty, what's the matter?"

Scotty forced a chuckle and ruffled the boy's hair. "Nothin'. Just changed my mind on somethin'."

Guy's lips formed a pout. "About the cookies?"

Scotty blasted a guffaw. "Nah. I'm still game on that. Let's go."

Chapter Seven

Hester

In spite of the unexpectedly stressful challenges of bringing three children into her household, walking Guy and Evelyn to school on a crisp, clear spring morning was a dream-come-true moment Hester would cherish for the rest of her life. She'd left Winnie in Scotty's keeping, uncertain how long it would take to complete enrollment. It seemed odd not to have all three children in tow, and the feeling told her that her heart was already binding itself to them.

She held Guy's hand and walked along the edge of the dirt street, where tires hadn't carved ruts. Guy swung Hester's hand the opposite way he swung his lunch box. He'd chosen a bright-red tin pail printed with a lithograph of a boy and dog sitting side by side on a creek bank. She heard the pint jar she'd filled with water rolling around in the pail because of the motion. The jar was probably mashing his cheese, pickles, and crackers, but she didn't scold. She didn't want to dampen his enthusiasm. Maybe some of it would rub off on Evelyn.

Other children walking to school waved or called hellos when their paths crossed. Guy returned each greeting, but Evelyn didn't bother to look in their direction. At least the girl had ceased arguing about going to school. And she'd been helpful that morning—clearing the breakfast dishes, brushing Winnie's hair and helping her dress, and offering to carry the bundle of tablets and pencils Hester had taken from her store's shelves. But through it all, Evelyn's frown remained intact. If she wore it all day, would she frighten off any would-be friends? Millersberg wasn't a large community. If the children branded Evelyn disagreeable, she'd be very lonely. Hester didn't want that for her.

As they approached the corner of Maple and Washington, Guy went on alert, no doubt captured by the sounds of chatter and laughter coming from the playground. Hester drew him to a halt at the intersection and paused to check for oncoming traffic. Not that there was much traffic to speak of when compared to New York City, but he and Evelyn would walk on their own tomorrow. She would demonstrate wise choices for them today.

When no cars were coming from either direction, Hester said, "All right, let's cross." As they stepped into the street, the early primary teacher, Miss Waddell, came out on the school porch and pulled the bell rope. At the resounding *clang! clang! clang!* children grabbed up lunch pails and books and raced for the doors. Hester double stepped the final distance, and the three of them trailed the other children entering the school building.

Miss Waddell secured the rope on a hook and smiled at Hester. "Good morning, Mrs. Haak. I heard we might be getting some new students today."

Hester swallowed a chortle. Word spread fast in Millersberg. "Indeed you are. This is Guy Sadler, who is in grade two. And this"—she gestured Evelyn closer—"is Evelyn Holbrook. She's in grade seven."

"But Winnie ain't comin' to school," Guy said. "She's too little. So she's at home with Uncle Scotty."

Miss Waddell laughed. "Well, when she's big enough, we will welcome her in." She held her hand in invitation for Hester and the children to enter. She latched the doors and then turned to Evelyn. "Evelyn, our secondary grade students meet upstairs. Climb that staircase at the end of the hall. It's all one big room up there, and you'll easily find the teacher, Mr. Herriott. He'll assign you a seat and get you enrolled."

Evelyn sent a frantic look at Hester. "Ain't you coming up?"

Hester's pulse skipped into happy double beats. "If you want me to, of course I will."

Evelyn shuffled the items in her arms and shoved two tablets and a trio of pencils at Guy. "Here's your writing stuff."

Guy juggled the items with his lunch pail, and Miss Waddell laughed again. "Goodness, such a handful! How about I take those for you? Let's go into your classroom, Guy, and we'll watch for—" Her expression turned apologetic. "Excuse me, what do the children call you?"

Hester wished she could say *Mama.* Scotty referred to her as such to the children, but so far Guy called her *ma'am,* Winnie tugged Hester's sleeve to garner attention, and Evelyn rarely addressed her at all. Until she knew for sure whether they were staying for good, she should keep things simple. "Mrs. Haak is fine."

Miss Waddell nodded. "We'll watch for Mrs. Haak to come back." She ushered Guy into the primary grades classroom and closed the door behind them.

Hester sent up a prayer for Guy to find friends and have a good day, then smiled at Evelyn. "Let's go."

Evelyn

Evelyn crisscrossed her arms over the stack of tablets, clutched her pencils in one fist, and dangled her pretty lunch pail from her other hand. She couldn't see her feet, which made stair climbing tricky, but her heart was thudding like a bass drum that might pop right out of her chest if she didn't hold it in. So she kept her arms real tight all the way to the top.

Like Guy's teacher had said, the upstairs was one big room. The wall parts without windows were filled with blackboards and maps and other pictures tacked into place. The attic schoolroom at the Mission Church Home had one smeary old blackboard and no pictures except students' essays and drawings. This room almost made Evelyn dizzy, as there was so much to look at.

A boy standing in front of the group said, "Please rise for the morning prayer."

Chairs squeaked and floorboards creaked with everybody getting to their feet. Evelyn felt like a ninny standing over by the stairs with Mrs. Haak while the rest of them bowed their heads and recited together, " 'Our Father which art in heaven, hallowed be thy name . . .' "

Mrs. Haak said the words with them. Evelyn could have. She'd heard the prayer lots of times at the home and even before that from Mama. But her mouth was as dry as if somebody'd stuffed it full of cotton, so she stayed quiet. At the "amen," the students all sat down. Mrs. Haak wiggled her fingers for Evelyn to follow her, and the two of them walked to the man behind the desk at the front of the room.

Evelyn stared at the coil of brown hair on the back of Mrs. Haak's head the whole way, but she didn't have to look aside to know that every student in the room was staring at them. And whispering about them. She heard it. Her face got so hot she wondered why her ears didn't catch fire. She held tight to her belongings and kept her back to the students while Mrs. Haak talked to the teacher.

"Good morning. I'm Mrs. Hester Haak, and this is Evelyn Holbrook. She recently moved here from New York City." More whispers, louder ones, rumbled behind Evelyn. "She is living with me at 103 West Washington Street. I'd like to enroll her in grade seven."

The teacher glanced at Evelyn. "Welcome, Miss Holbrook." He wasn't warm and smiley like the lady teacher downstairs. He pulled a card from a little box on the corner of his desk, picked up a fountain pen, and wrote down everything Mrs. Haak said.

While he was writing, Evelyn sneaked a peek over her shoulder. Sure enough, everybody was gaping at her. She recognized some of the kids from Sunday school, but the only one whose name she remembered was a girl with curly red hair—Rosemary. Their eyes connected, and Rosemary smiled big and gave a little wave. One side of Evelyn's lips twitched in reply.

"Rosemary?"

Evelyn turned around at Mr. Herriott's low voice. She heard a shuffle—Rosemary probably standing up again.

"Yes, sir?" The girl sounded a little nervous. Evelyn hoped Mr. Herriott wasn't going to be a mean teacher. Teachers at the home changed real quick, and some were nicer than others.

"It seems you're already acquainted with Evelyn. Am I correct?"

Evelyn stared at the corner of the teacher's desk, hugging her tablets so hard the edges dug into her chest.

"Yes, sir. We met in Sunday school yesterday." Now Rosemary's voice held a little note of excitement. Evelyn lifted her head a bit and peered at the teacher. He wasn't smiling exactly, but he didn't look grumpy, either. She loosened her grip on her belongings.

"Then I am appointing you as Evelyn's buddy." He shifted his attention to Evelyn and Mrs. Haak. "When we receive a new student, we assign them a buddy to help them settle in with our classroom routine and introduce them to their classmates. Evelyn, if there are questions Rosemary isn't able to answer to your satisfaction, please see me during our noon break and I will answer them for you."

Evelyn's head filled with questions, but her tongue seemed stuck to the roof of her mouth. She nodded.

Mrs. Haak touched Evelyn's arm and leaned close. "I'll be at the edge of the schoolyard when classes are finished for the day to walk you and Guy home."

When Evelyn was little, Mama always walked her to and from

school. Before leaving each morning, she kissed Evelyn on the cheek and wished her a good day. For a few seconds, she wished Mrs. Haak would do what Mama'd done. Then she remembered she wasn't little anymore and this lady wasn't her mama. "I can get Guy back to the house all right. You don't need to come."

The woman winced like Evelyn had poked her with one of her new pencils, but then her soft smile came back and she took a step away. "All right. I'll see you later, then. Have a good day." She hurried off.

"Have a good day." The same as what Mama always said. Guilt stabbed. She should let Mrs. Haak walk them home. She started to call after her, but the teacher cleared his throat.

"Evelyn, place your lunch pail on the shelf at the back of the classroom, and then take the seat next to Rosemary's. It's time to start our day."

"Yes, sir." Evelyn scuttled to obey.

During the first morning in her new classroom, knowing how many curious eyes followed her every move, Evelyn couldn't relax. Worse than the kids' unwanted attention, though, were the assignments Mr. Herriott gave the students in her grade. She'd never divided by two-digit numbers before, only single digits. Rosemary helped her, but the problems made her brain hurt. Then he put sentences on the board and called kids up to name all the parts. She'd learned to recognize nouns, verbs, adjectives, and adverbs at the home, but the teachers there never taught about such things as subjects, direct objects, indirect objects, or predicates. She nibbled her thumbnail all the way down to the quick. What would she do if he called her up there and she'd have to say in front of everybody that she didn't understand?

When the noon bell rang, she nearly collapsed with relief. She got her lunch pail and followed Rosemary out to the schoolyard. At least a dozen kids surrounded her, tossing out questions about New York so fast she hardly had time to take a bite of her lunch.

It was kind of scary to have so much attention, but it also puffed her up with importance. None of these farm kids had ever been anyplace as big as New York City. It was fun telling them about the city and watching their eyes go wide or their mouths drop open.

"Yep, the buildings there are so high you can't even see the top of 'em. They call 'em skyscrapers. Why, before I came here, they was working on one called the Empire State Building. It has over a hundred floors in it. My daddy was gonna take me to it and climb all the way to the top. Betcha we could've seen clear across the ocean from the top floor."

The kids oohed and aahed, and Evelyn thought of other things she could tell them to keep them oohing and aahing. She even added a few extra details to hold their interest. She hoped she'd be able to remember everything she said in case someone asked again. Of course, it might not matter. She wouldn't be in Millersberg very long. Just long enough to get ticket money for her and Winnie saved up.

Thinking about money for the train made her interrupt a boy's question. "Is there any place in Millersberg that'd hire a girl like me?"

Rosemary blinked at her. "You live with Mrs. Haak, right? How come you don't just help in her store? Seems like that would make the most sense."

Evelyn rolled her eyes. "She's already got somebody working for her. Besides, her store's small—nothing like the department stores in New York." She sniffed and fluffed her hair. "Not that I expect to find anything close to that here. But there's gotta be a store big enough to need some extra help now an' then."

"I dunno." The boy whose question she'd cut off shrugged. "I got enough chores at home to keep me busy. I wouldn't want to take on a job someplace else."

Others nodded and murmured their agreement.

Evelyn stifled a huff. They weren't helping very much. The bell rang, and everybody gathered up their lunch pails and sauntered toward the schoolhouse a lot slower than they'd come out of it. Rosemary and the two girls she'd introduced as her best-friends-since-forever, Bertie Mae and Norma, walked with Evelyn. They talked and laughed all the way up the stairs, quieting only when they slid into their bench seats.

Lunch break had passed too fast. Evelyn had never realized how nice it was to be with girls her age. At the home, she spent her time with Winnie. Plus, kids were always coming and going, so she hadn't made many friends. She liked being part of a group, giggling with the other girls. She wasn't ready for more studies, but Mr. Herriott didn't waste any time getting down to business. He told the grade seven kids to read a story from their primer, then told the grade eight kids to work on their maps, whatever that meant. He started talking to the oldest students about the essays they'd written on the Revolutionary War.

Evelyn opened the primer she'd been given, but instead of reading, she leaned sideways and whispered in Rosemary's ear. "If you hear about a job I could do, will you tell me?"

"'Course I will." Rosemary sent a quick look in the teacher's direction, then whispered from the corner of her mouth. "But how come you need a job so bad?"

"It's kind of a secret. Do you wanna come over to Mrs. Haak's after school? I'll tell you then."

"Evelyn and Rosemary?"

Rosemary jumped. Evelyn sat straight up on the bench.

Mr. Herriott was scowling at them from across the room. "Why are you talking instead of reading?"

Evelyn sucked in her lips. She hadn't meant to get Rosemary in trouble. She thought quick. "I was just asking her a question . . . like you told me I could."

Mr. Herriott folded his arms. "Did you receive an answer?"

Evelyn fought a grin. "No, sir. Not yet."

A few kids tittered.

Mr. Herriott stared at her for several seconds, as if trying to see underneath her skin. She resisted squirming. Finally, he nodded. "Rosemary, please give Evelyn the information she seeks, and then both of you return to your reading."

"Yes, sir," Rosemary and Evelyn chorused. Mr. Herriott turned his attention to the other students again. Evelyn exchanged a grin with Rosemary, then whispered, "So, can you come over?"

"Let's stop by my house after school and ask my ma. If she says yes, I'll come."

Evelyn nodded, squelching a happy squeal. She didn't plan to be here long. Not long at all. But while she was here, it would sure be nice to have a friend.

Chapter Eight

Hester

Hester tucked three biscuit-and-bacon sandwiches into each of the tin lunch pails on the counter. As she reached for the pint jars of water she always added, her gaze drifted to the calendar nailed to the wall next to the Frigidaire. She gave a start. She'd been so busy she'd neglected to change the month to April.

Wiping her hands on her apron, she crossed to the advertising calendar she'd been given by the Millersberg Bank & Trust Company last Christmas and tore away the page for March. Ordinarily, she'd discard the sheet. But she folded the page representing March 1931 and slipped it into her apron pocket, planning to put it in the cedar keepsake box Dale had given her for their first anniversary.

With her fingertip, she touched today's date—April third—and smiled. The children's tenth day of attending their new school. Tomorrow would mark two weeks of them living with her, and the day after that was Easter Sunday, their first holiday together as a family. Milestones, of sorts. Should they be celebrated? She hurried to Scotty, who sat at the table sipping coffee while the children finished their breakfast oatmeal.

"When you open the store this morning, would you please set aside one of the tinned hams and"—she cupped her hand and whispered into his ear—"three of the chocolate eggs?" She should have done it herself when the shipment came in last week. The cream-filled chocolate eggs decorated with candy flowers had been popular with her customers even though they were quite pricey at nineteen cents per eight-ounce egg. She hoped there were still three remaining in the display box on the counter.

Scotty swiped his mouth with his napkin and stood. “I’ll see to it right now, ma’am.” He ruffled Guy’s hair, winked at Winnie, saluted Evelyn in mock seriousness, then ambled out the back door, letting the screen door slap into its frame the same way the children always did.

She returned to the lunch pails and gave the water-jar lids one more check before placing the jars in with the biscuits. As she carried the pails to the table, Evelyn rose and began gathering up the bowls, cups, and spoons. Hester gave the girl her brightest smile. “Thank you, sweetheart.” Evelyn didn’t reply verbally, but her head bobbed in a brief nod.

Hester removed the dish towel she’d tied around Winnie’s neck as a bib and used it to clean the little girl’s face. To her amusement, there was even a small clump of oatmeal in the child’s hair. “Winnie, did you get any food in your tummy at all? You seem to be wearing most of your oatmeal.”

Winnie giggled and twisted her head back and forth. “You tickling me!”

Guy scrubbed his mouth with his red-and-white-checked napkin. “Oatmeal’s sticky. It’s hard to get off.”

Evelyn, running water in the sink, released a little huff. “If you didn’t try to shove half the bowl into your mouth in one bite, you wouldn’t get it all over your face.”

Guy shrugged. “I’m hungry in the morning. We’ve gone all night without eatin’. Besides, you take bigger bites’n I do. I’ve seen you.”

Evelyn flounced out of the kitchen, disappearing behind the sheet-turned-curtain shielding her sleeping area.

Hester lifted Winnie from her chair. “Please ask Evelyn to help you with your shoes.”

“Yes, ma’am.” Winnie skipped around the corner.

Hester smiled, watching her go. Such a sunny little girl, nothing like the screeching, scratching, bucking tornado she'd been in the train yard. The first few days alone with Hester and Scotty, she'd asked repeatedly for "Sissy," but she quickly adapted to the routine of going to the store while the other children were in school. Scotty put together a basket of odds and ends—empty spools, string, paper and crayons, a bundle of yarn strategically tied to resemble a doll, and a couple battered small tin cars he'd found somewhere. Winnie entertained herself for hours with the items in what she called her workbasket.

Suddenly Hester realized Guy was still sitting at the table, one arm draped over the chair's backrest and his feet swinging. "Guy, it's nearly time to leave for school. Have you brushed your teeth?" He turned his eyes toward the ceiling for a moment, then wagged his head back and forth. "Do so, please, and comb your hair. You have a rooster tail." He snickered, and she grinned at him. Amazing how much delight she found in uttering the same kinds of directions mothers all over town were likely giving to their children. For the first time in her adult life—including the years she'd shared with Dale—she truly felt as if she fit with the other women in the community.

At a quarter to eight, she walked the children to the edge of the street, as had become her custom over the past days. Evelyn hugged Winnie while Hester hugged Guy, and then Hester brushed Evelyn's sleeve with her fingers in lieu of the hug she longed to deliver. The two oldest children set off for school, Evelyn walking just a bit ahead of Guy.

Hester called after them, "Have a good day!" Guy turned backward and waved, then spun and trotted after Evelyn. Hester took Winnie by the hand. "Time for us to go to work."

Winnie smiled her crinkle-nose smile. She pulled loose from Hester's light hold and ran to the store. "Uncle 'cotty! I comin' to work now!"

Chuckling to herself, Hester followed. Scotty had already turned on the electric lights and propped open the front door with the rusty old iron doorstop shaped like a sleeping cat. Winnie ran straight to it. She crouched and petted the cat's head, the way she'd done every morning so far.

Scotty leaned on the counter, grinning at the child. He glanced over as Hester approached and bounced his thumb in Winnie's direction. "The way she's taken to that lump o' iron, think how she'd like a real fur-an'-purr cat. Or maybe a floppy-eared puppy dog."

Hester sent an indulgent smile in Winnie's direction. "I have enough to take care of without adding an animal to the household."

Disappointment seemed to purse Scotty's face. "Reckon so. Oh! Ma'am . . ." He lowered his voice to a whisper. "I put them eggs you wanted on a shelf in my room."

"Thank you." She would place them next to the children's breakfast plates on Easter Sunday. Wouldn't the table look festive with the eggs as decorations? Or maybe she should wait for dinnertime. If they ate something so sweet for breakfast, they might have tummy aches. So many things a mother had to consider.

"Good thing you said somethin'." He gestured to the display box. "There's only one left now. That'll surely be gone by day's end. Next year, you might wanna order two boxes of 'em."

"I'll make note of that in my order book. I wasn't sure if they'd sell at all, considering the nice selection of chocolates the drugstore always has available." She removed her gingham kitchen apron and laid it on the counter, then took her bibbed work apron from its hook and slipped it on. When she lifted the kitchen apron to fold it, the calendar page she'd put in the pocket slipped out and drifted to the floor. Scotty pinched it up and handed it to her. She thanked him and started to put it with the apron, but then she impulsively unfolded it and showed it to him. "Do you know what this is?"

He squinted at it. "Looks like a page tore off the calendar."

She turned the sheet so the numbers faced her. "You're right, but it's much more than that. It's a record of my time with the children thus far. The first days of being a mother." Winnie skipped by, humming, and Hester's heart swelled as she watched the happy child retrieve the yarn doll from her basket. "They've settled in well, don't you think?"

"Yep."

Although he gave an affirmative answer, something in his tone set her senses on alert. She looked at him. "Is something wrong?"

"No. I'd say everything's as right as rain." He stood upright and jammed his hands into his pants pockets. "Oh, now, that Evelyn, she's still standoffish or quarrelsome most o' the time, but she helps out. Does her schoolwork an' all far as I can tell." His gaze drifted to Winnie, and softness tinged his features. "But the little ones . . . why, it's like they never been no place else in their whole lives, the way they've took to bein' with you."

Hester slowly nodded. Maybe all the prayers she and Scotty had offered over the past three years about her taking in a child had paved the way for an easy transition.

Scotty cleared his throat. "How many days has it been now?"

Hester smiled at the calendar page, memories from each precious day represented rolling in her mind. "Tomorrow will mark two full weeks."

"Uh-huh." An ominous utterance.

She jerked her attention to him. The worry glimmering in his blue eyes ignited her own concern. "What is it, Scotty?"

"Should you ought to be hearin' somethin' soon from that place in New York about whether they'll git to stay or hafta go?"

Hester looked at the page for March again. On which day had she ceased fretting over the agreement she'd made concerning the children's placement? She couldn't remember. In the busyness of adapting her schedule to accommodate the children's needs, worry had slipped away. But Scotty's question brought it all rushing to the fore. "I . . . I suppose there's been sufficient time for the guardians to reach New York and turn in the paperwork. It could be very soon."

"How they gonna let you know?"

"I had no telephone number to give them, but I wrote my address on the paperwork. I presume I'll receive a letter." She chewed her lower lip. She fixed her gaze on little Winnie cheerfully building a tower of wooden spools. Her heart rolled over in her chest. Oh, how she loved the child. She'd agreed to the terms of a temporary placement, but how would she be able to give up Winnie, Guy, and Evelyn if the orphans' asylum directors ordered her to do so?

"You know . . ." Scotty's soft drawl pulled Hester from her inner thoughts. "That place in New York is closin'. Them people ain't gonna come back here an' check on things. Just 'cause they say you gotta take 'em to Marion don't mean—"

"Yes, I do." Her heart would shatter if she had to deliver them to the poor farm, but her conscience wouldn't allow her to break her agreement. "A person's word is her bond." He nodded, his expression so sorrowful that tears stung Hester's eyes. She patted his wrist. "I know you love them and don't want to see them taken away. But the directors could just as easily say nothing and allow things to remain as they are."

"I'm sure prayin' no letter comes." His solemn yet hopeful face and tone matched Hester's thoughts. "But even if it does come, I been thinkin' on it, an' . . . " He scratched his cheek. "At the poor farm, are the rules about adoptin' the same as that home in New York?"

Hester shook her head slightly, uncertain she understood the question. "What do you mean?"

He scrunched his face in a comical scowl. “Maybe I shouldn’t say nothin’, but it’s been weighin’ on me an’ I don’t have no way o’ gettin’ to Marion to ask the poor-farm folks.”

Scotty was never eloquent, but he’d never before delivered such a bungled speech. A laugh bubbled up in Hester’s chest and spilled out. “What are you asking?”

He pulled in a deep breath. “If the kids end up at the poor farm, can’t you—”

The screen door hinges squeaked, and then the little bell hanging above the door tinkled its announcement—a customer coming in. “We’ll talk later.” She hurried forward with a smile. “Good morning, Mrs. Noone. How are you today?”

New York City
Callum

The five o’clock whistle blew, loud enough to wake the dead. Like every other man on the factory floor, Callum yanked off his gloves, set aside his tools, and untied his leather apron. Heavy, bulky thing—what a relief to shed the protective cover. His stomach rumbled as he fell in line with the others heading toward the time-card machine to clock out and retrieve their weekly pay envelope.

“Holbrook!”

The factory foreman’s voice carried above the racket of scuffing boots and men’s jabber. Callum’s pulse skittered. Every time he’d been called over at the end of a shift, he’d been told his help wasn’t needed anymore. What would he do if he heard a don’t-need-you-no-more message today?

Legs quivering, he changed direction and crossed to the man. “Yes, sir?”

“About an hour ago, I took a phone call from a . . .” He scowled at a rumpled paper in his hand. “Miss Armstrong from the Mission Church Home for something else I didn't get written down."

Callum sucked in a startled breath. "What'd she say?"

The foreman lifted his scowl to Callum. "Said to come by after work. Something about your girls."

Callum grabbed the man's arm. "Did she say she found 'em?"

He shook loose. "You know how noisy it is in here. You're lucky I made out her name and part of where she was calling from. And I gotta tell you, I'm not in the habit of playing messenger to my workers. When you see her, tell her—"

Callum whooped, socked the air, and raced to join the workers clocking out. Hours seemed to pass before he had the chance to jam his card into the machine, return it to its slot, and take his pay. He pushed through the crowd, suffering a few muttered curses and lots of elbow jabs, but what did he care? He was going to get his girls.

On the subway ride, he clung to a post and fidgeted in place. Couldn't the car go any faster? Every day for the past two weeks, he'd fretted and stewed about the home sending his girls away to someplace unknown. Every night, he'd tossed and turned on his mattress in his big-enough-for-three apartment, wishing his daughters were with him, the way he'd worked so hard for. Every hour, he'd been tormented with regret for not fetching them before they got put on a train. What would Freida say if she knew how he'd let their girls get taken far away?

She'd tell him to pray.

The subway car screeched to a stop and he jolted. Or maybe the answer to his inward question jolted him. He left the car, the unwelcome reminder of the lifelong habit he'd abandoned needling him with every step. Prayers hadn't seemed to mean much after begging God to let his wife live and losing her anyway. Angry and heartsore, he hadn't gone to church again, either. But what about now? Freida would want the girls raised in the church. It'd sure seem strange to enter a place of worship again after years of staying away. Could he even do it? And why was he worrying about it now? First, he needed to get his girls back.

He trotted up the walkway to the Mission Church Home's front doors. He gave the solid door several hard whacks and then stepped back, counting the seconds. The door opened, and Miss Armstrong herself stood on the other side of the threshold. Callum blurted, "So, where are they?"

Chapter Nine

Callum

"Please come in, Mr. Holbrook."

The calm invitation went against the eagerness pulsing through Callum's veins, but he wouldn't get pushy with a woman. He whipped off his cap and stepped inside. Crushing the tweed cap to his pounding chest, he forced a calm tone to match hers. "Where are my girls?"

She turned and headed up the hallway. Callum followed, gritting his teeth in impatience. In her office, she picked up a piece of paper on the corner of the desk and held it out to him. "I've copied the information gathered from the guardians who accompanied the children on the last placement."

Callum took the paper and stared at the neat handwriting filling the center of the page.

"You'll see the name and address of the woman who took temporary custodianship of the children."

His head still low, he shifted his gaze to meet hers. "Temporary?"

Her lips puckered for a moment like she'd tasted something sour. "Yes. It's not our custom to place children in homes with only one parent unless there is a blood relationship. This was not the case here. But the guardians were reluctant to put the children in the county poor farm and so allowed"—she glanced at the page—"Mrs. Hester Haak to take the children with the stipulation she would deliver them to the poor farm if the home's directors rejected the placement." She made a *tsk-tsk* sound. "The board of directors has officially disbanded with the home's closing, but I didn't feel qualified to validate the guardians' decision. Thus, I've made contact with three of the five board members. All three expressed disapproval of leaving the children with this woman when they could very well be adopted into a family if taken to the poor farm. Given I already have a quorum as far as decision-making, I won't waste more time contacting the final two." She sniffed. "I've already listened to enough criticism for the guardians' decision."

So the lady who took in the girls wouldn't keep them. This was good news.

She gestured to another paper laid out in front of her desk chair. "When you knocked, I was in the process of penning a letter to Mrs. Haak, instructing her to transport the children to Marion immediately upon receipt. Since the letter will likely reach her before you're able to make arrangements for travel, we can surmise that you'll retrieve Evelyn and Edwina from the County Asylum for the Poor, located outside Marion, Kansas."

Callum had been looking at the words on the page, but now he raised his head and gaped at her. "You mean I have to go get 'em?"

She drew back a bit. "Well, of course, Mr. Holbrook."

Panic struck. "But you sent 'em there. Why can't you go fetch 'em back?"

The woman shook her head. "Mr. Holbrook, the Mission Church Home for Orphaned and Destitute Children is no more. There is no staff, no board of directors, no funding. The responsibility we possessed for the children in our care has been passed to various families and, in the case of Evelyn and Edwina, the tax-paying citizens of Marion County. If you want your children, you have to go after them."

"I can't go get 'em." His voice rose with the worry clawing up from his gut. "I finally have a good-paying job. If I leave it, they'll hire somebody else. Then, even if I get 'em back, how will I support them if I don't have a job anymore?" Callum's head spun.

When he'd asked the woman to find them, he'd thought for sure the same people who took the girls away would bring them back somehow. The big bubble of hope that filled his chest when the foreman said Miss Armstrong had called now burst. Helplessness took its place. "What'm I supposed to do?"

Miss Armstrong's mouth stayed shut tight, but she looked straight into Callum's face. And he looked at her. She didn't seem any happier about the situation than he was. Matter of fact, he was pretty sure she regretted what had happened.

She stayed quiet for a long time, and then her expression brightened. "Well, Mr. Holbrook, for starters, you are to be grateful." The corners of her lips twitched, the way his nose did when he needed to sneeze. Was she trying not to laugh? "Have you ever heard the expression 'God works in mysterious ways'?"

Freida had said it. She always saw God at work, no matter what. "Yes, ma'am."

A soft chortle shook her frame. "According to the guardians, there were couples at every stop who seemed interested in adopting Edwina. But each time, she behaved so reprehensibly, the couples changed their minds." She tilted her head, her forehead crinkling into a thoughtful frown. "Ordinarily, I would not applaud a child's misbehavior, but perhaps it was an angel—not Evelyn, as the guardians so frustratedly reported—who inspired her naughtiness. If official adoption documents had already been filed in the state of Kansas, you could have quite a legal battle to regain custody of the girls. As it is, if you show the administrators of the facility proof of relationship, you should be able to retrieve them quite easily from the poor farm."

Freida might've berated him for his attitude, but Callum wasn't ready to feel grateful. How long would it take him to save up enough money to travel all the way to Kansas and bring the girls back with him? And what about his job? Would the factory owner hold it open for him? He hung his head. Maybe he should let the girls be taken in by a family in Kansas, the way Miss Armstrong said could happen. Maybe they'd be better off.

"Mr. Holbrook?"

Callum gave a start. He'd drifted off so far inside his head that he'd forgotten Miss Armstrong was still in the room. She stood in front of him with a large brown envelope in her hand. On the outside of the envelope, printed in block letters, was EVELYN HOLBROOK (13); EDWINA HOLBROOK (4). She pressed the envelope into his hands, and he stared at the names, fuzzy images forming in his memory. A lump filled his throat. Freida's girls. *His* girls. He couldn't give up. He had to get them back.

He held up the envelope. "What is this?"

"We always pass the children's legal documentation and other records to their adoptive parents. Since Evelyn and Edwina weren't adopted, the guardians brought back the Department of Health Certificates of Birth we secured when you delivered them here four years ago. There is also a record of any illnesses they had while with us. Take the information with you. The documents will allow you to prove that you are their father."

Remembering how the girls held on to him the last time he was here, he figured their running and latching on would prove to the poor-farm people that they knew him. But maybe after all this time, they'd be too mad to run to him. He tucked the envelope inside his jacket. "Thank you, ma'am. I appreciate this."

"You're welcome." She smiled, but it looked more sad than anything. "I'm sorry I'm unable to do more, but at least you know where your girls are and that they are safe."

"As long as nobody adopts 'em before I can get to Kansas." He hadn't meant to sound bitter, but the comment came out that way anyhow.

Miss Armstrong tapped her chin with her finger. "I will add an addendum to the letter for Mrs. Haak concerning your plan to retrieve the children from the poor farm and ask her to pass the information to the asylum's administrator. Will that ease your mind?"

A mighty sigh wheezed from Callum's chest. "Yes. Thank you, ma'am. And"—he gulped—"ask that lady—Mrs. Haak—to tell my girls I'll be there as quick as I can."

Millersberg, Kansas
Evelyn

Evelyn fidgeted while Mrs. Haak prayed over their vegetable stew and biscuits. As soon as she was done, she blurted, "I gotta ask you something."

Mrs. Haak sent the same indulgent smile she always wore across the table. "Of course. What is it?"

Winnie reached for the plate of biscuits and nearly toppled her milk cup. Evelyn moved the cup away from Winnie's waving arm. "Be careful."

Winnie pouted. "But I want a biscuit."

Mrs. Haak aimed the smile at Winnie now. "I'll fix one for you. With butter or with jam?"

"Jam!" Winnie waved both arms in the air. "'trawberry jam!"

Evelyn sighed. "Ssssstrawberry. And there's only peach."

Mrs. Haak rose. "I have strawberry jam in the Frigidaire. I'll get it."

Evelyn gritted her teeth, counting the ticks from the wall clock while Mrs. Haak fetched the jar, broke a biscuit in two, and spooned strawberry jam onto each half. She placed the halves on Winnie's plate and glanced around the table. "Would anyone else like strawberry jam?"

Scotty swallowed a bite of stew and wiped his mouth with his napkin. "I'd ruther have peach." He picked up the bowl with peach jam and its spoon, then grabbed two biscuits. "I like how sssstrawberries"—he grinned at Winnie—"taste, but all them little seeds get stuck in my teeth."

Mrs. Haak laughed real light and airy like she didn't have a care in the world. She turned to Guy. "What do you like best—sssstrawberry or peach?"

Guy smirked, holding a dripping spoonful of soup close to his mouth. "G-g-g-g-grape."

The grown-ups laughed. Evelyn rolled her eyes. Guy hadn't said anything all that clever. And when would they stop talking about jam? "Excuse me, I have a question."

Mrs. Haak's cheeks went pink. "I'm sorry, Evelyn. Please ask it now."

"Today when me an' Guy went to the post office—"

"Why'd you go?" Scotty talked past a lump of biscuit in his cheek. "Ain't that Guy's chore?"

Guy crinkled his face. "I asked her to 'cause there was a big boy bothering me. But he don't bother me when Evelyn's with me." He sent an admiring grin at Evelyn. "She's tough."

Concern creased Mrs. Haak's brow. "Someone is bothering you? Who is it?"

Evelyn huffed. "His name is Wilbur. He's a grade ahead of Guy, an' he's always picking on the littler kids. I told him to leave Guy alone or I'd punch him in the stomach. Then I walked Guy to the post office to make sure the kid wouldn't follow." She expected Mrs. Haak to praise her for looking out for Guy, but the woman shook her head like she was disappointed.

"Evelyn, one must never use violence to solve a problem."

Punching would-be bullies in the stomach had solved a lot of problems at the home. Nobody picked on Evelyn or Winnie there. "I won't have to if he leaves Guy alone. Now, as I was saying . . ." She shot a scowl at every person at the table, daring them to interrupt again. "Today after I walked Guy to the post office, I saw a Help Wanted sign in the window at the big general store where we got our lunch pails. I went inside and asked the boss what kind of help, and he said toting crates for folks, dusting an' sweeping, putting stuff back where it belongs when somebody moves it . . . that kind of thing." She leaned forward a little bit, excitement making her tummy tremble. "He said the job pays ten cents an hour and I can start Monday if you gimme a note with permission. Can I have a note?"

"Evelyn . . ." Mrs. Haak's tone held a warning.

Evelyn knew what the woman planned to say. "It ain't for all day." She'd rather work all day than go to school. How much longer would Mr. Herriott wait to tell Mrs. Haak how Evelyn wasn't keeping up? If not for copying some of the arithmetic and history answers off Rosemary's papers, she'd hardly get any problems right. "After school and Saturdays, that's all."

Mrs. Haak set her spoon down. "What about your homework and your chores here? How will you finish those if you're at Ebright's so many hours?"

Evelyn had thought it all out on her walk home from the store. "I'll do homework from my morning classes at noon recess. Rosemary'll help me. Then I'll do my afternoon homework here when I'm done with my chores. I probably won't have time to listen to you read to us before bed, but I'm too old for that anyway." Some of the stories, though—like the ones about Jesus healing the lepers and the shepherd going after a lost sheep—reminded her of stories Mama read to her when she was little. She steeled herself against thinking about those bygone days. "I've only been listening so Winnie'd sit still for you. But she's so used to it now she'll sit still without me. Won't you, Winnie?"

Winnie shook her head.

Evelyn rolled her eyes. "She's just being ornery. She'll listen without me."

Winnie giggled.

Mrs. Haak gave Winnie that soft smile that made Evelyn wish she was still little and cute. "I'm sure she will, but I'm still uncertain about you taking on such a big responsibility. You won't have time for after-school visits with Rosemary, Norma, and Bertie Mae if you have a job."

Evelyn would miss time with her friends. They'd started calling themselves Little Women after the characters in the storybook. The others decided Evelyn was Amy because she was the feistiest one. She liked being part of their circle, but it was best to stop spending so much time with them. She'd leave for New York as soon as she had enough money. She forced a shrug. "I'll still see them at school, and I'll also see Rosemary at church."

"And I'm afraid your schoolwork will badly suffer if you're rushing through it at recess or right before bed."

It couldn't suffer any worse than it already was, but Evelyn didn't want to say so. She sucked in her lips and begged with her eyes.

Mrs. Haak made an *I'm sorry* face. "As much as I'd like to approve, I don't think it's a good idea."

Scotty stuck out his hand. "Miz Hester, I ain't meanin' to intrude on your decision-makin'. You're the mama, after all."

Evelyn bristled. Mrs. Haak was not her mama.

"But," the man went on in his slow drawl, "maybe you're bein' too hasty. Evelyn's growin' up. Takin' on a little more responsibility might be good for the gal." He looked real hard into Mrs. Haak's face. "Might even make her feel like Millersberg's her real home."

For several seconds, the two grown-ups stared at each other. Winnie and Guy went on eating, making smacking noises, dropping biscuit crumbs everywhere, and squirming in their chairs. Evelyn held her breath and waited, wishing she could read whatever silent words passed between them.

Finally, Mrs. Haak gave a little nod and turned to Evelyn. "All right, I'll give you the permission note."

A happy gasp escaped Evelyn's throat. She sucked in her lips again so another one wouldn't come out.

"But you must promise that if your schoolwork falls behind or you don't see to your chores here at the house, you'll agree to quit. Do you promise?"

Evelyn crossed her fingers in her lap. "I promise."

Mrs. Haak and Scotty exchanged another look, and then Mrs. Haak sighed. "Eat your supper now before it's stone-cold."

Evelyn spooned up a bite. The soup was already stone-cold, but she didn't care. She was going to make ten cents an hour! First thing tomorrow, she would ask Rosemary to help her figure out how many hours she needed to work to earn enough for train tickets to New York.

Chapter Ten

Hester

After Hester tucked the children into their pallets behind the sheets, she crossed the yard to the store and let herself in through the back door. Lamplight spilled from the storeroom doorway and painted a path across the floor. Good. If the door was open and the light was on, Scotty was awake. Remaining near the back door, she called his name.

Metal springs creaked, and then Scotty's shadow filled the center of the glow, followed by his lanky frame still attired in the work clothes he'd worn that day. A slow smile climbed his stubbled cheeks. He glanced beyond her. "Kids sleepin'?"

"They're in their beds, but they aren't asleep yet. I understand why Evelyn is restless. She's excited about her new job. But the little ones are wound up as well."

"Still? They was actin' like little monkeys at the supper table tonight."

Hester laughed at his apt description. "They were. But I'm not sure why."

Thunder rumbled in the distance, and Scotty angled his head as if trying to discern the direction from which it came. "Could be 'cause a storm's brewin'. That thunder don't surprise me a bit. Been feelin' a rain comin' on in my knees today. Do you reckon Guy an' Winnie sense it somehow?"

Hester hadn't considered that weather might affect children's behavior. "I suppose we'll know, if they're here long enough to go through more than one rainstorm."

The corners of his lips curved upward. "Reckon we will."

The approaching storm must be affecting more than his knees. His knowing grin made him seem cocky. Perhaps he was overtired. She should deliver her intended message and return to the house. "I'm sorry to disturb you, but I wondered if you'd take Guy to the barbershop tomorrow. I didn't purchase new clothing for the children for Easter Sunday." Why hadn't she thought about it before now? Easter and Christmas—those were the days she observed children wearing brand-new outfits to Sunday service. Now it was too late. "But a fresh haircut will look nice with the suit coat and knickers he brought with him from the home."

"I'm happy to do that, ma'am."

Hester's heart swelled. She couldn't recall a single time Scotty had denied a request. "Thank you. I appreciate it."

He scratched his nose. "What about the girls? You need anything for them?"

"When I send Evelyn to Ebright's with her permission note, she can purchase ribbons for their hair and some lace gloves. At least they'll have a little something special to wear."

"You're a right good mama, Miz Hester. I hope you know that."

His praise meant more than he could possibly know. Heat filled her cheeks, and she looked aside. "Thank you." She faced him again. "I admit, though, I would have told Evelyn no concerning the job if you hadn't spoken up. Why were you so adamant she should take it? You know what she plans to do with the money."

He chortled. "Oh, I know what she plans. But she ain't goin' nowhere. An' if you tell 'er no, she's gonna resent you. Besides, it won't take long an' she'll be tired o' keepin' up with her schoolwork an' chores, not havin' extra time with them friends o' hers. Let 'er figger it out for herself, though. It's a good way to learn."

Hester shook her head slowly, smiling at her friend. "You're very wise."

He lowered his head and snuffled. "Aw, now . . ."

"Truly, thank you for your help with the children." She took hold of the screen-door handle. "I'll go and let you enjoy the rest of your evening."

He took a step forward. "Wait."

She paused. "What is it?"

"There's somethin' I been wantin' to tell you, but seems we always got little pitchers listenin' in these days." He waggled his hands beside his ears.

She laughed. "That we do." But how much longer would that be true? She wished the letter from New York would come and end the speculation and worry.

"I know you're frettin' about what the New York people'll tell you about havin' to take the kids to the poor farm."

Another rumble of thunder came, this one louder. A breeze whisked through the screen door and carried the scent of rain. They needed to finish talking so she could return to the house before the storm descended. "I'm aware of the futility of worry, but you're right—I have worried." A lump filled her throat. She had to honor her word but didn't want to let them go.

"Lemme tell you what I been thinkin'." He inched forward, his face alight with the same excitement Evelyn displayed about her new job. "The poor-farm people . . . what're they gonna do with them kids?"

Hester recalled what the guardian she'd spoken with at the train depot told her. "Most likely, given Evelyn's age, she will be apprenticed out. As for Guy and Winnie, I suppose the poor-farm administrator will look for a family to—" She gasped, realization striking with the same force as a bolt of lightning. "Scotty!"

He grinned big, nodding. "Do you reckon they have rules about not lettin' a single lady adopt?"

She pressed her palms to her fluttering heart. "I . . . I don't know. But it would be easy to find out." She gazed at him in awe and admiration. "Why hadn't I considered this before? If so ordered, I can honor my agreement to turn the children over to the poor farm and then petition to adopt them. Oh, Scotty." She grabbed him in a hug. "Once again, you're my angel."

He patted her on the back, chuckling. "An' I gotta tell you somethin' else." He set her aside and pinched his chin. "Hmm, maybe two somethin' elses."

His serious tone and expression gave Hester a little chill unrelated to the cooling breeze whisking through the door's screen. "What is it?"

"First, when you know for sure them kids're stayin', would you consider lettin' Guy get a dog? I know how busy you are with the store an' the kids, but he wants a puppy bad. A boy ought to have a dog of his own, don't you think?"

When she met Dale, he'd owned a mixed shepherd dog that had been his faithful companion since he was a boy of twelve. His parents got him the dog as a reward for winning a county essay contest about one of America's former presidents. He named the dog Andrew Jackson after the president. When Jack, as Dale affectionately called him, died a few months into their marriage, he was heartbroken. Yes, the bond between a boy and his dog went deep. It would be good for Guy to have a dog to love and be loved by. "I'll ask around about puppies this summer when he will be home all day to take care of it."

Scotty beamed his approval.

A flash of lightning briefly lit the sky, followed by another roll of thunder. The rain would start soon. "What's the second 'something else'?"

He waved his hand at her. "It's fixin' to storm. Don't want you caught in it. The other'll keep for a while."

"All right." The scent of rain was filling Hester's nostrils. She fidgeted with the screen-door handle. "Since I'm now confident the children will be staying, would you think about how to make proper beds for them? Something nicer than pallets on the floor?"

"Sure thing. Now, scoot."

Laughing, she trotted across the yard and closed herself in the house just as the first fat raindrops fell from the dark sky. She slept well that night, lulled by the soft patter on the roof, the melodious roll of thunder, and the sweet assurance that, regardless of what the New York orphanage directors decided, she would be able to adopt the children.

Saturday flew by in a rush in its typical busyness. Guy looked handsome and grown-up with his new haircut. After Hester told him so, he strutted around like a peacock the rest of the day. Evelyn was in a rare cheerful mood, having given Mr. Ebright the note granting her permission to work at the general merchandise store. Hester gloried in the girl's change in attitude and was grateful Scotty convinced her to allow Evelyn to take the job.

When the children had eaten their fill of the chicken and rice Hester cooked for their supper, they took turns bathing. Afterward, Evelyn coiled strands of Winnie's hair and secured them with rag strips while Hester gave Evelyn's hair the same treatment. The girls might not have new dresses to wear to church for Easter Sunday, but their hair would be curly and adorned with brand-new bows—white satin in honor of Jesus's resurrection. Winnie insisted on wearing her new white lace gloves during the process, and she gently clapped and hummed while Evelyn worked. Hester memorized every second of the ministration, savoring what some might consider a duty but was for her a privilege and joy.

After ironing the children's nicest clothes, Hester gathered the trio on the living room couch and read the Easter story from the children's Bible storybook she'd gotten off a shelf in her store. As she read the angel's announcement "He is not here: for He is risen, as He said," she blinked back tears. Jesus had risen from the grave, conquering sin and death for all eternity. She would forever glory in the new life He offered when she was still an unwanted orphan longing for love. Even while she continued the story, she inwardly prayed that these precious children would grow to love and serve Jesus all the days of their lives.

The story done, she prayed with them and then tucked them into their pallets for the night. Humming to herself, she headed to the kitchen, where the ironing board waited. She still needed to press her nicest spring suit for tomorrow's service. Scotty, his face shiny and hair still damp from his Saturday-night bath, sat at the table with his finger hooked in the handle of a ceramic mug.

He raised the mug and gave her a sheepish look. "I'm still feelin' last night's rain in my bones, an' the hot coffee is right nice goin' down." He took a noisy slurp. "Hope you don't mind me havin' another cup."

Hester ran the iron over the wrinkles in her pale-pink skirt. "Of course not." She'd told Scotty when she hired him that he was welcome to anything in her cupboards or refrigerator as part of his room and board. He'd never taken advantage of her offer. People in town sometimes whispered about his ragged appearance. He wasn't fond of a razor, and he rarely tucked in his shirt. But he had a gentleman's heart. Hester trusted him completely.

He sipped while she ironed her skirt and jacket, neither speaking, but she enjoyed the companionable silence. She realized she was completely relaxed, so different from the frenzied Saturday evening two weeks ago. She and the children had grown together well in a short period of time, and she knew in the depths of her soul she'd done the right thing by bringing all three of them home with her. She silently thanked God for the blessing of her little family as she hung the suit on its hanger and hooked it on the curtain rod.

She unplugged the iron and folded the ironing board into the wall, cringing at the rusting hinges' discordant screech. She aimed a grimace at Scotty. "Do you suppose you could oil the hinges before next Saturday?"

"Yup. An' there's another thing I can likely do by then, if you agree to it."

She turned and folded her arms, her lips twitching into an amused grin. "Oh? What's that?"

He rose as slowly as if his hinges had grown rusty and carried his empty mug to the sink, his heels dragging. He turned and leaned against the counter, folding his arms the way she had. "You ever been on a ship?"

What an odd query. "Not that I recall."

"I have. Worked on one when I was a little shaver."

If he grew up working on a ship, it explained his lack of schooling. She'd worked all her growing-up years, but the Webers had allowed her to sit in on the private tutor's lessons with their children. She'd probably received a better education than most, something she wouldn't have had if she'd not been sent west on a train when she was a young child. A bright spot in an otherwise dismal childhood.

Scotty tapped the floor with his boot. "Yep, spent near eight years on a ship goin' back an' forth from New York to England, cartin' goods to an' fro. Slept most nights on the deck with the stars shinin' down, but when the weather was testy, I took a bunk down below with the crew." He snickered. "Them bunks, they wasn't made for comfort, but a fella stayed dry an' warm down there."

Hester enjoyed the opportunity to learn a bit more about her ordinarily closemouthed friend, but why had he chosen this evening to share this part of his past with her?

"Them bunks folded, kind o' like your ironin' board there, up against the wall by day, then down for night. There was three of 'em"—he chopped the air with his hand at three different levels from low to high—"so three men could sleep in the same space as one. Is that makin' sense to you?"

The entire recitation was starting to make sense. She moved to the counter and leaned next to him. "Are you considering building similar bunks for the children in their half of the bedroom?"

"Not the foldin' kind. Not sure I could figure all that out. But I could fix 'em to the wall real good." His shoulders rose and fell in a slow shrug. "It'd get 'em up off the floor. An' bunks take up less space than a row o' beds." He shrugged again, sighing. "Now, them bunks wouldn't be nothin' fancy. Evelyn'll likely do some fussin' about climbin' up an' in. But they'd be sturdy. Meant to last. Maybe they'd tell the youngsters that they're meant to be here for good." His lips scrunched to the side for a moment. "One o' them little pitchers must o' heard us talkin'. He's worryin' about where he might hafta go. A real bed, even if it's just a bunk bolted to the wall, might ease his mind."

She wanted the children secure in their new home. She didn't need to give Scotty's idea another moment of thought. "This should be done quickly. Monday, if possible." A plan formed in her mind. "Tomorrow after church, I'll ask Elizabeth Stafford if Winnie can spend Monday with her. If she agrees, we'll close the store for the day."

"Close the store?" He nearly squawked the question.

She hadn't closed the store for a full day since Dale's funeral and burial, but this was important. "One time won't hurt. It's our slowest day of the week anyway. After Evelyn and Guy have left for school, we can drop Winnie at the parsonage. Then you and I will drive to Marion. While I'm at the poor farm inquiring about the children's adoptions, you can take the car to the lumberyard and gather what you need."

He drew back. "It's gonna cost some to buy lumber an' such. Are you sure it won't cut you too short?"

She was frugal, a habit she'd learned from Dale, who'd learned it from his father. Dale called it being a good steward. Interesting the things that were passed from generation to generation. She wished she had some parental lessons of her own to bestow. But she could share lessons from God's Book. "Beds are not a frivolous purchase. I'll take what I need from my money jar." Thank goodness Dale had never utilized banks. When the stock market crashed and so many banks, including the one in nearby Quarry, were forced to close, their savings were safe in a jar in the corner of their wardrobe. "I wonder how much it will cost to buy enough lumber for two bunks on the girls' side and one on Guy's."

A teasing grin lifted the corners of his lips. "Are you sure I shouldn't build two on Guy's side? You might decide to take in another little boy. Guy'd likely enjoy havin' a brother."

Hester laughed and delivered a playful pat on Scotty's arm. "Guy will have to be happy with a puppy." She held up three fingers. "Three bunks, Scotty. My house is full." As was, for which she thanked the Lord, her heart.

Chapter Eleven

Scotty

Scotty gave the crank on the Model T a good twist. Soon as the engine sputtered to life, he ran around and jumped in behind the steering wheel. Miz Hester'd told him she was too trembly to drive. He hoped it was excitement instead of worry making her quiver from head to toe like leaves in a hurricane.

Truth be told, he was nervous right along with her. But not for the same reason. When he'd wandered into Millersberg in the winter of 1928 after being chased off the train at a watering stop, he'd prayed for a warm place to lay his head for just one night. But God led him to an angel who said he could stay as long as he wanted to. He'd figured out right quick she needed help, so he became her extra hands in the store and around her house. But mostly he gave her somebody to talk to. She was one of the loneliest people he'd ever met. And he'd met a lot of people in his time.

Old people. Young people. Rich people. Poor people. People with hearts of gold, like Miz Hester. People with hearts as cold as the inside of a Minnesota icehouse. He'd met 'em, and he'd prayed for all of 'em, because the way he saw it, what all them people needed more than anything else was somebody to love 'em the way Jesus did. So he did his best to shine a little bit of Jesus's love on 'em before moving on.

Miz Hester already knew Jesus real good. Shined Him real good, too. And now that Evelyn, Winnie, and Guy were there, Miz Hester had all the company she needed. She didn't need him no more. Except to build them bunks. Maybe what he'd been thinking lately was right. Thinking about it again made nervousness stir around in his belly. When he was all done putting in beds for the children, it'd be time for him to—

The right front tire bounced into a rut, then bounced out again. He got all four tires back on even ground and shot her a side-eye frown. "Sorry about that. Must not o' been payin' good attention."

She adjusted her hat. "It's all right. This road is terrible. Almost like being on a carnival ride."

He'd worked a carnival or two, but he'd never took a ride. He'd wanted to, though. But if them rides jarred a person the way this road did, maybe it was good he hadn't. The two of them went back to being quiet. He kept his thoughts on driving. It wouldn't do to flatten a tire. They had lots to get done today.

When they reached Marion, Miz Hester pointed out the signs for the poor farm. It was a ways outside of town, almost like it was embarrassed to be seen, but he didn't know why. The big rock building with its spindled porches and tall square turret was as handsome as any castle in England. He pulled up in front of the building and kept his foot on the brake so Miz Hester could get out.

She dug around in her purse. She pulled out some paper money and a few coins. "Take this to pay for the lumber and whatever else you need."

He held up his hands like he was under arrest. "No, ma'am. You know I can't figure what's right to pay. In Millersberg, folks who come to your store won't cheat you even if it's me they're payin'. But I don't know nobody at the lumberyard in Marion. It's best I pick the lumber, an' then I'll take you there after an' let you pay."

Her forehead pinched some. "It would save time if you buy

the lumber straight-out. I don't know how many other stops we'll need to make today."

He set his jaw. "Ain't gonna tote that money for you. Don't feel right about it."

She put it back in her purse. "All right, then. Will you be able to find your way here again when you're done at the lumberyard?"

He couldn't read words, but he read landmarks real good. "I'll do fine. You head on in an' git them kids settled." He gave her shoulder a clumsy pat. "I'm prayin' all goes smooth as a ship sailin' a calm sea."

A real smile, the first he'd seen that morning, lit up her face. "Thank you, Scotty. I'll see you soon." She got out.

He watched her climb the porch, looking timid yet determined at the same time. He waited until somebody answered her knock, and then he drove himself to the lumberyard. He only knew how to drive because she'd took him on some roads outside of town and made him learn. In case she ever needed him to run errands.

If the Model T was bigger, he'd drive to the Quarry train depot twice a month and pick up orders shipped in from the east. But she hired out the hauling to Joe Frager, the only fellow in town who owned a flatbed truck. Joe charged separate amounts for the driving and the loading, so Scotty rode along and loaded the goods to save her a little bit. He'd offered to take the truck on his own, save Joe the time it took to go back and forth, but Joe said no—he wanted to drive it himself. Probably didn't trust Scotty with his truck.

No matter how many times he drove Miz Hester's Model T, it still amazed him that she trusted him with it. Especially since her husband bought it a couple years before he died. "Lord," he said as he pulled up beside the fenced-in area with stacks of white pine shining under the sun, "let 'er keep them kids. There can't be a better mama for 'em anywhere in the world than Miz Hester." He shut off the engine, dropped the key into his trouser pocket, and ambled into the yard.

Right away, a man trotted over to him. "Howdy, mister. What do you need today?"

Scotty rolled his eyes heavenward, retrieving the list he'd created in his mind. "Gonna need six eight-foot-long two-by-fours." The man pulled a pad of paper and a stubby pencil from his pocket and started writing. Scotty watched the marks show up on the page as he talked. "Four twelve-foot four-by-fours if you got 'em, ten-foot if you don't."

"We got twelve-foot ones, all straight an' square." The man said it real proud. He aimed his pencil at the paper. "What else?"

"I need nine two-by-fours an' twenty-four one-by-fours, all three feet long. Then probably . . ." Scotty scratched his chin. "Two pounds o' three-inch screws an' a gallon can o' white paint. The shiny kind." He sure hoped Miz Hester had brought enough money.

The fellow frowned at the list, twisting his lips this way and that like he had a seed caught in his tooth. "Well, now, mister, we're gonna have to cut down some two-by-fours an' one-by-fours, an' we got two orders ahead o' yours. Might take, oh, an hour, hour an' a half, before I can get to it."

Scotty shrugged. "That's all right. I got other errands. I'll see to them an' then come back."

The man clapped Scotty on the shoulder. "Sounds good. What name's on the order?"

"Hester Haak."

The lumberyard worker smirked. "Your name's Hester?"

Scotty guffawed. "No, sir. But that's who the lumber's for, so it's her order. I'm just buildin' some bed frames for the kids she's adoptin'." Should he tell this fellow Miz Hester's business? Well, it wouldn't hurt anything. Besides, he was so happy for her he could nearly bust his buttons.

The man's expression changed to real interested. "You say she's adoptin' some kids? Are they from the train that came through here a couple weeks or so ago?"

Scotty drew back. "Uh-huh. How'd you know that?"

He snorted. "My cousin an' his wife in Quarry took in one of those kids, but they're wonderin' now why they bothered. He's run away three times already, every time back here to Marion."

Scotty whistled through his teeth. "That's a four-mile walk—quite a ways for a youngster. Why's he keep doin' it?"

"Tries to sneak on the train." The man snorted again. "He's not good at it, though. He always gets caught an' they cart him back to Quarry. I told my cousin they ought to send him back to where he came from, but I guess the place that brought those kids is closed up now, so they're stuck with him. Not sure what they'll do. Well . . ." He grinned and pocketed the pad of paper. "We'll get those boards cut nice an' neat for you. I hope this Hester Haak has better luck with the kids she's adoptin' than my cousin has." He strode off.

Scotty got the Model T started and drove to the poor farm. He drove slow, watching for the turns he'd took before. But his mind was turning, making it hard for him to think. He didn't know the boy the people from Quarry'd took in, but his heart hurt for him. He imagined him walking that dirt road, same way Scotty'd walked so many roads in his life. Why did the boy run away? Was the people mean to him? People could be mean. He knew that better than he wished he did.

He was still puzzling over the unknown boy when he pulled into the poor farm's yard. Miz Hester was sitting in a wicker chair on the porch. She bounced up and almost skipped down the steps and over to the auto. She climbed in and then gave him a great big smile. "Guess what?"

Her cheerfulness cheered Scotty a little bit. "I dunno, but it must be good."

"It's wonderful." Inside the car, the roof put her face in shadow, but her smile was so bright she might as well have been standing in full sun. "The superintendent has no interest at all in having the children live here. He said their rooms are full, the other residents are all elderly and in poor health, and children would be a disruption to his routine. So he signed a letter advising the county health department to grant me full custodianship of them." She waved a sheet of paper like a flag. "To the courthouse, Scotty! I'm going to be a mother today!"

Hester

Hester could not stop staring at the Certificate of Birth forms laid flat on the car's leather seat. Was the ink dry yet? She'd been advised not to stack them until the ink had completely dried or it might smear and render them unreadable. She didn't want to mar a single letter of these beautiful certificates. Her heart fluttered with pure joy as she read the carefully penned names on the official documents.

Evelyn Freida Holbrook Haak, born on June 16, 1917
Edwina Marie Holbrook Haak, born on August 23, 1926
Marion Guy Sadler Haak, born on September 5, 1922

She hoped the children would be pleased she'd included their former names on the certificates that legally granted her permanent guardianship. She didn't want to erase their lives before they became her children, but she wanted them feeling secure in her love for the remainder of her life. The words blurred, happy tears distorting her vision. She sniffed hard and blinked, then stared at the forms again, hardly daring to believe this moment was true. And it happened so quickly. Surely, it was God's will for all of them.

While she admired the forms, Scotty and a lumberyard worker loaded lumber into the back seat of the car. The helpful worker had placed several burlap bags on the seat and draped a pair of flour sacks over the window ledge of the passenger back door. "The boards are gonna stick out—nothin' we can do about that," he'd told her. "But we'll do our best to keep from scratching up your automobile, Mrs. Haak."

Hester appreciated his consideration. She had a dime left in her purse after paying the fees for registering the children's births with the Department of Health's Division of Vital Statistics and purchasing the materials needed to build the bed frames. Strange how the fee for each child was less than a third of the cost for each bed frame. Shouldn't it be the other way around? But she was happy she'd brought enough to cover the expenses plus be able to tip the kind man for his diligent efforts.

Scotty stuck his head through the open window in the back. "We're all done now. Might wanna put them papers away so they don't blow out the window when we're drivin'."

His comment could be taken as lighthearted, but his tone held an undercurrent of sadness. He'd behaved oddly since retrieving her from the poor farm, but he kept his thoughts to himself. She decided not to prod him. She gathered the certificates into a neat stack and slid them into the manila portfolio she'd been given at the courthouse. "I'm ready."

Scotty went around front. As he cranked, Hester rolled down the window and waved the lumberyard worker over. He trotted to the car and she pressed the dime into his hand. "Thank you very much. I appreciate the precautions you took to protect my vehicle."

He put the coin in his pocket and tipped his hat. "No problem, ma'am. Have a good day, now."

She smiled. "I already have."

The engine was sputtering. Scotty slid in behind the wheel,

and Hester waved to the lumberyard man as the automobile rolled forward. She hugged the folder to her chest the entire drive to Millersberg, a prayer of gratitude constantly rolling in her heart. When they pulled into town, she said, "Please take me to the Staffords."

Scotty shot her a frown. "Don't you wanna get this lumber out o' the way first?"

"No. I want to see Winnie. I want to see *my* little girl." Her voice broke and she closed her eyes against the sting of happy tears. "She can sit on my lap on the drive to the house."

Scotty gave the steering wheel a tug and drove to the parsonage near the church. He switched the gear to Park but left the engine running. Hester got out and half skipped up the walk to the house. Not until she lifted her hand to knock on the door did she realize she was still carrying the portfolio. She was softly laughing at herself when the door opened.

Elizabeth Stafford pressed a finger to her lips. "Shhh . . . Winnie just went down for a nap. We don't want to disturb her." Then she stepped out onto the porch, and a smile lit her face. "Why, you're practically glowing. Your errand must have been successful."

"It certainly was." Hester hadn't divulged the reason she needed to leave Winnie for the day, only that she had an important errand to run. But now she could tell the preacher's wife the full truth. She could tell everyone the truth. "As of 10:23 this morning, I am the proud mother of three beautiful children." The woman tipped her head, her expression curious. Hester laughed again. "I adopted Evelyn, Winnie, and Guy. The certificates with their new legal names are right here." She held the portfolio out the way a child might show off a perfect spelling test.

The woman squealed and caught Hester in a hug. The portfolio got caught between them, and Hester released a little cry of alarm. Holding her breath, she peeled back the flap and peeked inside.

Elizabeth looked, too. "Are they all right?"

Hester blew out a sigh of relief. "Not even a tiny crease." She offered the kind woman an apologetic look. "I'm sorry for being so picky, but I want the documents pristine when I surprise the children with them."

Elizabeth gently squeezed Hester's upper arm, her smile understanding. "Will you tell them after school?"

"Not until after supper. Evelyn starts a new job today at Ebright's General Merchandise Store. She won't be home until later." It was only a bit past noon. How would she be able to wait so long?

"My, my, the children will be so delighted, won't they?" The preacher's wife gasped and placed her hand over her heart. "Hester, I just had the most marvelous idea. But, of course, you must approve it."

Elizabeth appeared nearly giddy, stirring Hester's curiosity. "What is it?"

"Well, as you know, when women from the church have their first babies, others in the congregation shower them with gifts."

Hester'd brought many a little nightgown, embroidered bib, or flannel blanket for other women's babies, always hoping for the day when people would celebrate her baby's arrival in like manner.

"May I organize a gift shower for your Evelyn, Guy, and Winnie? I'm sure there are things you need, and it would be a true joy for our congregation to help provide items for the children."

Gratitude and joy welled up with such force Hester swallowed a sob. "Oh, Elizabeth, that is so generous and kind, but . . . won't people think it's strange? After all, none of my children are babies."

"They aren't babies, but they're your first children. I believe that deserves a celebration. Leave it all to me. I love organizing parties. We'll have it . . ." She tapped her chin with her finger. "The nineteenth of the month, directly after morning service. Two weeks will give everyone time to prepare. We'll enjoy a light lunch in place of cake and invite the other mothers and their children to attend."

The other mothers. Hester was now included in that blessed fellowship.

Elizabeth hugged Hester again, this time from the side to protect the portfolio. "Oh, Hester, I'm thrilled for you. May God abundantly bless your new family."

Chapter Twelve

Evelyn

The minute the dismissal bell rang on Monday, Evelyn darted down the stairs and out of school, not even caring how many people she bumped with her elbow or lunch pail. She ran the whole way to Ebright's General Merchandise Store, dodging puddles still left over from Friday night's rain as she went. No sense muddying up the floor since she'd likely be the one cleaning it. Her lunch pail banged against her hip, and her books got heavy on her arm, but what did she care? She was gonna get ten cents for every hour she spent in the store. She needed to get there fast.

She burst through the door, panting. "I'm here! What should I do first?"

The lady customer at the counter and the clerk both gave little jumps and looked at her like she'd burped real loud at Sunday dinner. Evelyn wiped her feet on the mat, then walked slowly to the counter. A nervous giggle escaped. "Sorry. Didn't mean to startle you. I'm just excited about starting my job."

The customer eyed Evelyn up and down. "Are you one of the children Mrs. Haak took in?"

Evelyn laid her books and lunch pail on the counter. "Yes, ma'am."

"Why aren't you working in her store?"

Evelyn resisted rolling her eyes. Nearly every kid she'd told about her new job asked that same question. She gave the same answer she'd given the kids. "'Cause she won't pay me ten cents an hour."

The clerk—Evelyn had learned her name was Mary when she came in on Saturday with her permission note—laughed, but the customer didn't. The lady dropped some coins in Mary's palm, picked up the brown paper-wrapped package of whatever she'd bought, and left the store.

Evelyn turned eagerly to Mary. "Is Mr. Ebright here?"

Mary put the coins in the cash register drawer and closed it with a firm push. "He ran an errand. But he told me what he wanted you to do."

A happy shiver rattled through Evelyn. "I wanna get started right away."

Mary winked. "Looking forward to your pocket change, huh?" Mary wasn't much older than Evelyn—maybe eighteen or nineteen years old. She reminded Evelyn of the glamour girls from fashion magazines with her pin-curled bobbed hair and bright-red lipstick. If they got to be good enough friends, Evelyn might ask her how to do her hair in a wavy bob. Mrs. Haak could only do rag curls. Rag curls were for little girls like Winnie.

Evelyn shrugged, grinning. "That's why I'm here."

Mary came around the counter. "Grab your things and follow me."

Evelyn picked up her books and lunch pail and trailed after Mary beyond a curtain where only the people who worked there could go. She puffed up with importance breezing past that thick green curtain. Mary led her to a closet-sized room. "Leave your stuff in here while you're working. Nobody'll bother it."

Evelyn sent a quick look around the space. Two brooms and a big metal bucket with a mop stuck in it lurked in a corner. Tin dustpans and a huge duster made from feathers hung on nails pounded into the wall. She'd probably use all those things in her job. On the opposite wall, pegs held aprons like the one Mary wore over her dress. Would she get to wear one of those so people would know she really worked here? She'd like that a lot.

A bench was pushed up against the wall underneath the aprons. A purse already sat at one end of the bench with a sweater folded beside it. Evelyn laid her things at the other end of the bench, then took off her sweater. She dropped it on top of her books and turned to Mary.

"What 'm I s'posed to do first?"

Mary unhooked an apron and handed it to Evelyn. "Put this on."

Swallowing a crow of delight, Evelyn pulled it over her head. It sagged below the hem of her school dress.

Mary huffed. "That's way too big. Here, lemme fix it." She folded the skirt part at the waist and then crisscrossed the ties behind Evelyn's back. She brought the ties to the front and tied them real tight over the fold. She stepped back and gave Evelyn a frowny look. "Well, it'll have to do. Come with me."

Evelyn trotted behind her, wincing. The ties cut in under her rib cage with every step. The shoulder straps slipped. Maybe she'd ask if she could work without an apron. But she'd wait until tomorrow. She shouldn't cause trouble on her first day.

Mary led Evelyn all the way to a back corner of the store, where shoeboxes were scattered on shelves built right into the wall. Mary put her hands on her hips. "A lot of people came in for new shoes before Easter, so things got a little messy back here."

Boxes sat this way and that, some two high and some all alone. Evelyn shook her head. "Looks like how pigeons line up on a roof ledge—all hither and thither."

Mary laughed. "Mr. Ebright wants you to unhither and thither them." She pulled one box down and pointed to writing on the end. "See this little square with a number? That's the size. Then down here's a description that tells if they're for men, ladies, or children." Mary gave her the box. "Arrange them by size with the men's shoes on the top shelves, ladies on the middle, and children on the bottom. Leave some space between the sizes because there'll be a shipment of more shoes in by the end of the week and we'll need room for them."

Evelyn sucked in her lips. She'd planned on sweeping. Or maybe dusting. Organizing all these boxes by size would take a lot of thinking. Too much like homework. "Wouldn't you rather I mop the floor? Folks drug in mud on their shoes. I could clean that up real good."

"We mop after the store's closed. When you're done with the shoes, come to the counter. Mr. Ebright should be back by then."

Strange to find him gone. Didn't bosses stay in their stores? Evelyn put the shoebox Mary had given her on the shelf. "Where'd he go?"

"To make a delivery to the Widow Phelps." Mary giggled behind her hand, the corners of her eyes crinkling. "He left a half hour ago. She gives pie and coffee as a tip to whoever delivers her groceries. That's why he made the delivery himself instead of sending me."

Evelyn pictured the man who'd told her she could work here. He was shaped like Humpty-Dumpty from the book of nursery rhymes Mama had read to her when she was little. "He must make lots of deliveries to the Widow Phelps."

Mary blasted a laugh. The screen door slapped into its frame, and a lady's voice called "Yoo-hoo?" Mary patted Evelyn's shoulder and then inched backward. "I gotta see to the customer. When Mr. Ebright gets back, he'll tell you what to do next." She hurried off.

Evelyn stared at the disorganized shelves for a few seconds, deciding how best to start. Maybe turn the boxes so the size and who they were meant for faced outward. She liked the idea. The silly straps of the apron slipped off her shoulders and tried to trap her arms while she worked. It aggravated her and slowed her down. But she kept at it, flipping boxes around, setting them nice and straight on the shelves, and making sure the numbers lined up from smallest to biggest. Mary hadn't said to go that direction, but it made the most sense in Evelyn's mind, so she did it that way.

While she worked, she heard the door open and close, people coming and going. Mary chatted with everybody who came in, but Evelyn was too far from the counter to understand what was said. It was lonely and boring back here in the corner. Mary got to have all the fun, talking with folks. Maybe after she'd worked here awhile, Mr. Ebright would trust her to work at the counter.

Mrs. Haak had told her that morning to be respectful and responsible at her new workplace. Evelyn didn't much like being told what to do, but it was good advice. If she was respectful and responsible, Mr. Ebright would let her keep working there. She needed to work for a long time if the figuring Rosemary did was right. She paused with a shoebox in hand, recalling her shock when Rosemary said a ticket would probably cost as much as thirty-five dollars per passenger. If she and Winnie both went, it would be double the amount. Plus, they'd need money to buy food on the train. Rosemary told Evelyn she should save eighty dollars to get from Marion all the way back to New York. Then she'd said with her eyes real wide, "You'll need to work eight hundred hours to earn eighty dollars."

She hadn't expected such a big number—eight hundred hours was a lot. Her brain hurt when she tried to figure out how many days it would take. It made Rosemary's head hurt too much to figure it out for Evelyn. They agreed it would be weeks and weeks. But if she got a better job here—like being a clerk—she'd probably earn more. Then she'd have her train fare faster.

She adjusted the very last shoebox on the children's shoes shelf and then stepped back and admired how nice the shelves looked. Mr. Ebright would be pleased. A little bit ago, she'd heard a man's voice. Maybe he was in the store now. Her tummy trembled as she imagined how he'd compliment her for doing such a good job with the shoeboxes.

She whispered what she wanted to hear. "That's the finest organizing I've ever seen, young lady. Why, you should be put in charge of organizing all the shelves. Tomorrow you'll be our new shelf-straightening girl an' I'll pay you . . ." She let her imagination soar. "Twenty-five cents an hour!"

Eager to hear it for real, she hooked the straps of the annoying apron with her thumbs and pushed them back onto her shoulders. Then she started in the direction of the counter. Two ladies stood in the middle of the aisle between shelves of canned goods, chatting. She turned sideways to skirt by them, and she heard one say, "Isn't that just like Hester Haak? I can't decide if the woman is a saint or destined for a loony bin."

Evelyn bristled the same way she had when Guy told her about Wilbur picking on him. Were these ladies talking mean about Mrs. Haak? She ducked around the end of the shelf and stood real close to the display of canned corn, her ear tipped in the direction of the ladies. If they said something else mean, she might forget about being respectful.

"Well, now, Florence, it might work out all right," the second one said. "After all, back when she took Scotty in, I worried she'd be murdered in her sleep. Nobody knew anything about him. But he's proved himself to be trustworthy."

The woman named Florence tittered. "Even if he does look like one of the men who jump off the train now and then. What do they call those men?"

"Hoboes."

"Yes, he looks like a hobo. But you're right. He's been a good worker in her store and goes to Sunday service every week like any other civilized person. But, Ida . . ." Florence made a clicking sound—her tongue on her teeth. Evelyn knew the sound well.

Miss Armstrong at the home in New York did it a lot. It meant she didn't like something. What did Florence not like? Evelyn tipped a little closer. "The woman is a widow. Does she really think she can raise three children on her own? Why, I had Harry to help raise our three and I sometimes got overwhelmed when the boys were little."

"But these children aren't so little. Elizabeth told me the girls are four and thirteen and the boy is eight."

Evelyn gasped. They weren't just talking about Mrs. Haak. They were talking about her, Winnie, and Guy!

"The oldest girl will surely help with the littler ones," the one named Ida went on. "Hester will be fine. I'm happy for her. I'm not a member of her church, but Elizabeth said any women from the community are welcome to attend the celebration."

Evelyn perked up. A celebration sounded fun.

"Spread the word about the adoption party to be held at the Baptist church on April nineteenth."

Adoption party? Evelyn's heart took up pounding so big it made her shake from head to toe. Her ears started to ring. The women went on talking, but she couldn't hear them over the buzz in her head. They must be wrong. Mrs. Haak couldn't adopt her and Winnie. They weren't orphans. She and Winnie were going back to New York. She bolted for the room where she'd put her books and other things. She almost plowed into Mr. Ebright. Her feet slid.

He caught hold of her shoulders and kept her from falling on her rump. "Slow down there, Evelyn. I appreciate your enthusiasm, but I'd rather you walked in the store."

Evelyn wriggled free of his grip. "Mr. Ebright, I hafta go home." No, not *home. Home* was with Daddy in New York. "I mean to Mrs. Haak's."

Her boss bent down and frowned at her. "Your face is bright red. Are you ailing?"

Did the ringing in her ears mean she was sick? "Yes. No. I don't know." She pressed her fingertips to her temples. The right-side apron strap caught on her elbow and pulled. She grunted and jerked the strap up, and then she untied the bow at her waist with impatient yanks. "I just gotta . . . go."

The man stepped aside. "All right. I'll record an hour for today. Tomorrow—"

Evelyn darted off. She didn't want to think about tomorrow. Not if what those ladies said was true. She grabbed her belongings, then scrambled through the store, out the door, and up the street.

Chapter Thirteen

Hester

Hester took the chocolate–sour cream cake from the oven and placed it on the windowsill, breathing in the wondrous aroma. She'd not had spare time for baking since the children came. She squeaked out hours for necessary things—making daily meals, keeping the house neat, washing their clothes and sheets each week—by getting up a little earlier and going to bed a little later. If she wanted to bake treats, it would take time from stories and prayer. Hester wouldn't sacrifice those precious minutes. But today with the store closed, she'd had hours to spare, so she decided to do something special. To celebrate.

She ran hot water in the sink and sprinkled in some washing soda. Baking the cake created a mess, but it was worth it. Bangs and thuds, along with Scotty's soft drawl and Guy's and Winnie's excited voices, carried from the bedroom. Scotty had decided to build Guy's bed first since it would be the quickest to put together. Guy nearly turned a cartwheel when they told him what the stack of lumber in the living room was for. Little Winnie got wound up because Guy was wound up, but Hester wasn't sure the girl truly understood what Scotty was doing.

Would Winnie understand the meaning of the certificates Hester planned to show the children before serving the cake? Evelyn certainly would, and Guy might. Whether the little girl comprehended the importance of the documents or not, Hester understood, and she gloried that she could now ask all three children to call her Mother. Her hands stilled in the water, contemplating. *Mother? Mama? Ma?* With each title, she heard a different voice in her head—first Evelyn, then Winnie, and finally Guy. She chuckled to herself. Whatever they chose, she would find joy in hearing it. In *being* it.

The back door slammed and Evelyn burst in, her chest heaving and her face as red as a beet. Hester grabbed a towel and hurried to the girl, drying her hands as she went. "My goodness, Evelyn, is someone chasing you?" Maybe the bully had gathered reinforcements. Then she glanced at the clock, and uncertainty joined worry. "Why are you home already? I thought you were to work until six."

Evelyn smacked her books and lunch pail onto the kitchen table and glared at Hester. "I left. 'Cause I heard something, an' I have to know it ain't true."

Winnie dashed from the bedroom into the kitchen and threw her arms around Evelyn's waist. "Sissy!"

Evelyn wrenched Winnie loose. "Go on, Winnie. I gotta talk to Mrs. Haak." She nearly spat Hester's name.

Winnie's lower lip puckered out. Even when Evelyn was fractious with everyone else, she was kind and gentle with Winnie. Her rough treatment startled Hester as much as it must have hurt Winnie's feelings. Hester smoothed Winnie's hair from her forehead. "Go back to Uncle Scotty, sweetheart. Evelyn will give you a hug after she and I have talked." Winnie hung her head and scuffed around the corner. Hester laid the towel aside and aimed a firm look at the older girl. "Clearly you're upset, but that's not an excuse to be unkind. Tell me what's troubling you, and then apologize to Winnie."

Tears—of anger or remorse?—shimmered in Evelyn's blue eyes. She clenched her fists and planted them on her hips. "Are the ladies in town planning a party to celebrate you adopting me, Winnie, an' Guy?"

Hester stifled a groan. News spread faster in Millersberg than a summer wildfire. Why hadn't she asked Elizabeth Stafford to keep the adoption a secret until she'd had a chance to tell the children? The woman hadn't meant any harm. She was only happy for Hester. Hester couldn't be angry with her, but she wished she'd been able to surprise the children.

She reached for Evelyn. The girl made a jerky sideways step that put herself out of reach. Hester sighed. "I planned to tell you children myself after supper. I drove to Marion today and filed paperwork at the courthouse to legally adopt the three of you. You're now"—her heart fluttered—"my daughters and son."

Evelyn shook her head hard, the veins in her neck showing purple. "You can't adopt Winnie an' me. We ain't orphans. I told you—we're going back to our daddy. We're his daughters, not yours!"

Hester took hold of Evelyn's upper arms and guided her to a kitchen chair. She pressed the girl onto a chair seat and then pulled her own chair close. She sat and placed her hands over Evelyn's knees. "Evelyn, I know you want your daddy to come for you. To be honest, it's what I want for you as well. I would have given anything to have my own papa fetch me away from the house where I grew up. But the home's director sent your daddy letters asking him to come. He didn't." She spoke softly, tenderly, inwardly praying Evelyn would set aside her false hope and that it wouldn't shatter her heart.

Evelyn's chin quivered and her eyes welled. "You're making that up."

"No, honey, I'm not. And I'm not the first one to tell you this. The director of the orphans' home told you. The guardians who brought you on the train told you. As hard as it is for you, you must accept it."

"No." One tear rolled down Evelyn's cheek. She swatted it away. "Just because your papa didn't come for you doesn't mean mine won't. Daddy loves us. He said he'd come for us." She turned her face aside and sucked in her lower lip.

Hester's chest ached worse than it had the day she was told her parents were dead. Worse than when the sour-faced old woman at the orphan asylum took baby Effie from her. Worse, even, than the horrible days after Dale passed away. She'd prayed and yearned for years for children. To be a mother. Now it was here, and instead of the day of joy and celebration she'd long anticipated, it had become a day of disappointment and sorrow.

She sent up a silent prayer for comfort and strength, then gently squeezed Evelyn's quivering knees. "Evelyn, even though you're now my legally adopted daughter, I don't expect you to forget your daddy. I don't expect you to ever forget the mother who gave birth to you, either. In fact, I want you to remember them. Winnie is too little to have her own memories of your mama and daddy. If you don't share yours with her, she won't know them at all." How she wished she could share her few, fleeting memories of her parents with her sister. The wish couldn't come true for her, but it could be fulfilled through Evelyn and Winnie. "Hold on to your memories. Treasure them. But please don't trap yourself in what used to be. Open yourself to this new life here in Millersberg with me."

She waited, but Evelyn didn't look at her. Hester swallowed the knot filling her throat. "I love you very much. I promise I'll be a good mother to you." She held her breath . . . waiting, hoping, praying this hurting child would accept the comfort she longed to give.

Evelyn bolted out of the chair. She rubbed the tears from her face with her sleeve and then lifted her chin. "I'm goin' back to Ebright's. It ain't closed yet. I can put in another hour or so, earn another ten cents. I gotta make lots of money so I can buy those train tickets and get me an' Winnie to New York." Her expression hardened. "We have a daddy, and we wanna be with him. We're gonna be with him no matter what you say." She marched stiffly out the door.

Hester stared after her. From the bedroom, giggles rang. But they didn't lift her spirits. She slumped forward and buried her face in her hands. The Lord had given her the deepest desire of her heart. Adopting the children was her dream-come-true moment. Why couldn't it have lasted more than mere moments?

Scotty

Scotty couldn't take no more of smelling whatever Miz Hester had in the oven without having a taste of it. Maybe it'd erase the bitter flavor he'd been carrying on his tongue ever since the lumberyard man told him about the boy who kept running away from his new home.

With Guy and Winnie prancing along behind him, he stepped into the kitchen. Miz Hester sat at the table all bent forward, holding her head. Thoughts of something to eat went skedaddling. He hurried to her. "Ma'am, are you sick? You need some analgesic powders or a cup o' water?" He waved his hand at Guy. "Fetch a glass an' fill it up for your mama."

Guy scampered toward the cupboard, but Miz Hester sat up. "Guy, thank you, but I'm fine. I just needed to . . . think for a minute."

The sad droop of her eyes pained Scotty something fierce. He'd carried a burden since they left Marion, but she'd been so joysome. What'd happened? Then he spotted Evelyn's lunch pail and books stacked on the table. Suspicion filled him. Mindful of the little pitchers underfoot, he chose his words careful. "Had a run-in, did you?"

She gave the most miserable nod he'd ever seen. Scotty put his hand on Guy's shoulder. "Guy, how 'bout you take Winnie out an' show her the bunny nest? Them babies've hopped off by now, but I betcha there's some tufts o' fur in there. Bunny fur's real soft. Let her feel it, okay?"

"Okay. C'mon, Winnie." He took the little girl by the hand and led her out the door. As soon as the screen door snapped into its frame, Scotty dropped into the chair facing Miz Hester. "I thought you was gonna wait an' tell the kids at the same time—give 'em a surprise. How come you told Evelyn already?"

"I didn't. She found out about it at Ebright's."

His mouth fell open. "Who told her?"

"I don't know." She flicked the pages of the writing tablet, her head low. "I should have asked Mrs. Stafford not to say anything to anyone until I'd given the go-ahead. Why would people not talk about an upcoming party for three adopted children? There hasn't been anything like it in all the years I've lived here."

Scotty snorted. "They should have more sense than to steal your thunder. I'm sure sorry, Miz Hester."

"It's not having my thunder stolen that troubles me." She lifted her face. Her eyes were all shiny and she blinked real fast. "It's Evelyn's reaction to it. She . . . she doesn't want to be my child."

Scotty tried to act surprised, but he doubted she believed it. He'd be more shocked if Evelyn took to the idea. Still, he'd hoped, for Miz Hester's sake, the girl would prove him wrong. "Aw, now, you know how she is. She ain't one to think much before she spouts off." He clumsily patted her hand. "Give 'er some time. She'll come around."

"I hope so." Then she tilted her head and fixed him with a frown. "Scotty, you've been very quiet since we left Marion. Are you worried I made a mistake by adopting the children?"

"No." He said it real firm and shook his head at the same time. "You did the right thing. Them kids need a mama, an' they're plain lucky to have you, whether they know it or not. No, I . . ." Should he tell her? Her heart was already smarting, and she was a kind woman. Knowing about the boy who come off the train would make her sadder. He didn't want to spin a fib, though.

He rubbed his finger under his nose. “I was just caught up thinkin’ about gettin’ them beds built.” That was true. ’Cause he’d figured when they was done, he should probably move on. But he’d keep quiet for now. Knowing her kind heart as good as he did, she’d be sad for him to leave. He couldn’t add to her sadness.

He stood, his back giving him a little catch. He wasn’t as young as he used to be, and some of them pieces of wood was heavy. “I best git to work on Guy’s bed.”

“Mrs. Haak! Mrs. Haak!” Guy come running in with Winnie right behind him. “Lookee here what we found in the bunny nest!” He shoved a clump of fur under the woman’s nose. Winnie moved close and leaned against Miz Hester’s knees, her eyes aimed at the gray furball. Her sweaty face beamed.

Miz Hester took the fuzzy wad, her lips forming an O of awe. “Why, just look at this. A mama bunny scratched this from her own hide so her babies would have something soft to lie on. Wasn’t that a good mama? And ohhh . . .” She smoothed it over the back of Winnie’s little hand, smiling when the little girl giggled. “It’s very soft, isn’t it? You found quite a prize, Guy.”

Scotty’s cheek twitched with a grin coming on. Seeing the three of them so content together gave his worried soul a boost. That bit of fur wasn’t much of a real prize, but the woman sure was for those kids. First chance he got, he’d tell Evelyn so. And he prayed the girl would listen.

Chapter Fourteen

New York City
Callum

The air horn blasted. Loud enough, Callum was certain, to be heard all the way on Rikers Island. As always, it made his ears ring. But today it also brought on the prickle of sweat from head to toe. His shift was done. Now to talk to his foreman about going to Kansas to fetch Evelyn and Winnie.

He ambled toward the man who stood with his arms folded, scowl in place, observing the workers take their pay envelopes from the time-card rack the same way he did every Friday at quitting time. Callum wasn't a small man. Freida had called him strapping, always with admiration in her tone. But he felt like a gangly youth next to the barrel-chested man who towered at least three inches taller and much more than three inches wider than Callum. He'd not seen one fight break out among the factory workers, different from the daily scuffles he'd witnessed on the docks. Probably because Boss Moore promised to knock together the heads of any men whose disagreements turned physical. More to protect the machinery than the men, most likely. Callum wished he didn't have to talk to him at all.

He stopped next to the foreman and cleared his throat.

Boss Moore glanced at him without turning his head—a quick shift of his hooded eyes. "Yeah?"

"Do you remember givin' me a message last Friday from a lady at the Mission Church Home?"

Now he looked Callum up and down. His bushy eyebrows tipped closer together. "Yeah. Holbrook, right?"

"That's right." Callum licked his dry lips. "Y'see, my girls've been livin' there since my wife—their mother—died more'n four years ago. But the home closed, an' the people there . . . they sent my girls west on a train."

Slowly, the foreman lowered his arms. He turned and faced Callum. "There some reason you're telling me this?"

The noise of shuffling feet, men's chatter, and the repeated *ka-chunk* of time cards in the machine made it impossible for a quiet conversation. Callum didn't want the whole place to know his business, but Boss Moore needed to hear him. He forced his tight throat to speak above the quitting-time racket. "Yes, sir. The director of the home says if I want 'em back, I have to go get them. From Kansas. I want 'em back. But my job . . ." Were his tonsils tied in a knot? It felt like it. He could hardly get the words out. "If I'm gone for a while, will I lose my job?"

"How long's a while?"

Callum had checked train schedules. "Three days out an' three days back. Probably a day in between to fetch the girls from the place that has 'em now. So . . . a week." He wished he still prayed—he'd ask for God's favor.

The man worked his jaw back and forth, his narrowed gaze aimed somewhere beyond Callum. Finally, he gave a little grunt and looked directly at Callum. "You're a good worker. Haven't missed a day. You show up sober, and there's no horsing around when you're here."

Callum hadn't realized how closely the man observed the workers. Observed *him.* Would the praise that'd been heaped on him make any difference now? He held his breath, hoping.

"I can hold your spot for a week."

Callum's wind whooshed out, and his knees went wobbly with relief. "Thank you, sir."

"When're you going?"

Callum's throat went tight again. "As soon as I can scrape up the train fare." It'd taken him three months to save enough to secure the two-bedroom apartment. He needed more than twice what he paid a month for rent to ride the train to Kansas and bring his girls back with him. "I . . . I can't rightly say when that'll be."

"When you have your ticket bought, come see me again. For now, head on outta here. You need to clock out before the next shift starts."

"Thank you, sir." Callum trotted to the time clock and jammed his card into the slot. As he dropped his card back in its place on the rack, the man who swept up between shifts sidled up beside him.

"Excuse me. Did I hear your name's Holbrook?"

"That's right—Callum Holbrook." The fellow was nearly as thin as the handle of the broom and as wrinkled as a prune. Callum had no idea what his real name was. The fellows who worked in the factory called him Scurvy because he always walked half bent over. Callum didn't want to call him that, though. "What's yours?"

"William Francis Shelton." He chuckled. "But my ma called me Billy. I like it best."

Callum gave a nod. "Billy it is. What do you need?"

"Well, now, I think it's more what *you* need." Sympathy glistened in his pale-gray eyes. "I overheard what you said to the foreman about rounding up the money to go get your girls." He tilted his head. "How many daughters have you got?"

Callum swallowed. "Two."

"How old are they?"

"Thirteen and four." Still children but growing up fast. And he was missing it.

Billy rolled his eyes skyward and pinched his chin. "So, one fare going out and three fares coming back . . ." He snapped his fingers and grinned at Callum. "I'm thinking a hundred twenty should cover it all with some left over."

Callum gaped at him. "How'd you know that?"

He grinned and leaned on the broom. "There's not much about trains I don't know. I was a porter on the New York Central Railroad even before the Civil War. Yes, sir, it was a dandy job. I'd still be there if I could pick up something heavier than a broom." He shrugged. "Age changes a man."

Callum tried to imagine Billy in a porter's suit and cap, standing tall and proud. The picture wouldn't form. "I reckon."

"How long has it been since you saw them—your girls?"

Why was this man so interested in his business? Maybe he was lonely. Callum knew what that felt like. He could spare a few minutes. "Over a year." Another wave of regret struck.

"Oh, that's a long time." Sadness pinched the old man's face. "You want to get to them soon, I'm sure."

"I do." Men were gathering outside the doorway, ready to come in for the next shift. He and Billy should get out of the way. "Well, it's been nice visiting with you, Billy, but . . ." He gestured to the wide opening.

Billy glanced over and gave a little start. "Oh, you're right. I better get busy." He took a shuffling step forward, pushing the broom in front of him. "Callum Holbrook, I'll be praying you get that money gathered up real quick so you can go after your girls."

Callum's heart warmed at the man's kindness. He gave a nod and headed out. While he walked alone to his tenement building, he thought on the brief conversation with Billy. It'd been nice to talk for a bit. When he'd shared a room with three other men, they'd played cards around their rickety table almost every evening, but they hadn't talked about anything important. Not the way he'd done with Freida. He hadn't realized how much he missed talking to someone.

Loneliness, as heavy as the leather apron he wore at work, bowed his shoulders. The deepening evening shadows darkened his mood. He'd never minded evening falling when Freida was alive, because she'd have a lamp burning in the window and a warm meal waiting. But now it only reminded him of what waited when he reached home—nothing but a shadowy, empty apartment.

"I'll be praying you get that money gathered up real quick so you can go after your girls."

Billy's parting words rasped in Callum's memory, and he sent a peek at the slice of gray sky visible above the buildings. If Somebody was really up there, he hoped Billy's prayers would be heard. And answered.

Millersberg
Evelyn

Mopping took longer than she'd expected. So many muddy footprints everywhere! Evelyn didn't get back to Mrs. Haak's house until almost seven, and she was still mad. She'd planned to not eat anything for supper. Mrs. Haak took so much pleasure in putting meals on the table for all of them she figured it would show her good if she went straight to bed. But when she went in, the smell of pork chops, stewed tomatoes, and fried potatoes made her stomach growl. So she sat in front of the plate waiting on the table and dug in.

She'd never admit it, but it was lonely there by herself. Now that she was working, would she sit alone and eat a cold supper every night while the others went on with their evening? A soft voice drifted from the front of the house—Mrs. Haak reading to the little kids. "Glad I don't hafta listen," she muttered around a bite of tomatoes and potatoes mixed together. They tasted good that way. But the good flavor in her mouth didn't mix very well with the jealousy in her chest. Story reading was for babies, so why did she miss listening with them?

She shoved in another bite of food to chase the feeling away. She picked up the glass of milk for a big swallow. A folded piece of paper was stuck to the bottom of the glass. She pulled it off, set the glass aside, and unfolded it. Mrs. Haak's handwriting filled the middle of the page. Evelyn read real soft, " 'Evelyn, when you've finished your supper, look in the icebox. You'll find a surprise.' " She'd drawn a little heart at the end of the sentence instead of signing her name.

Evelyn didn't have to look in the icebox. When she'd come in earlier, she'd smelled the cake. Had seen it cooling on the windowsill. So it wasn't a surprise at all. Not like the surprise she got at the store when those ladies spilled the beans about her and Winnie getting adopted. The note said to wait until she finished her supper, but Evelyn didn't have to mind Mrs. Haak. That lady was not her mother and never would be.

The promise of cake drew her to the Frigidaire like a magnet's pull. She yanked open the door. Next to the almost empty bottle of milk was a saucer with a big wedge of cake on it. She lifted it out with both hands, careful not to tip it, and bumped the door closed with her hip. Just as she sat and plunged her fork into the point of the wedge, Scotty ambled in from the bedroom. He stopped and looked from the cake plate to her supper plate to her. His hands went to his hips and he shook his head.

"What?" Evelyn jabbed the bite and shoved it into her mouth, glaring at him. Daring him to scold her for not finishing her supper. Guy and Winnie might call him Uncle Scotty, but he wasn't her uncle. He wasn't anything to her, no more than Mrs. Haak was.

He crossed to the table and sat in his usual spot across from her. He folded his hands together the way they all did when Mrs. Haak prayed over their food, and then he rested them on the table. The whole time, he never looked away from Evelyn's eyes. She aimed her fork at the cake for another bite.

"Go ahead an' eat. An' while you do, little girl, open up them ears o' yours an' listen good." He spoke quiet. Calm. His face didn't even change expression. Anybody looking in would think they were having a friendly chat. He was a wily one. "Miz Hester done a good thing for you, the best thing anybody can do for somebody else."

Evelyn snapped, "What'd she do?"

He leaned forward a little bit. "She chose to love you, girl. An' lemme tell you, you don't make it easy on her." A wry chuckle rumbled. "I've met a lot o' people in my time, an' you might be the most disagreeable one ever."

The cake didn't taste so good anymore. Evelyn slammed her fork onto the table and started to stand.

"Sit down."

He wasn't anybody to her. She didn't have to mind him if she didn't want to. But for some reason, she sat.

"Nope," he said, using that calm, kindly voice. "There ain't a single reason why the woman in there readin' to your little sister an' Guy should care about you."

Did he have to rub salt in her sore feelings? She should've got up and left.

"But she does anyway, 'cause she's got a big heart. Big enough to forgive the people who didn't love her one bit durin' her growin'-up years. Big enough to give a no-account drifter like me a home. Big enough to adopt a girl who pushes her away at every turn." He shook his head real slow, real sad. "She didn't do nothin' more'n open up her heart to you, Evelyn. You got no cause to be angry an' hateful to her."

Evelyn hated him in that moment. Mostly because he was right, and it made her madder than ever.

"You wanna be mad at somebody, why not be mad at whoever plunked you in that orphans' home an' left you there?" Then he let out a little grunt. "No, instead o' bein' mad, I'm thinkin' you ought to be grateful to 'em."

She jerked so hard her spine hit the chair's ladder back. "G-grateful?" Was he joshing her?

"That's right. 'Cause if they hadn't put you there way back then, you wouldn't be here right now. An', girl . . ." His eyebrows rose up, and he pointed at her. "Here is the best place you could be. It's the best place 'cause it's with Miz Hester. Think on that while you eat the rest o' the supper she left out for you." He pushed to his feet. "When you're done thinkin', give Miz Hester an *I'm sorry* for bein' mean to her. You owe her that much."

He stared at her until she squirmed and looked away. Then he sighed and headed out the back door in his slow way of walking. Evelyn watched him, and as much as she didn't want to, she couldn't help thinking about what he'd said. About who she should be mad at. If she was honest with herself, Mrs. Haak hadn't done anything wrong. The person who did wrong was—

She jumped up and grabbed the plates from the table. She wouldn't let her thoughts go there.

Chapter Fifteen

Hester

Troubled by Evelyn's angry response to being her legal child, Hester spent a restless night. But Dale's mother had told her many years ago that restless nights were made for prayer, so she used those awake hours to talk to the Lord. And early the next morning, Hester arose with a fresh resolve. The three official birth registration certificates, each bearing the surname Haak, proved the relationship was permanent. It was time to make some permanent changes in her home.

Scotty intended to finish the bed frames today and get the remaining boards out of the living room. The sturdy bunk-type beds secured to the walls lent evidence that the children were here to stay, but each child having a bed was only the beginning. Between tending to customers on Tuesday, she created a list of to-dos that would change her house from a widow's dwelling to a family home. When she reviewed it at the end of the day, the length brought to mind the list of chores she was required to perform for the Webers each week when she lived with them. But she reminded herself, just as she had when she was a child, she had a full week to get everything accomplished.

She whispered her favorite part of Isaiah 41:10, a verse Dale often quoted—" 'I will strengthen thee; yea, I will help thee.' " Bolstered by the reminder, she tacked the list to the kitchen wall next to the calendar and began making supper.

On Wednesday after Guy and Evelyn left for school, she chose two items from the list to accomplish that day. *Find a shelf for the children's belongings* and *Look for quilts.* Even before the store opened, she cleared off a small standing shelf Dale's mother had used to display potted plants and assorted bric-a-brac in the front window. She put the plants on the windowsill and boxed up the glass bowls and figurines. She asked Scotty to put the shelf in the children's area of the bedroom to hold the books and toys she anticipated receiving at the adoption party.

That afternoon while Winnie napped in Hester's feather bed, Hester left Scotty to tend the store, and she pulled down the folding ladder in the kitchen ceiling, which led to the attic. She carried the box of her mother-in-law's belongings up and added it to other items stored in the triangular space where the rafters met the floor. Then she made her way through gray shadows across creaky boards to a massive trunk situated beneath the gable's single square window.

She used her apron and whisked away the dust covering the lid of the stained-ash trunk. Writing burned into the wood came into view—"Haak, Kansas, U.S.A." and some numbers too faded to decipher. The trunk had been her father-in-law's pride and joy, handcrafted in Russia by his father and used to carry the family's belongings across the ocean to America in the early 1870s. He'd passed it on to Dale, who'd hoped to bequeath it to his own son someday. Would Dale approve of her passing the trunk to Guy?

Enough woolgathering. She had work to do. She raised the lid, grunting a bit against its weight, and leaned it against the window frame. The pungent scent of cedar rose from the trunk, mingling with a musty smell that made Hester's nose tickle. Crumpled tissue paper held down by cedar chips protected the contents. She gently gathered the chips in the paper and set it aside, then peered into the trunk. A happy gasp left her throat. Just as she'd hoped, several quilts, all sewn and stitched by Dale's mother, lay in a neat stack.

She made a quick count. Five in all. Her pulse skittered into happy double beats. She scooped up the top three, carried them downstairs, and placed them on the kitchen table. Then she retrieved the other two. She tucked the tissue paper over the remaining contents, scattered the cedar chips on top—it wouldn't do for moths to sneak in—and then closed the lid and descended the ladder.

Her muscles quivered as she folded the ladder and pushed it up into its frame. Dale always dealt with the ladder when he was alive. She heard his warning play in her memory. *"That thing's heavy, honey, and if it drops, it'll come down on your head. Let me do it."* She smiled, recalling how he always wanted to do things for her and teased her about being "stinkin' independent." Childhood experiences had instilled her independent tendencies, but she'd learned to let Dale gift her with helpful acts. Now that he was gone, the independence she'd learned as a young girl let her forge forward without him. Dale's mother often said God wasted nothing. Hester understood the statement more now than she had when the woman was alive.

With a little sigh of contentment, she reached for the quilts, then quickly drew back with a huff of aggravation. Her hands and sleeves were covered with dust. A glance down her front confirmed she needed to change her apron and her dress before handling those precious items.

She washed her hands at the kitchen sink, then tiptoed into the bedroom and changed into a fresh dress, keeping an eye on Winnie, who went on sleeping soundly. Clean again, she returned to the kitchen and took the quilts into the backyard. She strung them on her clothesline, humming as she worked. An afternoon in the stout breeze under the sunshine would chase the smell of storage from the colorful coverlets. And they'd be perfectly displayed for the children to each choose one for their beds. She gave the quilts one more admiring look and then returned to the store.

Scotty was taking a gumdrop from the fat jar on the counter as she came in. He turned a guilty look in her direction. "I'll add it to my tab, but that black one's been callin' my name since I got up this mornin'. Just couldn't resist no more."

She dismissed his words with a smile. "You're welcome to a gumdrop every day, Scotty, just as the children are." Guy always took a green one, Winnie an orange, and Evelyn a red. Good thing they didn't like the licorice-flavored ones or they might have to tussle with Scotty. The thought made her laugh.

"Whatcha laughin' at?" He spoke around the candy bulging his jaw.

She shook her head. "Nothing important." She crossed behind the counter and scanned the shelf beneath. "Has Mrs. Reames brought in eggs yet today?"

He gave two big chews and swallowed. "Haven't seen her. But she comes in every day, dependable as clockwork. She'll be here by an' by." He arched one eyebrow. "You needin' eggs to bake another cake? That one from yesterday was real good."

Hester's list included *Find time for more baking* and *Chickens?* She'd given the children tinned cookies for a treat most days since they'd arrived, but homemade were better. Single-handedly running the store took up time from a lot of things she'd rather be doing. "No, I wasn't thinking about baking. I was thinking about the wisdom of getting a few chickens of my own. Since the children arrived, I've taken a good number of the eggs from Mrs. Reames for our use, which sometimes means I don't have enough for customers wanting to purchase them. What do you think about putting a chicken pen behind the store? Then we'd have our own eggs, and any extras could be sold."

"I think it's a fine idea." His whiskered cheeks twitched. "What about milk? You gonna get your own cow?"

She burst out laughing. "Goodness, no! I'll rely on the milkman. But chickens? I think the children could take care of chickens."

"An' a dog." Scotty tossed the comment over his shoulder as he rearranged apples in the barrels. "Don't forget the dog."

Hester wakened Winnie shortly before the school bell would ring. As they walked to the store together, she glanced at the quilts flapping in the wind. She was eager to let the children each select one for their newly constructed beds, but she'd wait until Evelyn was back from Ebright's. As the eldest child in the family, she should have the privilege of choosing first. Maybe it would bring a smile.

When Guy returned that afternoon, he scuffed rather than scampered through the back door. Immediately concerned, Hester bustled around the counter and bent to his level. "Is something the matter?"

He thumped his schoolbooks and lunch pail onto the counter and then turned a sorrowful look on Hester. "I done somethin' real bad."

"Real bad?" She smoothed his tousled hair, hiding a smile. "That doesn't sound like you."

Tears swam in his eyes. "I got the mail like I'm s'posed to, an' when I come out o' the post office, I seen Wilbur comin' up the street, so I took off runnin'. An' when I got home just now"—a plump tear rolled down his cheek—"the mail wasn't with my books no more. The wind must o' blowed it away." He hung his head. "I'm sorry."

Hester pulled her handkerchief from her sleeve and wiped Guy's face. "Accidents happen, Guy. The important thing is you told me and didn't try to hide it. That took courage."

His eyes widened. "It did?"

"Indeed it did. Only a very brave person owns up to his mistakes. I'm proud of you." She picked up one of his books and opened the front cover. "Tomorrow when you get the mail, put it inside a book." She closed the cover and patted it. "Then it'll be safe from the wind."

He tilted his head. "What about the mail from today? I don't know where it is."

Probably in the next county, as gusty as it was out there. She put the book on the counter and tapped the end of his nose with her finger. "There's no sense in worrying about it now. Maybe someone will find it and bring it to us." She beckoned to Winnie to leave her toys and join them. "Get some gumdrops for you and Winnie," she told him, "and you may play in the yard for a while." She winked. "Try not to blow away."

Finally, a smile graced his face. "Thanks, Ma." He fished out two gumdrops, gave the orange one to Winnie and put the green one in his mouth, then herded the girl out the door.

Hester crossed to Scotty, who was lining up cans of peas on a shelf. "Did you hear all that?"

"I sure did. Poor little feller." He turned his attention on her, his face as puckered with worry as Guy's had been. "What if that letter you been waitin' on from New York was in today's mail?"

She held out her hands in a futile gesture. "There's nothing I can do if it was. But what difference will it make now, anyway? I met Kansas's stipulations for adoption." She flicked up fingers one by one as she shared what the clerk at the courthouse had told her. "Must be at least twenty-five and not older than sixty-five years of age, must have a dependable source of income, must have adequate housing. So the rules in New York don't matter one bit. In the eyes of the law, the children are already mine."

An approving smile bloomed on his stubbled face. "I'm real happy for you, Miz Hester. An' for them kids. You all are lucky to have each other."

"More than lucky, Scotty. We're blessed."

He gave an emphatic nod. "You sure are. An' I'm real happy you ain't worryin', 'cause you know for sure . . . it's done."

"It's done."

Scotty's simple comment became Hester's cry of encouragement, a reminder that the desire of her heart was fulfilled. Later, she whispered it to herself, battling happy tears, as Evelyn chose the lovely indigo-and-white Irish chain quilt, then helped Guy and Winnie put their choices—a scrappy nine-patch in every color imaginable for Guy, and Flying Geese in autumn shades for Winnie—on their beds. She recited the phrase with each task accomplished as she worked her way down the to-do list she'd created. She used it as a reminder of the finality of adoption when Evelyn announced at the supper table on Friday how much money she'd earned to apply toward tickets to New York.

As she climbed into bed on Friday evening, she sighed out, "It's done," an admission of weary satisfaction with the week's accomplishments. Were things perfect? Of course not. But every day was a little better, a little more settled, a little more organized. Motherhood might have been, as Scotty so humorously put it, dumped on her, but she was finding her way through this new life journey and loving every minute of it. Loving them—all of them—with a fierce love.

Before sleepiness lulled her to dreamland, she aimed a smile at the stars shimmering outside her bedroom window. "Thank You, dear Lord," she whispered to the accompaniment of deep breathing on the other side of the sheet curtains, "for the gift of my children. Draw us ever closer with Your bonds of love and affection."

Chapter Sixteen

New York City
Callum

Saturday morning, after a visit to the water closet down the hall and a cold breakfast of two pieces of nearly dried-out bread and a cup of water, Callum grabbed the cracker tin from the top shelf in the cupboard and sat down at the little table in his kitchen. He popped the lid and turned the container upside down. Coins clinked and rolled, and paper money fluttered out onto the tabletop. He scooped the coins and bills into a pile and then sorted them—pennies, nickels, dimes, quarters, half dollars, and dollars. He set aside what he needed to save toward next month's rent. He picked out seven nickels and seven dimes—money he'd use to buy cheese sandwiches and a bowl of soup for his lunches and dinners until next payday. Then he added up what was left.

He shook his head and added it again. The amount was the same. But shouldn't there be more? For a full week, he'd nearly starved himself, even skipping the three-cent cups of stout coffee sold by a street vendor on the corner every morning. At this rate, it might take him a full year to save up what he needed to go get the girls. He glanced around the apartment, hoping something of value he could sell or even pawn might magically appear. But everything in the place was scavenged from trash heaps in alleys behind tenements or bought secondhand.

Groaning, he slumped forward. Why had he bought a sofa, a table, and beds and a dresser for the girls? He'd be closer to what he needed if he hadn't spent that money. Remembering what he'd paid, he snorted under his breath. He wouldn't be much closer. But closer, even by a few measly dollars, would be better than where he was right now.

With jerky motions, he gathered up the money except the nickels and dimes and dropped it back in the tin. As he stood to carry the tin to the cupboard, somebody knocked on his door. It'd better not be the landlord telling him the rent was going up. Rental owners all over town were raising their prices, feathering their own nests at the expense of hardworking folks.

He plunked the tin onto the shelf and stomped to the door. He swung it wide. "Yeah? What do you want?" Then he blinked in surprise. "Billy?"

The broom pusher from the factory, wearing a baggy, pin-striped three-piece suit, snatched off his battered bowler and gave a nod. "Yes, sir, it's me. May I come in?"

Callum stepped aside. "Sure, come on in." Billy shuffled over the threshold, clutching his hat in both hands. Callum closed the door behind the man and cringed. "I'm sorry I don't have anything to offer you—no coffee or . . . or . . ." What had Freida given to visiting neighbors? "Cake."

Billy chuckled. "I don't need anything. I've had my breakfast."

Callum hoped it had been more substantial than dry bread and water. The old man was so thin it seemed like a stiff breeze could carry him away. What should he do now? He couldn't recall the last time he'd had a visitor come to call. "Well, then, why don't you have a seat?"

"Thank you, Callum." Billy crossed to the sofa and sat, lowering himself slowly. His eyes, pale in color but still lively, met Callum's. "You sit as well, my boy."

Callum dragged a kitchen chair across the floor and sat. He rubbed his nose with his knuckles. "You're the first person who's come calling since my wife died. I . . . I don't rightly know what to say to you."

The man grinned. "Then how about I do the talking?" He laid

his hat on the sofa seat beside him, planted his palms on his knees, and sat up as straight as his curved spine would allow. "After our conversation about your girls, I talked to my wife. She and I agreed . . . it's important for you to be with your children again. We did a lot of thinking on it."

Callum envisioned the money in the cracker tin and stifled a grunt. "I've been thinking on it myself."

"I'm sure you have." Sadness pinched the man's face for a moment, but then he tipped his head slightly like a curious child. "Are you a churchgoing man, Callum?"

Callum looked aside. "Well, sir, I used to be. When I was a boy and even after I got married. But then . . ." He faced Billy again. "I haven't darkened a church doorway since August twenty-fifth, 1926. That's the day we laid my wife in the ground."

"Mad at God, are you?"

The abrupt question took Callum by surprise for two reasons. One, the man was brighter than he'd realized. And for the first time, he admitted it wasn't so much a lack of belief but anger that had put a barrier between himself and the God his parents had taught him to love and serve. "I guess I am."

"You suffered a loss. Anger's a natural response. But staying there doesn't do you much good, does it?"

Callum forced a laugh to cover the discomfort the man's question raised. "Are you a railroad porter or a preacher?"

A rumbling chortle left Billy's throat. "A porter no more. Never a preacher. But something I always am is a servant of Christ." His expression turned serious. "At least, I try to be."

Uncertain what to say, Callum just sat looking into Billy's faded gray eyes with all the little lines—laugh lines, Freida would have called them—fanning from their edges. The man was old, hunchbacked, and frail. He had the lowliest job at the factory. But in the man's eyes, Callum glimpsed a peace he hadn't known in a very long time. It unnerved him, but he couldn't look away.

"Part of serving Christ," Billy went on, "is talking to Him in prayer, just as I told you I would. And while I was praying, God gave me an idea. Or a plan." He swished his hand in the air. "Whatever you want to call it. This past Monday, I put the idea to work." He reached inside his jacket and pulled out a fat envelope. "Here."

Callum scowled at it. "What is it?"

Billy pushed it closer to Callum. "Take it and see."

Callum took it. It was heavier than he expected. He gripped it tighter, puzzling over what he felt inside.

"Open it, Callum. Look what God has done."

Was his statement a challenge or an encouragement? Either way, curiosity got the best of Callum. He unwound the string holding the envelope closed and lifted the flap. He gasped and almost fell out of the chair. Clutching the envelope, he gaped at Billy. "Did you rob a bank?"

The man rolled his eyes. "No, I didn't rob a bank. I took up an offering." He grinned. "Hmm, that's something a preacher would do, now, isn't it?"

Callum was too shocked to joke with him. "There must be close to a hundred dollars in here."

"One hundred and seventeen, to be exact." Billy's eyes twinkled as brightly as Evelyn's had on Christmas morning 1925 when Callum splurged on the biggest baby doll in the Macy's store window. "It's a gift to you from your fellow workers and me."

"But I . . . they . . ." Callum shook his head. He shoved it at Billy. "I can't take this."

Billy's expression turned stern. "You can and you will. I prayed for you to be able to get to your girls quickly. God answered with an idea for raising the money. The men at the factory agreed to help. If you don't take it, it's the same as giving me, all those men, and God Himself a slap in the face." His brows lowered. "Would you really do such a thing, Callum?"

Even during the years he couldn't find a permanent job, he'd never taken so much as a loaf of bread that he didn't earn somehow. The people who gave this were mostly family men, all with their own bills to pay. If the can had been passed for one of them, would Callum have put a dollar in? To his shame, he doubted he would have.

Callum gulped. "But I . . . I don't deserve this."

Billy settled his hat on his head and pushed to his feet. "I can't think of a single person who deserves the blessings God chooses to bestow." He winked at Callum. "Accept it as grace, Callum Holbrook, and go get your girls."

Millersberg, Kansas
Scotty

Scotty felt less guilty about leaving Miz Hester to mind the store without his help now that Guy was there. The little fellow loved carrying bags for the customers, dusting, and sweeping up. Scotty teased that Guy was fast putting him out of a job. But his duty this morning was one Guy couldn't do—loading the goods Miz Hester had ordered onto Joe Frager's flatbed truck.

Scotty dozed on the short drive to Quarry. The truck bounced some, the way the ship's deck had on rough seas, but he had no trouble sleeping through it. A lot of those crates were heavy—he needed to be good and rested to tackle them. Joe wasn't much of a talker anyway, so it didn't bother him if Scotty slept.

Something whacked him on the arm, and Scotty sat up so fast his neck popped. He turned a look on Joe, who was grinning at him. "What was that for?"

"I turned the engine off a full minute ago and you went right on snoozing. I said your name twice and you didn't rouse." Joe shrugged. "I thought maybe you'd died. I had to check."

Scotty huffed a breath. He must've gone deep into sleep. Probably because he hadn't slept so good the past few nights, worrying about whether it was time for him to move on. The sooner he talked to Miz Hester about it, the better it'd be. For both of them.

"Hope it don't disappoint you, but I'm alive."

"Not disappointed at all. If you were dead, I'd have to load those crates." Joe slapped his knee and laughed loud and long.

Scotty hopped out and closed the door on the man's cackling. He got busy moving crates and bags and barrels from the loading dock to the bed. The breeze kept things cool, but by the time he was done, sweat had dampened his shirt and dribbled into his eyes. He slid the last box into place, swiped his forehead with his shirtsleeve, and then took up the rope he used to tie everything in place. He braced himself to toss one end of the rope to the other side. The sweat burning his eyes made his vision fuzzy. He wiped his eyes again, and when he opened them, a boy was standing next to him.

"Need some help, mister?"

Scotty suspected the kid was hoping for a tip. He shrugged. "Sure."

The boy grabbed the end of the rope and climbed up on the truck bed.

Scotty pointed. "Tie it good on that hook up at the front, an' then lift it over them boxes."

The boy followed Scotty's directions. Scotty went back and forth, hitching the rope on hooks all around the bed while the boy scampered like a spider weaving a web, crisscrossing the rope over the boxes and other things. When Scotty was sure everything was secure, he tied off the rope, then squinted at the boy. "Thanks for your help, son. Come on down now."

The boy leaped and landed flat-footed a yard or so from Scotty. He pushed his hair away from his forehead, gave a little wave, and plopped onto the edge of the loading platform.

Scotty dug in his pocket and found a nickel. "Here. Git yourself a soda at the drugstore." He tossed the coin in the boy's direction.

The boy clapped it between his palms, grinning. "Thanks, mister!"

Scotty climbed into the truck cab and flicked his fingers at the windshield. "All done. Let's go." He slumped in the seat and half dozed on the way back to Millersberg. No sense in going into full sleep and getting whacked again. When they pulled up in front of the Corner Store, Miz Hester came out on the porch.

Scotty slid down from the cab and gestured to the bed. "Got our work cut out for us, puttin' all this away." He said the same thing with every delivery.

She smiled. "That's how we stay in business." Her regular reply.

"Reckon so." Scotty started unsnarling the knot he'd made in the rope, and a movement on the bed caught his eye. He leaned sideways and looked between a pair of crates. Then he reared back. Was that what he thought it was? He moved a couple of feet closer to the cab and got a better look. Sure enough. The boy who'd helped him tie down the load was hunkered in there.

He put his hands on his hips. "You'd better come on out, son."

Miz Hester came over. "Scotty, what's the matter?"

Scotty pointed just as the boy stood up.

Her mouth dropped open. "Who is this? And why is he on the truck?"

Scotty shrugged. "I dunno. Reckon you gotta ask him."

Miz Hester cupped her hand above her eyes and looked up at the boy. "What's your name?"

"Beckett, ma'am. Nice to meet you."

Scotty shook his head in wonder. The boy spoke up like he hadn't done a thing wrong by sneaking onto the truck bed.

"Beckett, what are you doing on Mr. Frager's truck?" Miz Hester sounded plumb befuddled.

"I needed a ride." Beckett turned a half circle, looking here and there. He turned to Miz Hester again real quick. He didn't seem so sure of himself now. "Is this Marion?"

"No, it's Millersberg."

The boy's face fell, and all of a sudden Scotty knew who this boy was. Sympathy swelled in him, but the boy had done a reckless thing by sneaking onto the bouncy truck. He held his hand to Beckett. "C'mon down from there, son, an' let's have us a talk."

Beckett squirmed from between the crates, climbed over a barrel, and hopped from the end of the bed. He took one step toward Scotty and Miz Hester, but then he spun and took off running up the street.

Chapter Seventeen

Scotty

Miz Hester gave a little push on Scotty's arm. "Scotty, go after him."

Scotty thought about telling her he was sixty-three years old and he'd just loaded a truck all by himself, but she was right—somebody needed to catch that boy. He took two stumbling steps in the direction Beckett'd gone. Then Guy charged past Scotty like a hound dog after a fox, hollering, "Beckett! Beckett!"

To Scotty's relief, Beckett skidded to a stop and turned around. The boy stood still while Guy caught up to him. Scotty decided to stay put and see what happened, but he was braced to start running again if Beckett did. Miz Hester moved close to Scotty, and they watched the two boys. He couldn't hear a word that was said, but there was lots of hand flinging and head shaking going on. Then Beckett slumped low like the air had gone out of him, and Guy took him by the hand. The younger boy led the bigger boy right to Scotty and Miz Hester.

"This here's Beckett Ross. He lived at the home with Evelyn an' Winnie an' me." Guy looked up at Beckett and pulled on his hand. "Tell 'em what you told me. Mrs. Haak—she's my new ma—an' Uncle Scotty are real nice. They'll help you."

Scotty put his hand on the boy's shoulder. "Speak up, son. We ain't gonna hurt you."

The misery in Beckett's eyes just about broke Scotty's heart. "I gotta get to Marion. Gotta get on the train. I wanna go back to New York. I don't like livin' in Quarry."

Hadn't the people at the home told the kids why they was all being sent west? Maybe Beckett hadn't paid attention. Scotty gave Beckett's shoulder a little squeeze. "Well, now, you can't go back to New York. That home where you lived ain't open no more."

Beckett's chin quivered. "I know, but I can make do in New York. I lived on the street with a bunch o' other boys until a policeman took me to the home. I could've run away from there, but I liked the schoolin'. Never'd got any schoolin' before then." A weak smile curved his chapped lips. "I like readin' most of all." He sighed, and the light went out of him. "But the people who got me from the train, they say readin' is a waste o' time. They say I'm gonna be a farmer so I gotta learn farmin' instead. They make me work all day. They call me lazy an' good-for-nothin' when I get tired." Tears swam in his eyes. "I might not get any more schoolin' in New York, but at least I won't get worked like a dog. I was happy back then. I wanna be happy again."

Miz Hester was staring at Beckett with her eyes real wide. "Are you sure your new parents are keeping you out of school to work? You're not just making up a story because you're upset about having to do chores?"

Beckett shook his head real hard. "I'm tellin' the truth." He made an X on his chest with his finger. "Cross my heart an' hope to die."

A crooked smile formed on Miz Hester's face. "You needn't go to that extreme." She got serious again. "Who adopted you from the train?"

Beckett set his lips real tight and turned his face away.

Guy shrugged. "He wouldn't tell me, neither. 'Cause if he tells, you can take him back there. He don't wanna go back."

Miz Hester exchanged a look with Scotty. Then she smoothed Guy's hair into place. "Guy, take Beckett into the store and let him choose a gumdrop."

"Can I have one?"

She tilted her head. "May I . . . ?"

Guy grinned. "May I have one?"

"Yes, you may."

"Thank you, ma'am." Guy yanked Beckett onto the porch. "C'mon, Beckett."

Miz Hester watched after the boys until they went inside, and then she turned the fiercest face on Scotty he'd ever seen. "If that boy's telling the truth, we can't take him back to the people who adopted him. They've broken their agreement."

Scotty started to ask what agreement, but Joe ambled around the rear of the truck and put his hands on his hips.

"You gonna get this stuff off so I can move on?"

Miz Hester wrung her hands. "I'm sorry, Mr. Frager, but we have a small emergency to address."

Joe glanced toward the store. "You mean the boy who hitched a ride?" He scowled. "You aren't gonna ask me to drive him back to Quarry, are you?"

Scotty looked at Miz Hester. She looked at him. Then she looked at Joe. "No, I'm not."

Scotty blew out a breath, half relieved and half worried. If she didn't send Beckett back, what would she do with him? Like it or not, them people in Quarry had guardianship, same as Miz Hester had guardianship of Evelyn, Winnie, and Guy. Did they even have a choice?

Hester

Hester peeked between the gap in the sheets. Finally, all four children were asleep. Mercy, what an ordeal to get them settled tonight. She felt as worn-out as if she'd been dragged through a knothole backward. And she still needed to iron Guy's clothes for tomorrow's church service. She trudged to the kitchen.

Scotty was at the table dipping tinned shortbread cookies into the remaining coffee in his mug. He glanced up. "They sleepin'?"

Hester nodded and crossed to the ironing board. A weary laugh found its way from her throat. "Beckett's unexpected arrival certainly disrupted our routine." Yet she wasn't unhappy about him being there. If all he said was true, he deserved a safe place to sleep, if only for a night or two. She unfolded the board and plugged in her iron.

"Disrupted's a good way o' sayin' it. Guy was bouncin' around like a puppy dog, Winnie did more whinin' than I ever heard from her before, an' Evelyn even got worked up. Not mad worked up, but excited worked up." He dunked a cookie in his coffee. "They ought to sleep like logs tonight."

Hester hoped so. The girls and Guy had their new beds with fluffy down-stuffed mattresses from Ebright's. Evelyn actually commented on how comfortable hers was. Hester had laid out a straw-filled tick on the floor next to Guy's bed for Beckett, and he hadn't said a word of complaint. Maybe it was better than what he'd been provided at the house in Quarry.

"Scotty, what do you make of what Beckett said about being kept from school to work all day?" She applied the iron to Guy's knickers as she spoke. "The agreement I signed included a stipulation that all children adopted from the home must be educated to the highest level provided in their new community. Quarry's school only goes to the ninth grade, but Beckett said he's eleven. He has many years of schooling ahead of him. Do you suppose the people who took him decided they don't have to honor the agreement since the home from which he came is no longer functioning?"

Scotty aimed a thoughtful look in her direction. "Could be they don't care about breakin' the agreement. Could be they ain't got much schoolin' themselves an' figure he's had enough."

Dismayed, Hester shook her head. "I can't imagine anyone in this day and time thinking a fifth-grade education is enough."

Scotty shrugged and put the lid on the cookie tin. "I didn't even get that far. I've made do with the good Lord's help, but it ain't been easy." His forehead crinkled with frown lines. "I don't hardly know Beckett at all, but I want better'n that for him. Seems them people who adopted him, who hafta know 'im better'n we do, would wanna do right by him."

"I'd love to know their reasoning." Hester draped Guy's pants over a hanger and laid out his suit on the board. "I'd ask them myself, but until Beckett tells us who they are, we're stuck."

"Yep, you are, 'specially since, like you said, that home's closed up now. There ain't nobody to ask."

Hester gave a little jolt of realization. She set the iron aside. "Scotty, why didn't I think of it before? The couple from Quarry must have registered Beckett at the county courthouse, the same as I did with Evelyn, Guy, and Winnie. The clerk will have the name of the adoptive family." She lifted the iron and pressed the placket until it created a crisp fold. "I'll drive to Marion on Monday and ask to review adoption records from March. If there's more than one adoption registered to folks in Quarry, I'll see which is for a boy named Beckett." She paused and heaved a sigh. "I hate to leave you alone in the store again, but the courthouse isn't open on Sundays."

Scotty hung his head. "I'm sorry I can't do that errand for you, ma'am. But I can't read them records."

How difficult it must be for the proud man to admit such a thing. "It's all right. I know I'm leaving the store in very capable hands." She hoped her confidence in him would lift his spirits. Oddly, he didn't even glance up. She went on. "I'll go after Evelyn and Guy leave for school. Will you be all right with both Beckett and Winnie? I could take Winnie with me if you'd like."

He looked up, fondness softening his expression. "The little one's no trouble at all. An' I can keep Beckett busy carryin' bags an' such for folks the way Guy does after school. Don't worry on me, Miz Hester. Just take care o' that boy."

"Thank you, I will." She flopped Guy's suit around and ran the iron over the back. The girls' dresses didn't need a freshening touch-up. They were careful with their clothes. But Guy must scrunch the fabric and then lean on it to create such a tight cluster of wrinkles. She shook her head in indulgence. "Until I'm able to determine who took Beckett in, we must keep him here. We can't risk him running off and actually getting on a train for New York. A boy his age shouldn't be left on his own."

Scotty grunted. "I'm with you there, Miz Hester. I'll keep a close eye on him, 'cause the boy has a habit o' runnin' off."

She looked up in surprise. "He does? How do you know?"

A sheepish grin appeared. He scratched his chin. "When I was at the lumberyard gettin' the wood to build the kids' beds, a feller there told me about a boy who kept runnin' off from his new parents, tryin' to get on the train. Don't take much reasonin' to figure that same boy's now sleepin' in the other room with your kids."

Hester set the iron aside and stared at Scotty. "What else did the man say?"

Scotty rolled his eyes upward and pursed his lips. "Said them new parents were plumb fed up with him runnin' away an' thought on sendin' him back. But they couldn't 'cause the home was closed." His mouth dropped open. "Miz Hester, he said the ones who took Beckett was his cousins. He can tell us their name."

Hester laughed and crossed to the table, amazed at how easy it would be to solve the mystery of Beckett's placement. "Will you drive to Marion on Monday and talk to the man at the lumberyard again? Ask him for the name of the family who took Beckett in." An unpleasant thought formed in the back of her mind. "But can you do it in a way that doesn't let on we know where Beckett is? I'm not willing to take him there until I'm convinced he'll be educated and well cared for."

Scotty stood, resolve in his stance and expression. "I'll for sure do that." He angled his head slightly, his gaze narrowing. "But what're you gonna do if you find out everything that boy's said is true—that they're workin' him like a dog an' not gettin' him any schoolin'?"

What would she do? Hire a lawyer and have their adoption revoked? Did she have enough money to pay for such a service? If the adoption was revoked, where would the judge send Beckett? Would the new placement be any better than his current one? There were too many questions Hester couldn't answer. "I don't know. I'll have to pray on that."

He nodded slowly, somberly. "I'll join you in that prayin'."

Chapter Eighteen

New York City
Callum

Callum clocked in for work Monday morning, same as usual. Except it wasn't a usual Monday. He wouldn't work a full week before leaving for Kansas. He already had his ticket, bought on Saturday, safe in the cracker tin with the rest of the money Billy gave him. He still couldn't believe the men from the steel factory had been so generous. As soon as he told Boss Moore his leave-taking date, he would put the note of thanks he'd written on the announcements board for everyone to see.

The boss usually stood outside his office and watched the men clock in, but Callum didn't see him. He crossed to the office door and peered through the window. The man was at his desk, writing on something. He seemed busy. Callum started to turn away, but the boss looked up and waved him in.

Callum opened the door and stepped inside. The action reminded him of the day he came to the factory looking for a job. He was sure he'd be told no. He'd heard no so many times that he'd lost all hope of a yes. But Boss Moore had said yes and matched him up with a seasoned grinder, and Callum learned a new trade. And now, because of being here, he had the money to go get his girls and bring them back to live with him. Freida would tell him, *"God worked things out for your good."* She'd also add, *"And His glory."*

He shook off the thought as he crossed to the desk and pulled his cap from his head. "Sorry to bother you, sir, but you told me to let you know when I'm leavin' for Kansas. I got my ticket. I leave Wednesday morning."

"Leaving Wednesday. So are you coming in tomorrow?" He wrote something else on the paper, his head low.

Callum nodded. "Yes, sir, if that's all right with you." He'd been given a five-day leave. He wouldn't burn one of those days lollygagging in his apartment. Not that he'd done a bit of lollygagging since Billy'd handed him the envelope of money. He'd visited the railroad depot, examined the train schedules, and secured a ticket. He'd packed his best clothes in a drawstring laundry bag he borrowed from the woman who took in wash from people who lived in his building. A smaller bag, the one he used for grocery shopping, already held cheese, dried apples, and crackers—enough for the three days it would take to reach Kansas. Having all that money had tempted him to buy something better, like jerked beef or tinned sardines, but he hadn't squandered so much as a penny of it.

The foreman put down his pen and met Callum's gaze. "I figured you'd catch the soonest train. Why'd you wait? Are the rates cheaper on Wednesday?"

They were, by $1.50, but Callum hadn't used only that for his decision. "The factory's not open on Saturday or Sunday. I had to come in today so I could tell you when I was going."

"That was a responsible thing to do, Holbrook."

Pleased yet embarrassed, Callum shrugged off the compliment. "Savin' some money was a nice surprise. An' speakin' of money . . ." He slipped his fingers into his shirt pocket and pulled out the note he'd written. "Can I pin this on the announcements board so the workers know how thankful I am for what they gave? I"—he swallowed the knot in his throat—"would've lost another year, maybe longer, of being with my daughters if they hadn't been so generous."

"That's fine." Boss Moore rose and came around the desk.

"Most of our workers have youngsters of their own, so they could imagine how you feel." He ushered Callum out the door, snickering. "Besides, Scurvy went around quoting a Bible verse about if you give, God'll give to you. Yep, ol' Scurvy is pretty persuasive."

All across the floor, machines were powering to life. Men were hollering greetings or playful insults to one another. Callum had something to say, and he'd have to say it loud, which meant more ears than Boss Moore's would hear. He might take some ribbing, but he'd say it loud anyway. "William Francis Shelton is a good man. I'm proud that Billy, as he likes to be called, is my friend."

The boss's eyebrows rose. He gave a nod. "I'll have a short-pay envelope ready for you tomorrow. Good luck to you, Holbrook. Now, get to work."

Millersberg
Scotty

Monday morning, Miz Hester gave Scotty money to buy materials from the lumberyard in Marion to build a chicken shelter and pen. Then they prayed that the same fellow who'd helped with the lumber for the beds would wait on him today. He prayed it again on the drive to Marion and once more as he pulled up close to the lumberyard office and shut off the engine.

As he climbed out of the automobile, the worker he remembered ambled up with a big smile. Scotty sent a grateful glance skyward and then stuck out his hand to the fellow. "Howdy. Remember me?"

The man gave Scotty a firm handshake, eyeing him careful. "Oh, yeah. You were gonna build bed frames for the lady who adopted some kids."

God was showing up real strong, swinging the door wide for Scotty to ask about Beckett. But he'd better get business settled first. "Yup, that's right. Those materials worked real good, so she sent me back to get a roll o' chicken wire an' some more wood. Those kids she took in are nearly eatin' her out o' house an' home." He laughed and the man joined in. "She's needin' a chicken coop for her own flock."

"I reckon we can help with that." The man opened the wire gate to the area where stacks of boards of every kind filled the fenced yard, and Scotty followed him in. "How big a coop do you need?"

Scotty scratched his cheek. "Well . . . she's figurin' on gettin' four or five hens an' a rooster. How big should the coop be for a half-dozen birds?"

"Four by four, six feet high ought to work fine. That'll give the chickens some space to peck around and make it easy to get in there, collect the eggs, an' clean the coop." The worker picked up one board a little longer than Guy was tall, propped it upright, and braced his forearm on it. "You got a drawn-out plan to follow?"

"Nothin' drawn out, but I got one in here." Scotty tapped his temple with his finger. He pictured the coop in his mind, built on short stilts so no rainwater could puddle inside, with a little ladder leading to a swinging door and windows east and west for ventilation. He even saw shutters for folding back during nice weather or latching shut to seal against bitter cold.

The fellow tossed the board aside. "Did you make a list of materials?"

Scotty cringed. "No. I just know I need wood, posts, an' chicken wire. You got some idea of what all it takes to build a four-by-four coop six feet high?"

He grinned. "My dad keeps a copy of all the orders we write up for folks. I'm sure we can find one that shows what other people've bought to build a chicken coop. Let's go into the office."

Once again, Scotty followed the worker. "Didn't you say your cousin adopted one o' the kids from the train, like Miz Hester did?"

"Yep, they did. A boy." His arms pumped while he walked, his gaze straight ahead.

Scotty mimicked his gait. "Do you mind givin' me your cousin's name? My boss . . . she's curious."

They reached the office door. The man turned the knob and pulled the door open, angling his head toward Scotty at the same time. "Sure, mister, I don't see any harm in that." He ushered Scotty over the threshold. "I'll write their names down on your order. Will that do?"

Scotty swallowed the shout of victory building in his chest. "That'll do fine. Thank you very much."

Chapter Nineteen

Evelyn

The end-of-the-school-day bell clanged, and Evelyn bounced out of her seat with a sigh of relief. She shot a smile at Rosemary as she gathered up her books, but Rosemary was already turned around talking to Norma and Bertie Mae. Evelyn stifled a huff. Seemed like lately those three had forgotten there were four Little Women. "Hey!" she hollered over the noise of kids' feet tromping across the floorboards and voices jabbering.

Rosemary jolted sideways and gave Evelyn a startled look. "What?"

Now Evelyn didn't know what to say. Should she tell the others she didn't like being left out? They'd probably tell her it was her own fault for always being at work when they wanted to get together. She'd been working at Ebright's for only a week, but it'd sure changed things with her friends. And why did it matter since she was going to leave Millersberg anyway? She didn't know, but it bugged her to be ignored. When they were all in the same place, she wanted to be part of things. She pulled in a big breath. "I want—"

"Evelyn?" Mr. Herriott interrupted Evelyn's announcement. "Would you come here, please?"

Evelyn hugged her books, zinging her gaze between the girls and her teacher. "I . . . I gotta get to my job."

"It won't take long."

Rosemary, Norma, and Bertie Mae scooted to the staircase. Rosemary sent a peek over her shoulder and mouthed, *Good luck.* They disappeared behind the wall.

Evelyn scuffed to Mr. Herriott's desk. "Yes, sir?"

He laid out several papers in a line across his desktop. "These are some of your assignments from last week. What do you notice about the letter grade on each?"

Evelyn winced. "Well, sir, they're all the same."

His dark eyebrows pinched into a V. "Indeed they are. What else do you notice?"

Wasn't it humiliating enough to be failing without having to say it? She pursed her lips and stared at the reflection of the overhead lamp in the round lenses of his glasses.

He scooped the papers into a stack. "I've delayed speaking with your mother—"

"She ain't my mother." The words burst out, and then she clamped her mouth closed again. The V between his eyes got deeper. Evelyn swallowed. "I call her Mrs. Haak."

He cleared his throat. "I've delayed speaking with Mrs. Haak, hoping I would see improvement. But you've been here three weeks now, which is sufficient time to settle in, and your grades are getting worse instead of better."

It was because now that she was working, she didn't have enough time to copy hardly anything from Rosemary's papers. But she couldn't tell him that. She searched for a good excuse. "I . . . I'm sorry, sir. I don't have much time for studying because I work after school an' all day Saturday at Ebright's store. I gotta work 'cause . . . Mrs. Haak can't buy everything I need." She inwardly praised herself for the clever reply. She'd told the truth without telling the whole truth.

"I see." He stared at her while the clock's pendulum went back and forth, back and forth, and she curled her toes in her shoes to keep from running out of the room. Finally, he sighed. "I'm sorry, but your success as a student is my main focus. Clearly, you are not keeping up with grade seven material. If by the end of this week I don't see a marked improvement, I will talk with Mrs.

Haak about placing you with the grade six students to finish this school year and try grade seven again next year."

She was stuck in Millersberg until she'd earned enough money for tickets. It'd take a while, and she wouldn't even get to have lunch with the other Little Women if he moved her downstairs. "Please don't do that. I'll do better. I promise."

He held up one finger. "One more week." Then his stern expression softened. "If you're truly struggling with the material, it isn't fair to you to keep you in this grade. A change to grade six isn't a punishment, Evelyn. It's meant to be a help."

He could say that. He wasn't the one being marked as too dumb to learn. "Can I go now? I'm late for work."

He gave her the papers. "Yes, but take these home with you. Mrs. Haak needs to be aware of your progress. Have her sign one of them and return it to me tomorrow so I know she's seen them."

Evelyn jammed the assignments between her books. "Yes, sir." She darted for the staircase. Worry and anger battled in her chest during her walk to Ebright's. No matter what Mr. Herriott said, she would not go to grade six. Everyone would make fun of her. She had to stay in grade seven.

Or did she?

Even though she was already late, she slowed her pace. What if she didn't go to school at all? If she worked all day at Ebright's, she'd earn money for train tickets a lot faster. And why did she need more schooling? Mr. Ebright hired her even though she was only in grade seven. Didn't that mean someone in New York City would do the same? Daddy would be so proud if she brought money in every week. Maybe with her help, they could even get a real nice apartment away from the smoke smell from the factories and fishy smell from the water.

The plan chased away her worry, and she ran the rest of the way to work. She dashed past the lady customer at the counter, calling to Mr. Ebright, "I'm sorry I'm late—my teacher had to talk to me. I'll get my apron on an' get busy right away." She swatted the curtain aside and plopped her books and things on the bench. The books slid, and the assignments Mr. Herriott gave her peeked out.

She growled under her breath. If she showed all those to Mrs. Haak, she'd make her quit this job. She couldn't show them. But if she didn't bring back a signed paper, Mr. Herriott would talk to Mrs. Haak and she'd be found out anyway. So what to do? Another idea popped into her mind. She grabbed the whole stack, pulled out one math assignment, and put it inside her arithmetic book. Then she tore all the others to shreds. She dropped the pieces of paper in the waste can by the back door.

"Evelyn?" Mr. Ebright's voice carried past the curtain. "I need you to carry these packages to Mrs. Tipton's car for her."

"Coming!" Evelyn grabbed an apron and tossed it on while she raced for the counter. She gave her boss and the customer her brightest smile. "Here I am. Lemme get those for you, ma'am." As she gathered the paper-wrapped bundles into her arms, she said to Mr. Ebright, "Can I talk to you about something? It's real important."

He flicked his fingers at her. "Yes, but later. Mrs. Tipton is ready to go."

"Yes, sir." When she came back in, Mr. Ebright was already helping someone else. For some reason, his usual clerk, Mary, wasn't there. But things were too busy for her to ask about her. Or to ask anything else.

At a little past six, Mr. Ebright closed the door behind the last customer, pulled down the shade on the door's window, and then turned the cardboard sign to Closed. He headed in the direction of the counter.

Evelyn trailed him across the floor. "Mr. Ebright, can I talk to you now?"

He leaned against the counter with a long sigh. He folded his arms above his belly and looked full at her. "You may."

She'd been holding her words inside for almost three hours, and they came spilling out in a rush. "I really like working here. If you say so, I'll work here whenever you're open instead of only after school and on Saturdays. Can you maybe use me all the time instead of just some of the time?"

Mr. Ebright held up his hand like a traffic cop. "Slow down there. Am I hearing you right? You want to work full-time here?"

She nodded hard, gripping her hands together. "I do."

"But you're what . . . thirteen years old?"

"Almost fourteen."

"I don't know, Evelyn." He shook his head. "Now, it's not like I couldn't use the help. Mary up and quit on me."

"She did?" Why hadn't she told Evelyn she planned to quit?

"She's marrying a boy from Hillsboro and moving there real soon. So I'm looking for somebody to come on full-time."

She nearly danced in place. "I could do it. Ain't I done a good job for you so far?"

"You've done fine."

She beamed at him.

"With stocking and cleaning."

Her lips quivered and lost the smile.

"But you haven't run the cash register, haven't done inventory, haven't made out order forms, haven't done deliveries . . ."

"I could do all those things if you teach me."

Now he scowled. "All those things are meant for someone older. Someone who can already drive an automobile, who's had more than seven years of schooling." He put his hand on her shoulder. "And I don't have time to teach you. Mary might've been able to, with time, but she isn't here anymore." He dropped his hand and folded his arms again, peering at her through squinted eyes. "Have you talked about this with your mama?"

Would people stop calling Mrs. Haak her mama? "No, sir. But I was going to after I talked to you. Didn't see the sense of it unless you said yes."

"Well, I can't even consider it unless she gives her permission. You're too young to decide on something as serious as dropping out of school and going to work full-time." He went around behind the counter.

Evelyn followed him with her gaze. "But if she says yes, you'll hire me for full-time?"

He blew out a mighty breath and faced her. "If she says yes, I'll think on it. But I'm not promising anything." He gestured to the curtain. "We'll put off mopping and so forth until tomorrow. For now, get your things and go home. I can see you're champing at the bit to talk to your mama."

Evelyn came close to correcting him, but she didn't want to aggravate him. Not when he said he'd think about hiring her. "Yes, sir!"

She walked through the back door of Mrs. Haak's house just as everyone else was sitting down to eat supper. Winnie pulled away from Scotty, who always lifted her onto her seat, and ran to Evelyn with her arms outstretched. "Sissy!" Evelyn dropped her books and lunch pail next to Guy's on the counter in the pantry and gave her a hug. She took Winnie by the hand, and they went into the kitchen together.

Mrs. Haak smiled big. "You're early. It will be nice to have you with us while we eat."

Evelyn liked not having to sit at the table all alone eating a cold supper, but she kept the thought to herself for some reason. She helped Winnie onto her three-legged stool, then sat and scooted her chair up between Winnie's stool and the apple crate turned on its end that Beckett sat on. With six of them now around the table, it felt crowded. How long would Beckett be here?

Mrs. Haak said a blessing for the meal. She stood up and

plopped spoonfuls of baked beans with chunks of fatty pork on each plate. Then she sat and passed the basket of cornbread muffins. Scotty crumbled his muffin over his beans. So did Beckett and Guy. Winnie didn't take one, but Evelyn and Mrs. Haak put theirs on the side of their plates. Mrs. Haak broke off pieces with her fork. It looked like a neater way to eat, but Evelyn didn't want to look like she was copying, so she picked it up and ate it the way she'd eat a cookie.

Beckett nudged her with his elbow. At first she thought he'd done it by accident, they were so crammed together. But when she glanced over, he was smiling at her. She said, "What?"

"Guess what I did today."

Evelyn shrugged and stabbed two beans and a piece of meat with her fork. "Something funner'n going to school, I bet."

His face clouded. "I like goin' to school. I hope I'll get to soon." He brightened again. "I helped Uncle Scotty dig holes an' put posts in the ground."

Uncle Scotty, huh?

"Guess what he's buildin'."

She shrugged.

"A chicken coop!" Guy blurted the answer. His eyes danced with excitement. "Soon as it's done, we're gettin' chickens."

Evelyn looked across the table to Mrs. Haak. "That so?"

The woman wiped her mouth with her napkin. "It is. We'll have plenty of eggs to use for baking. If the chickens lay well enough, I'll even boil some for you children to take in your lunch pails in addition to fruit, cheese, and crackers."

Guy licked his lips. "Mmm . . ."

Scotty added another scoop of beans to his plate. "'Course, before you all can eat them eggs, we gotta git the coop built. Guy an' Beckett, there'll be enough sunlight to see good for another hour or so. You wanna come out with me after supper an' git started on the floor?"

Both boys whooped. Then Winnie did, and Guy frowned at her. "Winnie, you're too little to build a chicken coop."

"Am not! I can build a chicken coot!"

Everybody but Evelyn laughed.

Mrs. Haak shook her head, but her eyes were smiling. "All right, now, settle down and finish your supper. There's work enough to go around, but you should fill your bellies first."

They all dug in. While Evelyn ate, she tried to figure out the best way to tell Mrs. Haak she wanted to work at Ebright's full-time. She also needed to get a signature on that paper so Mr. Herriott wouldn't come calling. She still hadn't thought up a good plan by the time she finished eating, so she stayed quiet and cleared the table without being asked.

Winnie sat on the edge of the counter and chattered while Mrs. Haak washed the dishes and Evelyn dried them. As soon as Evelyn put the last plate in the cupboard, she drew in a big breath and faced Mrs. Haak. "Ma'am?"

At the same time, Winnie threw her arms in the air. "Get me down, Mama. I wanna go hewp build the chicken coot."

Evelyn went still as a statue. Had she heard right? Did Winnie really call Mrs. Haak *Mama*? When Mrs. Haak laughed and scooped Winnie into a hug, Evelyn knew it was true. She went cold, then hot, then cold again. Memories of her own mama paraded through her head. Mrs. Haak wasn't their real mama. Just because Winnie never knew her real one didn't mean she could replace her with any lady who came along. She had to get Winnie out of here fast.

Chapter Twenty

Hester

The joy of hearing the title *Mama* come out of Winnie's mouth carried Hester on a wave of bliss the remainder of the evening. Before tucking the children into bed, she chose the story about God answering Hannah's prayers with the arrival of baby Samuel. She fully understood Hannah's song of praise now that two of her children had openly accepted her as their mama. Just as Hannah later was blessed with the arrival of other children, surely Hester would eventually find blessed acceptance from Evelyn.

She delivered a kiss on each warm cheek, even Beckett's, then closed the curtains with a whispered "Sleep well, children." She and Scotty hadn't yet had a chance to talk about the family in Quarry, and she was eager to do so. She'd told him she would come out to the store when the children were safely in bed. She started toward the back door, but halfway across the kitchen, the patter of footsteps sounded behind her. She turned and found Evelyn.

She touched Evelyn's gown sleeve. "Honey, what are you doing up? It's bedtime."

"I gotta talk to you."

She took a look at the girl's sullen expression and braced herself. Evelyn's shock at Winnie's exclamation hadn't escaped Hester's attention. She'd anticipated an outburst. "What is it?"

Evelyn went into the pantry, then returned holding a piece of paper against her bodice. "Mr. Herriott gave me this and said I had to have you sign it to prove you saw it." She turned it around and thrust it at Hester.

The glaring F at the top of the page momentarily stole Hester's breath. "Oh, my." She took the paper, but she set her gaze on Evelyn's unsmiling face. Although the grade pointed to a lack of effort, Hester knew from Scotty's experiences that sometimes effort wasn't enough. Sometimes a person lacked understanding. If that was the case, then she'd failed Evelyn. She guided the girl to the table, and they sat.

Hester laid the paper between them. "Tell me the truth. Did you do poorly on the assignment because you hurried through it without much thought, or is it because the problems are beyond your ability right now?"

Evelyn hung her head and shrugged.

Hester suspected it was a combination of the two. She could fix both issues. Evelyn needed to give up the after-school job at Ebright's, and Hester needed to review and help her correct her homework assignments before they were submitted for grading.

Evelyn suddenly sat up. "I wanna quit school and work all the time for Mr. Ebright. He said I c-could if you gave me permission."

The stutter hinted that the girl might be stretching the truth, but Hester decided not to address her suspicion. "I don't believe leaving school at your age is a good idea, Evelyn. But even if I did, I couldn't grant permission."

Evelyn's gaze narrowed. "Why not?"

She placed her hand on Evelyn's wrist. "I signed an agreement with the Mission Church Home that any child in my charge would be educated to the highest level provided in my community." She gently squeezed Evelyn's wrist. "You will stay in school until you've completed grade twelve."

Evelyn yanked free. "They won't know if I'm in school or not."

"No, they won't. But I will. And, most important, God will." Hester hoped Evelyn was taking in her words and would remember them. "When we make a promise to any man, God is listening. As His children, we are called to integrity. I gave my pledge to house, provide for, educate, and love you, Guy, and Winnie. I intend to keep my word."

Evelyn's jaw jutted and she crossed her arms. "The people who took Beckett gave the same pledge, but they didn't send him to school."

"Just because someone else does wrong doesn't give me permission to do the same. Wrong behavior is wrong no matter how many people choose to do it. Surely, you understand that." Hester waited, hoping Evelyn's posture would relax. It didn't. Stifling a sigh, she got up and fetched a pen. She wrote on the bottom of Evelyn's math assignment, "Mr. Herriott, I hold some accountability for Evelyn's performance. I will check her papers for errors before she turns them in from now on." She signed it, then slid the paper in front of Evelyn.

Evelyn's gaze dropped to Hester's note, and her cheeks blazed red. "You're really gonna do that?"

"Yes, I am. It's my responsibility as your—"

Evelyn bolted from the chair. "You ain't my mother!" She stomped out of the kitchen and threw the curtain aside. Moments later, the creak of wood told Hester she'd climbed into her bed.

Hester chewed the inside of her bottom lip. Should she go in and try to reason with the child or let her sleep off her anger? As if a night of sleep would eradicate Evelyn's ire. The girl carried the emotion the way some people carried change in their pockets. It was always there, but sometimes in greater quantity than at other times. She would talk to her again tomorrow. There'd likely be an increase in her fury when Hester told Mr. Ebright that Evelyn would no longer work in his store, but she hadn't adopted children to be their friend. She was, whether Evelyn liked it or not, her mother, and she would do what she deemed best for the girl. She rose, intending to go see Scotty.

The back-door hinges squeaked. He was coming to see her. He ambled into the kitchen and plopped into the chair Evelyn had vacated. "I was startin' to worry. Everything okay in here?"

"Not really." She told him about Evelyn's failed assignment and how she intended to deal with her schoolwork in the future.

Scotty whistled through his teeth. "Hoo boy, I reckon she didn't take it so well."

Hester released a rueful chuckle. "You are correct."

He gave her a couple pats on the shoulder. "At least you got a plan to make things better for her. You got any ideas on how to make things better for Beckett?"

Hester moved the arithmetic paper to the center of the table, gave herself an internal reminder to spend some extra prayer time on Evelyn before turning in, and shifted her focus to Beckett. "My foremost desire is to get him out of his current placement and into a home where he'll be more than a workhorse. But I realize there needs to be more proof than one young boy's report of neglect."

Scotty's eyebrows rose. "Don't you believe him?"

"Of course I do," Hester answered quickly. "But sometimes children exaggerate to get their way. If someone asked Evelyn about me, she might paint me in a bad light because she disagrees with my decisions."

He nodded slowly. "I see your point. Well, then, how're you gonna find out how much o' what Beckett's sayin' is true an' what ain't? You don't expect them folks who adopted him to be all the way honest, either, do you?"

Sadly, Hester did not. When she was growing up, a representative from the asylum from which she'd been sent made a wellness check at the Webers' home every other year. Mr. and Mrs. Weber always convinced the woman that Hester was treated like their very own child even though she was an unpaid, sometimes overworked servant in the household. If the family in Quarry benefited from Beckett's free labor in the fields, they would no doubt try to convince Hester all was well. But there was a place where people were more prone to provide truthful answers.

She leaned forward slightly. "Scotty, what kind of person, after placing his hand on a Bible and vowing with God's help to speak the truth, would willingly lie?"

"Only a low-down skunk, that's who." His eyes went wide. "Are you thinkin' on makin' that boy an' his folks answer in front of a judge?"

She couldn't discern from his reaction whether he approved or found the idea scandalous. "Do you think I should?"

He pinched his chin and sat quietly for several seconds, staring past Hester. Finally, he sighed. "If you're wantin' the full truth, I reckon it's the best place to go." He stacked his forearms and leaned on the table, bringing his worried face closer to her. "If we find out Beckett's been spinnin' a tale, the judge'll send 'im back to Quarry. But if the judge decides what he told us is true about workin' instead o' goin' to school, what'll happen to 'im? I can't hardly stand to think of him bein' put in another orphan home somewhere."

The corners of his lips tipped downward. "When he was helpin' me dig holes for the posts this afternoon, he wanted to know what was in that tank out back, so I told 'im to peek. He did, an' he thought all them minnows scurryin' around were right funny. He got sad, though, when I said they was bait for bigger fish. He wanted to know how come we kept 'em an' didn't let 'em grow up an' swim in a big lake instead. Said they'd be better off if they wasn't cooped up in the dark tank." He drew in a deep breath and then released it as a long sigh. "The boy's got a tender soul, Miz Hester, an' he don't belong locked up inside a city buildin' anymore'n he ought to be toilin' all day when he's still just a tadpole."

Tears winked in Scotty's blue eyes. "What'll happen to 'im if the judge takes 'im away from them people in Quarry?"

Perhaps it was unrealistic, but Hester said the first thing that came to mind. "I'll ask if he can stay here with us."

Scotty blinked away the moisture swimming in his eyes and sat straight up, a smile growing. "Well, then, when I'm all done with your chicken coop, I'll git to addin' another bunk on the boy side o' the room."

Hester held up her hand. "No, not until we hear a decision from a judge. I don't want to give him false hope. He's suffered enough disappointments already."

Scotty's bright expression didn't change. "All right, I'll hold off, but for sure I'll be buildin' him a bed by an' by. 'Cause no judge worth his salt'd tell you no."

Evelyn

When Evelyn woke up on Tuesday morning, she was still mad. Mad about Winnie calling Mrs. Haak *Mama.* Mad about everything she'd heard Mrs. Haak and Scotty talk about last night. It didn't matter that she was planning to leave this place. That lady was gonna make her quit her job? And take in Beckett? Wasn't it crowded enough already? But she couldn't say anything about it because then they'd know she listened in. In fact, she was afraid if she opened her mouth at all, she'd give something away. So she didn't speak during breakfast. She didn't even act like she heard when Scotty asked for somebody to pass the salt. She didn't answer when Mrs. Haak reminded her to take that signed arithmetic paper to Mr. Herriott.

But as she was walking out the door with Guy to leave for school, an idea swooped in on her and she couldn't hold it inside. She spun around and blurted, "Beckett, wanna walk to school with us? You ain't allowed to go inside the school . . . yet . . . but maybe you'd like to see the place where me an' Guy go."

Mrs. Haak gave her a funny look, but she turned to Beckett. "If you'd like to walk with them, it would be fine."

Beckett yanked the napkin from his shirtfront, threw it aside, and bounced up from his crate seat so fast he toppled it over. "Sure!" He darted to Guy and Evelyn, calling, "See you later, Uncle Scotty an' Mrs. Haak!"

Evelyn hugged her books to her chest and counted the steps until the three of them got to the street. Then she nudged Guy. "Hey, if you run ahead, you'll have some time on the swings before the bell rings. I know you really like playing on those swings."

Guy swung his lunch pail. "Uh-huh, I do, but I wanna walk with Beckett."

Evelyn swallowed a growl and made her tone nicey-nice. "You'll see Beckett after school, but those swings get took real fast at recess. That ol' bully Wilbur makes sure of it. You probably won't get a chance to play then."

Guy looked back and forth at Evelyn and Beckett and then shrugged. "All right. See you later, Beckett!" He shot off.

Evelyn moved in front of Beckett and stopped him in his tracks. "Listen, I thought you'd like to know this . . ." She glanced around in case anyone was close enough to overhear. "Mrs. Haak an' Scotty were talkin' last night. They're gonna take you to see a judge. I reckon you can guess what the judge is gonna make you do."

Beckett's brown eyes went wide and scared. "Go back to Quarry?"

"Don't see any other way of it since those people over there adopted you an' you're theirs now."

His chin wobbled like he might cry. "But I don't wanna go back to Quarry."

Guilt tickled for scaring him, but she had to get herself and Winnie away from Mrs. Haak as fast as she could, and she needed help. Beckett was big enough and strong enough to help. "Then you gotta run away from Mrs. Haak. It's the only way to keep from being took to the judge."

Beckett hunched his shoulders. "Think I should run off right now?"

Evelyn rolled her eyes. "Of course not, silly. If you don't go back to the house this morning, they'll send out a search right away. No, you gotta wait until you won't be missed for a longer time. Like at nighttime." She put her hand on his arm. "I'm gonna help you, Beckett."

His eyes squinched half shut. "How come?"

"'Cause I wanna get to New York as much as you do."

"You do?"

She huffed. "Why are you so surprised? I never asked to be took away from there anymore'n you did. Why should grown-ups we don't even know tell us what to do?"

Beckett stared at her with his mouth open.

"The best thing for us is to go back to New York an' make our own way, right?"

Beckett's mouth snapped shut. "Right. But . . . how? I've tried sneakin' onto the train five or six times already. The bull always finds me an' makes me get off."

Evelyn had planned to buy tickets, so she hadn't worried about being bothered by the fellow hired to keep hoboes from catching free rides. Those bulls were mean. She shivered, imagining coming face-to-face with one. "Lemme think on it today. By the time I get back from working at Ebright's, I'll have a plan for us and Winnie to go to New York. Okay?"

Beckett nodded.

"But don't tell anybody! Mrs. Haak and Scotty can't find out we know what they're doin'." And she couldn't let them get wind of what she was planning. The school bell clanged. Evelyn started walking backward. "Just keep quiet, Beckett. We'll all be safe in New York soon enough."

Chapter Twenty-One

Scotty

Scotty minded the store in the morning so Miz Hester could go to the post office and use the telephone to call the Marion County Courthouse about Beckett's situation. She wasn't gone long—not more'n half an hour—so Scotty had an easy time of it. He wanted to ask right away what she'd found out, but with Winnie and Beckett underfoot, he couldn't. Even though Beckett wasn't as little a pitcher as Winnie, he still had ears, and there was things he shouldn't hear. So he kept his questions to himself and went out back to the pile of boards and the drawing he'd been given by the man at the lumberyard.

He felt a little guilty about putting Beckett to work on the chicken coop with him. The boy did everything Scotty asked without offering a single word of complaint, but over and over, he turned a longing look in the direction of the school building. Maybe they shouldn't have let him walk with Evelyn and Guy that morning. It must've put ideas in his head he couldn't shake out.

When the sun was shining almost straight down, Scotty took a step back and gave the coop a good look-see. Four posts held a planked floor a foot and a half off the ground. One wall on the east and a partial one on the west snugged up against the back side of the store. Good progress so far.

He nodded, satisfied. "Yup, it's comin' along, Beckett, thanks to your help." He flopped his arm across the boy's narrow shoulders. "It's lunchtime. I got some jinglin' money in my pocket. The drugstore in town makes a real good egg salad sandwich.

How 'bout we go have us one with a bottle o' grape soda pop? That sound good?" He waited for Beckett to lick his lips or light up at the idea of eating at the drugstore.

Beckett shrugged. "I guess so."

Scotty caught hold of Beckett's chin and lifted his face to look him in the eyes. "What's troublin' you, son? Ain't hardly been a word out o' you since breakfast, an' before that you jabbered like a magpie. Is it 'cause you ain't at school with the other kids? 'Cause Miz Hester's doin' her best to fix that."

Beckett gave a little jerk. "She is?"

"She sure is."

"But Ev—" He snapped his mouth shut on his words as fast as a snapping turtle on a fish.

Scotty gave him plenty of time, but he didn't open it again. It didn't matter, though. Scotty'd heard enough. He turned Beckett in the direction of the store. "Come with me." He herded him into the store, past Winnie and her pile of spools and right to the counter. Miz Hester was busy adding up purchases for Mr. Groate. The old widower did no cooking at all, only ate things straight from cans or tins. And he came in only once a week to gather up enough vittles for seven days' worth of eating. That made for a lot of cans. So it took a while to get him settled. Then it took time, even with Scotty lending a hand, to load all the cans into the man's rattletrap coaster wagon. But finally they sent him on his way, and Scotty didn't wait another minute.

"Ma'am, we got us a problem."

Miz Hester shot a worrisome frown from Scotty to Beckett and back again. "What kind of problem?"

"This boy here has been as quiet as a clam since comin' back from his walk with Evelyn an' Guy this mornin'. There's somethin' heavy wearin' on 'im. I can't rightly say what it is, but I think it'd do some real good if you went ahead an' told him how come you went to the post office first thing this mornin'."

She cringed. "Scotty . . ."

He waved his hand. "I know you wasn't wantin' to give 'im false hope, but I'm pretty sure somebody gave 'im a false*hood* that's got 'im scared. He's a big boy." Out of the corner of his eye, he saw Beckett push out his skinny chest and lift his chin. "He needs to hear the truth, an' it ought to come straight from you." Miz Hester shook her head slightly, like she was a little put out at him. Maybe he had overstepped his bounds. But Evelyn needed to be reined in before she created bigger troubles than any of them could fix.

Miz Hester came around the counter. "Beckett, I called the courthouse in Marion this morning and told a deputy sheriff where you were."

"She was right! I knew it!"

Beckett bolted, but Scotty caught him around the middle. The boy tried to break free, but Scotty scooped him up and wrestled him back. He planted him in front of Miz Hester and pointed at him real stern. "Stay right there an' listen."

Beckett's lower lip quivered, but he didn't move.

Miz Hester put her hands on the boy's shoulders. "The authorities needed to know in case your adoptive parents alerted them that you'd run away. It isn't right to let them spend time searching for you when you aren't in the area. It takes time away from other people who might need their help. Do you understand?"

Beckett bobbed his head once. The betrayal in his eyes tore at Scotty, but when he heard the whole reason, he'd feel better.

"I also reported everything you told Uncle Scotty and me. The deputy is going to pay a call on the Biehls. He'll ask them their side of the story, and if it differs from yours, you might have to go to a courtroom and tell a judge why you ran away." She gave the boy a tiny shake. "If you weren't truthful with us, now is the time to say so. Going to court is serious business."

Tears dotted the boy's lower eyelashes. "I told the truth."

Miz Hester pulled him into a hug. "I believe you, Beckett." She kissed the top of his head and then stood him in front of her again. "The people who adopt children from the Mission Church Home are bound by a contract to send them to school. The deputy will remind the Biehls of the requirement in the agreement they signed. If they promise to honor it, then a sheriff's official will retrieve you." Now tears filled her eyes. "You deserve to be educated, and you deserve to be loved." Her gaze drifted to Scotty for a few seconds before landing on Beckett's face again. "That's what Uncle Scotty and I want for you. We're doing all we can to make sure you receive what you deserve."

Scotty was pretty sure Beckett wouldn't run off now. He moved beside Miz Hester so he could look the boy in the face. "You satisfied, or do you still got questions?"

Beckett snuffled and wiped his nose with the back of his hand. "How'd you find out who took me in? I didn't tell you."

Scotty explained how he figured out who he was and how he got the family's name.

Beckett's lips twitched a little bit like he was trying not to smile. "Pretty smart."

Scotty wanted to puff up. Felt real good to be called smart. "Anything else?"

Beckett nodded. "If the Biehls say they will but they really don't send me to school, what then?"

Miz Hester said, "The authorities in Quarry will report to the court whether or not you're enrolled in school and attending regularly. There are people who will make sure the Biehls honor their word."

Beckett wiped his nose again. "An' what if they say no, they don't wanna send me to school? What'll happen to me?"

Scotty shouldn't answer that question, because he didn't have any real say-so in it. He might not even be around to see it happen. But he answered anyway. "A real good home'll open to you. I guarantee you that."

Beckett sighed so big that Scotty felt the relief with him. He'd answered the boy's questions. Now he had a question to ask. He curled his hand over Beckett's shoulder. "What exactly did Evelyn tell you to git you so upset?"

Beckett blinked several times. His cheeks blotched. "She . . . she said you was gonna take me to a judge who would make me go back to Quarry."

Scotty and Miz Hester exchanged a look. Was she thinking what he was thinking? He couldn't ask in front of the boy. He ruffled Beckett's sweaty hair. "Go wash your hands an' comb your hair. Then I'll take you for that egg salad sandwich. Okay?" Beckett nodded and darted off, giving Winnie a playful tap on the top of her head as he went by.

Scotty waited until the back door closed behind the boy, and then he said, "How'd Evelyn know about you plannin' to ask a judge to help Beckett?"

She looked as befuddled as Scotty'd ever seen her. "I have no idea. You and I talked about it after the children had gone to bed."

He raised one eyebrow. "To bed, but maybe not to sleep, huh?"

She let out a short laugh that didn't hold an ounce of humor. "You're right. The curtain offers little privacy. Clearly, we can't—"

"Mama?" Winnie pulled on Miz Hester's apron skirt and looked up with big blue eyes. "My tummy is making noises. Like this." She made a growly sound.

Scotty laughed and picked her up. He settled her on his hip. "I'll take her with me an' Beckett for a sandwich at the drugstore. Give you some time to figure out how to fix your"—he cleared his throat—"problem with a bigger pitcher's ears."

They finished their talk just in time, because the bell above the front door *tink-tink*ed and Miz Reames came in carrying a basket of eggs. He gave the woman a nod of hello, bounced Winnie on his arm, which made her giggle, and then headed for the house to fetch Beckett. He'd do some thinking himself about what should be done with Evelyn. She wasn't his child, and he didn't really have no business poking his nose in, but he couldn't stand by and let the girl stir up trouble for Miz Hester. The woman deserved better.

And he made a decision right then and there. Even though Miz Hester had lots of company now, she still needed help. He wasn't going nowhere until he could rest easy that Evelyn would behave herself. Even if that meant staying until she grew all the way up and moved out on her own.

Hester

A few minutes before three, Hester called Scotty in from his work on the chicken coop to mind the store. She told him, "I'm going to Ebright's. Please say a prayer all goes well." His solemn nod communicated understanding. She gave Winnie and Beckett a motherly reminder to be good for Uncle Scotty and then set out with a determined stride.

Nervousness quivered in her belly. Evelyn could very well cause a scene in Ebright's. They'd be the talk of the town for days if she did. But the sight of tulips and crocuses waving their colorful heads in a surprisingly gentle breeze and the greening lawns gave Hester's heart a lift. Even as a child, she'd appreciated Kansas's changing seasons. Fall's leaves, winter's snows, spring's flowers—they came and went outside the walls of the Corner Store while she made a living. Not all widows inherited not only a home in which to live but also a business to sustain them. Ownership of the Corner Store was a blessing. But what delight to be outside on this calm spring day, basking in the beauty God placed in the world.

She turned from Pine Street onto Main Street. Millie Clancy

was sitting on the bench in front of the drugstore. The woman waved at her.

"Hester! Come sit for a minute."

Although Hester needed to waylay Evelyn, she had a minute to spare. She sat down. "Good afternoon, Millie. How are you today?"

"Fair to middlin'." Concern pinched her features. "Are you all right? Not going into the drugstore for a tonic, are you? I've never seen you away from your store this time of day."

Hester liked Millie Clancy, but the woman was known to wag her tongue. She wouldn't give her fodder for gossip. "I have an errand at Ebright's, but I'll be back at my store very soon."

Millie gave Hester's knee a light pat. "Good. Good." Then she rolled her eyes and tipped closer to Hester. "Just so you're prepared, Harv Ebright is on the warpath. He lost his clerk, so he's doing everything on his own. We need to pray he finds another clerk real quick before he gives himself apoplexy."

Concern for Ebright's clerk overrode everything else. Evelyn had mentioned how kind the young woman was to her. "What happened to Mary?"

The woman pursed her lips. "She's getting hitched."

Millie's odd behavior confused Hester. "Isn't marriage cause for congratulation, even if it does leave Mr. Ebright without a clerk?"

Millie *tsk-tsk*ed. "Hester, you don't understand. It's a"—she lowered her voice to a whisper—"have-to wedding. Her pa is fit to be tied."

Hester had no time for such twaddle. "I need to see to my errand. Have a good rest of the day, Millie." She hurried off. But Millie's report about Mr. Ebright handling the store single-handedly caused a prick of guilt. Making Evelyn quit was best for Evelyn, but would it cause additional angst for the store owner? She paused outside the door and sent up a plea for discernment.

Evelyn and Guy appeared at the other end of the block. Guy darted across the street, heading to the post office, and Evelyn moved in Hester's direction, her head down and heels dragging. Hester waited, watching and praying for God's wisdom to prevail. Evelyn's head came up. Her gaze latched onto Hester. Her cheeks blazed red. She jogged the remaining distance.

"What're you doing here?"

The accusatory tone made Hester wince. "I'm here to tell Mr. Ebright that you can't work at his store anymore. Your schoolwork must be priority."

"But that ain't fair!" Evelyn stomped her foot. "If I hafta quit something, it ought to be school. I'm not good at it anyway. But I'm good at working in the store. Mr. Ebright said so."

Hester took hold of Evelyn's elbow. "We made an agreement that if your schoolwork suffered, you would give up the job. You need to honor your word."

"I didn't sign nothing, and Mr. Ebright needs me. Especially now that Mary's gone." She tossed her head. "I'm gonna be his new clerk."

Evelyn's wishful imaginings were going too far. The girl needed a dose of reality. Hester turned her toward the door. "Let's go talk to him about that." Evelyn squirmed, but Hester kept a grip and escorted her over the threshold.

Customers milled the floor. As Millie had indicated, Mr. Ebright was taking care of them by himself. Perspiration dotted his forehead, and his lips were set in a tense line—nothing like the smiling businessman Hester had encountered on previous visits. Was it kind to deliver another blow?

Hester pulled Evelyn to a corner and turned a stern look on her. "Clearly, this is not the time to talk to Mr. Ebright. Put on your apron and go to work, but I'll return at six o'clock. We will talk then."

Evelyn wrenched her elbow free and marched off.

Chapter Twenty-Two

Evelyn

Evelyn kept an eye on the clock while she wrapped and toted packages, fetched items from the storeroom and shelves, and did anything else Mr. Ebright asked. He stayed behind the counter and did all the adding up and money taking. Every time she scooted close to gather items for another order for somebody, she couldn't help peeking into the cash drawer. The dollars stacked up in there like flapjacks on Scotty's plate Sunday morning. But they looked even better than Mrs. Haak's flapjacks. She couldn't buy a train ticket with flapjacks, but she sure could with those dollars. If only they were hers and not Mr. Ebright's.

The hands on the clock got closer and closer to pointing at six o'clock. Evelyn chewed the inside of her cheek while she scooped sugar from the barrel into the scale's bowl. One thing about Mrs. Haak, if she said she was gonna do something, she did it. She'd show up here and tell Mr. Ebright that Evelyn couldn't work anymore. Before she did, Evelyn had to talk to him. To make him see the sense of her working in the store. To convince him to convince Mrs. Haak to let Evelyn come on full-time. To—

"Evelyn, you're going to overflow that bowl." Mr. Ebright's sharp voice broke into Evelyn's thoughts. "Look what you're doing."

She looked. She'd filled the bowl to the top. She wouldn't be able to convince her boss that she was capable of working here all the time by doing silly things like this. And now she couldn't remember how much sugar Mrs. Mackey had asked for in the first place.

She sent a sheepish look at the woman standing on the opposite side of the counter. “Um, how much were you wanting, ma’am?”

Mrs. Mackey laughed a little bit. “Two pounds, please, Evelyn.”

Evelyn poured the whole bowl—mercy, it was heavy!—back into the sugar barrel and started again. When she handed Mrs. Mackey her two-pound bag of sugar, the lady winked, and Evelyn smiled her thanks. But her smile went away fast. As Mrs. Mackey went out, Mrs. Haak came in. Evelyn pretended she didn’t see her and went on wrapping up packages with brown paper and string and carrying items to the counter for customers.

One by one, the people buying things left. When the door closed behind the last one, Mr. Ebright heaved a great big sigh. “What a day.” Then he made a little jerk. “Oh. Mrs. Haak, I didn’t realize you were still here. What can I get for you?”

Mrs. Haak came up to the counter. “I’m not here to shop, Mr. Ebright. I’d like to talk to you about Evelyn.”

Evelyn started in the direction of the little room where the brooms and such were stored. “I’ll get started sweeping now.”

Mr. Ebright snapped his fingers. “Hold up, there.” Evelyn stopped. “Turn yourself around and come here.” With a stifled groan, Evelyn did as he said. When she stood next to him, he said, “All right, Mrs. Haak. What is it?”

Evelyn sucked in her lips and folded her arms real tight across her chest while Mrs. Haak tattled about her failing grades and complained how working at the store stole study time. “She enjoys her job, and it gives me no pleasure to take it away from her, but I believe it’s in her best interests to quit.”

“I’m sure sorry, Mrs. Haak.” Mr. Ebright glanced at Evelyn. “I knew she was wanting to drop out of school and work all day, but I didn’t realize it was because she’s not doing well there. If I had, I would’ve told her no straight-out instead of saying I’d think about it." He snorted. "Why, I didn't even let my own youngsters work here until they were all the way done with school for the same reason you said—the studies don't get done."

"Thank you for understanding." Mrs. Haak made an *I'm sorry* face. "I saw how busy it was in here. I hate to leave you shorthanded. If it will help, I'll let Evelyn come in after school for a couple hours each day until you find someone to take her spot."

"It's always busy when I mark the canned goods three for a quarter." He waved his hand. "No worries about finding somebody part-time. All I have to do is put the sign in the window and somebody'll show up. It's the full-time clerk position I need to fill since Mary quit." He shook his head. "Just as well, I suppose. Given the circumstances, I would've had to let her go even if she wasn't moving to Hillsboro. It's a shame. She was a real good worker, but . . ."

Miss Armstrong at the home always said children were to be seen and not heard, but Evelyn had never been good at staying quiet for long. Especially if somebody was being picked on. Mr. Ebright's comments about Mary didn't make a lot of sense, but they didn't sound nice. "Mary never treated me like a dumb kid, the way some girls do when they're a little older and real pretty. It wouldn't bother me a bit to be like her when I'm all the way grown-up."

Mr. Ebright's lips pinched tight. He went behind the counter and opened the cash drawer. Evelyn heard a few clinks and shuffles, and then the drawer snapped shut. He came around again and pressed a bill and a few coins in her hand. "There's your final pay. Sixty cents for yesterday and today and a dollar bonus for your good work."

Evelyn stared at the money in her hand. Her aggravation with him melted in a heartbeat. "Thank you, Mr. Ebright."

"You're welcome." He put his hand on her shoulder. "Now, young lady, when you've graduated from school and have picked up some clerking skills from watching your mama in her store, you come back and see me. I might be able to use you full-time then." He turned to Mrs. Haak. "Unless you'll be putting her to work at the Corner Store, ma'am."

Mrs. Haak smiled that soft smile she sometimes gave Guy or Winnie when they'd done something cute. "That will be up to Evelyn. By then, she'll be old enough and wise enough to make her own choices on where she wants to work or what she wants to do."

Mr. Ebright gave Evelyn's shoulder a pat. "Listen to your mama and do what she tells you. She's a smart lady. Now, fetch your things from the back room and head home. You've got studying to do."

Hester

After supper, Hester asked Beckett to take Guy and Winnie into the living room and read to them. "Let them each choose a story, please." She trusted the children to select long ones. Anything to postpone bedtime.

Beckett grinned. "Yes, ma'am!" He herded the two youngest children out of the room.

She and Evelyn stacked the dishes in the sink, but she didn't run water. She instructed Evelyn to sit at the table, and she sat next to her. Scotty sent Hester a wink and a nod, then ambled out the back door, leaving the two of them alone.

Evelyn jammed a hand in the air. "If you sat me down here to tell me you're sorry for making me quit my job, don't."

Hester took hold of Evelyn's hand, guided it to the table, and placed her hands over it. "I have no reason to apologize for that. I made the right decision for your good. The only thing for which I'm sorry is not realizing how much you were struggling with your schoolwork. I should have been more attentive, and I will do my utmost to help you from now on." The girl rolled her eyes, but Hester pretended not to notice. "I need to talk to you about what you told Beckett this morning. You caused a great deal of unnecessary anxiety for him."

Evelyn's eyes grew wide. She looked toward the living room, her mouth hanging open. "That sneaky rat. I should've known he'd come squealing to you."

Recalling Evelyn's threat to punch someone in the stomach if they wronged her, Hester spoke quickly. "He didn't come to me. Uncle Scotty brought him to me when it was clear something was bothering him. The problem is, Evelyn, you repeated something that should have been kept private. And you repeated it in such a way that you frightened him."

Evelyn tilted her head into an inquisitive angle. "What'd he tell you I said?"

"That I was taking him before a judge."

"Is that all?"

Hester nodded.

Evelyn released a little puff of breath.

If Hester read the reaction correctly, the girl was relieved. Suspicion rose in the back of Hester's mind. For now, though, she needed to settle something with this child of hers. "You had no business repeating part of a conversation that wasn't meant for you to hear."

"It ain't my fault I heard you. You were talking right here"—Evelyn bounced her finger on the table—"and my bed's around the corner. I hear everything from in there."

"If you heard everything Uncle Scotty and I said, why did you choose only a small portion to share with Beckett? You deliberately misrepresented the intention of meeting with a judge." She scooted her chair closer and placed her hand on Evelyn's tense shoulder. "Proverbs 12:17 tells us that the person who speaks truth shows righteousness, while a false witness only shows deceit. If you want to be trusted, you need to speak truthfully, not use words as tools of deception."

Evelyn sat in stony silence, glaring at Hester.

Hester stared back, unrelenting. "You've betrayed my trust by not honoring your word about quitting the job on your own if it interfered with school and by sharing misinformation with Beckett. As a consequence, you must be watched."

Evelyn spluttered something nonsensical and pushed Hester's hand from her shoulder. "What's that supposed to mean?"

"It means either Uncle Scotty or I will walk you and Guy to school each day and meet you afterward to walk you home again. It means you will not be allowed to spend time alone with any of the younger children. It means you will do your homework in the store under my supervision."

Evelyn gaped at her. "If I'm not working anymore, I wanna do my homework with Rosemary, like I used to."

Hester shook her head—firmly—without lifting her gaze from Evelyn's stormy face. "You will not be allowed to go to Rosemary's or any other friend's house on the weekends or evenings."

Evelyn huffed. "For how long?"

"Until I am convinced you can be trusted to make wise decisions."

"But—but—"

"Hush."

The girl sucked in her lips, but her eyes spit fire.

Hester prayed for God to guide her remaining words. "I know you're angry at me right now. You probably don't even like me." Evelyn's derisive sniff confirmed it. Hester felt a small smile tugging at the corners of her lips. "But I can live with that. What I cannot live with is not being able to trust someone I love very much and want the very best for. You are my child, Evelyn. It's my God-given responsibility to teach you to honor God and His ways. Deception and dishonor displease Him and are of no benefit to you. The sooner you work to adopt those characteristics, the sooner I will be able to trust you."

Evelyn sat still and silent for several seconds, seeming to hold her breath. Then she pushed her chair backward and stood, glowering at Hester. "It don't matter if you trust me. And it don't matter if you keep me away from everybody, because I'm not gonna be here much longer anyway. I'm going to New York to my daddy. I'm taking Winnie with me, and you ain't gonna stop me."

Hester stood and gripped Evelyn by her upper arms. Temptation to shake her until her teeth rattled nearly got the best of her, but one of the proverbs she memorized while under the Webers' tutor's guidance tiptoed through her memory—*"A soft answer turneth away wrath: but grievous words stir up anger."*

She relaxed her hold. "Evelyn, you must stop nursing a fantasy and accept the truth. You have a new life here in Millersberg. It can be a good one if you set aside your resentment and open your heart to it."

Tears broke loose from Evelyn's eyes and painted trails down her flushed cheeks. "No." She pulled loose and ran to the sleeping area.

Hester sank back into her chair and put her head in her hands. What would it take to finally get through to Evelyn? She was almost fourteen, fast leaving childhood behind. Were these habits of choosing make-believe over what is and twisting truth to benefit her own needs so deeply ingrained they couldn't be changed?

Another proverb found its way from the depths of her memory to the forefront of her thoughts—*"Train up a child in the way he should go: and when he is old, he will not depart from it."* Resolve straightened Hester's spine. She aimed her gaze at the bedroom doorway where Evelyn had disappeared from view. No matter how hard the girl fought her, she would train this daughter of hers in God's ways. And she would trust Him to work in Evelyn's heart.

A wry thought crossed her mind. "Lord," she whispered lest Evelyn overhear, "I don't know what You meant by 'old,' but it would be fine with me if we defined it as 'age fourteen.' "

Chapter Twenty-Three

New York City
Callum

Callum tossed his clothing bag under the bench, tucked the sack of goods next to his hip, then scooted down until the back of his head met the rolled top of the velvet seat back. He wished he could prop his feet on the bench across from him, but he didn't figure the train porter would approve. He planted the soles of his freshly polished boots flat on the floor, wide apart, so his knees didn't bump the other seat. Then he closed his eyes.

He had the little berth to himself, but on the return journey, Evvie and Winnie would be with him. His heart lurched. Was he really heading to Kansas to get his girls? The address Miss Armstrong had given him was safe in his shirt pocket under his jacket along with the paper money Billy had collected for him. The plan was simple.

Today, tomorrow, and Friday—ride the train.

Saturday—retrieve the girls from the poor farm by showing the papers Miss Armstrong had given him.

Sunday—board the train again and be back in New York Tuesday evening.

He wished he didn't have to go to work the morning after. It'd be nice to have a day at the apartment with his girls. To help them settle in. To sit at their secondhand table and eat together. Did Evelyn know how to cook some simple meals? He should've asked Miss Armstrong if the girls learned such things at the home. Whether she could have dinner ready or not, it would be real nice to have people waiting when he got off work. Real nice to have them in the house when he woke up in the morning. Real nice to be a family again instead of a man living all by himself in a big city.

The seat underneath him started vibrating, the way the floor at the factory did when all the machines were running at once. He popped his eyes open, sat up, and looked out the window. It seemed like the depot was sliding aside, but he knew better. The train was moving. Excitement pulsed through him, as powerful as the locomotive's steam engine. He was on his way.

He waved farewell to people standing outside the depot even though he didn't know a one of them. As he waved, he whispered, "Hang on, girls. Daddy's comin'."

Millersberg, Kansas
Hester

Hester, Beckett, and Winnie walked Evelyn and Guy to school Wednesday morning. Guy ran circles around the group as they went, as exuberant as a spring lamb. Beckett chased him once or twice but always returned to Hester's side. Winnie gave little jumps every few steps, her giggle ringing. Evelyn plodded along, gaze straight ahead, lips set in a grim line.

After breakfast, during which Evelyn refused to acknowledge anyone at the table despite Winnie's and Guy's attempts to involve her in their chatter, Scotty had advised Hester not to give Evelyn any attention for pouting—"No sense in rewardin' her by tryin' to coax her out of her sour mood. She'll get tired of it by an' by." So Hester pretended not to notice Evelyn's behavior and chatted with the children as if all of them walking together was a usual happening.

Hester wanted so much to grow as close to Evelyn as she already was to Guy and Winnie. Even Beckett, who'd been with them only a few days, seemed more at ease with Hester than Evelyn did. Would the official come today to take him back? It would be very hard on all of them to let him return to Quarry.

Throughout the rest of the day, Hester kept watch for someone with a badge to come through the door, but only her usual customers came and went. Scotty and Beckett worked on the chicken coop, with Winnie occasionally getting underfoot. The little girl was so excited to have chickens in the yard she asked Hester repeatedly, "When're the chickies comin'?" Hester always answered, "When the coop is all done." And Winnie would run out to check the progress and stay outside until Scotty shooed her back in.

At a little before three, Hester asked Scotty to mind the store, then invited the children to walk to school with her to retrieve Guy and Evelyn. Both Winnie and Beckett opted to stay with Scotty, so Hester walked on her own. But she didn't mind. Strange how, in these past few weeks, she'd learned to enjoy a few minutes of solitude. As a lonely child sleeping in her attic room, far from the members of the family who'd taken her in, she'd longed for company. After Dale died, she thought she'd wither up from loneliness. Scotty's arrival helped, but as much as she treasured his friendship, it wasn't the same as having a life partner.

An image of Dale's handsome face flitted across her mind's eye. Would he have loved Evelyn, Guy, and Winnie as much as she did? She wanted to think so, but she'd never know. Maybe God would bless her with another husband who would grow to love these children of her heart. A chortle left her throat. What a silly thought. She knew everyone in Millersberg. The few widowed men were as old or older than Scotty. The only two bachelors near her age, the Tipton twins who lived on a farm south of town, were set in their ways. Besides, was there another man who could measure up to Dale? She doubted it. She'd be content to raise her children and eventually enjoy the gift of grandchildren. It would be more than enough.

The school bell clanged, and children spilled from the building. Hester searched the group until she spotted Guy and Evelyn. Guy came running to her as if escaping a raging bull, but Evelyn sauntered across the school grounds, surrounded by her trio of friends. Hester suspected Evelyn was going to ask to go to Rosemary's house. She probably thought Hester would approve since she had an audience. If so, she'd be disappointed.

Hester put her hand on Guy's shoulder and waited for the group to draw near. "Good afternoon, girls." She skimmed each face with a smile. "Did you have a good day?"

All four giggled, and despite Hester's frustration with Evelyn, it did her heart good to see her in a circle of friends. Norma, the girl dubbed as the character Jo, nudged Evelyn's arm. "Tell her who sat with you at lunch break."

Evelyn's face glowed pink and she looked aside. "Huh-uh."

Bertie Mae blurted, "Fred Ash. He's in grade eight." The girls giggled more, and Evelyn's face grew as red as a ripe tomato.

Hester shook her head, but she couldn't help smiling. "All right, let's not embarrass Evelyn." She brushed her palm down Evelyn's dress sleeve. "We should head home. Tell your friends goodbye now. You have studies to do."

Evelyn quickly faced Hester. "Can they come to our house? We hafta do our homework together."

Hester raised one eyebrow. "You have to?"

The girl nodded hard. "Yes. Mr. Herriott let us pick our own groups for a history project. We're supposed to make a . . . a . . ." She whirled her hand in the air and turned to her friends.

"Diorama," Rosemary said. "Of the Plymouth Colony."

"Yes, a diorama." True excitement seemed to glimmer in Evelyn's eyes. "We need a box and modeling clay and paints and some scraps of fabric. You have all those things, don't you?"

Hester drew in a breath. "I believe I do, yes. But—"

"Could we make it there?" Evelyn's expression turned pleading. "If I don't help, I won't get credit for the project. We'll be right there in the store. Right where you are."

Hester hesitated. Would granting permission give the message that she was already going back on the punishment she'd given Evelyn?

"It's okay, Evelyn." Bertie Mae shrugged. "Us three'll make it at my house, and we'll just put your name on it."

Before Hester could voice a word of protest, Evelyn huffed. "No!" She sighed. "You guys make one together, and I'll make one by myself." She angled her gaze at Hester. "Is . . . that okay?"

Hester examined each girl's face by turn. Had they plotted this request to coerce her into changing her mind about Evelyn coming straight home and being supervised? She didn't see a hint of guile in any of their expressions. She tucked a strand of hair behind Evelyn's ear, and the girl didn't even flinch. "It's fine if you and your friends make the diorama at the store."

Cheers exploded from the little group, and Guy groaned. "Oh, no, so many girls."

The girls laughed harder, and even Hester had to join in. She turned Guy toward home and delivered a light pat on the seat of his britches. "Go tell Uncle Scotty we have company coming, and please gather up some empty crates for the girls to use as a table before you fetch the mail."

"Yes, Ma!" He shot off.

Hester followed the girls, observing their interactions. Isolated at the Webers' home, spending most of her day involved in housework, she'd had no time for friends. But watching Evelyn laugh and joke was almost as good as being part of it. She'd made the right decision.

The girls set up the crates in the small foyer by the store's back door within Hester's sight and hearing. Although giggles often broke out, Hester also overheard serious discussion about how to paint the box so it seemed the colony was next to the sea, whether or not sand would stick to glue, and how large to craft the Pilgrims from modeling clay. Although they had fun, they were also working. Hester wandered by frequently enough to remind Evelyn she was being observed but not so often she disrupted their focus.

At half past four, Norma and Bertie Mae left, promising to meet again the next day to work more on the project. Rosemary stayed, though, and she and Evelyn laid out their books on the crates and bent their heads over the assignments. Hester caught bits and pieces of their conversation. To her delight—and relief—the two stayed on task.

Thursday followed Wednesday's pattern. No sheriff's official arrived to retrieve Beckett. Evelyn and her fellow Little Women worked on homework in the store after school. But Scotty and Beckett completed the chicken coop and strung the wire fence, so Thursday evening, they all piled into the Model T and drove to the Tipton twins' farm, where each child selected one hen from those Marvin Tipton offered for sale. Scotty, at Hester's insistence, chose the rooster.

The drive back to town was as lively as a three-ring circus, with children squealing, hens clucking, feathers flying . . . And Hester savored every minute of it. At home, they wrestled the chickens into their new coop and then washed for dinner.

The excitement of buying the chickens wound everyone up, turning dinnertime into a raucous affair. Hester couldn't help wondering if the joy and exuberance of this evening hinted at what to expect on future Christmas mornings. She treasured the thought. They finished eating, and Hester and Evelyn washed the dishes while the boys went to the side yard and tossed a ball back and forth. Scotty asked Winnie for a new picture to hang in his room, so Winnie used crayons and scribbled up a sheet of drawing paper at the table. The ordinary activities reined in their wild excitement, and after stories and prayers, the children settled into their beds and quickly drifted off to sleep.

Hester returned to the kitchen and poured herself and Scotty cups of coffee. She sat across from him and took a couple of sips, enjoying her first chance to simply sit and do nothing since rising that morning. Crickets sang outside the half-open kitchen window, and an occasional cluck from a hen added harmony. She might have sat there basking in the quiet forever if Scotty hadn't cleared his throat.

"Now that the coot's all done"—she smiled at his adoption of Winnie's word—"seems like I should put my hands to another project."

She set the cup on the table and aimed an indulgent look at him. "What are you thinking now?"

He grinned. "Them kids're here to stay. At least, three of 'em."

When would they hear something from the officials in Marion about Beckett? She would go to the post office tomorrow and make another call. If they weren't coming for him soon, he should be enrolled in school. If the school would allow it, considering he wasn't a resident of Millersberg.

"Miz Hester?"

She gave a little jolt. Scotty was waiting for her acknowledgment. She pushed her thoughts aside and focused on him. "Are you thinking the sheet curtains need to be replaced with something permanent? Something that provides more privacy for them and me?"

He nodded. "I can put walls where them sheets've been hangin', but"—he blew out a *whew!*—"it makes some mighty small spaces for youngsters to grow up in." He glanced at the painted beadboard ceiling. "I've been in your attic a time or two. The floor's real solid. Whoever built the house used two-by-sixes instead o' two-by-fours for ceiling joists. Smart choice, even if it likely cost 'em more. They might've even been thinkin' ahead to usin' that space for somethin' more'n storage someday." He pointed at her, raising one steel-gray eyebrow. "That's to your favor now."

"How so?"

"If a fella was to put—" Scotty's whiskered face screwed into a scowl. "Whadda they call them special kinda windows that poke out from a roof's angle?"

Hester took a guess. "Dormers?"

He snapped his fingers. "That's it! Dormers. If a fella was to put dormers up there, good-sized ones—maybe twelve foot wide—on each side o' the house, it'd make a real nice room for the boys. An' you'd still have storage space at the front an' rear o' the attic."

She tried to envision it. She could picture the room itself, but . . . "How would they access it? I don't care to leave the ladder down all the time and step around it while I work in the kitchen."

"I'm thinkin' you could put in a staircase right here." He pointed to the corner closest to the bedroom doorway. "There's a way o' doin' it so the steps climb around the corner instead o' havin' a landing. I did some figurin' in my head, an' I'm purty sure there's enough room if you make it a narrow staircase. Nothin' grand."

Hester winced. "Like the stairs leading from servants' quarters to the kitchen?"

He nodded, oblivious to the memories he'd just stirred to life in her mind. "That's right." He leaned closer, a satisfied smile softening his expression. "Why, you could probably git two good-sized rooms up there in case you wanna adopt more kids later on."

Her heart fluttered. More children? Oh, to have a houseful, the way she and Dale had dreamed. But how likely was it? The trains from New York weren't running anymore. She should count her blessings—Evelyn, Guy, Winnie—and be content.

"I like your idea, but it sounds like a pretty major undertaking." How to phrase her concern without stomping on his feelings? Scotty was a proud man. "Are you sure you want to tackle such a project? You've already done so much." A knot filled her throat, and she couldn't resist reaching across the table and placing her hand over his gnarled knuckles. "I don't want to take advantage of your friendship."

"Aw, now, there ain't no chance o' that happenin'. Why, we're kind o' like family, ain't we?"

She playfully shook her finger. "Not kind of, Scotty. We *are* family. In the best sense of the word."

He ducked his head and rubbed his finger under his nose. Then he chuckled and met her gaze. "It's mighty nice o' you to say so." He stood slowly, yawning as he rose. "I reckon I ought to turn in. Tomorrow I'll do some drawin' on a paper. Then, if it's all right with you, I'll drive over an' talk to that feller at the Marion lumberyard about what you'd need to put some rooms in the attic."

"How about instead of taking the Model T, ask Joe Frager if he'll drive you over in his flatbed truck. I imagine you're going to need more lumber than my automobile can hold."

His jaw dropped. "You already know you wanna do it? Even before knowin' what it'll cost?"

She shrugged. "You're right that the children need a better space. Why not go ahead and get it done? Isn't that what parents do—meet their children's needs?"

He slapped his thigh. "All righty then, I'll do it." Admiration glowed in his eyes. "Miz Hester, you make a right fine mama."

Her face heated. She rose, rounded the table, and caught

Scotty in a hug. "Thank you for everything you do for me. I appreciate you more than you know."

He gave her back a few light pats and then pulled loose. "G'night, now. Sleep well." He sauntered out with his head held high.

Chapter Twenty-Four

Hester

After walking Evelyn and Guy to school Friday morning, Hester went to the post office and placed a telephone call to the Marion County Courthouse. She asked for the same deputy she'd spoken to previously, but he wasn't available. The clerk didn't know of any new developments concerning Beckett's situation, so Hester returned to the store with no more information than she'd had before. She wanted to keep Beckett. He was a fine boy, wise beyond his years, but he had gone too long without formal education.

By the time she reached her store, she'd decided if there'd been no word by the end of the day, she would enroll Beckett in the Millersberg school on Monday morning. He wasn't her adopted son yet, but she would proceed as if he would be.

Midmorning, Elizabeth Stafford breezed through the door with a smile on her face. She delivered a hug, then stepped back and beamed at Hester. "Everything is in order for Sunday. There will be sandwiches and cake, fruit punch, and of course lots of gifts."

Hester blinked, confused. Then she inwardly berated herself. She'd completely forgotten about the adoption party the minister's wife promised to host. She took hold of Elizabeth's hand. "You're so kind to arrange this for the children and me."

The back screen door slapped into its frame, and Beckett shot around the corner. "Mrs. Haak? Uncle Scotty wanted me to ask if—" He stopped, and a flush climbed his cheeks. "Oh, I'm sorry. I didn't mean to interrupt."

Hester gestured him closer. "It's all right. You remember Mrs. Stafford from church, don't you?"

"Yes, ma'am. Hello again, Mrs. Stafford."

Elizabeth returned the greeting, and Hester asked the boy, "What does Uncle Scotty want?"

"He said the chickens need some fattening up an' dried meal-worms from the feed store'll do it. Is it okay if me an' Winnie go with him to buy some?"

"Of course. Enjoy your outing."

"Thank you." He nodded at Elizabeth. "Nice seeing you again, ma'am." He made a hasty exit, hollering, "We can go!"

Elizabeth watched after him. "What a polite boy. When you introduced him at Sunday school, I didn't realize he was staying with you permanently."

Hester laughed lightly. "I'm not sure that he is. It's a rather complicated story. But if at all possible, I want him to stay here."

Elizabeth tapped her chin, her brows furrowing. "Hmm, it wouldn't be fair to have gifts for your other children and nothing for him. It's short notice, but I'm sure I can round up some-thing." She fixed Hester with a bright look. "What does he need? And what does he like?"

Hester hesitated. Was it fair to ask people to provide items for Beckett when he might very well carry them all off to another home? But how could she let him sit at the party while the others opened gifts and he had none? "Well . . . he came with only the clothes on his back. I've been washing them out every other day, but he could use another set of clothing. He loves to read, and he's fascinated by Scotty's whittling. I think he's responsible enough for a penknife." Then she placed her hand on Elizabeth's forearm. "But please don't feel obligated to purchase gifts for him. You've been more than kind already."

Elizabeth patted Hester's hand. "Leave it to me. He looks a bit younger than my Timothy. I'll cull a few of his still nice outgrown clothing, and I'm sure we can locate some books, a penknife, and maybe even a toy or two." She blew out a little breath, her eyebrows high. "I'm so glad he came in when he did! I'd hate to leave him out." She turned toward the door, waving over her shoulder. "Have a good weekend, Hester, and we'll see you Sunday."

Evelyn

Evelyn hadn't minded being under Mrs. Haak's watchful eyes after school because she had her friends with her. Then the kids and grown-ups were all together in the house in the evening, so those hours didn't bother her much, either. But she thought sure that by Saturday, the lady would decide Evelyn didn't need watching. That she'd be able to do her chores and then walk to Rosemary's to talk about Fred Ash. She couldn't talk about boys in front of Mrs. Haak. Or talk about how she was gonna get to New York. She wasn't ever gonna give up on going there. She had $3.20 saved from working at Ebright's, but she needed a lot more. Rosemary was real smart. She might have some good ideas.

But right after washing their breakfast dishes, Mrs. Haak said, "Evelyn, choose a schoolbook or two to bring to the store. You can study in between helping me with customers."

Evelyn gawked at her. "But it's Saturday."

"That's right, and you have catching up to do."

Evelyn put her hand on her hip. "What about chores? How'm I gonna do my chores if I'm out in the store all day?"

"We'll work together this evening to complete your chores. Now, gather your books and come with me."

Evelyn huffed real loud, but Mrs. Haak just stood there holding Winnie's hand. Evelyn stomped into the bedroom, grabbed the whole stack, and followed Mrs. Haak to the store. Inside, Winnie pulled loose, ran to the front door, and started crooning to the iron cat doorstop. Evelyn rolled her eyes at her sister's silliness and smacked the books onto the counter. "What about the boys? Do they gotta stay in here with you all day?"

Mrs. Haak tied on an apron. "Beckett has a list of chores, and Guy is going along to Marion with Uncle Scotty for a load of lumber."

"The boys get to have all the fun." Evelyn eyed the apron. Mrs. Haak's work aprons were made from flowered feed-sack material instead of heavy twill like the workers at Ebright's wore. They were pretty, even nicer than some of the dresses she'd brought from the home. Evelyn wouldn't mind wearing one. She rested her elbows on the counter, then propped her chin in her hand. "If I'm working in here, do I gotta wear an apron?"

"That's up to you."

"I reckon it'll keep me from mussing my dress." Evelyn sauntered real casually around the counter. There were two on hooks. She liked the one sprinkled all over with little pink rosebuds better than the one with blue and yellow morning glories. "Does it matter which I take?"

Mrs. Haak glanced up from doing something with a leather-bound book. She gave her one of those soft smiles—almost like a hug. "Evelyn, you're my daughter. Everything I have is yours as well, so choose whichever one you like."

The smile and kind words stirred a yearning she didn't understand in the center of Evelyn's chest. Uncomfortable, she grabbed the rosebud one. She sidled up to Mrs. Haak while putting it on and peeked at the book. The page had a name at the top, then a list of items and dollar amounts. "What is that?"

Mrs. Haak slid it closer to Evelyn. "This is the charge ledger. See? These people came in earlier this month and charged their purchases rather than paying for them at that time."

Evelyn gaped at her. "You let people take stuff without paying for it?"

She laughed and put her arm around Evelyn. "It's a fairly common practice in most stores. Especially when you know your customers well and trust them to pay when it's due."

Evelyn stared at the amounts in the book. "When's it come due?"

"My customers pay off their accounts the second and fourth Saturdays of the month."

Evelyn glanced at the calendar and gave a little jolt. "So all this"—she ran her finger down the line of amounts due—"is coming in next Saturday?"

"Mm-hmm."

"You're gonna be rich!"

Mrs. Haak laughed, but not like she was making fun—like Evelyn had said something clever. "A good bit of that will be used to purchase more stock for the shelves, but you're right that I'm rich. I'm rich in blessings." She aimed another of those soft smiles at Evelyn before closing the book and putting it on the shelf under the counter. Then she handed Evelyn a feather duster. "Would you please dust the tops of cans and boxes? With the door open most of the day, the wind carries in quite a bit of grit. I don't want my merchandise to look old."

Evelyn took the duster and headed for the shelves, still thinking about the dollar amounts written in Mrs. Haak's ledger. Then she remembered Mrs. Haak saying, *"Evelyn, you're my daughter. Everything I have is yours as well."* Did she mean even the money in the cash register? If so, she didn't need to talk to Rosemary. She had an idea of her own.

Marion, Kansas
Callum

Callum paused at the end of the lane leading to the Marion County poor farm. He was sweaty, tired, and achy from three days of staying in one small space, followed by a seven-mile walk to this overgrown house built from stone blocks. He wanted a cold drink and a bath. But mostly he wanted his girls.

His heart pounded so hard it hurt his chest. Would they remember him? Would they want him as much as he wanted them? Winnie wouldn't know him. How could she? Evvie, though—she'd know him for sure. But Freida always said that girl had his spunk. She might be plenty sore about him being gone so long, for letting her and her baby sister be taken so far away.

"Don't be mad, little girl." He practiced how he'd cajole her if she started spitting fire. "I came as quick as I could." He was here now. Why stand out here when his girls were waiting inside?

He put his feet into motion and trudged all the way up the curving lane to the big front porch. He dropped his bags of belongings at the bottom of the stairs and then climbed the risers, setting his feet firm as he went, anticipation growing with every step.

At the door, he thumped with his fist and stepped back so whoever answered could swing the door wide. A man wearing gray pinstriped pants and a matching vest over a white shirt with a yellowed collar opened the door. Except for him standing straight up and sporting a potbelly, he reminded Callum of Billy with his suit, warm smile, and white hair. "Can I help you?"

Callum nodded. "Yes, sir. My name's Callum Holbrook." He reached inside his jacket and pulled out the packet Miss Armstrong had given him. "I'm here to collect my daughters, Evelyn and Edwina Holbrook. I have all their papers—birth registries and such. They were brought here by a lady from"—he peeked at the note Miss Armstrong wrote—"Millersberg."

The man's smile turned upside down. "Mr. Holbrook, I'm afraid there's been a mix-up. Please come in and we'll try to straighten it out."

Callum gulped. Had he come to the wrong place? He followed

the man inside. They passed a parlor, where three women sat doing handwork and a pair of old men played checkers. The man led him into a little alcove under a spindled staircase wide enough for three big men to climb up side by side. He gestured to a chair with a scene of deer in a forest stitched into its backrest, and he sat in a matching chair close by.

Callum didn't want to sit. He wanted to take his girls and go. The walk back to Marion would take longer than it had for him coming out if he ended up carrying Winnie while Evelyn toted the bags. He still needed to find a better place than the park for them to sleep, and that could take some time. But the man was sitting there quiet, his hand held out to the chair like he wasn't sure Callum had seen it yet. Resigned, Callum dropped the packet onto the little table between the chairs, sat, and leaned against the deer picture.

The man let out a big sigh. "Mr. Holbrook, I had a visit from a woman concerning some children from an asylum in New York."

"The Mission Church Home?" Callum didn't figure there'd be another one, but he wanted to be sure.

The man nodded. "That sounds right. Apparently, the asylum directors instructed her to deliver them here, but she requested permission to adopt them. Since I didn't have room available for the children, I passed guardianship to her."

Callum gripped the armrests and came half out of his seat. "You gave away my girls?"

The man drew back. "I didn't know you were coming to take custody of them. I couldn't keep them here, and she met every requirement for adoption in Kansas. It seemed the best thing to do at the time."

Callum slumped into the chair, his pulse pounding like a bass drum in his ears. He couldn't be mad at this man. He'd only done what he thought best for the girls. It was all his own fault.

He should've gone back sooner to get them. Then they wouldn't have been sent to Kansas in the first place. He sucked in a deep breath and let the air ease out, willing the thud in his head to ease with his slow exhale. "What's the name of the woman who took them?"

He rolled his eyes upward. "Hmm . . . It started with an *H* and was unusual. Hack? Hawt?"

Callum grabbed the envelope and pulled out the note from Miss Armstrong. "Haak? Hester Haak?"

The man smiled. "That's it. Yes. Mrs. Hester Haak from Millersberg."

So the woman who took them from the train figured out a way to keep them even though the Mission Church Home said she couldn't. Pretty sneaky—or pretty smart. Callum jammed the packet and crumpled note into his jacket pocket and stood. "Well, then, I guess I'll go there and get them."

The man scrambled to his feet, his eyes wide. "Sir, if the children have been adopted, you can't take them. You'll be charged with kidnapping."

Callum gaped at him. "Kidnapping? My own children?"

"If the adoption's been finalized, yes. In the eyes of the law, they're Mrs. Haak's children now." He spoke like he knew what he was talking about. "You'll have to petition the court to have their custody returned to you."

A low groan scraped past Callum's throat. "I don't have time for that. I've gotta be back at my job in New York by Wednesday morning."

The man looked as unhappy as Callum felt, but he shook his head. "I'm sorry, but the courthouse isn't open on weekends. You won't be able to talk to a judge until Monday, and that's if he has time to see you. You might have to return to New York without them and come back at a later time."

"I can't." He didn't have enough money for a second trip, and he couldn't ask Billy to pass another collection can. He had to get his girls now. Today. "Is there a bus or a taxicab that can take me to Millersberg?"

"I'm afraid we don't have bus or taxi service here. But Marion's a fairly busy town on Saturdays. People from surrounding communities, including Millersberg, often come in for shopping. You might be able to find someone to give you a ride."

Callum spun and marched toward the front door, arms pumping. He had to hightail it to town and ask every person with an automobile if they were from Millersberg. He had to get to his girls. He had to convince this clever, conniving Mrs. Hester Haak to give his children back to him.

Chapter Twenty-Five

Scotty

Scotty leaned on the bumper of Joe's truck and watched the pile of lumber on the bed get taller. Miz Hester had done the measuring and wrote it all down on paper. Scotty trusted her numbers, but now he had to trust that the fellers stacking these boards knew what they was doing. He sure hoped the money in the leather pouch she'd given him to pay for all this would be enough when they was done.

Joe Frager stayed in the cab of the truck, but Guy darted back and forth in excitement, sometimes getting in the way of the men. Scotty didn't scold him, though. Neither did the workers. Scotty was glad of that. The little boy was so happy about getting a new room. Scotty didn't want some impatient person stomping out his joy.

While he waited, cars and a wagon or two drove by. Their wheels stirred up dust that mixed with the sawdust coming off the lumber. Marion was sure busier'n Millersberg. More businesses. More automobiles. More people. More everything. Not as much everything as he'd seen in big cities, but still a change from the peacefulness he'd found in the little town eight miles up the road.

He chuckled to himself. He sure hadn't figured on being there this many years when he took the job at Miz Hester's store. But then, he hadn't ever figured on having anything close to a family. Her saying they was family had plumb chased away his itchy feet. He reckoned he'd be content for the rest of his life to stay in the little room in the back of her store, helping out with customers and making sure her needs was met. Was his feelings for Miz Hester the way a father felt toward his child? If so, it was a good feeling. Lord willing, he'd like to keep it.

The man whose cousin had took in Beckett dropped a few more two-by-fours on the bed, then stepped back and swished the sawdust from his clothes. "Well, now, that's the last of it." He turned to the other two men who'd come to help. "Rope it all down, fellas." They came forward, and he turned to Scotty. "Let's go inside an' I'll tally up your bill."

Scotty caught hold of Guy as he went darting past. "Hop back in the truck, now. We'll be headin' home here in a minute."

"Yes, sir, Uncle Scotty!"

Scotty waited until Guy closed himself in the cab, and then he caught up to the man. He patted his thigh with the leather money bag, nervousness making him want to twitch, while the worker added up all the numbers. His pulse seemed to chant, *Be enough. Be enough.* Finally, the fellow straightened, set the pencil aside, and announced the total.

Scotty opened the bag and held it out. "This here's what I got. Can you tell . . . is there enough to pay for it all?" His face went hot. So shameful, being his age and not able to know how to make the bills and coins match the amount wrote down on paper. He had to trust this lumberyard man's honesty.

The man took the pouch and fingered through it. Then he gave Scotty a nod. "There's enough with some to spare."

Scotty nearly wilted with relief. Not only because there was money enough to pay, but because the man didn't make fun of him for not knowing it himself. "Go ahead an' take what you need."

The fellow plucked out several bills and a few coins, then handed the pouch back. "All right, there you go. Good luck with that buildin' project."

Scotty jammed the much-thinner pouch inside his shirt,

tipped his hat, and headed outside. The bright sunshine after being in the building made him squint. He almost walked into a fellow standing between him and the truck. A hobo, most likely. The man's wrinkled clothes, few days' growth of whiskers, and pair of bags slung over his shoulders gave him away. The bull had probably put him off the train. Scotty wouldn't treat the man badly because of it. Lord knew, he'd been there himself more'n once or twice.

Scotty tipped his hat to him. "Howdy."

"Hey," the man said back.

Scotty stepped around him and took hold of the door's handle.

The hobo hurried over. "Excuse me, where are you going?"

Scotty flapped his hand toward the road. "Headin' north, endin' in Millersberg."

The man's whiskered face lit up. "Mind if I hitch a ride?"

It wasn't his truck, so Scotty probably should ask Joe Frager, but what harm would come from giving this footsore-looking fellow a ride for a few miles? "Ain't room in the cab, but if you don't mind sitting on the wood, climb aboard."

The man smiled a thank-you. He tossed his bags on top of the lumber, clambered up, and took a seat.

Scotty gave him a little salute. "Hold tight. It's a bumpy road." He squeezed into the cab and leaned forward a bit to catch Joe's eye. "Let's go."

Callum

Bumpy road was right. Callum gripped the rope holding the lumber on the truck's bed the way a mounted policeman held the reins while in pursuit of a criminal. His backside would likely be black-and-blue by the time he reached Millersberg, but what difference did it make? He'd found a ride.

While he rode, he hatched a plan. As much as he wanted to see his girls right away, he'd gotten a reflection of himself in a plate-glass window. The sight had almost scared him. He should find a place to clean up, shave, and put on fresh clothes. If he was presentable, the woman who had Evvie and Winnie wouldn't see him as unfit. That was important. If she'd really adopted them, he'd have to do some fancy talking to convince her to let them go. Nicer clothes, a smooth face, and a good scrubbing with a bar of soap would help. If Millersberg had a hotel, he'd rent a room. Even if it cost dear, it'd be worth it.

He stretched out on the boards, hoping it might mean less bumps. They could use some bricked roads out here. Flat on his back, he still got jarred, but from this position, he got a good view of an almost cloudless sky. The blue seemed to stretch forever. In New York City, so many buildings stood in the way that a fellow got only peeks at the sky. And it always seemed gray with factory smoke hanging like a veil over the city. This view was pretty, as was the land rolling as far as he could see. The waving grass kind of looked like a green ocean.

And the quiet . . . He sighed. The quiet was real nice. Oh, the truck was making some noise, but not enough to cover up birdsong and the wind whispering through all that tall grass. If he wasn't bouncing around like a rubber ball on concrete, he might be soothed to sleep with the gentle sounds of nature around him. He settled his clothing bag under his head, gripped ropes in his fists, and watched clouds float in that great big sky.

Brakes squealed, and the truck gave two shudders as it slowed down. Callum sat up and peered over the top of the cab. They were coming up on a town. A sign posted on the road said "Millersberg, Inc., 1884" in neat black letters on a white background. Simple but nice. The people here must take pride in their little town.

Rows of buildings, some with clapboard fronts and some of stone blocks like the poor-farm building, lined both sides of a wide dirt street. He didn't see any business with a Hotel sign, but a couple of the buildings were two-story. They might have rooms to let. He took hold of his bags and scooted to the edge of the bed. When it slowed enough, he'd get off and put his plan into motion. His heart double thumped in eagerness. In an hour, maybe two, he'd see his girls.

The truck's brakes announced another slowdown. He braced himself, took a deep breath, and leaped. He landed flat-footed, stinging the soles of his feet something fierce, but he kept himself upright. A hand popped out the passenger window and waved. The old man who'd given him permission to ride must've seen him hop off. Callum waved the almost empty food bag and gave a nod he hoped would serve as thanks. Then he tossed the bags over his shoulders and set off up the street.

Millersberg
Scotty

Scotty gave Joe Frager a hearty clap on the back. "Thank you for roundin' up fellers to help git all that wood off your truck. It would've been too much for me to handle all by myself."

Joe shifted his hat back and forth. "Aw, no problem, Scotty. That's what neighbors are for, right? Besides"—he nudged Scotty with his elbow and grinned—"I've got another run to make before my wife puts supper on the table, so it was a help to me as much as to you to get it cleaned out." He climbed into the cab. Moments later, the automobile revved to life and rolled up the street.

Dust billowed behind the truck's tires and filled Scotty's nose. He headed inside the store, coughing. Miz Hester sent him a concerned look. He waved his hand. "I ain't comin' down with nothin'. Just good ol' Kansas dust makin' me cough is all."

She laughed. "There's a pitcher of Kool-Aid in the Frigidaire. Go have a glass and chase the dust out of your throat."

It was his nose giving him trouble, but a cold drink sounded good. "What's Kool-Aid?"

"A flavored powder you mix with water. I got some samples in the mail several weeks ago and came across them again this morning, so I mixed up a batch. The children liked it. I might start stocking it."

Flavored powder? Scotty huffed a laugh. "What'll they think of next?" He started toward the back door, but he heard her say, "Oh!" He turned back. "Somethin' wrong?"

"It's been so busy this morning, I forgot . . ." She bustled from behind the counter. "Mr. Maddox has a fever that's left him unsteady on his feet, and Mrs. Maddox is reluctant to leave him by himself. I know her usual list, and I can have Evelyn fill a carton."

Suddenly Evelyn popped up from behind the counter. She was wearing one of Miz Hester's aprons and looked right grown-up in it. Scotty couldn't help sending her a grin. "I thought you was a jack-in-the-box there for a minute. What're you doin' back there?"

She made a face that proved she wasn't so grown-up yet. "Homework."

Miz Hester wriggled her fingers at the girl, and Evelyn came around the counter. Miz Hester slid her arm around Evelyn's shoulders but looked at Scotty. "When the order is filled, would you mind taking it to the Maddox house?"

Evelyn let out one of those little *huh* sounds. "I could carry it to her."

Miz Hester shook her head. "I want you to stay here and study."

Scotty had to admire the woman. She was sticking to her guns about keeping Evelyn focused on schoolwork and under her watchful eye. "I'll do that for you, after I git me a drink o' Kool-Aid."

"Thank you, Scotty." Miz Hester gave Evelyn's shoulder a little pat. "You'll find last week's orders under the counter in the wooden tray. Look for one with Martin and Dorothy Maddox at the top and duplicate it on a new order. Then fill a carton with those items, please."

Evelyn scuffed off.

Miz Hester turned to Scotty again. "It'll take at least thirty minutes to fill the order, so enjoy a little break, but please be quiet. Winnie is napping in there. I think she played too hard this morning, because she was pretty cranky by noon." She swiped her hand over her forehead. "It's been a good day—lots of shoppers—but I'll be ready to sleep tonight."

Scotty went on into the house and opened the Frigidaire. He gave a snort of amusement. The youngsters must've liked the Kool-Aid a lot. The pitcher was near empty. He poured the last of it in a glass and drank the fruity liquid in one long draw. Smacking his lips, he put the cup and pitcher in the sink. Plates scattered with bread crumbs were stacked in there, proof that the kids'd eaten sandwiches for lunch. He might as well have a sandwich, too. He slapped some cheese on bread, sat at the table, and ate slow, giving Evelyn plenty of time to gather the groceries. When a half hour had eased past, he headed for the store's back door.

The boys were leaning against the minnow tank, each chewing a blade of grass. If they didn't look the picture of laziness. Wasn't there something they could do to help Miz Hester? He started to call to them, but Miz Hester was all of a sudden next to him.

She touched his sleeve. "Did you happen to check on Winnie while you were in the house?"

"I didn't. But she must be sleepin' sound. There wasn't even a peep from the other side o' the curtain."

"No worries. I'll go check on her." She seemed to notice the boys. "Have you two finished hoeing the garden plot as I asked you to do?"

They shot each other sheepish looks and bounded up. "No, ma'am."

"Please get to it. It won't be long, and I'll want to put seeds in the ground."

"Yes, ma'am!" The pair galloped toward the little shed on the corner of the property.

Miz Hester gestured toward the store. "The Maddox order is all ready for you. Thank you for taking care of it." She hurried off.

Scotty opened the screen door and let himself into the store. As he rounded the corner, Evelyn lurched away from the cash register. His scalp prickled, and unease rolled through his gut. He approached the counter, his gaze latched on the girl's pink face. "What were you doin' back there?"

She acted real innocent, but the pink didn't go away. "Dropping a nickel in the drawer." She pointed to the door. "One of the kids from the neighborhood came in for some penny candy. He bought three gumdrops and two peppermint sticks. He just left if you wanna look. He rode off on a bicycle, but he couldn't have got too far yet."

Scotty went behind the counter and pushed the button that opened the drawer. Every section had money in it. Quite a lot in some sections. More than a little relieved, he closed the drawer and gave her a firm look. "Next time, let your mama see to droppin' money in here. The till ain't nobody's business but hers."

"That's not what she told me."

"Oh, yeah?"

"Yeah." She tossed her hair. "She said whatever's hers is mine, 'cause I'm her daughter."

Scotty raised one eyebrow. "I'm purty sure she wasn't meanin' the money folks pay for groceries. That's hers an' only hers. You best remember it."

Evelyn flounced to the books stacked on a crate behind the counter. She plopped down on another crate and opened one of the books.

The box of groceries for Mrs. Maddox was on the floor by the front door, but Scotty didn't pick it up. He'd wait until Miz Hester came back from the house.

Chapter Twenty-Six

Callum

Callum awoke with a start. He sat up, the mattress springs twanging loudly, and looked around in confusion. Where was he? Realization crashed down—in a room above Miss Sally's Dress Shop in Millersberg, Kansas. He pulled himself out of bed and stumbled, sleep muddled, to the window. He yanked the shade, and it whizzed up and spun on its roller. He looked out on a nearly dark, nearly empty dirt street.

He slapped his forehead. How had he slept so long? Granted, he'd caught only short snatches of sleep on the train. Always sitting up, so much noise from the wheels on the track and people yakking all around him, frequent whistle blasts . . . How could a body relax and sleep hard enough to feel rested afterward? But he'd meant to close his eyes for just a few minutes. What time was it? He squinted at the windup clock on the bedside table. He groaned. He'd laid down more than six hours ago.

He sank down on the edge of the mattress, raising another complaining squawk from the springs. He couldn't show up at Hester Haak's door past eight o'clock in the evening. It wouldn't be decent. And who would be willing to drive him and the girls to Marion at this hour? He'd have to wait and go in the morning. Surely, he'd find someone with an automobile who'd accept a dollar or two in exchange for a trip to Marion. He'd miss the earliest train for sure, but maybe, if he was lucky, they'd catch one that would still get him back in New York before he had to clock in Wednesday morning.

His stomach growled. He pushed himself up and turned his

food sack upside down over the bed. One wrinkled apple strip, two crackers, and a hardened lump of cheese fell out. None of it looked appetizing, but it was better than nothing. He ate every bit of it, even the cheese, although it felt like a chunk of tar in his mouth. When he was done, he returned to the window.

Callum's stomach ached, and it wasn't because of the food. Somewhere out there, a woman he didn't know was probably tucking his girls into bed right about now. Did she sing and pray with them the way Freida had? He'd always watched from the doorway, his heart swelling as his wife knelt beside the bed for a nighttime prayer and then sweetly sang a lullaby. A melody trickled through his memory, but he couldn't remember the words to the song.

He tried humming it, but after a few notes, he made a face and stopped. He'd keep a child awake with his off-pitch crooning. Winnie was so little yet. Someone should sing her to sleep. Maybe Evvie would do it.

He lowered the shade and flopped sideways across the mattress, arms flung out and stockinged feet on the floor. He stared at the slowly circling blades of the ceiling fan. Odd that the room had an electric fan but no electric lamps. He could light the kerosene lantern on the bureau, but what was there to see in this small square room? He was stuck until morning. Stuck in a town that shut itself down at sunset. But as soon as the sun came up, he'd go straight to Mrs. Haak's house and sweet-talk her out of his girls. Until then . . .

He shifted around on the bed, rolled to his side, jammed the pillow under his head, and waited for more sleep to claim him.

Hester

On their first Sunday together, Hester had driven the family to church. They'd walked every Sunday since. But today the children would receive gifts at the celebration. Uncertain if they'd be able to easily carry everything home, she instructed everyone to get in the car. The boys whooped and galloped out the door, and Scotty ambled after them. Evelyn reached for Winnie's hand as she always did when they were all going somewhere, but Winnie shook her head and backed away.

Evelyn frowned, seemingly more puzzled than upset. "C'mon, we're going to Sunday school."

Winnie shuffled to Hester, arms upraised. "Carry me."

Too startled to do otherwise, Hester picked her up. The little girl laid her head on Hester's shoulder. Hester gaped at Evelyn, and Evelyn gaped back. Then Evelyn stomped out, and Hester followed. Although Evelyn must be seething inside, Hester relished carrying Winnie to the Model T.

Scotty was waiting at the front of the vehicle, ready to turn the crank for her, as he always did. An amused grin creased his face as she approached with Winnie in her arms. "The little one's legs not workin' this mornin'?"

Evelyn huffed and slammed herself into the back seat with the boys.

Hester laughed softly and rubbed Winnie's back. "She just needs some cuddles. She'll be fine. But why don't you go ahead and drive?" She slid in on the passenger side of the front seat and settled Winnie beside her.

Scotty gave a good crank, and the Model T chugged to life. He hopped in and drove them to the church. He parked in the closest open spot to the porch, saying with a shrug, "It'll make loadin' the kids' stuff easier afterward."

They fell in with friends and neighbors walking across the lawn to the church doors, Winnie clinging to Hester's hand. Once inside, the three oldest children headed for the basement. Hester started after them with Winnie, but the little girl dug in her heels. Winnie looked up at Hester with tear-shiny blue eyes and a wobbly lower lip. "I don't wanna go to sunny school. I wanna stay with you."

Hester waved the other children on. Then she ushered Winnie away from the flow of folks coming in and crouched down to her level. She smoothed Winnie's freshly curled hair. "Are you having a sad day, sweetheart?"

Winnie sighed and hung her head.

Scotty came near. "Somethin' ailin' her? I'll take her back to the house if you want."

Hester gently tweaked Winnie's nose and earned a tiny smile. She straightened. "I think she's just a little out of sorts. I'll keep her with me for now. I'd hate to have her miss the party, but if she isn't up to staying for it, I can send her with you when you walk home after the service."

Scotty ran his hand over Winnie's gold-brown curls, smiling tenderly. "Aw, by the time church is out, I reckon she'll be fine."

"Yes, I'm sure she will be." Hester picked her up, placed a kiss on her rosy cheek, and carried her into the sanctuary.

Callum

Callum checked the address on the piece of paper from Miss Armstrong, then looked again at the numbers painted above the door of a clapboard building with *Corner Store* painted across the top of its false front. He'd found the place he needed and without much trouble, even on his own.

He could have asked for directions from the lady who'd delivered a breakfast of two hard-boiled eggs, three biscuits, and a slice of cold ham to his room that morning. But when he'd requested coffee, she got a little put out and told him she didn't have time to go after it—not on a Sunday morning. He figured giving directions would take time she didn't want to spend. He appreciated being fed, though, even if she was a little grumpy about feeding him. He ate every bit of the cold breakfast, enjoying a full belly for the first time since leaving New York. Then he put the key in the door's lock and his empty plate on the floor in the hall, as she'd instructed, and left the building by an outside staircase. It dumped him in an alley. There he'd stood for a minute or two, unsure which way to go.

As it turned out, once he walked between buildings and landed on Main Street's boardwalk, it hadn't been hard at all. Pine Street intersected with Main Street. He'd followed Pine Street west one block and located the right address. Odd, though, that the address seemed to be attached to a gas station instead of a house.

He jammed the paper into his clothing bag and stepped up onto the porch. He peeked in the windows. Even though the store was small, there were quite a few shelves holding a variety of items. This wasn't a gas station, as the pump near the street led him to believe. It was an actual grocery store. Did his girls live here? If so, they weren't home. It was dark—not a soul around.

He turned away from the door and moved to the short concrete path connecting the dirt street to the store's porch. A slender dark-haired boy perhaps fifteen or sixteen years old rode around the corner on a bicycle. Callum dropped his bag and ran to the edge of the street. "You there! Can you help me?"

The boy stopped and planted one foot on the street, the other still on its pedal. "Maybe. Whatcha need, mister?"

Callum gestured to the building behind him. "Is this where Mrs. Hester Haak lives?"

"Well, not exactly. She runs the Corner Store, but her house is behind it." He leaned forward on the seat and pointed. "That's where she lives."

Callum walked to the other side of the gas pump and looked where the boy had pointed. A narrow house with a tiny porch centered between two windows sat well beyond the street, half hidden by the store. No wonder he hadn't seen it. He turned to the boy. "Thank you." He grabbed his bag and started toward the house.

"Nobody's gonna be there, mister. Mrs. Haak's already gone to church."

Callum swallowed a groan. He should've thought of that. Even though he didn't go to services on Sundays anymore, other folks did. Callum reversed direction and approached the grinning boy. "What church does she go to?"

"The Baptist church on the north end of town, corner of Maple and First Street. You can't miss it—there's a great big cemetery beside it. It gets out at noon, but most of the ladies in town are going to a party there after today's service. Mrs. Haak'll stay for that."

Callum considered what he'd heard. He didn't want to attend the service. "I guess I'll go to the party." He was really talking to himself, but the boy laughed.

"The party's only for women and kids." He pushed off with his foot, calling over his shoulder. "You'll have to wait until she gets back. I gotta get to church now or my ma'll chew my hide. Have a good day, mister."

Callum yanked off his cap and slapped his leg with it. Church? Then a party? It'd be at least midafternoon before he could even talk to Mrs. Haak about his girls. Would he still be able to catch a train today? He'd made such careful plans, had such grand dreams of reunion, and everything was crumbling. Unless . . .

He put on his cap, shoved his bag under a bench on the corner of the store's porch where it wouldn't get much attention, and then took off in search of First Street.

Hester

Surrounded by the women from the town she'd claimed as her own as a new bride, her children playing with their children, laughter and happiness bursting in every corner of the decorated basement room, Hester experienced a sense of community even greater than the day the townsfolk gathered to lay Dale to rest.

When they finished eating, Elizabeth Stafford called Evelyn, Guy, Beckett, and Winnie to the center of the floor. Chairs encircled the area, with smiling women and bouncy children occupying each seat. Hester sat closest to the center with Winnie on her lap. Evelyn went shy, sending embarrassed grins at Rosemary. Guy bounded over with his usual exuberance. Beckett inched forward with uncertainty, but he sat cross-legged on the floor with Evelyn and Guy.

Evelyn looked at her little sister and patted the floor beside her. "C'mon, Winnie."

Winnie hadn't left Hester's lap since arriving—not during Sunday school or the service or while they ate. Now she buried her face in Hester's bodice. "Go ahead, honey." Hester gave the child a gentle nudge. "You'll get to open presents."

Winnie burrowed hard.

Elizabeth patted Winnie's small shoulder. "If she wants to stay with you, it's all right. I imagine all this activity is a bit overwhelming. She can open her gifts from there."

Hester appreciated the woman's understanding. Typically, Winnie napped after lunch, so it didn't surprise Hester that the little girl slumped against Hester's chest while peeling paper from the items people had brought for her. Over time, even though the church basement stayed cooler than the sanctuary, she got uncomfortably warm with Winnie's little body nestled against hers. But Hester had never cradled a baby of her own. Holding Winnie was as close as she would get. Before long, Winnie would be too big to hold this way. So Hester cuddled her and kissed her warm cheek again and again while she watched the children open at least a dozen gifts each. Not everything was new, which didn't bother Hester, given the difficult times in which they all lived. The generosity and love behind each choice touched her deeply.

When the children finished unwrapping everything, Hester gloried in giving a motherly prompt. "What do you tell everyone, children?"

Evelyn, Guy, and Beckett chorused, "Thank you," and the attendees applauded as if they'd made a grand speech.

Elizabeth also thanked everyone for coming and immediately gave directions for the cleanup. Since the party was in her children's honor, the least Hester could do was assist in straightening things. She tried to slide Winnie to the floor, but the child wrapped her arms around her neck and refused to let go. Hester joggled her loose despite her whines of protest and looked into her face. Her cheeks wore rosy patches, and her eyes were glassy and droopy. The child was more than tired—she was feverish. How had Hester not realized it sooner?

Carrying Winnie, she wove between others to Elizabeth. "I want to stay and help, but I think Winnie is sick."

Elizabeth looked into Winnie's flushed face, and sympathy puckered her lips. "Oh, it does appear she's not feeling well." She turned Hester toward the door. "Take her to your car. I'll ask Lillian and Andrew to help your other children collect the gifts and carry them out. You can be on your way quickly." She touched Hester's arm. "I'll pray it's nothing more than a spring cold."

Hester thanked the woman and climbed the stairs, Winnie in her arms. As she stepped out onto the church's porch, she spotted a man standing at the edge of the churchyard. She'd never seen him before, and his intense pose—as if braced for a race—gave her pause. He was clean-shaven and wore clean, if somewhat rumpled, clothing. But he was out of place, and it unnerved her to be outside alone with him.

She ducked back into the foyer and waited for the children. In a few minutes, the clatter of feet on the stairs alerted her to their approach. She peeked out the door. The man was still there, still staring at the church. How she wished she hadn't told Scotty to go home. She would feel much safer if he or any of the other men from the congregation were there. Andrew Stafford would have to do. Although he was only a young teen, from a slight distance his gangly height might give the illusion that he was a grown man. If the stranger made any threatening moves, Andrew could waylay him while Beckett or Guy ran for help.

She sent up a quick prayer for their safety and then led the group out of the church and down the stairs. The group of young people were all chatting and laughing, their gaiety bringing a smile that chased away Hester's earlier apprehensions. But suddenly one voice—Evelyn's—rose above the others in an excited shout.

"Daddy!"

Chapter Twenty-Seven

Hester

Hester whirled around. Evelyn, sobbing and laughing at the same time, dropped her armload and raced across the lawn to the man. He caught her in a hug and swung her in a circle. Beckett, Guy, Lillian, and Andrew gawked at Evelyn, then at Hester, and then at Evelyn again. Their identical open-mouthed expressions and perfectly executed synchronization of their heads turning would have been humorous if Hester's heart hadn't suddenly forgotten how to beat.

She gasped for breath, holding Winnie tight. "Lillian, please fetch your mother."

Lillian placed her stack of gifts on the ground and ran inside the church. Andrew also put his items down and stepped close to Hester, as if sensing she needed reinforcement. Beckett and Guy, their arms still full, moved behind Hester and Andrew. They all stayed there in a little huddle, silent save the heaving breaths that painfully rattled Hester's entire frame.

Arm in arm, Evelyn and the man she'd called Daddy started across the grass. At the same time, Elizabeth clicked down the steps and trotted to Hester, her eyes wide in disbelief. She squeezed between Hester and Andrew, sliding her arm around Hester's waist.

"Hester," she whispered, "is this truly the girls' father?"

Evelyn's fanciful forays into make-believe could lead her to claim a stranger as her daddy, but Hester couldn't imagine a strange man impulsively participating in a charade. The closer they came, the more she glimpsed Evelyn's nose, eyebrows, and hair color on the man. She released a shaky sigh. "Yes. Yes, I believe he is."

Elizabeth tightened her hold, which was as good as a hug—something Hester desperately needed. Hester offered the preacher's wife a small smile of gratitude and took a forward step. The man stopped only a yard or so away, his gaze locked on Winnie.

"Ma'am, I'm Callum Holbrook." His deep voice somehow held both strength and uncertainty. Although he addressed Hester, he didn't lift his attention from Winnie's small form. "I'm Evvie an' Winnie's daddy. I've come from New York to take them home."

Evelyn danced in place. "I told you! I told you he didn't leave us for good!"

He slung his arm around his daughter and snugged her tight to his side. She circled his middle with her arms and placed her cheek against his chest, smiling at Hester. He had yet to look directly at Hester. "I'm obliged for the good care you've given 'em. I can see they're well fed and clean and happy. But it was an awful mistake, them being sent to Kansas on that train. We've gotta right that wrong now."

Hester's heart had rediscovered its ability to beat. It did so in double time, making her quiver from head to toe. "Mr. Holbrook, this isn't a conversation to have in the churchyard. Winnie is not feeling well, and I need to take her h-home." She glanced over her shoulder at Elizabeth, and the woman immediately came to Hester's side. "Elizabeth, would you bring the children's gifts to my house? I don't think I can get them all to fit with six people in the Model T."

Elizabeth rubbed her back. "Of course." Her eyes shifted in Mr. Holbrook's direction for a brief second and returned to Hester. She whispered, "Would you like me to send Thaddeus instead?"

Hester appreciated the woman's concern, but there was no

need to trouble Reverend Stafford. "Scotty is there. I'm sure I'll be fine. But . . ." Should the children be witnesses if the discussion turned heated? "Maybe Guy and Beckett could go to your house for a little while."

"Excellent idea." Elizabeth's palm drew another quick circle on Hester's shoulder blade. "And that will leave enough room in your car for the gifts." She turned and clapped twice. "Boys, let's load these presents into the back seat of your mama's car. Then you can come to my house and spend some time with Timothy and Andrew."

Mr. Holbrook set Evelyn away from him. "I saw you carrying packages. Some of 'em must be yours. Go help." She turned a pleading look on him, but he flicked his fingers. "I'm not goin' anywhere. Help out."

She scuffed off.

Finally, the girls' father angled his head and his eyes met Hester's. Eyes as blue as Winnie's and Evelyn's. Blue like the expansive, cloudless sky. "You're gonna need to drive your automobile. I don't see how you can do it while you're holding Winnie. How about I take her?" He held out his arms, his expression entreating her. His Adam's apple bobbed, and he abruptly shifted his focus to Winnie again. "I . . . I sure would like to hold my baby girl."

Hester swallowed a knot of agony. Although she was reluctant to release Winnie into the keeping of someone she didn't know even if he was the girls' father, his comment about her driving was true. She gently peeled Winnie from her shoulder and laid her in Mr. Holbrook's waiting arms. He drew her close, staring down at her flushed face with such love and joy it hurt Hester to witness it.

She turned sharply away and hurried to the car. "Is everything loaded? All right, Evelyn, get in. Boys . . ." She cupped the boys' cheeks and delivered kisses on their sweaty foreheads by turn.

"Be good for Mrs. Stafford." Her lips wobbled into a smile she hoped was convincing. "I know you're eager to play with your new toys. I'll come for you soon."

Elizabeth put her hands on the boys' shoulders and gave Hester an encouraging nod. "I'll let Thaddeus know about"—she glanced at Mr. Holbrook—"this situation. We'll be in prayer."

Callum

Callum examined Mrs. Haak's profile out of the corner of his eye as she pulled away from the church and aimed her automobile in the direction of her store and house. He wouldn't say she was as beautiful as his Freida. What woman could be? But she was a comely woman. There was a softness to her that most any man would find appealing.

He'd had himself prepared to hate her. She'd stolen his girls—she must be a monster. But when he'd seen her come out of the church with her cheek tipped against his daughter's hair, any anger he'd harbored whisked away like a dandelion seed on a stout breeze. He wasn't the smartest man in the world, but he knew love when he saw it. The woman holding his baby girl made a fetching picture that unsettled him to his core. He hadn't expected it to bother him to take Evvie and Winnie away from this stranger who'd wrongfully claimed them as hers, but already his heart was twinging for the pain Mrs. Haak would feel when the girls left.

She pulled into the gravel alley alongside her store and then parked behind the house next to a stack of lumber. She'd no more than shut off the engine when the tall, lanky gray-haired man who'd given Callum permission to catch a ride from Marion ambled around the side of the house. He carried Callum's bag. Mrs. Haak opened her car door, and Callum heard the fellow say, "This was layin' on the store porch when I got back from church.

It's got some men's clothes an' a razor an' comb an' such in it. Do you know how it got there?"

Callum leaned forward so he could see out, careful not to mash Winnie. "I put it there."

The man bent down and looked into the car. His face went confused real fast. "You again? What—"

Evelyn threw her door open and jumped out. "He's our daddy, and he's come to take Winnie and me back to New York."

The man bolted upright. "He's come to do what?" He sounded fighting mad. "Miz Hester, what's goin' on?"

Callum needed to explain himself. But not from inside the car. He turned sideways on the seat and pulled himself out. Even being careful, he jarred Winnie when he stood up. Her eyes popped open. She looked into his face. Her entire body tensed. Then she pulled in a big breath and screeched, "Mama!" while turning into a little wildcat, legs and arms flailing.

Mrs. Haak hurried around the hood of the car, reaching for Winnie. "It's okay, sweetheart. I'm here. You're all right."

Callum tried to turn Winnie around and lay her head on his shoulder, like she'd done with Mrs. Haak, but she pushed at him, crying and coughing all at once. Afraid she'd fight her way out of his arms and fall to the ground, he handed her over to the woman she called Mama. Winnie wrapped her arms and legs around Mrs. Haak's neck and waist the way she'd wrapped herself around his leg the last time he'd seen her. Jealousy hit him harder than if a load of bricks'd landed on his head. He stood by helplessly while Mrs. Haak rubbed Winnie's little back and soothed her into silence.

When she was calm again, the woman offered a meek smile. "She's usually a very happy child. But it's well past her nap time, and I think she's running a slight fever." She turned and moved toward the back of the house. "Please come inside. We can talk after I put her to bed."

Callum followed, Winnie's distrustful eyes peering at him over her shoulder. Evelyn grabbed his arm and stuck close to him. Plodding footsteps behind him proved that the man who'd picked up his bag was coming along. If the fellow hadn't called Mrs. Haak *Miz Hester,* he'd think he was her father, given his protectiveness.

They entered the house and walked through a pantry into a small but cheerful kitchen. Mrs. Haak turned partway. Her gaze skipped past him and landed on Evelyn. "Take your father into the living room, please. I'll join you as soon as I get Winnie settled."

Evelyn yanked on Callum's arm. "C'mon, Daddy, through here."

Mrs. Haak slipped between some sheets hanging from the ceiling, and Evelyn pulled him past a four-poster bed all neatly made up with a woven coverlet. His gaze skimmed across the marble top of an oak mirrored dresser. A silver brush, comb, and mirror set, similar to one Freida got as a wedding gift, was laid out on a doily with a hatbox on one side and some bottles with colored water on the other. An open wardrobe holding women's dresses filled the corner of the space. He suddenly realized Evelyn was parading him through Mrs. Haak's bedroom. He sped his feet and almost burst into the living room of the house.

This room wasn't as personal as a bedroom, but little touches that seemed to fit well with the home's owner still left him feeling like an intruder. He stood stupidly in the middle of the floor, unsure what to do.

Evelyn flopped down at one end of a camelback sofa and patted the spot next to her. "Sit with me, Daddy."

Callum seated himself, but he jumped up again when Mrs. Haak, followed by the scowling old man, came in. He yanked his cap from his head and twisted it in front of him. "Ma'am, I'm sure my coming here is a shock. And I'm real sorry you were misled into thinking my girls were orphaned. As you can see, I'm alive and I—" He remembered something. He couldn't stop a scowl from forming. "But didn't you already know it? The matron at the home, Miss Armstrong, sent a letter telling you I was coming."

Mrs. Haak and the old man exchanged a look Callum couldn't read. She touched the man's elbow. "Scotty, I've changed my mind. I think it would be best if Reverend and Mrs. Stafford joined this conversation. Take the Model T and fetch them. Quickly, please." Her voice cracked on the last word.

The man named Scotty sent a blistering glare in Callum's direction, but he marched out. The woman pulled in a breath that straightened her spine, and then she moved with both grace and purpose to a rocking chair in the corner. Callum's heart lurched as she settled herself in the chair's seat. Did she rock Winnie to sleep in that chair?

Callum sat again, propping his elbows on his widespread knees. He looked hard into Mrs. Haak's unsmiling yet somehow calm face. She didn't strike him as someone who'd be deceptive. He cleared his throat. "Ma'am, did you get a letter from the home?"

She folded her hands in her lap—a ladylike pose. "No, I didn't. I expected one. But only to tell me if the home's board of directors would allow the children to stay or instruct me to take them to the poor farm." Her forehead pinched. "If I'd known you were coming, I . . . I . . ." She hung her head. She pulled a handkerchief from her dress sleeve and dabbed her eyes.

Callum's chest went tight. Seeing her pain didn't give him an ounce of pleasure. Even though he needed to get out of there with his girls, he also wanted to comfort her somehow.

Evelyn pulled on his elbow. "Daddy, should I pack me an' Winnie's stuff?"

Mrs. Haak winced, and so did Callum. He looked into his

daughter's eager face. Didn't she feel anything for the woman who'd taken her in and cared for her these past weeks? Or was she just so happy to see him everything else was forgotten? Either way, he felt selfish answering her question. But he had to be truthful. "Yeah, go ahead."

She let out a little squeal, kissed him on the cheek, and scampered around the corner.

Callum faced Mrs. Haak again. Her cheeks had gone pink. Now heat flooded his face. He wasn't from high society by any means, but she seemed like a proper lady. He probably should've kept Evelyn in there with them as a . . . what? He couldn't remember the right word. Somebody who made sure nothing inappropriate happened. He sat back real quick to put more distance between them.

"Mr. Holbrook . . ." She spoke so soft he tilted his ear toward her. "According to the state of Kansas, the girls are legally my daughters. I . . . I love them dearly. But knowing that you're alive and desire to care for them, I—" A sob cut off her voice. She pressed her handkerchief to her mouth for a few seconds, then jerked it downward, sniffed hard, and raised her chin. "I can't find it in my heart to keep them from you." She pushed herself out of the chair so slowly and stiffly it seemed she'd aged fifty years in the past minutes. "I will fetch the girls' birth certificates and send them with you so you're able to legally revert their names when you return to New York."

Callum stood on shaky legs, mangling his cap in his hands. "Thank you, ma'am. I can see it's a real sacrifice for you."

She nodded, swallowing. "It is. I . . . I feel as if my heart is splintered. But I can't be selfish enough to deny Evelyn and Winnie the one thing I longed for all my growing-up years."

He pondered her odd statement. Before he could ask about it, an automobile—her Model T—roared by the room's east window. A second car parked right outside the window. A man and the woman he'd seen in the churchyard got out of the parked car. Moments later, they appeared on the porch outside the door.

Mrs. Haak let them in, and at the same time, Scotty clomped into the living room from the bedroom doorway. Callum glanced across each face. Scotty looked fit to be tied. The man and woman who'd come both seemed worried. And Mrs. Haak . . . He gulped. Mrs. Haak's eyes swam with tears that made her irises as green as clover. But even then, she seemed more calm than distraught. She was one impressive woman.

She talked real soft to the three other people, too soft for Callum to hear. While she talked, the others shot glances holding remorse and, in Scotty's case, no small amount of fury at him. But then they all gave Mrs. Haak hugs and pats, and before Callum knew what was happening, they joined hands and bowed their heads. He watched, fighting an odd desire to be part of the circle. He heard the man who'd come in the front door murmur, "Amen," and they all lifted their heads and turned to him.

Mrs. Haak smoothed a lock of brown hair from her cheek and moved toward the bedroom doorway. "I'll get those certificates now."

The rest of them stayed over on their side of the room, looking at Callum. He remained by the couch, wringing his cap and trying not to look at them. It seemed like an hour dragged by, and he was getting twitchy. He glanced out the window and spotted the parked automobile. He jerked his gaze to the minister. "Would you be willing to take me and my girls to the Marion train station? I'll give you some money for gasoline. I've got to get on the train."

Scotty's hands balled into fists, but the other man offered a slow nod. "I could do that for you."

Callum's lips quivered into a weak smile. "Thank you." He couldn't wait to get away from these people and the strange feelings stirring in him. He hoped Mrs. Haak would hurry. And just like that, she stepped into the living room. But she wasn't holding any papers. She darted past him to the couple, and this time Callum heard every word.

"Reverend Stafford, please go get Dr. Ash. It's Winnie . . . she's terribly sick."

Callum's kind thoughts dissolved. What kind of game was this lady trying to play?

Chapter Twenty-Eight

Callum

Callum jammed his cap into his back pocket and entered Mrs. Haak's bedroom for the second time. Keeping his eyes averted from her personal items, he pawed at the sheets hanging from the ceiling until he found an opening. When he pulled the sheet aside, he found Evvie kneeling on the floor beside a handmade bed frame. It must be Winnie's bed, but he didn't see his little girl. Evvie's pose brought a rush of worry, and he touched her shoulder.

She bolted to her feet and threw herself against him. "Daddy, Winnie's head is real hot and sweaty, and she's crying."

Only then did Callum hear the soft whimpers coming from underneath a pile of covers—his baby girl's weak, rasping voice. He set Evvie aside and went down on one knee by the bed. He put his hand on Winnie's chest and leaned close. "Daddy's here, honey."

She swatted at him, the swing so slow and soft it might've been a butterfly brushing past his arm. "Want Mama . . . Mama . . ."

Mrs. Haak hurried into the room and pushed in front of Callum. He stood but stayed close as she sat on the edge of the bed and stroked Winnie's flushed cheek. "I'm sorry you feel so bad, sweetheart. The doctor is coming. He'll make you all better again."

Winnie coughed and lifted her arms to the woman. "Hold me."

Callum stumbled backward, coming up against one of the

sheets. He watched Mrs. Haak tenderly cradle Winnie in her arms and rock back and forth, murmuring, "Shhh, shhh, baby." He didn't want to watch. The sight was turning his gut inside out. But he couldn't tear his eyes away. Mrs. Haak loved Winnie. He'd clearly seen it. But not until that moment did he accept how much Winnie loved Mrs. Haak.

He reached blindly for Evvie and pulled her against his side. They needed to go. To leave right away. He had to get them settled in their apartment. He had to return to work. There wasn't time to spare. But he didn't make a move or speak a word. His heart was torn in two. Could he really take Winnie away from the only mama she'd ever known?

Somebody tugged the sheets aside. Callum took a sideways step, drawing Evvie with him. In one long stride, Scotty moved past both of them. He put his hand on Mrs. Haak's shoulder. "Doc's here, Miz Hester. Put Winnie in your bed. It'll be easier for him to tend to her there."

She rose immediately, cradling Winnie. Whoever this man was, he was important to Mrs. Haak. She didn't even look Callum's way as she, with Scotty close beside her, went to the other side of the curtain.

Scotty paused at the opening. He turned to Callum, and his thick gray eyebrows came together in a worried frown. "Winnie's got all the help she needs. Evelyn, take your daddy an' go sit in the livin' room."

Evelyn stiffened. "I wanna—"

Callum gave her a squeeze. "No, Evvie. He's right. We'll be in the way. Come on." He delivered a light nudge on her spine that sent her moving. He followed closely, but he couldn't help sending a look in the direction of the four-poster bed, where Winnie seemed so small and helpless.

The image taunted him even as he returned to the sofa and pulled Evvie down beside him. The reverend and his wife were still there. They sat in chairs across the room and asked him about New York and his job and other things people brought up when they didn't know what else to say. Callum answered to be polite. The man was a preacher, after all. But he wished they'd hush so he could hear whatever was being said on the other side of the wall behind him.

Finally, the doctor came into the living room. Callum and the Staffords jumped up at the same time. Only Evvie stayed sitting, but she turned sideways and leaned on the armrest, looking up at the doctor with wide scared eyes.

Mrs. Stafford hurried to the doctor. "What is it, Dr. Ash?"

"I'm certain Winnie caught the influenza that's making its way through the county."

Mrs. Stafford clutched her hands at her throat. "Oh, my. Will she be all right?"

"Influenza tends to be hardest on the very young and the very old, but Winnie is a strong, healthy little girl. I believe she'll recover nicely with bed rest and lots of fluids." The doctor directed his words at the Staffords and Scotty. "I've given Mrs. Haak instructions for bringing her fever down, which will make her feel a little better. In a week or so, she should be up and playing as usual."

A week or so? Callum moved into the doctor's line of vision. "She's got to rest for a week?"

Dr. Ash gave a start. "Excuse me, we haven't met. You are . . . ?"

Evvie jumped up and eased in front of Callum. "He's our daddy."

Callum reached around his daughter's shoulder. "Callum Holbrook, sir."

The doctor gave his hand a quick shake, but confusion lingered in his expression. "Yes, to answer your question, rest is imperative for a smooth recovery."

Evvie tossed her head, making her curls bounce. "Daddy and

me and Winnie are going to New York today." She tilted her head and gave Callum a confident look. "She can sleep on the train, right, Daddy?"

"Absolutely not," the doctor said.

Evvie huffed. Callum planted his hands on her shoulders. "Hush now." She folded her arms, and Callum turned to the doctor. "Why can't she get on the train? It's three days to New York City, and there's nothing to do that whole time except sit and rest."

The man folded his arms like Evvie. "You don't seem to understand. Influenza spreads. If you take Winnie onto a train car, you'll expose every person she encounters to the sickness. Besides, when I say *rest,* I mean quiet and bed rest. She can't get quality rest while riding on a train."

Callum couldn't argue with the doctor's final statement. His six-hour nap when he finally had a chance to lie down proved it. "You're sure it'll be a week before she's well enough to travel?"

"If she follows the same pattern as the others in town who've contracted it, yes."

Callum turned away from the group and jammed his hand through his hair.

Mrs. Stafford's voice broke into Callum's thoughts. "I think we need to be very grateful that Winnie's sickness was discovered before she boarded a train."

"I agree." The doctor's firm tone coaxed Callum into facing him again. "Without proper treatment, influenza can turn into pneumonia, and pneumonia is often deadly."

A chill exploded through Callum's frame. For the first time since he could remember, he wanted to thank God for a delay in his own plans. At the same time, worry gnawed at him. What would he do now?

The doctor picked up the hat and jacket he'd discarded on a side table in his rush to Mrs. Haak's bedroom. He settled the hat over his graying hair, then shrugged into his jacket, the movements brisk. "Reverend and Mrs. Stafford, I'll give you some instructions to prevent you or your children from contracting the illness. Winnie's is the third case so far in Millersberg. We don't want an epidemic in our community."

Reverend Stafford gripped Callum's forearm, the pressure comforting. "Elizabeth and I will pray for little Winnie. I'm sorry you aren't able to travel as you planned, but as my wife said, discovering this now is truly a blessing in disguise." He and his wife left with the doctor.

Callum wanted to check on Winnie, but he couldn't make himself enter the bedroom again without being invited. He sat on the edge of the sofa and ran his hand down his face, his thoughts whirling.

Evvie sat beside him and rested her temple against his shoulder. "Daddy, you won't go back to New York without us, will you?"

He might not know what else would happen, but he did know the answer to this question. He grabbed her in a hug and kissed the top of her head. "I'm never leaving you or your sister again. I promise."

Hester

As soon as Scotty retrieved Guy and Beckett from the Staffords' on Sunday afternoon, Hester sat the boys, Evelyn, and Scotty down at the kitchen table for a serious chat. Mr. Holbrook came in and stood behind Evelyn's chair. Hester couldn't send him away. He was concerned about Winnie, and he needed to hear the doctor's cautions. But his presence was distressing—a constant reminder of what she was giving up. She tried not to look at him while she repeated everything Dr. Ash had told her.

The children made faces about needing to wash well with soap after each encounter with Winnie or anything she touched. Hester nearly had a mutiny on her hands when she said they'd all need to take baths when they were finished talking. Guy reminded her, as if she needed reminding, he'd just had a bath the night before. She informed him—and Beckett, who was also making a sour face—that it was the doctor's orders and they all would scrub with soap from head to toe before supper.

"And," she said, "because of the risk of carrying germs, until Winnie has been without a fever for two days, you will bathe every morning before leaving for school."

Evelyn shrugged, her expression smug. "I won't have to, because I'm not going back there anymore. No need to. Daddy's taking me and Winnie to New York as soon as she's well."

Hester pretended she hadn't heard Evelyn. "Beckett, I've put off enrolling you in school long enough. You'll go tomorrow with the others. It will be safer for you there than here all day."

Beckett socked the air in excitement, but Evelyn huffed. "I told you I—"

"Evvie, hush." Mr. Holbrook shook her by the shoulders a tiny bit, a gesture Hester read as more an attention grabber than a punishment. "Mrs. Haak's right about you kids being better off away from the house. Besides, you need to get as much studying in as you can while you're here in Kansas. Once you're home, you'll be housekeeping and watching over Winnie."

Hester blinked several times, stunned by his statement. Would he really pull Evelyn out of school? What a preposterous plan. She momentarily forgot the purpose for their gathering.

Scotty patted her hand. "Miz Hester, is that it, or is there somethin' else we need to do so we don't git sick or make nobody else sick?"

Hester needed someone to give her a little shake to rattle loose the frustration coursing through her. "No, that's it as far as the children are concerned. Keeping their distance from Winnie and practicing lots of cleanliness." She stood. "Guy, you go first in the bathtub. Remember, use soap."

He sighed. "Yes, Ma."

She recalled something else. "Take clean clothes in with you. Leave what you're wearing now in a pile on the floor—don't touch them after you've bathed. I'll carry them out and wash them this evening."

Guy came around the table and looked mournfully at Hester. "If you pick up our dirty clothes, will you get sick?"

Hester's heart melted. She ran her knuckles down his cheek in lieu of a hug. "I'll be very careful and do a lot of washing afterward. Now, fetch some clean clothes and take your bath."

While Guy, Beckett, Evelyn, and Scotty took turns in the bathroom, Hester cut a length of sheeting into twelve-inch squares and folded them longways into fourths. The doctor had said to keep cool cloths on Winnie's forehead to help control her fever. She filled a basin with water and carried it, along with the cloths she'd prepared, to her bedroom.

Before he left, Dr. Ash had given Winnie a small dose of aspirin to help her rest. To Hester's relief, it had taken effect. The little girl slept soundly with her rosebud lips parted. Hester put the items on her bedside table and then dipped one folded cloth, wrung it well, and laid it gently across Winnie's forehead. The child didn't even stir. Hester backed away, being as quiet as possible.

She needed to scrub her hands and put supper on the table, but she should strip Winnie's bed first. She went behind the sheet and removed everything down to the mattress. Her arms full, she bumped the curtain aside with her elbow and gasped. Callum Holbrook filled the kitchen doorway. She'd forgotten he was still there.

He stepped backward. "I'm sorry I startled you, ma'am. I was waiting to talk to you."

Hester eased past him and went to the pantry. Gathering her

wits, she made a show of placing the wadded ball of bedding on the counter. The other three children, their hair still damp, were sitting around the table. Scotty must have retrieved the gifts from the car, because Evelyn was applying a crochet hook to pink yarn, Beckett was caught up in one of the books he'd been given, and Guy rolled a pair of little metal cars back and forth while making engine noises. She needed Scotty's stalwart presence. Where was he? Splashing sounds from the bathroom answered her internal question.

Drawing in a breath, she entered the kitchen and crossed to the sink. She lathered her hands with a few dishwashing flakes, dried them on a fresh piece of toweling, and then went to the Frigidaire. To her angst, Mr. Holbrook followed her.

He rested his forearm on the refrigerator's rounded top edge and cleared his throat. "Ma'am, if I'm gonna be held up here in Millersberg while Winnie's getting over her sickness, I need to let my boss at the factory know." He spoke loudly enough for her ears only. He had a pleasing voice, smooth and deep, not at all raspy even in a half whisper. "He gave me a one-week leave, but I'll need more than that. Do you have a telephone so I can call him in the morning?"

A troubling thought struck. "You don't intend to stay here tonight, do you?"

His cheeks blotched. "No, ma'am. I've got a room above the dress shop in town. I'll come back in the morning."

She'd rather he stayed in his rented room. "I don't have a telephone. When I need to call anyone, I use the one at the post office."

"Ah."

She opened the door to the refrigerator, hoping he'd step back. He didn't. He peered at her over the top of it.

"Well, then, I'll go to the post office tomorrow morning and make the call."

"All right." She rustled around in the Frigidaire, seeking the ingredients for an easy yet filling supper—eggs. Thanks to the chickens, she had quite a few of them. Scrambled eggs and toast should do. She pulled out the bowl of eggs and the smaller bowl of butter. She went to bump the door closed with her hip, as was her habit, but he gave it a push. Her hip kept going while her feet stayed still, and she nearly tossed the bowls.

Callum Holbrook darted to her side and rescued them from her hands. "I'm so sorry, ma'am. I meant to help."

She glanced at him. Was he fighting a grin? Well, who could blame him? She must have looked like a clumsy fool. She took the bowls and marched to the counter. Her back to him, she said, "Do you have a key to get into Miss Sally's?" She hoped he'd take the hint.

He ambled to the far end of the counter and leaned against it, his arms folded. "The door off the alley isn't locked, so I can let myself back in easy enough. But if you don't mind, I'd like to wait awhile. Spend some time with Evvie. Maybe hold Winnie a little bit." A pained expression crossed his chiseled face. "She doesn't really know me. I need to fix that."

Hester hung her head. She was being petty. Of course he wanted time with his girls after their long separation. And the girls—well, Evelyn, at least—wanted time with him. He wouldn't be able to find a meal in Millersberg today. Everything was closed. Would she really send him away hungry? She had to set aside her resentment toward him.

Lord, help me. I know it's wrong, but I wish he hadn't come.

The bridge of her nose stung, a sure sign that tears were threatening. She sniffed hard and removed the urge to cry. "Well, you can stay for supper, but after . . ." She made herself fully face him. "I'm a widow, Mr. Holbrook, residing in a small town. I don't wish to have my neighbors see a strange man leave my home after dark and make incorrect speculations."

Irritation momentarily darkened his eyes, but then his expression turned contrite. "You're right, ma'am. I won't be in town long, but this is your home. I don't want to create unpleasantness for you. I'll tell Evvie good night and leave now."

While he bent down on one knee and spoke softly to Evelyn, Hester grabbed the bread and cheese from the icebox and quickly assembled two sandwiches. From the corner of her eye, she watched Evelyn shake her head and grab on to his neck, but he pulled her arms loose and said something else Hester couldn't hear. Then he kissed her forehead, stood, and strode to Hester.

Guilt smote her for making him leave, but she only held out the sandwiches.

He took them with a bob of his head. "Thank you, ma'am. That's very kind." He pulled his cap from his back pocket and settled it over his hair. "If it's all right with you, I'll come by midmorning and look in on Winnie. I'll help as much as I can without"—the corners of his lips twitched and a teasing glint briefly lit his eyes—"causing speculation. Good night now." He left the kitchen through the pantry. The slap of the screen door announced his departure.

As the screen door closed, the bathroom door opened and Scotty, fully dressed with his gray hair mussed, looked in the direction of the screen door, then turned to Hester. He raised one eyebrow. "He gone?"

Hester nodded.

"For good?"

"He'll be back tomorrow morning."

"Humph." Scotty exited the same way Mr. Holbrook had.

Hester sighed. *Humph,* indeed.

Chapter Twenty-Nine

Hester

After sending Evelyn, Guy, and Beckett to bed, Hester sat down with Scotty at the table, coffee cups in hand. She found comfort in his presence. Especially now, when she was losing her daughters.

Scotty didn't agree with her letting them go. *"Fight for 'em,"* he'd told her. But she couldn't—or, more accurately, she wouldn't—deny them a relationship with a loving earthly father. She wasn't sure Scotty agreed with her reasoning, but she understood why he wanted her to fight. He loved Winnie as much as she did. Evelyn? He was trying, but the girl didn't make it easy on him. Even so, he was more patient than most would be.

"It's going to be a difficult week, Scotty." She released a weary sigh. "Winnie requires diligent, round-the-clock care. I'll sleep on the sofa so I'm close by but can still distance myself a bit."

Sympathy pursed his face. "You ain't gonna get good rest out there. An' you can't take Winnie to the store with you, so how're you gonna keep an eye on her all day?" Then he gave a start. "Can you even open the store? What if you share the influenza with folks who come in?"

She'd specifically asked about the store and had been greatly relieved when the doctor told her if she took proper precautions before going out, she needn't close it. She shared that with Scotty, then added with reluctance, "Mr. Holbrook being in town might turn out to be a blessing. He can see to Winnie, rebuild his r-relationship with her." She tried to swallow the knot of agony that rose each time she thought about losing the sweet child who called her Mama, but it remained wedged. It might be there forever. "I'll check on her as well, but you and I will be free to operate the store." She glanced at the ceiling. "I'd hoped to have you start on the upstairs rooms, but now it should wait until Winnie is well. The noise would disrupt her sleep."

Scotty took a draw of his coffee, his eyes pinned on her face above the rim of his cup. "I'm kinda surprised you wanna go ahead an' build them rooms, seein' as how the girls're leavin'."

Although he didn't say so, they both knew Beckett could eventually leave. But Guy wouldn't be a little boy forever. He would need a private space to call his own. She'd already purchased the lumber. It made sense to utilize it even if for only one child.

Only one child.

She was going to dissolve into tears if she didn't think about something else. "The lumber can't be returned, so we might as well proceed as planned. When Winnie is well and . . . and . . ." She didn't know what else to say.

Scotty reached across the table and patted her hand. "Miz Hester, I'm right proud o' you."

She choked out a puzzled laugh. "Proud of me? For what?"

His eyes shimmered. "I know your heart's breakin', but look at you stayin' strong. Movin' forward instead o' crumblin'. I don't know why God let Mr. Holbrook come when He did. To be honest with you, I'm plenty put out about it. Put out with myself, too, for lettin' him hitch a ride to Millersberg."

She dismissed his last statement with a shrug. "He would have come anyway, and you did a kind thing by agreeing to let him ride."

He huffed. Not as dramatically as Evelyn, but his regret was evident. "I s'pose. You know, you could be railin' at me, railin' at the Almighty, but seein' how you ain't givin' way to despair, why, it helps me stay strong right with you."

His dear face wavered as tears distorted her vision, but she smiled and turned her hand to grasp his. "I love you, Scotty. I hope you know that."

He gave her fingers a quick squeeze. "Aw, now, I reckon I do. I love you, too." He sighed deeply. "We're gonna be all right. Ain't we?"

"We are."

Over the next few days, Hester questioned the firm assurance she'd given Scotty. Deep down, she wasn't all right. She'd been blessed with the gift of children, and now her daughters were being taken away. She thought about the bedtime story she'd read the Saturday night before Mr. Holbrook arrived. Job, while in the depths of despair, was encouraged by his wife to curse God and die. Yet he rebuked her and held to his faith. She remembered telling the children, *"No matter what we encounter in life, God gives us strength. You can always trust your heavenly Father."* Hester believed what she'd said. She'd learned through life's challenges that her Father God was her greatest source of strength. She wouldn't reject Him. But she couldn't help questioning Him.

They all rose earlier than usual for baths before Scotty walked the children to school. The children's crankiness at the change in their routine started her days on a sour note that lingered. She'd expected Mr. Holbrook to take full care of Winnie while she ran the store, but each time Winnie wakened, she cried so hard for Mama that the man fetched her inside. Each contact with the child required a change of clothes and thorough wash before returning to the store. She nearly ran herself ragged going back and forth and seeing to loads of laundry each day in addition to her other responsibilities. She wore weariness like a cloak.

The frequent encounters with Mr. Holbrook wore on her as well. Having him spend so many hours in her home made her uneasy, as if she were the interloper rather than the other way around. She told herself again and again that his presence was a blessing. He was very helpful not only with Winnie but also in keeping Evelyn on task with her studies. He seemed to be a good-hearted man—tender with Winnie, patient with Guy's bounciness, gentle yet firm with Evelyn. His graciousness extended beyond the children. Without being asked, he washed the breakfast and lunch dishes each day and swept the kitchen floor. She appreciated these things, yet she couldn't relax around him. She both longed to have him gone and dreaded the day he'd leave, because he wouldn't leave alone. Her emotions changed directions as unpredictably as the stout Kansas wind, which left her unsettled and stole hours of sleep.

Scotty suggested forgoing evening story time so everyone could go to bed earlier, but Hester refused. The day was fast approaching when she wouldn't have the joy of gathering on the sofa together for a Bible story. She intended to take advantage of every precious minute with all her children.

By Thursday, to Hester's and Mr. Holbrook's relief—although for different reasons—Winnie showed evidence of improvement. She asked for noodles in her broth, she wanted to sit up, and she requested the yarn doll from her workbasket. Hester rejoiced at the signs pointing to recovery, but on joy's heels came a wave of mourning for what full recovery meant.

After settling Winnie in for her afternoon nap, Hester escaped to the store to nurse her sore heart. As she entered through the back door, the front door opened and the long-awaited sheriff's official sauntered to the counter. Scotty clomped from behind the counter to Hester's side, already bristling even before the man said a word. Hester slipped her hand through Scotty's bent arm, grateful for his support not only emotionally but also physically.

She met the officer's unsmiling gaze. "If you've come for Beckett, you'll need to wait a few hours. He's at the schoolhouse with the other children." The sound of her calm, steady voice surprised her. Her heart pounded a wild beat in her chest.

"Well . . ." He dragged the word out as if he had all the time in the world to deliver his message. "I won't be taking him . . ."

Hester gasped and held her breath, stifling an exultant shout.

". . . today."

Her breath escaped in a huff, removing her strength with it. She might have dropped to her knees if not for her grip on Scotty's arm. "What do you mean?"

"The Biehls, like you said on the phone, never sent the boy to school."

Hester drew back in surprise. "They admitted it?"

"They did. When they were told it's against the law not to send him since he's not yet sixteen years old, they made the excuse that school's nearly out for this term so they were gonna wait and send him next term."

Scotty grunted. "Sounds fishy to me."

The officer nodded. "I won't argue with you on that. They figured we'd bring him back to them right fast, but the judge isn't so sure about it. He's afraid they'll just work him hard through the summer, get whatever they can out of him, and then maybe give him up. Judge Banks wants some time to decide whether or not to trust the Biehls, so he's got a couple of us goin' around asking people to either speak for 'em or speak against 'em. Once he's got a good grip on who these folks are, whether they're trustworthy or not, he'll decide whether to send 'im back to their farm."

Scotty squinted at the officer. "An' what about now? If you ain't takin' 'im, does that mean he'll stay here with Miz Hester until the judge decides?"

"If Miz Hes—er, Mrs. Haak is willing to let 'im stay for now, the judge says the county'll pay two dollars and fifty cents a week for his keep. That is, if you'll send 'im to school and see to his needs."

Scotty harrumphed. "She's already doin' all that."

Finally, the man smiled. "I kinda figured. Anybody'd who'd take in three kids all in one fell swoop and enroll 'em in school right away isn't likely to mistreat a fourth one. Besides, everybody we asked spoke real highly of you, ma'am."

Hester exchanged a look with Scotty. Scotty asked what she was thinking. "You checked 'er out?"

"'Course we did. Had to make sure there wasn't some unsavory reason she was tryin' to get the boy away from the folks who took him in. But like I said, the judge feels real good about letting Beckett stay with you until a final decision's made. In fact . . ." He jammed his hands into his pockets and rocked back on his heels, puffing out his chest. "I've been instructed to ask if you'd consider openin' your house to other kids, if need be. Y'see, with so many people struggling, parents in some parts of the state are handing their kids over to orphan asylums just so they're fed every day."

Sorrow for the parents and their children created an ache in Hester's heart. She pressed her palm to her bodice. "You must be kidding."

"No, ma'am. Asylums are all filled up. The state's looking for other places for kids to go." He shrugged. "Something for you to think on. We can talk about it again when the judge makes up his mind about Beckett. Goodbye, now." He strode out in the same nonchalant manner in which he'd entered.

Hester stared up at Scotty, her mind whirling. "It breaks my heart that children right here in Kansas need homes. I thought children being abandoned was a big-city problem."

"A sign o' the times, I reckon." Scotty scratched his stubbly cheek. "With Evelyn an' Winnie goin' back to New York, would you maybe take in another girl or two?"

Hester winced. Would it be coldhearted to replace Evelyn and Winnie? It felt so in that moment. But was God opening a door for her to reach out to other hurting children, bringing beauty from the ashes in which she found herself now? Could she take them in knowing it was temporary? Could she risk her heart that way? She shook her head, closing down the erratic thoughts. In her tired state, she couldn't make sound decisions.

She patted Scotty's arm. "I need to pray about it, but I'm not averse to the idea." A humorless laugh trickled from her throat. "Of course, it needs to wait until Winnie is completely free of influenza. My poor water tank is barely keeping up with the current residents now."

Scotty threw back his head and laughed. "There's the spunky Miz Hester I know." Mrs. Reames entered, and Scotty headed in her direction. "How can I help you today, ma'am?"

Leaving Scotty to see to their customer, Hester stepped into the storage room and sent heartfelt thanks heavenward that Beckett wouldn't be immediately removed and Winnie was feeling better. She thanked God for the community's kind endorsement of her character and asked for His wisdom about bringing other children into her home.

Over the past days, busyness had shortened her time speaking with her Father. It felt so good to spend time with Him she didn't want to stop. She sank down on the end of Scotty's cot, bowed her head, and poured out her pain about losing her daughters, the desire to keep Beckett—not temporarily, but always—and finally her mixed feelings each time she was forced to come face-to-face with Callum Holbrook.

"Lord," she whispered, "he seems like a decent man, dedicated to his children and honorable in his dealings. His concern about leaving his boss in New York shorthanded speaks to dependability. But I'm troubled that he doesn't see the value in Evelyn continuing her education. Will he truly keep her home from school in New York? I'm troubled that when I pray with the children each night, he holds himself aloof. Will he teach Evelyn and Winnie to love and serve You? And I'm troubled"—her throat went tight, and she swallowed—"about my ill feelings toward him. It's wrong of me. I'm called to love as You love, and I know You love him unconditionally. But, dear Father, he's taking my children, and—"

"Mrs. Haak?"

Hester sat up so quickly the room momentarily spun. Callum Holbrook stood just outside the storeroom doorway. She rose, heat filling her face. Had he heard her private prayers? "W-what do you need?"

"Winnie woke up and wants"—he gritted his teeth for a moment—"Mama to make some Kool-Aid. I don't know what she means or I'd do it myself."

Hester nodded and hurried toward the door. He moved aside, and she double stepped to stay ahead of his long-legged stride on the way to the counter. Scotty's and Mrs. Reames's muffled voices carried from the far corner of the store.

Her hand trembled as she selected a packet of the cherry-flavored powder and held it out to Mr. Holbrook. "Here you are. Mix this in a tall pitcher of water with a cup of sugar. You'll find sugar in the canister marked as such next to the sink. Pitchers are in the upper cupboard above the canisters."

He took the packet, his gaze low. "Thank you, ma'am. If . . ." The word caught. He cleared his throat. "If she insists on you giving it to her, will you come in?"

Unexpectedly, compassion filled her. How hurtful it must be each time Winnie refused his ministrations. Hester had suffered enough rebuffs from Evelyn to know how it felt. Impulsively, she brushed his sleeve with her fingertips. "Yes, but I'll pray she accepts it with no fuss."

His eyes lifted and met hers. He stared at her in silence for the count of three heartbeats. Then he nodded and strode out of the store.

Chapter Thirty

Callum

Callum jogged to the house and let himself inside, his pulse thrumming a beat that had nothing to do with the short run. Freida would have some choice words about him intruding upon someone's prayers. But the pain in Mrs. Haak's voice when he heard her confess, *"But, dear Father, he's taking my children,"* and he knew the *he* meant him . . . He'd had to stop her before she said something else that would pierce his heart.

He mixed up the Kool-Aid the way she'd told him, then carried a glass to the bedroom for Winnie. But she'd drifted off to sleep again. He took a draw of the drink. Ugh, too sweet for his taste. He left it on the bedside table for when she woke up. He touched her cheek with the backs of his fingers. A breath of relief left his lungs. Still cool to the touch. Same as when he'd gotten there that morning. If she stayed fever free today and again tomorrow, he'd be able to hire a ride to Marion and get on board the train tomorrow evening, Saturday morning at the latest.

"Dear Father, he's taking my children."

He shook his head, silencing the anguished plea. No matter what Mrs. Haak thought, Evvie and Winnie weren't her children. No matter the papers she'd given him with the surname Haak on them, they were Holbrooks. They were *his.* They belonged with *him.*

Winnie twisted her head slowly, her mouth stretching in a yawn. Her eyes fluttered open, and her gaze landed on him. It held for a few seconds, and then she searched the room. "Where's Mama?"

Did a knife thrust through the center of his heart? He touched his chest. No knife, but it sure hurt. Callum forced a smile. "She's in the store. But here's your Kool-Aid." He helped her sit up and gave her the glass.

She kept her blue eyes fixed on him while she slurped it down to halfway. She lowered the glass and let out a little burp followed by a satisfied sigh. "Done. I want Mama now."

Callum took the glass and set it on the table. Slowly. Very slowly, giving himself time to get a grip on his emotions so he wouldn't snap at his baby girl. "Mama can't come. But Daddy's here. Do you want some paper and crayons? Your doll? Some buttered bread?" She should eat to get her full strength back now that the fever had passed. "I'll butter a piece of bread and sprinkle some sugar and cinnamon on it." Evvie loved that when she was little.

"No." Winnie's eyes begged. "I want Mama."

Callum stroked her tangled hair. "I'm sorry, baby, but Mama's working and can't come. I'll fix you that bread." He ducked around the corner before Winnie's quivering lower lip made him give in.

He fetched two slices of bread so they could each have a snack. As he slathered on butter, he told himself that Winnie'd get over leaving Mrs. Haak. He and Evvie had adjusted to losing Freida. He was okay now. And Evvie was okay. In time, Winnie would be fine, same as him and Evvie. It was good they'd be leaving tomorrow before Winnie got even more attached to Mrs. Haak. This evening, he'd figure out where the preacher and his wife lived and pay a visit so he could ask them about driving him and the girls to Marion as soon as Evvie got home from school tomorrow. Or maybe he'd keep Evvie home. She could pack up all their belongings. Yes, that'd be best. A full day with him, Evvie, and Winnie together would let Winnie see how good they were, just the three of them. Everything would be fine once they were back in New York in their apartment.

He held to his inner assurance the remainder of Thursday,

telling himself again and again how fine they'd all be. Over the afternoon, each time Winnie asked for Mama, he distracted her with books and toys and excuses that Mama was busy. He watched the clock, eager for it to be three, when the other children returned from school, imagining Evvie's joy when he told her they'd be able to leave tomorrow.

Finally, the squeak of the back screen door's spring alerted Callum to the children's return. He patted Winnie's leg. "Sissy's home." He stepped into the kitchen as the boys dropped their books onto the table. They darted to the cookie jar on the corner of the counter, the same way they'd done all the other days this week. Every day, Evvie went to the jar with them. But today she sagged into a chair at the table, set her books down, and then laid her head on the stack.

The boys raced out the back door, cookies in hand, and Callum crossed to his daughter. "Is something wrong?"

She sat up, grimacing. "I don't know. I feel sort of . . . achy. In my bones."

Callum sat next to her and looked hard into her eyes. They seemed a little glassy, and her eyelids drooped. Holding his breath, he placed the back of his hand against her forehead.

Warm.

He pushed away from the table. "Lemme get you a glass of Kool-Aid, see if that helps." But it wouldn't help. He'd keep her home from school tomorrow, but not to pack. And they wouldn't be getting on any train after all.

As much as Callum didn't want to ask Mrs. Haak to leave work again, he didn't have a choice. He told Evvie to go to bed, and he went to the store. He waited until she finished seeing to a customer, and then he told her that Evvie most likely had a fever.

"Oh, no. This delays your leave-taking, doesn't it?" Sympathy was evident in her expression and tone.

If she'd chortled with glee or appeared even the tiniest bit happy about having another week with the girls, he would've taken it better than he did her concern. Her genuine reaction of remorse gave him a prick of guilt he didn't want to accept. He pushed the emotion aside and nodded. "Yes, ma'am. And I've gotta let my boss know."

She came around the end of the counter, calling for Scotty. He appeared from behind some shelves, and she asked him to man the register. Then she turned to Callum. "Go make your call. I'll stay with the girls while you're gone."

He ran all the way to the post office. He stepped up to the counter, and the clerk gave him a smile. "Hello again, Mr. Holbrook."

How did the man remember him? He'd been in the post office only one other time. He wished he could recall the postman's name. "Hello. I'm sorry to bother you, but I need to use the telephone again. It's important."

The fellow waved in the direction of the phone mounted on the wall. "Help yourself."

Callum lifted the earpiece and turned the crank a few times. An operator came on the line and asked for the number. "I don't know the number, but I need the Remington Metalworks Factory on Westchester in New York City."

"Just a moment, sir."

The minutes stretched long while he waited, but finally the operator's voice came again. "Your call's going through." He listened to three blaring rings before a click signaled the phone being picked up at the other end. He heard his boss's gruff "Moore here" over the line's crackle.

"This is Callum Holbrook. Sir, my littlest girl's doing a lot better, but now my oldest girl came down with the influenza. I'm gonna be stuck here awhile longer."

"I'm sorry to hear that, Holbrook, but you're puttin' me in a hard spot. I can't leave your machine unmanned for much longer."

Callum cringed. "I know, and I'm real sorry. But we can't get on a train until everybody's well."

"Can't you come back now and have whoever's got your girls send them later?"

As much as Callum needed his job, he wouldn't risk sending the girls so far on their own. And he couldn't ask Mrs. Haak to bring them. She had a store to run. He sought another solution but came up empty. "I . . . I don't think so. I'm gonna have to wait until both my girls are well."

A disgruntled snort came through the line. "Well, I'll give you until the end of the month. But I can't wait longer'n that."

"I understand, sir." Callum hung up, then stood for a moment, worry holding him captive. What was he going to do?

Pray.

The prompt came out of nowhere, startling him into action. But not into prayer. God hadn't done so great at fixing his problems in the past. He'd figure this out himself. He went to Miss Sally's Dress Shop. The owner was bent over a noisy sewing machine. He waited a minute or two, but she didn't look up. He tapped her shoulder.

She spun around. "Mr. Holbrook! I nearly sewed my thumb to the garment."

"I'm sorry, ma'am. My other daughter's got the influenza now, so I've gotta be here a few more days. Can I keep renting that room upstairs?" Every day meant handing over more of the money he needed for train tickets. He hoped Evvie's sickness didn't last a full week.

"That's fine. I don't imagine anyone else will need it." She faced the machine and went back to pumping the pedal.

He left, grateful to have a place to stay. But worry about the cost of the rented room hung like a cloud over his head on his return to Mrs. Haak's. He should give some money to Mrs. Haak for feeding him lunch and dinner every day. She hadn't asked for anything, but it was the right thing to do, especially considering how many others she fed.

Why was the woman so nice to him? She didn't have to be. He was taking something precious away from her, after all. But she shared her food. Talked kindly to him. Even thanked him for seeing to little things around her house. He'd watched her with Evvie and Winnie and he couldn't fault a thing she'd done in caring for them. Yes, she was quite a lady. One who could hold a man's thoughts captive without effort.

This little town in Kansas had its draws, too. Even while carrying his woes, he enjoyed the smells filling his nostrils. Fresh smells. He appreciated how whoever he met on the street gave him a smile and wave instead of pushing past to get wherever they were going. He liked the open spaces. Not only between houses, but all around—the sky above him and the rolling prairie stretching toward the horizon—instead of buildings hiding whatever lay beyond. He'd never realized how many different ways clouds looked. Sometimes thin and flat, other times fluffed like big cotton balls, and other times swirly like cream blending into a cup of coffee. In the evening, when the sun lit the clouds up pink and orange, the sight could almost steal his breath. Millersberg was a good town, a fine place to be. Maybe a better place for his girls than in an apartment in the Bronx.

He stumbled to a halt. What was he thinking? Would he really go back to New York without his girls? Yes, Mrs. Haak was a good person—a good mama—living in a good town. But New York was his home. And he'd promised not to leave Evvie and Winnie again. He'd keep his promise.

Chapter Thirty-One

Hester

The familiar *chug-chug* grind of Joe Frager's truck filtered through the screen door and reached Hester's ears. She heaved a sigh of relief—Scotty was finally back with her weekly order of goods. Having three children, one of whom was so happy to be out of bed she couldn't sit still, underfoot in the store all morning without Scotty's assistance had proved quite taxing. Maybe unloading the truck with Scotty would settle the boys down. And if they settled down, perhaps Winnie would follow their lead. At least, she could hope.

She excused herself from helping Mrs. Tipton and called the boys to her. They galloped over, nearly colliding with Mr. Maddox on the way. She gave them a frown. "Boys, slow down. This isn't a playground." Their sheepish expressions begged forgiveness. She granted it with a smile and gestured to the door. "The truck is here. Go help Uncle Scotty, please." They poised to run. "But walk!"

They sauntered to the door, then darted out. Sighing to herself, she turned to Mrs. Tipton. "All right, ma'am, you wanted two pounds of navy beans?"

"Yes, and a pound and a half of—"

The door smacked open and Guy charged in. He ran straight to Hester and grabbed her by the arm. "Ma! Come quick!"

Hester's patience reached its end. She snapped, "Guy, please, I'm busy."

He yanked on her. "It's Uncle Scotty. He's hurt."

Hester dropped the bean scoop and raced off. Joe Frager was

standing next to the open passenger door of his truck. She ran to his side. "What happened?"

He pointed inside the cab. "This ol' man forgot his age. He was hauling boxes and crates faster'n he should've been, and he lost his balance. Fell backward and whacked his head on the edge of the loading dock. It bled quite a bit, but the depot clerk got it stopped. Even so, he ought to have Doc Ash take a look. He might need stitches."

Hester pushed past Mr. Frager. Scotty was slumped in the seat, his eyes closed. She took his hand. "Scotty, are you all right?"

He didn't open his eyes. "I'll be fine if somebody'll take the hatchet out o' my head. It's hurtin' me somethin' fierce."

Mr. Frager tapped Hester's shoulder. "I'm gonna go round up some help to get the stock unloaded."

Scotty snorted and struggled to sit up. "That's my job. Help me out."

Hester put her hand on his arm. "Stay put." She turned to Beckett and Guy, who stood behind her with tears swimming in their eyes. "Boys, run to the doctor's office and tell Dr. Ash we need him right away." The pair took off up the street, and she fixed her attention on Scotty again. "I'm going to get Mr. Holbrook to help you to your room."

He shook his head, then winced. "No. Don't want that sidewinder's help."

Mercy, he was stubborn. And Mr. Holbrook wasn't a sidewinder. But now wasn't the time to address his obvious resentment toward the girls' father. "Please, Scotty, for me—let him help you."

He snorted again, but he fell back against the seat.

Hester went into the store and quickly informed her customers that she needed to step out for a few minutes. Concern showed on every face, warming her toward her neighbors. She told Winnie to stay with Mrs. Tipton and then jogged to the house. Mr. Holbrook was at the counter, assembling sandwiches. She wasted no time on a preamble. "Scotty's been injured. Would you help me bring him into the store, please?"

He dropped the butter knife and came at once, wiping his hands on his pantlegs. "What happened?"

She repeated what Joe Frager had told her, then added, "He's a very proud man and doesn't want to admit he needs help. Please be patient with him."

"Of course. I will."

His prompt agreement brought a rush of gratitude so great that tears pricked her eyes. She sent him a wobbly, genuine smile as they reached the side of the truck.

He leaned in and slid his arm behind Scotty's back. "I hear you got a knock on the noggin. Well, as tough as you are, a good nap ought to cure you. But for now, toss your arm over my shoulders and let's get you out of the truck."

Scotty muttered, but he did as Mr. Holbrook asked. Once he was on his feet and away from the truck, Hester scurried to his other side. She tucked herself under his arm, and three abreast they entered the store. While her customers looked on, worry etched into every brow, she and Mr. Holbrook walked Scotty to his cot. He sank down, moaning, and put a hand to his head.

Hester knelt beside him. "Stay still, Scotty. Dr. Ash is on his way."

Scotty waved his arm, the movement weak. "Don't get the doc. It costs too dear. Just lemme rest."

Hester bit the inside of her lower lip. Scotty was a grown man who should be able to make his own decisions, but what was best?

Mr. Holbrook took hold of her elbow and drew her aside. "Mrs. Haak, when I worked the docks, there was a man who got hit on the head real hard. He went to sleep and didn't wake up again." He spoke quietly into her ear, his warm breath brushing her temple. "A doctor should check Scotty out."

A shiver of awareness that had nothing to do with her worry over Scotty wiggled down her spine. Hester crossed to the opposite side of Scotty's cot and then faced the girls' father. "Would you please let the customers know I'll be out as soon as the doctor comes? Then you can see to Evelyn."

An unrecognizable emotion—irritation or hurt?—flickered in his eyes, but he nodded and left the little room.

Hester sat beside Scotty and held his hand, silently praying until the doctor's arrival. As Mr. Frager had suspected, he needed a few stitches to hold the wound closed. It took some time to clean it and then stitch it, and she stayed close until it was done. Hester then observed Dr. Ash as he looked into Scotty's eyes, listened to his heartbeat, and checked his reflexes.

After putting his instruments into his bag, he folded his arms and aimed a stern look on Scotty. "When you hit your head, did you lose consciousness?"

Scotty gave the slowest shrug Hester had ever seen. "If you mean did I see stars an' then did things go dark as midnight, yep, I did."

"For how long?"

"I can't rightly say. Only recall fallin' backward, seein' stars, then comin' awake on the grass with a hatchet in my head."

The situation wasn't funny. Not even close to funny. But his description painted a picture in Hester's mind, and a burble of laughter threatened. She squelched it and gently rubbed Scotty's shoulder.

"Your remembrance tells me all I need to know." Dr. Ash directed his attention to Hester. "It's highly likely he suffered a concussion. He's going to want to sleep, which is normal, but over the next twenty-four hours, you'll need to wake him every other hour. Have him drink water—a full glass, if he'll take it—each time he wakes. No food, though, until the end of the twenty-four hours. Do you have any questions?"

Still reeling from the doctor's somber recitation, she couldn't think of anything to ask. She shook her head.

"If you think of something later, send one of the boys for me." He put his hand on Scotty's shoulder. "Scotty, did you hear everything I said?"

"Yeah, yeah, but could you not talk so loud? You ain't doin' my head any good."

The doctor chuckled. "I'm sorry. We'll let you rest. But lie on your side so you don't aggravate the wound." He helped Scotty turn sideways on the cot. Hester lifted his feet and Dr. Ash supported his upper body as he lowered his head to the pillow. While Hester tugged off his socks and covered him with a blanket, the doctor bent down and shook his finger in Scotty's face. "Now, Scotty, stay put. No joggling around, no lifting anything, no walking farther than to the toilet for the next twenty-four hours. I'll come check on you tomorrow, and we'll decide if you're ready to be up and doing. But you're to rest until I've told you otherwise."

Scotty snuffled and closed his eyes. "You sure are bossy."

"Indeed I am." Dr. Ash picked up his bag. He followed Hester out of the room and closed the door behind him. The concern in his expression increased Hester's worry. "Remember, wake him every two hours. Ask him his name, where he is, what happened to him. If he's unable to wake up or answer those questions correctly, send for me at once."

Hester clutched her hands at her throat. "Doctor, will he be all right?"

Dr. Ash's stern expression softened. "I imagine he's been clunked harder than this a time or two, but he's not as young as he used to be. It's best to be cautious." He glanced in the direction of the store floor. "You've got customers waiting. Can I do anything else for you before I go?"

"Not that I can think of. Thank you for coming, Doctor."

"You're welcome." He shook his head. "Influenza and now a concussion." He raised one eyebrow in a wry grin. "Superstition warns that things always come in threes. You might want to stay alert."

Influenza and Scotty's concussion were the second and third blows, the first being Callum Holbrook's arrival. Or was that really a blessing? She pushed aside the thought and walked the doctor to the door. Winnie pulled loose from Mrs. Tipton's hold and ran to Hester. Hester lifted her onto her hip, then sent a shaky smile over the shoppers.

"Dr. Ash said Scotty has a concussion. I'll need to keep a close eye on him, but he should recover well with rest." She released a half laugh, half sob. "Pray I can keep him down long enough to heal. We all know how headstrong he is."

The others nodded and chuckled. Mr. Maddox ambled close. "How can we help you, Mrs. Haak? You've got those children to take care of, and now Scotty can't work in the store. What do you need?"

Mrs. Tipton hurried forward. "I know what she needs—all the groceries from the crates and such Mr. Frager and the other men put on her front porch brought in and the contents put on the shelves."

Mrs. Harper marched over to Mrs. Tipton. "You and I have shopped in here since Delbert and Lela Haak ran the place. Dale didn't change things much when he took over. We know where everything belongs. If the others'll tote it in, we can direct folks to where things need to go."

A murmur broke out among those in the store, heads nodding and feet shifting, their eagerness to help palpable. Before Hester knew what was happening, her customers took charge. She put Winnie down and reached for a crate, but they shooed her aside and instructed her to rest. Mrs. Harper told her, "Hester, you've been carrying the full load of this place ever since Dale died, always making sure your customers have what they need. Let us repay you a bit today. Take that little girl of yours into the house and have a bite of lunch together." Tears glistened in the old woman's eyes. "Store yourself up a memory."

Mrs. Harper's words and the sorrow on her face told Hester word had spread about Mr. Holbrook's purpose in coming to Millersberg. She blinked back tears herself. Time with Winnie was exactly what she needed most. She thanked the woman with a smile and guided the girl toward the back door, weaving between those already dragging in crates from the porch. At Scotty's door, she put her finger to her lips in a silent warning to Winnie, then cracked the door open. She peeked in. He was asleep on his side, snoring with his mouth hanging slack.

Winnie grinned up at Hester and whispered, "Uncle 'cotty is growling."

Hester whispered back, "He is." She closed the door, then took Winnie's hand and walked across dappled patches of shade cast by the sun sneaking through branches on the single cottonwood tree in her yard. She kept her gaze on Winnie as they moved toward the back door, memorizing the child's lighthearted gait, her penchant for swinging her arm as she walked, and the way sunlight ignited strands of gold in her light-brown hair. They reached the back stoop, and Hester reached for the door handle. She froze mid-reach.

Callum Holbrook was on the other side of the screen door. He pushed the door open, a shy smile lifting one side of his lips. "I was just coming to see if you wanted some lunch." He pointed over his shoulder with his thumb. "The boys're already eating. I hope you don't mind me feeding them, but they said they were hungry." His eyes lit on Winnie, and a tenderness entered his gaze. "I made peanut butter sandwiches, Winnie's favorite."

Hester put her hand on the back of Winnie's head, storing away in her memory the feel of the child's sun-warmed hair to replace the odd flutter in her chest his smile evoked. "Th-that sounds good."

Suddenly his brows pinched together. "How's Scotty? Does he need a sandwich?"

She stuttered a bit as she shared the doctor's instructions, unnerved by the man's intense focus and her unexpected reaction to it. She finished, "I'll take him some water when I go to wake him in another hour."

"Come in for now and get something to eat." He moved aside, still holding the door open.

Hester sent Winnie in, but she flapped her hand in the direction of the store. "I—I usually give the children an apple with peanut butter sandwiches. I'll . . ."

He caught her elbow and held her in place. "Mrs. Haak, I'll fetch some apples to go with the sandwiches. Sit down and eat with the kids."

His hand on her arm—the touch both gentle and masculine, so different from when the children grabbed on to capture her attention—left her flustered. Had the blow to Scotty's head somehow rendered her insensible? She stood in the middle of the pantry, uncertain what to do.

He lowered his hand. "How many apples? Only for the kids, or did you want one, too?"

"I'd like one. Thank you."

He nodded. "I'll be right back." He shot off, letting the screen door slam into the frame behind him.

Chapter Thirty-Two

Callum

Not until Callum was halfway to the store did it occur to him that if Scotty was sleeping and Mrs. Haak was in the house, there wasn't anyone watching the store. Had she closed it for the day? Given the circumstances, he wouldn't blame her. But Evvie'd told him Saturdays were the busiest days. Could she afford to lose the business a Saturday brought in?

He neared the chicken coop built onto the back of the store. The chickens were restless, flapping around in their pen. He glanced skyward, wondering if a hawk circled. He didn't spot a predatory bird, but there was noise—scraping and bumps and clanks. From inside the store. Was someone in there clearing out the place?

He broke into a run and burst through the back door, fully expecting to tackle a robber. He slid to a stop and stared in amazement. A whole passel of folks, most of them older, were pulling canned and boxed goods from crates but not heading out the door with them. Nope, they were stocking Mrs. Haak's shelves.

A feeling swept over him—a feeling of things being right in the world. Which didn't make a lick of sense with Scotty laid up and Evelyn sick and him stuck far from home. But he felt it all the same, and he wanted to hold on to it. He shuffled forward, staring at the activity.

One of the men caught his eye and grinned. "Hello there. Did you come to help?"

"I came for some apples." Callum felt stupid after he said it, but why should he? It was the truth. Then, adding to his confusion, he realized he wanted to help. To work alongside these good-hearted, honest people. To get to know them better. But why? This wasn't his town. They weren't his neighbors. And Mrs. Haak wanted apples to go with the peanut butter sandwiches. He should get them and go.

He lined four apples on his forearm, anchoring them against his ribs. He turned to leave and then grabbed out a fifth apple for himself. He left the store slowly, taking in the sight of Mrs. Haak's customers enjoying themselves. He returned to the house, still pondering the acts of kindness he'd witnessed.

Mrs. Haak looked up as he entered. A frown pinched her face. "Mr. Holbrook, are you all right?"

He crossed to the table and handed the apples around. "I'm fine. Why do you ask?"

"You seem a little . . . disquieted."

So had she when he'd let her in the back door. Maybe they were all tired from the past week's happenings. "I'm fine." He sat and lifted his apple to his mouth.

Winnie pointed at him. "Daddy, no!"

He paused, his heart rejoicing. She called him Daddy. It added to the good feelings he'd experienced in the store. But did she think he'd lied about being fine? He swallowed. He might have. " 'No' what, honey?"

She crinkled her nose at him. "You're 'posed to pray before you eat, like this." She folded her hands and squeezed her eyes shut. "Thank You, God, for my food. Amen." Her blue eyes popped open, innocent and somehow wise.

"That's okay. I'm not eating." Callum put the apple on the table and rose. "I'm going to check on Evvie." He escaped his baby girl's sad gaze.

Hester

Hester's windup alarm clock clanged, intruding upon a dream. She pawed it off, then flopped back on her pillows for a moment, gathering the strength to walk to the store and wake Scotty. Beside her, Winnie slept soundly, but there were whispers behind the boys' curtains.

She sat up and slid her feet into slippers over the stockings she'd worn to bed. Smoothing wrinkles from her skirt, she crossed to the curtain and whispered, "It's still nighttime, boys. Go back to sleep."

Truthfully, she reminded herself as she filled a glass with water at the sink, it wasn't nighttime. It was four in the morning, and this was the eighth trek to Scotty's room. He'd been uncharacteristically gruff during the two o'clock visit. Not that she blamed him. His head hurt and he wanted to sleep it off. But Dr. Ash said to wake him, so she would wake him.

She scuffed across the moonlit yard, yawning. How many more times would she need to do this until noon, when the doctor would return and the critical twenty-four-hour period was past? Four. Only four. She could do this four more times.

The hens' sleepy clucks serenaded her as she unlocked the store's back door and flipped on the electric lights. She winced against the onslaught, then opened Scotty's door wide enough to slip through. A soft band of light fell across his sleeping form. She touched his shoulder.

He snuffled, shrugging away her hand. "I'm Scotty. I'm in Millersberg, Kansas. I conked my head. An' I'm right sorry I did."

Hester choked back a laugh despite her tiredness. She patted his shoulder. "Well done. I brought you some water."

"Not thirsty. Lemme sleep."

He'd downed a full glass at two. She decided not to force it now. She put the glass on the orange crate he used as a bedside table and let herself out. As she turned from locking the door, something flickered in her peripheral vision. She turned her head sharply. One of the upstairs windows of the house across the street seemed lit by a lantern. She frowned. Had someone purchased the Klein house? She hadn't heard any talk about it, and surely someone would have mentioned it. The stately house had sat unoccupied now for almost five months following Mr. Klein's death last winter.

She blinked at the glow. Had a hobo broken in? She should go over and check. But what would she do if she found an intruder? A man brazen enough to enter someone else's house without permission might be dangerous. While she stood debating with herself, the light went out. Maybe she'd imagined it. She was, she acknowledged with a rueful sigh, nearly asleep on her feet. And she'd be up again at six for another check. The children would probably awaken then, and she wouldn't get any more sleep. She needed rest more than she needed her curiosity appeased.

She headed for her bed. When Dr. Ash came to check on Scotty, she'd tell him what she'd seen. If he was concerned, he'd send someone over to investigate. At ease with the plan, she set her alarm to ring at six o'clock, nestled against her pillow, and quickly fell asleep.

All too soon, the alarm roused her yet again. This time, Winnie stretched and yawned. Hester walked the little girl to the bathroom and then settled her at the table with a glass of milk. The boys wandered out in their nightshirts, and she instructed them to pour themselves some milk and stay with Winnie until Hester returned from checking on Scotty.

Scotty sat up and drank the water. He wiped his mouth and gave a little snort. "All this drinkin' all night's got my bladder full to bustin'."

In all her years of acquaintanceship with the man, he'd never said anything so earthy. Her face heated, but she put on a nonchalant air. "Would you like me to help you inside to the bathroom?"

He shook his head. "All that wakin' up all night long's got me weak as a kitten. I'll use my thunder bucket."

First his bladder, now the chamber pot. Apparently, the knock on his head had erased any semblance of decorum he might have previously possessed. She inched backward. "All right, then. I'll return after I feed the children their breakfast."

Still sitting, he lifted his hand in a wave. "I know you will. I ain't been fussed over so much in all my days." Then he angled his head slightly, a weak smile appearing on his whiskered face. "Thank you, Miz Hester. You got a good heart."

All discomfort fled. She returned to the cot and kissed his prickly cheek. "Please rest, Scotty." And she hurried back to the house.

While Beckett, Guy, and Winnie ate oatmeal with raisins and chopped walnuts, she looked in on Evelyn. The girl's face was flushed, a sign that fever was still present. She brought her some water and then put a cool cloth on her forehead. Evelyn's eyelids fluttered, but she didn't fully wake. Which gave Hester the freedom to smooth her hair and kiss her temple, the way she'd so often wanted to do but hadn't out of fear of being rebuffed. She filed the memory away to savor later.

Scotty was able to answer the trio of questions at eight, but he complained of his head hurting. Dr. Ash hadn't given her permission to administer medicine, so she apologized and encouraged Scotty to drink more water, hoping it might help.

She couldn't go to Sunday school or church because she needed to check on Scotty again at ten, but she saw no reason why Beckett, Guy, and Winnie couldn't at least go to Sunday school. Beckett was responsible enough to walk the younger children to church and back. She dressed Winnie and instructed the boys to put on their nicest clothes. She sent them out the door with hugs and kisses, reset her alarm, and then flopped across her bed for a quick nap. It seemed she'd barely closed her eyes when someone knocked on the front door. Even before she answered, she knew who would be there—Callum Holbrook, coming to take care of Evelyn.

Groaning under her breath, she trudged through the living room and opened the door. "Mr. Holbrook. Come in."

His jaw dropped. "Goodness' sakes, ma'am. You look like you've been to war."

Well, *that* wasn't a greeting any woman wanted to hear. She turned on her heel and went into her bedroom. But when she got a glimpse of her reflection in the mirror on her vanity, she gasped. Hair stuck out in every direction from the bun she'd fashioned yesterday morning. Dark puffy pillows bagged beneath her bloodshot eyes. Why hadn't the children or Scotty told her how awful she looked? She clapped her hands to her face and gaped at herself for several seconds, mortified. And then she burst out laughing. It was laugh or cry, and laughing seemed the better choice.

The sound of a clearing throat caught her attention, and she turned again. Mr. Holbrook peeked into the room, his feet still planted in the living room. His eyes twinkled with either humor or orneriness—she couldn't discern which. She reined in her laughter and finger combed her hair, blindly smoothing the wild strands into place.

"I seem to recall my wife telling me during a particularly trying time in our first year of marriage, as long as a person could still laugh, he was all right." A grin dimpled his cheek. "You, Mrs. Hester Haak, are all right." Then his face flooded red. He ducked behind the sheets of the children's quarters, and moments later she heard him speaking softly to Evelyn.

She grabbed a clean dress and her hairbrush and beat a path to the bathroom. Behind the locked door, she changed her clothes and fashioned her hair in its usual bun. She brushed her teeth and then sat on the edge of the bathtub and held a cold wet washcloth to her eyes for several minutes. The ministration couldn't erase the exhaustion that weighted her limbs, but it revived her enough that she felt capable of facing the man who'd had a full night's sleep in his room above Miss Sally's and seemed as perky as a spring robin.

When she came out, she found him scooping aromatic grounds into the basket of her coffeepot. Was he really making coffee in her kitchen, as bold as if he had every right to do so? She waited for indignation to rise, but only gratitude came to the fore. She went to the pantry and added the dress she'd worn for the past twenty-four hours to the basket of clothes needing to be washed. She gave the overflowing wicker basket a scowl. The container hadn't been empty for more than an hour in nearly two weeks. No wonder she was tired.

She gestured to the covered pot on the stove as she crossed to the table and sat. "There's still some oatmeal left from breakfast. Help yourself."

"Thank you, but Miss Sally brings me a breakfast every morning." He put the coffeepot on the stove, selected a match from the tin holder hanging from a nail on the wall, and lit the burner, all the while talking. "Two boiled eggs, three dry biscuits, and a shriveled piece of fried ham . . . cold. I'm starting to understand why the woman is still a spinster." He blew out the match and, after running a little water on the charred, smoking tip, tossed it into the rubbish bin. "Worst part? She doesn't bring coffee. I hope you don't mind me making some." He glanced at her. "I figure you could use a cup yourself."

She probably should find insult in his final comment, but he spoke so kindly she couldn't fault him.

He leaned against the counter and folded his arms. "How was Scotty during the night?"

She coughed a short laugh. "Irascible yet lovable. It will take more than a few stitches and a concussion to keep him down."

Mr. Holbrook smiled. "I'm glad."

She tilted her head and squinted at him. "You are, aren't you?"

He nodded.

"Even though he calls you a sidewinder?"

His brow puckered. "What's a sidewinder?"

Coming from New York, he'd probably never encountered one. At least not in the literal sense. "A rattlesnake that travels sideways. Thus, it sneaks up on a person, and its bite can be deadly." She cringed. "When it's used in reference to a person, it isn't exactly a compliment."

He laughed. "He's made it pretty clear he doesn't like me, but why should he? I arrived uninvited and I'm taking something"—he swallowed, the humor fading from his eyes—"precious from you. As much as he doesn't like me, he loves you, and it's clear he loves the kids. It's gonna be hard on him when Evvie and Winnie leave. Maybe even harder'n it'll be on you."

She couldn't believe he could acknowledge such a thing, and so openly. "Why harder on him?"

The muscles in his jaw tightened for a moment. "Because not only will he miss the girls; he'll witness you missing the girls. Seeing someone you love in pain can be worse than hurting on your own."

Now she understood. When Dale had suffered with his final illness, she suffered alongside him, helpless to heal him. "You say that with certainty, as if you've experienced it yourself."

He shrugged and moved to the window. "My wife died after Winnie was born. All the bleeding . . . it was too much." With his back to her, it almost seemed he was remembering the event aloud instead of talking to her. "I knew she was slipping away, and I couldn't stop it. I was her husband—I was supposed to protect her. But I couldn't protect her against death."

He turned abruptly. “Ma’am, I’m not taking my girls back to New York because I want to bring you pain. I promised I’d fetch ’em. I’ve been working and planning and dreaming for years about the day I could keep that promise. They’re all I have of Freida. Do you understand?”

“Yes, I do.” The admission grated out, her tight throat aching. “And they need their father as much as you need them. That’s why I’m not fighting you for them.” Even though she could. “But I would like to extract some promises from you.”

Mr. Holbrook took two slow steps in her direction. “What kind of promises?”

She pointed to the chair across from her. Not until he sat did she consider the impropriety of their situation. Evelyn was in the house and Scotty close by, but both were asleep. She hadn’t turned on the electric lights, and very little sunlight entered the kitchen. The dove-gray shadows combined with the quiet of the room lent itself to intimacy. She should turn on the light, but her weary bones resisted carrying her to the push buttons a few feet away. She would speak quickly and then go out to the store. She could go over her accounts while waiting for Dr. Ash.

She cleared her throat. “Please don’t pull Evelyn out of school. She was behind the other students when she came, but she works hard on her assignments and she’s making wonderful progress. She’ll tell you she doesn’t want to go to school, but underneath I think she’s proud of her forward strides. She’s a bright girl. She deserves an education. Will you send her?”

He glanced toward the room where Evelyn slept, then lowered his gaze for a moment. When he looked up, he nodded. “You’re right. When I was a youngster, it was pretty common to leave school and work to help the family. But the world’s changing. I should change with it.” He drew in a breath that strained the buttons on his shirt and sighed it out. “When Winnie’s old enough to go, they’ll both go.”

Relief brought an effortless smile. "Thank you, Mr. Holbrook. Now . . . will you have the girls write to me now and then?" She linked her fingers and squeezed, battling a wave of melancholy. "It'll be a while before Winnie knows her letters, but she can send me pictures. She loves to draw. I . . . I would like to be part of their lives even if only as a distant pen pal."

"Of course."

His immediate agreement inspired a wave of joy and gratitude. "And finally . . ." This request would likely be the least palatable based on her observations, but she had to ask for the girls' sakes. "Will you take the girls to church? Or at least send them? Evelyn remembers going with her mother, and both girls have soaked up the Bible stories I read at night. Their souls need that nourishing." As did his, but she might insult him by saying so. For some reason, she didn't want to spoil this fleeting affinity. She watched his expression, waiting for anger or sorrow or some kind of response. He remained as still and unemotional as a statue.

The coffee basket rattled inside the pot, an indication that the water was boiling. She rose and turned down the fire under the burner. Then she went to the cupboard, took out two cups, and filled them. She carried them to the table and put one in front of each of their chairs. She sat and lifted her cup to her lips, but he held his between his palms and stared down at the steaming liquid.

"Mrs. Haak . . ." He raised his gaze and met hers. "I appreciate your concern for my girls. And I promise I'll do what I think's best for them." His forehead pinched into furrows, as if a sudden pain gripped him. "But when it comes to God and churchgoing, I can't promise you what that 'best' will be."

Chapter Thirty-Three

Callum

An alarm clanged, and Callum jerked, sloshing coffee over the rim of his cup. He went to the sink for a cloth, and Mrs. Haak got up and stumbled in a rush into her bedroom. The clamor stopped, and after another few seconds, she reappeared from behind the doorway.

"I'm going to check on Scotty." She left the house without glancing his way.

A feeling of loss fell on him with her exit. For a while, it'd seemed he and Mrs. Haak were bound together by their mutual love for Evvie and Winnie. He'd likely ruined that by refusing to grant her third request. But his conscience wouldn't allow him to make a promise he might not keep. And he hadn't decided about churchgoing when they got back home. Right now he had more pressing things to think about.

He took a sip of the hot, strong brew, hoping it would awaken some grand plan in his mind. It was the twenty-sixth of April already. For him to be back in New York by the end of the month, he needed to put himself and the girls on a train tomorrow, Tuesday at the latest. And Evvie still had a fever. How much longer would it last? Every day in this town meant more money squandered. And he really wanted to give Mrs. Haak at least a token payment for feeding him so many times.

Worry gnawed at his gut. If he didn't show up at work on May first, he wouldn't have a job. If he didn't pay his rent on May first, he wouldn't have an apartment. The coffee must've taken effect, because he suddenly remembered he'd left enough money for another two weeks of rent in the cracker tin in his apartment. Did Billy have a telephone? If Callum reached out to him, Billy'd give the money to the landlord for him—Callum knew it without a doubt. Because Billy honored God in his dealings, like Mrs. Haak did.

And now he was thinking about God again.

A big gulp of coffee washed the God thoughts away and brought his troubles back to mind. Billy could make sure the apartment was waiting for him. At least for a little while. But nothing would hold his job if he wasn't back on duty the first of May. He downed the last of his coffee, rinsed the cup, and peeked in on Evvie. She'd rolled to her side on the lower of the two beds secured to the wall and curled into a ball. She was probably cold. She'd kicked her covers down, the same way she'd done when she was Winnie's age. He pulled them to her chin, tucked them tight, and then tiptoed out of the curtained area.

He let himself out the front door and jogged to the dress shop. He rummaged in his bag for the sock holding what was left of the money Billy had collected and emptied it onto the bed. He counted it, then figured up the cost for returning to New York. Tickets for him and Evvie, because she was over twelve years old, were $30.00 each, but Winnie could travel the same distance for $18.00. So for tickets, $78.00. They'd need food on the way. If they ate as simple as he had coming out, he'd likely spend $.50 a day each for three days' travel—$4.50 in all. He added it all up in his head—$82.50. The money on the bed totaled $83.85.

He cringed. If he stayed in Millersberg even another day, he'd have only a measly ninety cents to give Mrs. Haak for food, and no money to pay for someone's gasoline. Which meant he couldn't stay in Millersberg one more day. Whether Evvie was still feverish or not, he didn't have a choice. They had to get on the train before nightfall.

He might as well have been wearing cement shoes, as hard as

it was to make his feet carry him back to Mrs. Haak's. At the corner, he spotted Guy, Beckett, and Winnie coming up the street from the direction of the church. Winnie held Beckett's hand, and Guy hopped beside them like a little toad. Callum stopped and waited for the children to catch up, hoping Winnie might let loose of Beckett and come running to him. She didn't, but he gave her a big smile anyway when they reached him.

"How was Sunday school?" he asked as they walked up the alley toward the house, more for something to say than out of real interest.

Guy galloped sideways next to Callum, grinning. "Real good! The story was about a boy named David who fought a giant named Goliath. Goliath had all these weapons. Spears an' swords an' bows an' arrows." He pantomimed their use as he listed them. "But all David had was a slingshot an' some rocks he found in a creek. An' you know what David did with just one little stone?" The boy's eyes bulged, and he started swinging his arm as if wielding a sling of his own. "He hit Goliath right in the middle of his forehead, an' that big, mean ol' giant fell flat on his face an' died!"

Callum had heard the story when he was a boy, but he said, "Is that so?" to keep Guy talking. The boy was doing a fine job of distracting him from his troubles.

"Yep! An' then the Izz . . . Izz . . ." He looked at Beckett.

"Israelites," Beckett said.

"Israelites all went runnin' at the Flippa-eens—"

Beckett huffed. "Philistines!"

"They went runnin' at the Flippastines"—Guy didn't miss a beat—"an' God's army wiped them enemies out! All 'cause David was brave enough to fling a stone." He beamed at Callum.

Callum couldn't resist ruffling the boy's straw-colored hair. "That's a fine story, Guy."

Guy came to a halt at the edge of the front stoop, and his expression turned solemn. "Mrs. Stafford told us we prob'ly won't ever have to go up against a giant like Goliath but we'll have big problems sometimes. But if we trust God, the way David did, He'll help us overcome." He tilted his head. "Mr. Holbrook, what's *overcome* mean?"

Callum was finished with the Sunday school lesson. "That's a question for your mama, Guy."

Winnie lifted her sweet face to Callum. "Where's Mama?"

Callum felt as though a stone settled in his windpipe. He forced a smile. "Probably in the house. Let's go see."

But she wasn't in the house. Evvie was awake, though, and wanted a drink. Winnie trailed Callum to the kitchen sink and then tried to follow him behind the sheet. He stopped her. "No. Evvie's sick. You need to stay out here." But how silly was his directive? They'd all be cramped together on the train soon enough.

Beckett hustled over. "Hey, Winnie, I bet Ma's out in the store with Uncle Scotty. Let's go say hi."

She trustingly placed her hand in his, then beckoned to Guy. "C'mon." Guy sighed, but he took her other hand and the three left together.

Callum's chest ached as he watched them go. Winnie was attached to the ones she viewed as her big brothers. She was attached to Mrs. Haak and to the man she called Uncle 'cotty. It would tear her little heart out to leave them all behind. But what other choice did he have?

"Daddy?" Evvie's croaky voice pulled him from his thoughts.

He stepped behind the curtain and found her sitting on the edge of the bed. Sitting up was a good sign, wasn't it? He gave her the water. "Are you feeling better?"

She took a long, slow drink. As she lowered the glass, she shook her head. "Maybe some. But I'm real achy, and my throat hurts, and I'm"—she yawned—"so tired."

He sat on the edge of the mattress, leaning forward so he wouldn't bump his head on the bottom of the upper bed. They weren't very far apart. "Too achy and tired to take a train ride?"

Her eyebrows lifted, but her eyes remained dull. "Today?"

"If I can find someone to take us to Marion." If he gave someone money for gasoline, there wouldn't be anything left for Mrs. Haak. But he could mail something to her when he got to New York. The thought eased his conscience.

She rested her head on his shoulder. The heat from her cheek went through his shirt to his flesh. "I wanna go, but . . . maybe not today."

He took the glass from her and stood. "Well, catch another nap before lunchtime. After you've slept some more and had some broth and crackers, I bet you'll feel better." *Please, please feel better,* his thoughts begged. But he wasn't praying.

She slid under the covers again. "All right, Daddy."

He left the glass on the windowsill and then followed the path the children had taken to the back door of the store. He let himself in, took two steps, and looked into Scotty's little sleeping space. Scotty was sitting up on his cot with the boys on either side of him and Winnie perched on one knee. Guy was retelling the David-and-Goliath story, "Flippastines" and all. But Mrs. Haak wasn't with them.

He moved past Scotty's doorway to the main part of the store. There she was behind the counter, leaning heavily on her elbows and poring over the pages in a book. He crossed to the opposite side of the counter. "Mrs. Haak, there's something I gotta talk to you about."

She looked up. "Yes?"

He frowned. Her face was pale except for her bright cheeks. Little dots of perspiration peppered her forehead. Why hadn't he noticed when they were inside? Probably because she now stood underneath one of the electric bulbs hanging on a wire from the ceiling. He didn't want to ask, but he had to know. "Are you . . . achy?"

"Of course I'm achy. I got very little sleep last night."

The tart retort spoke volumes. The knot of worry in his belly doubled in size.

She pressed her fingertips to her brow for a moment and then turned a repentant look on him. "Please forgive me. It's been a rather stressful week."

"And now you're sick." Callum said it as much to himself as to her.

She frowned. "I'm not sick. I'm merely—"

"Tired." He said it for her and shook his head. "No, Mrs. Haak, you're sick. I can see it. Couldn't you tell when you touched your forehead? It was hot, wasn't it? You've got a fever."

"I appreciate your concern, but I believe I'll allow Dr. Ash to make a diagnosis." She slapped the book closed. "Now, what did you need to speak with me about?"

He didn't want to tell her his plan to leave that day. If she was really sick, she didn't need bad news. "Um . . . it can wait until after lunch." He gestured to the book stamped with Ledger in gold letters on its black-leather cover. "Finish what you were doing. I'll go to the house and . . ." He was going to offer to make lunch, but all he knew how to fix was sandwiches. She might want something nicer for Sunday. But was she up to cooking?

He gave the shelves a quick scan for something he could make. Cans of Campbell's Beefsteak Tomato Soup were lined up as straight as soldiers during inspection next to canned vegetables. He pointed. "I'll heat up some of that tomato soup for everyone."

"That sounds fine, Mr. Holbrook." The agreement added to his certainty that she'd caught influenza. "The directions say to mix the contents with water, but please use milk. It's more flavorful and hearty with milk. The children need something hearty."

Even when feeling poorly, she thought of the kids. Callum's heart twisted in his chest. She was such a good mama. His girls were lucky to have her. He backed up in the direction of the canned goods, escaping the thought more than the woman. "Yes, ma'am. I'll use milk."

"Please also put crackers and cheese on the table." She put her hand to her head again, pursing her lips. "Such a sad Sunday dinner, but given the circumstances, it will have to do." Lowering her hand, she sighed. "Thank you for seeing to it, Callum."

"Sure thing." He took four cans from the shelf and then grabbed a cracker tin. Suddenly he realized she'd called him by his first name. He gaped at her, but she was bent over the ledger again, seemingly unaware of her blunder. Well, it was likely her fever talking. He wouldn't point it out.

He got a good grip on the items in his arms and headed for the door, her tired yet sweet voice echoing his name in his mind. He didn't speak a word as he left, but inside his head, he answered, *You're welcome, Hester.* He wished he could say it out loud. To know what her name sounded like when it left his lips. To see how she'd respond if she heard him speak it.

Chapter Thirty-Four

Callum

After feeding the children, Callum carried a bowl of soup draped with a cloth napkin across the lawn and entered the store. Dr. Ash's low voice carried from Scotty's room, bringing Callum to a halt in the little foyer next to the open door.

"You can't get up and act like nothing's happened. A concussion is a serious thing. Your brain got bounced inside your skull, and it'll take it a while to heal. It's important for you to take it easy."

"For how long?" Scotty's question emerged on a growl.

"At least three days. But maybe as long as two weeks."

Callum gulped. How would Mrs. Haak manage if Scotty was laid up for two weeks?

"I know that'll be hard," the doctor went on in a sad yet firm tone, "now that Mrs. Haak's come down with influenza, but listen to me. If you start feeling weak or your vision blurs or you're suddenly dizzy, don't ignore it and push through. Rest when your body warns you it's had enough. Otherwise, you'll make things worse."

How could it get any worse than Mrs. Haak being sick at the same time Scotty'd hurt himself? The whole situation wasn't right. Callum released a snort of aggravation.

Silence fell on the other side of Scotty's door, and then the doctor peeked out. "Oh, Mr. Holbrook, it's you."

Callum's face heated. He hoped the man didn't brand him an eavesdropper. "Sorry to interrupt, but I brought Scotty some soup."

"Well, bring it on in."

Callum entered the room and crossed to Scotty's cot. The man was sitting up with his stockinged feet set wide on the planked floor. He met Callum's gaze, but he didn't smile. Callum held out the bowl. "The kids were worried about you going hungry. So . . . here you are."

Scotty set the bowl on his knee. Callum pulled a spoon from his shirt pocket and offered it. Scotty took it and then sat with it gripped in his fist. "Thanks," he finally said, but not with any warmth.

Callum backed up a step and faced the doctor. "Um, Doc? What about Mrs. Haak's store?" Worry made his throat go dry. "And the boys? Who'll take care of them while she's sick and Scotty isn't able to be up and doing?"

Dr. Ash gathered up his instruments from the end of Scotty's cot and put them in his bag. "As soon as I tell my wife about Mrs. Haak's situation, she'll round up folks from town to lend a hand. At least in helping with the house and the children. As for the store . . ." He grimaced. "It might have to close for a few days until Scotty's able to run things again."

The doc turned to Scotty. "I'll leave you now so you can eat. I imagine you're hungry after going so long without food. If you rest this afternoon, you'll be able to go to the house for supper. And"—he cleared his throat—"a bath before bedtime. All right?"

Scotty grunted, but he nodded.

Dr. Ash left the room, and Callum followed after him. As soon as the back door closed behind them, Callum caught the doctor's sleeve. "Doc, can I . . . talk to you?"

The man turned and faced Callum. "What about?"

Callum had never been one to burden a friend, let alone a stranger, but these were uncommon circumstances. "I'm in a bind. I've gotta get back to New York before the end of the month or my job at the factory'll go to another man. I never expected to be in Millersberg for more'n a day. I don't have money to stay and still pay for train tickets to get my girls and me home again."

To his credit, the doctor seemed concerned. "I'm sure sorry to hear about your troubles. What is it you want from me?"

"I need you to tell me Evvie's ready to travel."

His dark eyebrows formed a V. "I can't do that. Until she's completely free of fever, she belongs in bed, not on a train."

Callum huffed a sigh. "I figured that's what you'd say, but I was hoping . . ."

The doctor's scowl faded. "I'm not unsympathetic to your problem, Mr. Holbrook. These days, jobs are dear. Maybe you should return to New York on your own with Winnie, and Evelyn can come when she's well."

"I can't take Winnie without Evvie because there's nobody to watch her while I'm at work." Callum gave the doc a hopeful look. "Isn't there some way to stop Evvie's fever?"

The doctor laughed softly. "That would be wonderful for lots of people, but a fever has to run its course. Evelyn's on the fourth day. It's possible her fever will break tomorrow. But she'll be weak for a day or two even after it's gone—not really fit for travel."

"I don't have the time or money to stay for days on end, but I can't leave." Callum rammed his fingers into his hair. "Why is God doing this to me?" He hadn't meant to ask the question aloud, but it was out, and the doctor seemed to take it seriously.

"Mr. Holbrook, I can't speak to this particular situation, but I can share my experiences. In the past when I felt as though God threw a barrier into my path, I eventually discovered He had something else—something better—in mind for me." The man's solemn yet kind tone held Callum's attention. "Maybe God is protecting you from something or is guiding you in a new direction." He put his hand on Callum's shoulder. "You see, God is always working on behalf of His children. I don't always understand His ways, but I've learned that I can always trust His heart."

Callum hung his head. "I thought that once."

The doctor dropped his hand and stood quietly for a few minutes, staring past Callum's shoulder. Then he cleared his throat. "Mrs. Haak mentioned she saw a light shining in one of the windows at the Klein house during the night. She thought perhaps a hobo had broken in there. I'm the only Klein relative, indirect as it may be, living in town, so I've been tasked with keeping an eye on the place until Silas's one remaining son sells it. I admit, I haven't been diligent about it. Would you mind walking over with me and giving the house a good perusal?"

Callum shrugged. "I can't go anywhere else."

Dr. Ash set his bag on the grass near the road. Then the two crossed the street and the doctor pointed south. "Please check the front door—make sure it's still locked. I'll check the back."

"Sure." Callum angled toward the side of the house that faced east, giving the structure's exterior an inspection as he went. He sure hoped the house hadn't been broken into. It was a fine house, with lots of gingerbread trim and bowed windows. It reminded him of some of the smaller houses in the Flatbush section of Brooklyn. Back when he and Freida were young and starry-eyed, he took her on a carriage ride through that area and they fantasized about living in such a house someday. All he'd been able to give her was an apartment in the tenements of the Bronx. But she'd never complained. Something she had in common with Hester Haak.

He shook his head, dislodging the odd thought. He climbed the stairs to the wraparound porch and opened the spindled screen door. He jiggled the knob and pushed. The door didn't open. Nobody'd jimmied the front lock. He headed around the house on the far side, checking windows on the way. None open or broken. He rounded the back of the house. There was a small porch all closed in with lattice panels. He peered inside. The door leading from the porch into the house stood open.

He went on in and found himself in a good-sized kitchen. "Doc?"

"I'm upstairs," came his voice. "Use the maid's staircase in the northeast corner."

Callum went up the narrow enclosed staircase and entered a hallway. "Where are you?"

The doctor stuck his head out one of the doorways springing off the hall. "In here."

Callum entered the bedroom and released a little *whew* of admiration. Evvie would love this room with its pink-flowered wallpaper, maple furniture, and brass bed. "Pretty fancy."

The doctor was opening and closing dresser drawers. "Apparently, someone else agrees with you. The lamp on the table by the bed has fresh oil in it, the bed's been recently slept in, and there are clothes in this bureau. There shouldn't be. When Carrie Klein married my father, she took all her personal belongings with her."

Callum gawked at him. "So a hobo did break in?"

The doctor held up a ruffly blouse. "I don't know of any hobo who would wear this." He dropped it back in the drawer and closed it. "There doesn't appear to be anything missing, and nothing's damaged, but I don't like that a stranger has been in here."

Callum didn't either. His girls were right across the street.

Dr. Ash strode to Callum. "Mr. Holbrook, where have you been staying since you came to town?"

"I took a room above Miss Sally's Dress Shop."

The doctor glanced around the room again. "What would you think about staying in this house? The electricity is disconnected, so you'll have to use oil lamps, but there's water. The pipes are connected to a private well."

Callum took a small step backward. "I can't afford to stay in a place like this." He couldn't even afford to stay at the dress shop anymore.

"You don't understand. As long as you're still in town, I'd like to hire you as a . . ." Dr. Ash rolled his eyes upward for a moment. "A caretaker of sorts. If the house appears occupied, no one else will bother to come in."

Callum considered what the doctor had offered. "You'd hire me?"

"Yes. How does twenty-five cents a day sound?"

"Better than spending forty-five cents a day."

The doctor laughed. "Then you agree?"

"Yes." Callum held up his finger. "Until Evvie is well enough to travel."

The doctor headed for the hallway, talking as he went. "It shouldn't take more than a few days to convince whoever has been sneaking in here to stay away."

Callum followed him down the staircase—the one he said was for a maid. What would it be like to have money enough for a house like this and a maid? He couldn't imagine. He just wanted money enough to go back to New York with his daughters.

They exited through the back porch. The doctor picked up a painted brick lying next to the door. A key was underneath it. He gave the key to Callum. "Pocket this. You'll use it to get back in later." He snorted, staring at the brick. "The intruder must have figured out Grandfather Klein's old hiding place. I won't use that again." He turned to Callum and gave him a sad smile. "I know you're eager to leave town, but I appreciate you being willing to help me until you go."

Callum shrugged. "At least I'm real close to my girls here. And I can give Scotty a hand if need be."

"That would be good. I'm concerned he'll try to do too much too soon." Dr. Ash crossed the street, and Callum stayed alongside him. "By the way, I noticed how gruff Scotty is with you. That's not his usual demeanor. He's a very compassionate, honest, hardworking man who has been a real godsend to Mrs. Haak since her husband's untimely death."

Callum hoped he wouldn't sound nosy, but he was curious. "What happened to her husband?"

"Pneumonia." The doctor paused, sorrow obvious in his expression and tone. "He was a good man, very well respected in the community. It was a blow to the whole town when he died. Mrs. Haak has carried on in his stead, even in her grief and loneliness, serving her neighbors by operating the Corner Store. We were all thrilled for her when she adop—" His cheeks blotched red. "I've said too much. Thank you for guarding the Klein house, and thank you for helping Scotty. Have a good rest of the day, now, Mr. Holbrook." He picked up his bag, climbed into his automobile, and drove away.

Chapter Thirty-Five

Callum

Sunday evening, an older lady Scotty greeted as Mrs. Maddox knocked on the front door. She handed a kettle of chicken and dumplings to Callum and asked to see Hester. While she checked in on Mrs. Haak, the rest of them—except Evvie, who wasn't hungry—had a fine supper.

After they all ate, Scotty and Beckett saw to the dishes. Callum, with Guy getting in the way, tacked more sheets to the bedroom ceiling to shield Mrs. Haak's bed. Sheets on both sides of the doorways created a hall and didn't make him feel like he was invading Mrs. Haak's personal space. Then, with Mrs. Haak's permission, he sent Evvie in with her and changed the bedding from the lower bunk so Winnie could sleep there. Winnie pouted about the change. She liked sleeping "in the big bed with Mama," as she put it. But Scotty sat her on his knee and explained that Mama was sick and might make Winnie sick again. His little girl still wasn't happy, but she accepted it. Callum wasn't sure whether he appreciated or resented Scotty's interference, but at least the subject was settled.

Scotty took a bath and then returned to his room at the store. Callum sent Beckett, Guy, and Winnie in by turn for baths. When they were done, he bathed in tepid water. They'd nearly emptied the hot-water tank. And Winnie'd left a big mess behind that he had to clean up. Apparently, she'd never bathed unattended and enjoyed her freedom a little too much. He'd remember that for tomorrow's bath time.

When they were all in their nightclothes, he put his hands on his hips. "All right, kids, off to bed."

Guy's mouth dropped open. "Ain't you gonna read us a story?"

Callum glanced at the clock. It was already past eight—he should make them go to sleep. But Freida had always read to Evvie. He wished Scotty was still there to take this duty, but maybe it was a way to draw close to Winnie. He flicked his fingers at Guy. "Get the storybook, then." He herded Beckett and Winnie into the living room, and they settled on the sofa with Winnie pressed close to Callum's side and Beckett perched on an armrest.

Guy darted in and thrust a thick book titled *Bible Stories for Children* at Callum. "Find the one about David and the giant. I wanna hear it again."

Callum located the story and read it. At its end, he blew out a grateful breath. "All right, bed now."

Winnie blinked up at him. "Huh-uh. We gotta pray."

He might've read about David and Goliath, but he wasn't going to talk to David's God. "Go ahead, then."

Without pause, Winnie folded her hands and closed her eyes. The boys did the same. But Callum kept his eyes wide open and focused on his baby girl's face as she thanked God for a good day, asked Him to bless each family member by name—including Daddy, which brought the sting of tears—and finally asked Him to make Uncle 'cotty, Mama, and Sissy all better again. At her "amen," her blue eyes popped open, and she scooted off the sofa. "Night night." She and the boys went to their beds.

Callum stayed there alone with the storybook heavy on his lap and the memory of Winnie's sweet prayer heavy on his mind until he was sure everyone was asleep. He hated to leave when the only adult in the house was sick, but he had to go. Partly to protect Mrs. Haak's reputation, and partly because he'd promised to guard the Klein house.

He exited the front door rather than traipsing through the dark bedroom and disturbing the others. He unlocked the back door at the big house and let himself in. He'd already decided he wouldn't sleep in one of the bedrooms on the second floor. If he stayed on the first floor, he'd be more likely to hear someone come in. That is, if someone had the nerve to come in with him there. He walked slowly through heavy shadows to the parlor, kicked off his shoes, and stretched out on the settee beneath the big front window. Serenaded by crickets and a hoot owl, he quickly fell asleep.

Monday morning when he headed for Mrs. Haak's, he found the Kleins' kitchen door ajar. He froze in place for a few seconds. Hadn't he locked it last night? He thought he had, but he'd had a lot on his mind. Inwardly berating himself, he made sure he locked it as he left and then put the key in his pocket. At Mrs. Haak's house, he woke the three youngest children and fixed them a simple breakfast of toast with peanut butter and glasses of milk. Scotty didn't come in, which worried Callum some, but he figured it was better to check on Evvie than see to Scotty. Evvie was drenched with sweat, but her forehead wasn't hot—a good sign, he thought.

Another lady showed up as he was sending Guy and Beckett to school, so he asked if she'd keep an eye on Winnie while he ran to the post office to make a telephone call. She shooed him off with a cheerful "Don't worry about us. We'll be fine."

But Boss Moore wasn't cheerful when Callum told him he was still stuck in Millersberg. "Holbrook," he said, "I understand your dilemma, but you aren't giving me much choice. Come Friday morning, if you aren't here at starting time, I'll have to put up a notice about hiring." He didn't need to mention how fast the spot would fill—men were hungry for jobs. Callum told his boss he wouldn't hold it against him even though panic clawed at him. Then he asked if he could leave a message for Billy.

Boss Moore snorted, "Call the man himself—he has a telephone at his house."

"But there's no phone for me to use past quitting time."

The boss agreed to tell Billy what Callum needed. His errand complete, Callum hung up and jogged back to Mrs. Haak's. He thanked the neighbor and told her she could go if she wanted to.

The lady smiled. "I'll be here through lunchtime, and Mrs. Stafford's coming for the afternoon and suppertime. Mrs. Ash has a whole list of folks willing to come help Hester and Scotty, so don't worry about meals or anything else. Your little girl can stay with me, and I'll see to the bigger girl and Mrs. Haak." She patted his arm. "Why don't you go help Scotty in the store? He's determined to run it, but"—she lowered her voice even though it was just the two of them—"he can't do the books. He needs somebody to write things down. Can you do that?"

Callum had never kept books before, but if somebody told him what to write, he could record it. He shrugged.

She smiled as if he'd wholeheartedly agreed. "Go on, then." She put her hand on Winnie's uncombed hair. "We're fine in here."

Callum left the breakfast mess and responsibility for the three females to the kind lady whose name he hadn't even asked. He found Scotty in the chickens' enclosure using his shirttails as a pouch for the eggs. Callum stopped outside the wire fence. "Dr. Ash's wife has ladies coming to see to Mrs. Haak and Evelyn. The one in there now said to come help you."

Scotty angled a scowl over his shoulder. "Thinks I need keepin', huh?"

Callum tamped back a chuckle. "Nah. No keepin'. Just helping. The two of us together probably won't be half as good at runnin' the store as Mrs. Haak does by herself, but I figure we can at least give her customers what they need."

Scotty stared at him for a few silent seconds, then gave a brusque nod. "Reckon so."

That Monday in the store, Callum experienced community in ways he hadn't known existed. Every customer who came in asked how Scotty was doing, asked after Mrs. Haak and even Evvie. Many told Callum how sorry they were about him being stuck for a while. At first he wasn't sure how to take their concern. Should it bother him that the whole town had been talking about his reason for being there and his eagerness to return to New York? But their sincerity won him over. They cared. They cared about Mrs. Haak and Scotty, but they also cared about him and his daughters. He was nothing more than a stranger who'd broken Mrs. Haak's heart, but they were kind. It reminded him of the feeling he'd gotten when he saw so many people emptying the crates and filling the shelves—a warmth under the skin that he wanted to hold on to.

Working with Scotty let Callum see the older man's heart, too. Oh, he wasn't kindly toward Callum. Clearly, Scotty resented him for stealing Evvie and Winnie. But his fierce loyalty to Mrs. Haak and his genuine affection for the children earned Callum's respect. Under other circumstances, the two might've been friends.

Tuesday morning, Evvie awakened completely fever free and ravenous. She stayed home from school and worked on the assignments Beckett had carted home for her. To Callum's surprise, she didn't complain even once about the schoolwork. At supper that night, she told everyone she couldn't wait to see her friends.

Callum cleared his throat. "Honey, since you're all well again, we could catch the train tomorrow morning." That'd get them to New York by Friday night, giving them the full weekend to settle in. And then he'd hustle to the factory first thing Monday and try to reclaim his job before someone else snagged it.

Her face fell. "But, Daddy, I wanna at least tell my friends and Mr. Herriott goodbye. I can't do that if I don't go back."

One more day would get them to New York by Saturday. That was good enough. "All right. We'll wait until tomorrow after school."

She tipped her head. "Will Mrs. Haak be better by then? We shouldn't leave while she's still sick. And Uncle Scotty—he ain't over his concussion yet."

Scotty spluttered and clanked his fork onto the table. "Don't be spendin' no worry time on me. I'm fine."

Evvie rolled her eyes. "Says you. I see your hand shaking when you're trying to stab your green beans. An' don't tell me you're just tired. I know better."

Scotty grunted, but the corners of his lips turned up a little bit, like he appreciated Evvie's concern.

She gave Callum a sorrowful look. "Mrs. Haak took real good care of us. Even when I wasn't very nice to her. She only got sick because Winnie and me got sick. We ought to take care of her until she's all well. It's the right thing to do."

Callum couldn't deny Evvie's claim, but he wasn't going to make any promises about staying longer. He told her to finish her supper and help Winnie with her bath. That night, Evvie offered to read the bedtime story, freeing Callum to leave for the Kleins' a little earlier. He needed some quiet thinking time. He let himself into the big house and headed for the parlor, picturing a calendar in his mind.

He trusted Billy to make sure the apartment was his until May fifteenth, but he'd have to earn some money before then to pay another week's rent on the sixteenth. Which meant being at a job at least by the eleventh. The timetable shook him. There weren't enough jobs in New York City to go around these days. He'd gone almost a full year before hiring on at the factory. It would be a miracle if he found something that paid as well in such a short amount of time.

He removed his shoes and leaned against the sofa's tufted

back, staring at the ceiling. Should he disappoint Evvie by leaving tomorrow after school? The ladies in town had already proved their willingness to take care of Mrs. Haak. And Scotty could handle the store. Not the books, but it would only be for a few days. Maybe one of the ladies would do the books for him. He'd ask whatever lady arrived in the morning. If she said yes, then he'd beg a ride to Marion tomorrow afternoon.

It was a good plan. A plan that would take care of everybody. So why didn't he feel good about it?

He started to stretch out on the sofa, but a rustling sound—someone rifling through a drawer or closet—above his head brought him to his feet. He shouted, "Who's up there?" Footsteps clattered down the maid's staircase. He took off for the kitchen. When his stocking-covered feet left the parlor rug and met the hardwood floor, one foot went east and the other west. He went down hard. He pushed himself up and scrambled through the hallway, but by the time he reached the kitchen, the back door was open and the intruder gone.

Growling, he stared into the dark yard. Now he knew why he'd found the door open that morning. The person had slept upstairs right above his head last night and sneaked out before he awoke. Some guard he'd turned out to be. He closed the door, made sure the lock was turned, and went to the parlor again. Tomorrow he'd tell Dr. Ash what happened and give his key back, because he'd be on his way to New York by the end of the day. He lay on the sofa and fell into a restless sleep.

On Wednesday, Evvie headed off to school with Beckett and Guy, a happy bounce in her step. Watching her go, Callum was glad he'd promised to send her to school in New York. After thanking the newest helper—Mrs. Phelps, an elderly widow who lived in the little house next to the Klein house—for coming, Callum went to the store.

Scotty hadn't come in for breakfast, but Mrs. Phelps claimed she'd seen him collecting the eggs. Heading across the dewy grass, Callum smiled, imagining the girls' surprise when he told them they'd be leaving that very afternoon. But first he had to tell Scotty he needed the day to pack their things.

He entered the store by the back door and called, "Good morning, Scotty."

No response.

Was he still outside somewhere? He stuck his head out the doorway and looked. No sign of him. Which meant he had to be inside. He passed Scotty's little room, glancing in at his rumpled cot as he went, and entered the sales area. "Scotty?" A groan from behind the counter met his ears. Callum darted around to the back and found Scotty sprawled on the floor, broken eggs all around him.

He dropped to one knee and touched Scotty's shoulder. "What happened?"

"Dunno." Scotty lifted his hand to his head. "I . . . I came around to put the eggs in the basket, an' the world started spinnin' like a top. Threw my feet out from under me." He grimaced. "I sure made a mess o' the eggs. A plumb waste." He rose up on one elbow, revealing a smear of blood on the floor. "Help me up, would you?"

Callum gently pressed him down again. "I don't think so. Your head's bleeding. You must've bumped it when you fell. We'd better have Dr. Ash take a look before you get up."

The man scowled. "You want me to stay here layin' in slimy eggs? Gimme some dignity, would you?"

Whether it was undignified or not, Callum wasn't going to move the man until the doctor said he could. He stood, careful to avoid stepping in the egg goo. "I'm going after Dr. Ash. Please stay put. Promise?"

Scotty closed his eyes. "All right, all right, but hurry, will you?" His voice sounded weak.

Callum raced to the house, told Mrs. Phelps what had happened, then took off. Thank goodness it was a small town. He only needed a few minutes to reach the doctor's little office on Main Street. Dr. Ash was just arriving, and his obvious concern when Callum said Scotty was dizzy enough to fall and break open his wound raised Callum's worry. The doctor told Callum to get in his auto, and they drove to the store.

The doctor went in, but Callum stayed on the porch. He'd give Scotty privacy to collect his pride. He paced, though, sending glances through the plate-glass window. Finally, he saw the doctor walking Scotty around the counter and toward his little room. Several minutes later, Dr. Ash joined Callum on the front porch.

"The stubborn old goat." Callum heard no insult in the statement, only deep worry. "Did you know he moved lumber yesterday?"

Callum gaped at him. "Lumber? No."

The doctor folded his arms. "Well, he did. Said his knee was telling him rain is coming and he wanted the lumber they purchased to build bedrooms under cover. Before he went to bed last night, he moved roughly half the lumber against the side of the store, where it would have some protection." He snorted. "I've cleaned up his wound, helped him into fresh clothes, and ordered him to three days of bed rest. I hope you'll make sure he stays there." Then he gave a little jolt. "Oh, I forgot. You intend to leave as soon as Evelyn is well."

"She went to school this morning." Guilt he didn't understand struck hard. "I was gonna pack the girls' things today and hitch a ride to Marion this evening."

The doctor's forehead puckered into a thoughtful scowl. "In that case, I should take Scotty to the surgery room at my office, where I can keep an eye on him for the next few days."

A worrisome thought captured Callum. "What about the store, though? Shouldn't somebody keep it open?"

"Given it's Mrs. Haak's means of livelihood, yes, but . . ." Dr. Ash held his hands out in a helpless gesture. "I don't see a choice other than to close it for now."

Evvie's sad face appeared in Callum's mind's eye. Her voice whispered in his memory. "*We ought to take care of her until she's all well. It's the right thing to do.*" She'd confessed that Mrs. Haak was kind even when Evvie wasn't. How could Callum be uncaring enough to walk away when she most needed help?

Before he could talk himself out of it, Callum said, "I'll run the store until Mrs. Haak's on her feet again. And I'll get the rest of that lumber moved so Scotty won't try to finish the job."

The doctor gave his shoulder a solid pat. "Thank you, Mr. Holbrook. You're a godsend."

Callum wouldn't go that far, but he'd made the commitment. He'd stick to it. Starting with cleaning up the eggs on the floor. Dr. Ash left, and Callum located a bucket and rags. As he filled the bucket from the spigot behind the store, he glanced across the street at the Klein house and groaned. He hadn't told the doctor about the person he'd chased out of the house last night. Well, he'd tell him later. He had work to do.

Chapter Thirty-Six

Evelyn

If somebody'd told her the first day she stepped foot in this school that she'd be sad about having to leave it, she would've laughed herself silly. But it was true. When she'd come back after being sick, Rosemary, Norma, and Bertie Mae surrounded her with hugs and joy that she was well again. The whole day long, all she could think about was how she liked being a Little Woman with her friends. How Mr. Herriott cared enough to teach the kids day after day, unlike the teachers at the home who sometimes didn't even last a full week. How nice it was to be noticed by Fred Ash, the cutest boy in grade eight. How much she'd miss everybody when Daddy took her back to New York.

If somebody'd told her even last week that she would want Mrs. Haak to be her mother, she would've denied it. But the first night Daddy had said she should sleep in Mrs. Haak's bed because they were both sick, she'd woke up coughing so hard it hurt her chest. She started crying because she felt so bad. Mrs. Haak rubbed her back and called her "sweetheart" and told her she'd be okay soon. Mrs. Haak was sick, too, but she tried to make Evelyn feel better. She called her "sweetheart," even though she'd been anything but a sweetheart. Only a real mother would do those things for her child. How many times had Evelyn told herself she didn't want a new mother? Lots of times. But now she did, and she wanted it to be Mrs. Haak. And that confused her so much she didn't know what to do.

When school let out, she told Beckett and Guy to go on ahead, and she walked with the other Little Women. They were talking, laughing some, even teasing her a little about Fred, and Evelyn was joining in the fun. Until Rosemary said, "When's your daddy taking you and Winnie back to New York?"

Evelyn stopped right there on the street and blinked real hard to hold back tears. "When Mrs. Haak feels better again. So it'll be soon, I guess. But . . ." She sucked in her lips, gathering enough courage to say what she really felt. "I don't wanna go. I wanna stay here."

Bertie Mae gasped. "You do? But you said you love New York, that it was more exciting than any city anywhere and Millersberg was too dull for words."

Evelyn blinked some more. She wasn't a crybaby, but she wanted to cry over lots of the dumb things she'd said. "I know I did, and I was wrong. I only said it because I missed Daddy. But now, if I leave, I'm gonna miss all of you. And Guy and Beckett. And Mrs. Haak. And even Uncle Scotty."

Norma's eyes twinkled. "What about Fred Ash?"

Evelyn hunched her shoulders and giggled. "Well . . ."

They all laughed. Rosemary slung her arm across Evelyn's shoulders. "It seems to me if you wanna stay, you need to tell somebody."

"Why, sure." Bertie Mae put her fist on her hip and tossed her blond curls. "You're big enough to decide on your own where you want to live. Tell your daddy you wanna live in Millersberg."

Evelyn hugged her books to her chest. "But Daddy wants to live in New York. I love him. I've missed him so much. I don't wanna be apart from him again. But I don't wanna go away from everybody here, either."

Nobody was laughing anymore. They stood in a silent circle, looking at one another with sad faces. Then Rosemary gave Evelyn a squeeze. "Remember when we were reading *Little Women* and Jo talked about her castle in the air?"

Evelyn nodded. "Yes. She had a castle and a key." She'd been fascinated by the way Jo said she knew she had what she needed to accomplish her goal to become a writer.

"Evelyn, you've got a key the same way Jo did. You've just gotta be brave enough to use it and unlock the door."

Evelyn drew a deep breath. "You mean I should tell Daddy I want to stay in Millersberg?"

"That's exactly what I mean." Rosemary shrugged. "Or tell Mrs. Haak. She can talk to your daddy for you."

Evelyn chewed her bottom lip, thinking. "She's pretty sick right now. I shouldn't bother her."

"I think if you tell her you wanna stay, she's gonna feel a lot better right away." Rosemary dropped her arm from Evelyn's shoulder and gave her a light nudge. "Tell her, Evelyn. Use that key and unlock your castle in the sky."

Norma, Bertie Mae, and Rosemary all beamed at her, nodding.

Evelyn squared her shoulders and closed her fingers around her imaginary key. "All right, I'll do it. I'll tell Mrs. Haak I want to stay." She sniffed back the tears threatening to flow down her cheeks. Words poured out without her even thinking about them first. "And you all pray real hard that my daddy won't go away. Because I want us both to be here."

Norma gave a firm nod. "We will, Evelyn. In fact, everybody, put your stuff down." Exchanging confused glances, they put their books and lunch pails on the ground. Norma held out her hands. "Grab hold. Let's pray right now."

Evelyn took Rosemary's and Norma's hands and held tight. As her friends prayed for her, Daddy, and Winnie to be able to stay in Millersberg, Evelyn's chest ached the way her gums hurt when a molar was breaking through. Then the ache splintered and fell away. Tears rolled, and she didn't even care. Because for the first time since Mama died, she felt like she could really breathe again. And she knew why.

Thank You, God.

Callum

The clock on the wall chimed five times. Closing time. Callum crossed the floor in three long strides and flipped the little sign on the front door of the store to Closed. He turned the lock and then scuffed to the counter. He slumped against the sturdy fixture, spent. Had he worked this hard at the factory? It seemed as if manning a grinder should tax a fellow more than operating a little store in a small town, but he couldn't remember the last time he'd been this tired. Of course, part of his tiredness was due to lack of sleep. Worry about the unknown intruder sneaking into the Klein house kept him from fully resting. And over the past days, he'd done more than take care of customers, count change, and record sales and receipts in the ledger.

He rotated his shoulders, groaning as his muscles pulled. How had Scotty unloaded and stacked all that lumber all by himself? Callum had struggled to finish moving the stack. He'd done it to keep Scotty from doing it, but it'd seemed a little silly. Here it was, Thursday evening, and the rain Scotty's knee predicted hadn't come. But at least the lumber was out of the way of the children's play area. Guy, Beckett, and Winnie needed space to run. Too bad there wasn't a grassy area outside his apartment building for Winnie. She liked chasing the boys as much as they liked chasing each other. And if there was grass, they might be able to have a garden.

Yesterday evening, he'd caught Beckett chopping at weeds with a hoe in a rectangular patch at the back corner of the yard and asked what he was doing. The boy sheepishly admitted Mrs. Haak wanted the area cleared to plant vegetables soon but he hadn't gotten it done. He wanted to surprise her with it all ready for seeds when she wasn't sick anymore. Callum thought it a fine idea, so when he wasn't taking care of customers, checking on Scotty, or moving lumber, he'd put his hand to preparing the garden plot. After all, he owed her something for the tender care she'd given his daughters and all the meals she'd shared with him over the past two weeks. He'd never worked in the dirt before, but he discovered he enjoyed turning the soil, inhaling the rich aroma rising from the ground, and watching clods dissolve. He hoped Hester would be pleased with his efforts.

Hester . . . He thought of her as *Hester* now. Improper? Maybe. But *Mrs. Haak* was too stuffy. More than half the people who came into the store used her given name. Scotty called her *Miz Hester,* but even that was less formal than *Mrs. Haak.* In his mind, even though he hadn't laid eyes on her since he put up the sheets on Sunday to section off her side of the room, she was *Hester.* He hoped he didn't slip up and call her that to her face.

He pushed away from the counter and fetched the broom from the corner. While he swept the grit peppering the floor into a pile, he kept his ear tuned for the doctor's arrival. The man had promised to check on Scotty before suppertime. Callum needed to give him a report on things at the Klein house. He hadn't heard anybody else in there since Tuesday evening, and to his knowledge the door had stayed locked. Still, he couldn't shake the notion that he wasn't alone in the house. He wanted the doctor to go over with him after he'd seen to Scotty and nose around. Dr. Ash was more familiar with what should or shouldn't be in there.

He paused and leaned on the broom, releasing a heavy sigh. He hoped the doc would ease his worries. Then maybe he'd relax enough to really rest. He couldn't arrive in New York all worn-out if he was going to pound the pavement in search of a job. It wouldn't be long now. Surely, he and the girls would board the train by Saturday, Sunday at the latest.

He waited for eagerness to rise in his chest. It didn't. He must be more tired than he'd realized. Yes. That was it. He was tired.

Just tired. Once they were on the train, his excitement would come back.

Sure it would.

Hester

Hester awakened and released a startled gasp. Evelyn was sitting at the foot of the bed, staring at her with her lower lip sucked in. Hester swallowed against her dry throat. "Good morning." She sounded as croaky as a bullfrog.

"Good morning." Evelyn spoke softly, hesitantly. Although unsmiling, she wasn't prickling with resentment. Unusual. The girl scooted closer by a few inches. "Mrs. Reames is here, fixing breakfast for everybody. I told her I'd check in on you. H-How are you feeling?"

Hester lifted her hand, amazed at how heavy it seemed, and laid the back of her fingers against her forehead. To her relief, although her hair was sweat matted, her skin was cool. The fever was gone. She could be up and doing again. Maybe. "Weak as a kitten, but I think the worst has passed. Are you all better?"

Evelyn nodded. "I went back to school on Wednesday already."

Hester frowned. "What is today?"

"Friday."

Five days had slipped by while she lay alternately shivering and sweating in her bed. She had fuzzy memories of people coming and going, of being given cool water and warm broth, but she hadn't realized how long she'd been sick. Suddenly Evelyn's words sank in. "You're attending school? Why are you still here? I thought your daddy was taking you girls back to New York as soon as you recovered."

An odd half smile appeared on Evelyn's face. "I told him we couldn't go until you were all well again. Especially with Uncle

Scotty down, somebody had to take care of the store and of you."

"Scotty is down? I thought he was doing better."

Evelyn rolled her eyes, a familiar gesture. "He was until he did too much. The doctor made him go to bed and stay there. If Dr. Ash says he's okay, he'll be up again tomorrow. I've been praying he'll be all the way better soon."

Evelyn had been praying? And she sat here talking to Hester without bristling? Was Hester dreaming? She reached out and put her hand over Evelyn's. "Sweetheart, are you all right?"

Tears brightened Evelyn's blue eyes. "No, ma'am, I'm not. I've been waiting until you were well again to talk to you." She sniffled, her chin quivering. "Because now that you're well, and especially if the doctor says Uncle Scotty can get up again, Daddy will take Winnie and me away, and I don't want to go. I want to stay in Millersberg."

Hester must be dreaming. She closed her eyes, counted to three, and opened them. No, Evelyn was still sitting there, looking at Hester with agony in her eyes. But she still wondered if she'd heard correctly. "You want . . . to stay?"

"I want all of us—Winnie and Daddy and me—to stay in Millersberg." A single tear rolled. "I'm sorry I was so awful to you. Uncle Scotty tried to tell me you didn't do anything wrong—all you did was love me. And I knew he was right. But I thought if I loved you back, I'd be . . . unfaithful, I guess . . . to Mama. And I wanted my daddy so bad." Another tear slid down her cheek. "But Mama is gone. And you're here. And if you still love me even after as bad as I was, I want . . ." She gulped. "May I call you *Mother*?"

Mother. The very title Hester had imagined Evelyn would choose. "I love you very much, Evelyn, and nothing would make me happier." She opened her arms, and with a little sob, Evelyn fell against her chest. She held the girl, kissed her hair, murmured to her, all the while thanking God for this amazing answer to prayer.

After a few minutes, Evelyn sat up and wiped her cheeks with the backs of her hands. "Rosemary and the others've been praying with me about getting to stay. They said I need to tell Daddy, but I'm afraid I'll hurt his feelings. That he'll think I don't want to be with him. But I do. I want to be with both of you. He's been staying in the big house across the street. If he keeps staying there, he'd be real close. Me and Winnie would see both of you every day." She pulled in a shuddering breath. "Would you talk to him for me?"

How could she refuse this plea? Hester cupped Evelyn's cheek. "Yes, I will. But you need to understand . . . I didn't have a father when I was growing up, and I always longed for one. You have a daddy who loves you and wants you. I've already told him I won't stop him from taking you girls with him. If he refuses to stay, I'll keep my word."

Evelyn nodded, a sad sigh escaping her lips. "I know. You always keep your word." She peered at Hester through her moist eyelashes. "But you'll try, Mother?"

Joy exploded in Hester's heart. Even if Mr. Holbrook took the girls, she would have the memory of her daughter uttering her name. "I will. And if he says no, I won't forget you. I'll write to you every day. You'll always be my daughter, in here." She laid her palm on her heart.

Evelyn's quavering smile erased the last vestiges of tears. "And you'll always be my mother."

The sheet whisked aside, and Mrs. Reames peered in. "Evelyn, come eat your eggs. They're getting cold." Evelyn rose, and Mrs. Reames smiled at Hester. "Good to see your eyes wide open. You hungry? There's still plenty of eggs in the skillet."

Hester couldn't honestly say she was hungry, but she needed to regain her strength. "Eggs and coffee sound wonderful, Mrs. Reames. Thank you."

The woman left, and Hester stared at the ceiling. She marveled at Evelyn's change in attitude. Her most heartfelt prayers concerning the girl were being answered, and she praised the Lord for His hand of healing in their relationship. But had it come too late?

Chapter Thirty-Seven

Hester

Hester couldn't believe how wonderful it was to sit at the table with Scotty and the children for supper Friday evening. Mrs. Fleming had prepared a big batch of tomatoes, beef, and elbow noodles before she left, which left Hester feeling completely spoiled. Tomorrow, though, she would do her own cooking. Dr. Ash approved it but cautioned her about tending the store until after the weekend.

"Your body needs time to recuperate from the fever. You'll be on your feet all day in the store. I don't want you overdoing and suffering a second bout," he'd told her before leaving. She promised to be wise, but it would be hard. She was ready to resume her usual activities.

For tonight, she relished Winnie's giggles, the boys' tales about what took place at school, and Evelyn's shy smiles from across the table. She hadn't forgotten the promise she'd made to Evelyn that morning upon waking. She planned to speak to the girls' father after the children went to bed that evening. Over the day, between short naps, she'd sent up at least a dozen prayers for God to guide her words and for Callum Holbrook's heart to be receptive to his daughter's desire—and, Hester admitted, her desire as well. Though she'd never say it out loud, she didn't wish to bid farewell to the girls' father. But she wouldn't allow herself to explore the reason too closely.

Your will, Father, her heart whispered while she helped the older children with their homework, read their bedtime story, and prayed with them before kissing their cheeks—including Evelyn's—and tucking the covers beneath their chins. Then she sat at the table with Scotty, content to enjoy a cup of coffee in the quiet of the evening. But when she finished her cup, she rose and pushed in her chair.

"I need to go to the Klein house and talk to Mr. Holbrook. Would you come along, please?"

He raised one eyebrow. "You askin' 'cause you think I'll get up to mischief while you ain't lookin'?"

She laughed, delighting in his ornery side. The concussion might have temporarily taken his strength, but it hadn't stolen his pluck. "Not that you haven't given me reason for concern in the past, but no. Not this time. I need your support. It's going to be a hard conversation."

He stood and rounded the table. "Then let's go."

They crossed the street with her hand in the bend of his arm, as if they were going out for a stroll. A lamp burned in the front parlor window, its glow welcoming and soothing. Could any kind of altercation break out under the soft yellow light cast by a hand-painted oil lamp?

Scotty knocked on the door, then stepped aside. Within seconds, the door opened. Mr. Holbrook, wearing trousers over long underwear and with his suspenders dangling, stood framed in the doorway. His gaze met hers, and he yanked the suspenders into place. Then he pushed the screen door open.

"Hes—" He cleared his throat. "Mrs. Haak. And Scotty. C'mon in."

Hester entered first, and Scotty came in on her heels. They followed Callum into the parlor. She couldn't resist sending an appreciative look around the room. Before Ruby Klein passed away, she'd invited Hester for tea a few times on Sunday afternoons. The place was dusty, and cobwebs decorated the overhead chandelier and corners, but it was still beautiful, still grand.

Hester sat in one of a pair of wingback chairs flanking the fireplace, and Scotty plopped into the second one. Mr. Holbrook went to the sofa and sat on the center cushion. He rested his elbows on his widespread knees and linked his hands, his pose casual. But his knuckles glowed white, indicating nervousness. His gaze moved back and forth between Hester and Scotty and then rested on Scotty. "What brings you over?"

Scotty pointed at Hester. "Her. I'm along so the neighbors don't whisper."

Hester released a short laugh of both amusement and embarrassment. "I wanted to talk to you when the children weren't close by."

Scotty gave a solemn nod. "Little pitchers have big ears."

Hester stifled another chortle. This was a serious topic and laughter didn't belong here. Maybe she should have left Scotty at home. "Yes, well, I'm sorry it's so late. I'm sure you're weary."

"That's okay. I wasn't sleeping. Just sitting here . . . thinking."

His hesitation before the final word made Hester wonder what had been going through his mind. But she'd come to talk, not ask questions. "Mr. Holbrook, this morning Evelyn asked me to speak to you about remaining in Millersberg. She's happy here. She likes school and has made good friends. And she"—her throat went tight as she relived the glorious moment Evelyn called her Mother—"wants to remain near me."

His jaw muscles twitched, but he didn't say anything.

Hester went on. "That's not to say she doesn't want to be with you. She loves you very much and is so happy to have you in her life again. She doesn't want to give that up, but she wants both her father and the one she's accepted as her mother." She hadn't meant to get emotional, but tears threatened. She blinked the temptation away. "She wanted to tell you herself, but she was afraid she'd hurt your feelings by asking to stay in Millersberg. Thus, she came to me."

Mr. Holbrook lowered his head slightly and rubbed his finger under his nose. When he looked up, she searched his eyes for signs of anger or disappointment. She saw only confusion. He swallowed, his Adam's apple bobbing. "I understand why she wants to stay. It's a nice little town. The folks here have been friendly to me"—his gaze flicked to Scotty and back so quickly she thought she might have imagined it—"even though my coming meant one of their own was gonna suffer a big hurt. I'll be honest with you. I've considered making Millersberg my home."

Hester's pulse leaped. "You have?"

"Yes, ma'am." He swallowed again, and his thick dark brows came together. "But I was born in New York City. I don't know anything else. Would you be able to pack up and leave Millersberg because somebody else wanted you to?"

Scotty snorted. "'Course she wouldn't. Her store an' house're here. Her husband's buried in the cemetery here. She's got ties to here."

"And I've got ties to New York. My folks and my wife are buried there. New York's my home the same way Millersberg is your home." Regret gruffed his tone. "I don't wanna pull Evvie or Winnie away from people they love, but I can't stay here. I've got no place to live. I don't have a job. I've gotta go back, and I want them with me. They're all I have." He shook his head, aiming his gaze downward. "I'm sorry, but . . . no. It'll be hard on the girls, but they'll adjust in time, the same way they adjusted to the orphans' home and then being here. They'll be okay." He raised his head enough to lock eyes with her. "Will you be okay, Hester?"

If he'd called her Mrs. Haak, she would have been able to answer him. But she hadn't heard her name delivered in a masculine voice laced with such tenderness since Dale died. Chills exploded across her frame, and it seemed cotton filled her mouth. She couldn't speak, entranced by his simple utterance of *Hester*. His hands remained linked—he hadn't even lifted a finger toward her. Yet she felt as if he'd gently stroked her cheek.

Scotty released a soft snort, breaking the spell. "Miz Hester'll be fine. She's the strongest lady I've ever knowed. Her heart'll break when you take them girls, but she'll lean on her Maker an' find her healin' in Him." He stood. "I called you a sidewinder when you come. Then I thought maybe I was wrong when you took over the store an' things while Miz Hester was sick an' I couldn't stand up. But I wasn't wrong. Sidewinders sneak up an' cause pain, an' that's what you done here. To Miz Hester an' me an' to your girls. For that, you ought to be ashamed." He held his hand out to Hester. "C'mon, Miz Hester, he ain't gonna do nothin' for anybody but himself. We might as well—"

A crash overhead ended his words. All three in the parlor looked up, then at one another.

"What was that?" Hester gasped.

"My intruder." Mr. Holbrook lurched between Hester and Scotty and dashed up the hall.

Hester grabbed onto Scotty's arm lest he follow. Dr. Ash said he shouldn't joggle himself, and running would definitely joggle his brain. Within seconds, they heard a shrill shriek followed by a scuffle, and then Callum came up the hallway toward them. He held someone short and slender—a child?—by the upper arm. Not until they cleared the shadowed hallway did Hester realize the person was a young woman. And then she recognized her.

She released Scotty and staggered forward, stunned. "Mary?"

Callum

Callum gaped at Hester. "You know her?"

"Of course I do." She gathered the young woman in her arms, frowning at Callum over the girl's shoulder. "This is Mary Kornelson. She was the clerk at Ebright's General Merchandise Store until . . . until . . ."

Callum took hold of the girl's arm again and pulled her loose.

"You wanna tell me why you're sneaking in and out of this house? And how're you doing it? I've got the key."

She sent him a withering glare. "I have my own key. I got it from my grandpa."

Callum snorted. "Why would your grandpa have a key to the Klein house?"

"Because," Hester said with an unruffled tone, "Mary's grandfather is Silas Klein's half brother."

"That's right." The girl sounded smug. "Grandpa left the key with my folks when he moved to Topeka so they could get in here if they wanted to. Some of his things from boyhood are still in the attic."

Callum wasn't ready to let her go yet. She'd been sneaking around, and people only sneaked around when they were up to no good. "Do your folks know you're staying here?"

She turned her face away fast.

Callum nodded. "Just as I thought. They don't know where you are, do they?"

Mary twisted her arm free and lunged at Hester. Once again, Hester held her, comforting her the way she might Winnie or Evvie if they were hurt or frightened. The sight turned Callum's gut into a knot.

He walked over to Scotty. "Dr. Ash said Mr. Klein's son put him in charge of keeping an eye on the house. That's why he asked me to stay here. But if she's got a right to be here, I should tell him—"

"No!" Mary barked the word. "Don't tell Dr. Ash."

Callum turned around. "Why not?"

"He'll tell my folks." She aimed her frantic look at Hester. "I don't want them to know. I'm only staying until I can figure out how to get far away. I have to before I . . . before I . . ." Her hands went to her belly, and Callum's gaze followed them.

Freida's belly had pooched that way in the beginning months

of carrying Evvie and Winnie. Mary's ring finger, absent of a band, spilled the rest of the story. No wonder she was hiding away. Most times, girls in her predicament didn't get sympathy.

Hester took hold of Mary's hands. "I thought you were marrying your beau from Hillsboro. Why are you here and not with him?"

Tears washed down the girl's cheeks. "Pa told me to go to Hillsboro because Gerry was responsible for me now. But Gerry's mama and daddy sent him to Cincinnati to stay with his aunt and uncle. Until he forgets about me, they said. They're as mad about us being in a family way as my pa is. I need to go someplace where nobody knows me, but I don't have any money." She flicked an uncertain look in Callum's direction. "Great-Uncle Silas and Great-Aunt Ruby had lots of money. My grandma used to laugh that Uncle Silas hid it all over the place to keep Aunt Ruby from spending it. I . . . I hoped I'd find some here, but I haven't yet."

Hester slipped her arm around the girl's waist. "Well, you're not going to do any more searching tonight. With Mr. Holbrook spending nights here, you can't stay."

Callum battled with himself. Should he leave? Now he knew it wasn't a hobo or transient breaking in. This girl had a familial connection to the Kleins. But where would he go? Especially at this hour. He looked at Mary's tearstained face, and despite his aggravation about the worry she'd caused, he couldn't help but feel sorry for her. What was her father thinking? He couldn't imagine throwing out his own child, no matter what she did. She needed a safe shelter.

He could toss some blankets on the floor at the store. It'd only be a night or two before he and the girls left anyway. Before he could offer to sleep in the store, Hester went on.

"Come to my house tonight. I'll put Winnie in with me, and you can take her bed. Evelyn will be so happy to see you. She always spoke highly of you."

Mary hung her head. "She won't anymore. Nobody will."

Hester set her lips in a firm line. "Enough of that. We'll talk more tomorrow about what you should do next." She turned to Callum. "Dr. Ash forbade both Scotty and me from working in the store tomorrow. Might I prevail upon you to fill in one more day? It will give me time"—she blinked rapidly—"to gather up a few more memories before y-you go."

Nausea struck, carried on a wave of guilt. He swallowed and nodded. "I already told Dr. Ash I'd stay until you were fully on your feet. I'd be happy to help tomorrow." But, he confessed to himself as the others left, happy was not how he felt.

Chapter Thirty-Eight

Evelyn

After Guy prayed over their breakfast Saturday morning, Evelyn went to the Frigidaire to fetch peach jam for Uncle Scotty. She put the jar on the table, and Mother caught hold of her hand. "Evelyn," she said just loud enough for her to hear over the boys' chatter, "I talked to your daddy yesterday evening. He wants to go back to New York, and he wants you and Winnie to go with him."

Evelyn dropped to her knees and sobbed with her head in Mother's lap for a solid five minutes. The whole time Evelyn cried, Mother patted her back, smoothed her hair, and murmured soothing words. But when Winnie started crying, Evelyn bit down on the inside of her lower lip and brought her tears to an end. Her chest ached something fierce, holding it all in, but she shouldn't upset her little sister. If Mother could set aside her hurt to comfort Evelyn, then Evelyn could do the same for Winnie.

As she went to her chair, she paused and kissed the top of Winnie's head. "Don't cry, honey. Sissy is sad right now, but I'll be okay. So will you." They would be. Because she would ask God for strength, the way Mama had and the way Mother did.

Winnie's lower lip quivered and tears swam in her eyes, but she stopped wailing and went back to eating her biscuits and "'trawberry" jam.

Evelyn slid into her seat, and Mary patted her hand, giving her a sad smile. Evelyn smiled back to say thank you. She'd sure been surprised to find Mary sleeping in Winnie's bed when she woke up. Nobody said why she was there, but Evelyn knew Mother well enough to figure Mary needed help. Mother had the biggest heart of anybody she knew—big enough to love everybody in the whole world, probably. And if she didn't think about something else, she was gonna start crying again. She grabbed a biscuit and took a bite.

The talk that'd stopped when Evelyn broke into bawling picked up again, and pretty soon they were laughing and jabbering like nothing was wrong. Would she, Daddy, and Winnie talk and laugh around the table in New York? Kids hadn't been allowed to talk at the table at the home, and this was so much nicer. She'd make sure they talked and laughed for Winnie's sake.

Only one biscuit remained on the platter in the middle of the table. Both Uncle Scotty and Beckett reached for it at the same time. Uncle Scotty pulled his hand back. "Go ahead. Eat up."

"That's okay. You can have it." But Beckett's hand hovered over the biscuit like a bumblebee above a marigold.

Mary pushed her plate toward Beckett. "Here. Eat mine. I haven't taken a bite of it yet."

"Thanks!" Beckett grabbed Mary's biscuit, and Uncle Scotty picked up the platter and carried it to the sink, munching the last biscuit as he went.

Mother frowned at Mary. Not an "I'm mad" scowl, but an "I'm worried" one. "Are you feeling poorly?"

Mary shrugged. "A little . . . queasy. It'll pass."

Mary and Mother exchanged a look that made the fine hairs on the back of Evelyn's neck prickle. Something was wrong, for sure. "You should go see Dr. Ash. I bet he could make you feel better." Her family'd kept the doctor real busy lately.

Mary sighed. "No need. He can't fix what ails me."

More tingles attacked, and Evelyn couldn't resist rubbing Mary's shoulder real soft. "I'll pray for you." My, how wonderful to say something like that and not feel silly about it or worried about it not doing a lick of good. When she went to New York with Daddy, would she slip back into not believing in God? It'd be easy to do if Daddy didn't believe. She'd have to pray enough for her and Daddy both until he believed again.

The boys were stirring, ready to dash off. She stood and sent a stern look at them. "Carry your plates to the sink so I can wash 'em." She'd do the dishes without complaining. If this was her last day in Millersberg, she wanted it to be a real good one for everybody. Especially for Mother. A lump filled her throat.

Beckett picked up his plate, but he stayed there grinning at Mother. "There's a surprise in the backyard for you. Come out and see!"

Evelyn huffed, dislodging the lump. "Don't you remember what the doctor said? Mother isn't supposed to be moving around a lot today." His smile faded fast, and Mother raised her eyebrows. Evelyn winced. She needed to be kinder in how she talked. She made her voice gentle. Like Mother's. How Jesus probably talked to people. "Go ahead and tell her what it is. She doesn't have to see it to be excited about it."

Beckett's eyes lit up again. "Mr. Holbrook helped me, and we got the garden all dug up and weeded. It's ready for plantin' things."

Mother steepled her hands under her chin and broke into a big smile. "That's wonderful! I'll give you some money, and you children can walk to Ebright's and buy seeds."

Beckett strutted to the sink with his plate, and Guy scampered after him.

Evelyn stacked everyone else's plates on hers and took them to the sink. As she set them down, she thought about something. She hurried back to the table. "Mother, Daddy didn't come in for breakfast, and we ate all the biscuits. May I toast some bread and take it to him?"

Mother squeezed Evelyn's elbow. "Of course, sweetheart." She rose and quirked her finger at the boys. "Come, let's make a list of the seeds we need and send you on your way. By the end of the day, we'll have them all planted."

Uncle Scotty had been leaning against the counter, watching her like he wasn't sure he knew who she was. Now he lurched upright and pointed at Mother. "I'll let you supervise, but you ain't gonna do any diggin'."

Evelyn nodded at him. "That's right."

He winked at her, and it felt so good to be in cahoots with him she went warm from the roots of her hair to her toes. She finished making Daddy's toast and put the slices on a plate. She told Uncle Scotty, "Leave them dishes. I'll see to 'em when I get back."

"Yes, ma'am." He poured himself another cup of coffee and ambled to the table.

Evelyn darted out the back door as fast as she could go without dumping the toast. She went past the hens clucking in their pen and into the store. "Daddy?"

He popped out from between two shelves. He was holding a feather duster, and it looked so funny in his hand that she couldn't stop a giggle from spilling. She shoved the plate at him. "I brung you some breakfast. It ain't much, but we ate all the biscuits Mother made."

He gave a little jerk, like somebody'd bumped him from behind. Then he jammed the handle of the duster into his back pocket and took the plate. "That's all right. Toast and jam'll do fine." He picked up one piece, but he didn't carry it to his mouth. He kept looking at her, his lips shifting back and forth like he wanted to ask something but wasn't sure he should.

Evelyn had an idea what he was thinking. "Mother told me you want us to go back to New York."

He put the toast on the plate. He walked to the counter and set the plate down, then held out his arms. At first she wasn't sure she wanted his hug. But the look on his face—so sad and hopeful—

sent her flying across the floor. She laid her cheek against his chest, and his arms closed around her. His chin rested real light on the top of her head. "Evvie, I'm sorry to take you away from your new mother. But New York's our home. It's where we belong."

Evelyn pulled back a little bit so she could see Daddy's eyes. "Are you sure?"

For a second or two, his forehead pinched hard, the way hers did when she was puzzling over something. But then it cleared and he nodded. A slow, single, hardly there bob of his head. "I'm sure."

She sighed and wriggled loose. "You're my daddy, and I'll do what you say. But . . ." She sucked in her lips and silently asked God for courage. "I know you're wanting to leave as soon as we can, but tomorrow's Sunday. Church day. Can we at least wait until after church? I wanna go to Sunday school so I can thank Mrs. Stafford for being such a good teacher. Then I wanna sit with Mother and Uncle Scotty and the boys and Winnie for the preaching. And . . ." She didn't want Daddy to get mad, but she had to ask. "Would you go with us? I'd like to have my whole family with me on a church pew before we have to leave town."

Daddy's expression didn't change. He didn't even blink—maybe didn't even breathe. Just stared straight into Evelyn's eyes while the clock on the wall *ticktock*ed slow and even and she waited for him to say yes or no.

All of a sudden his breath whooshed out and his shoulders went limp. "All right, Evvie. Yes. I'll go."

Callum

Callum checked his reflection in the standing mirror in what had probably been Silas and Ruby Klein's bedroom. Even after almost a full week of staying in the house, he still hesitated before walking into rooms. But if he was going to attend a worship service in a church building, he should make sure he looked halfway decent. He hadn't gone to church in so long he didn't even own a suit anymore, but he'd put on the nicest of the trousers and shirts he'd brought with him. He shook his head at his image in the mirror. Not even a string tie to dress things up.

He turned his back on the mirror and groaned. Would folks turn up their noses at him? Maybe he shouldn't go. But he'd told Evvie he would. He could put up with a few snubs for his daughter's sake.

He locked the back door and crossed the street just as Hester, Scotty, and the children came out of the house. He got a good look at them and winced. Scotty wore a suit, and even the boys wore jackets with their knickers. Did Scotty have a jacket Callum could borrow? He sped his steps, intending to ask, and he suddenly realized someone was missing from their little group—Mary. Even though she'd given him lots of anxious moments, worry about the girl chased away his concern about his clothes.

He trotted the final distance and stopped next to Scotty. "Isn't Mary coming?"

Evvie took hold of his hand, sadly shaking her head. "She doesn't feel good. I still think Dr. Ash should come take a look at her, but Mary says no."

Callum caught Hester's eye, and the two seemed to silently agree a change in subject was best. He tucked a strand of Evvie's hair behind her ear. "I'm sure she'll be fine."

Guy was swinging his arms as if trying to take flight. "We're takin' the Model T this morning so Ma an' Uncle Scotty don't get worn-out."

Callum looked at the group and then the shiny vehicle. He arched one eyebrow. "Who's going to ride on the bumper?"

Hester laughed. "We can all crowd in, but Evelyn asked to walk to church, the way we usually do. I'm sure you'll want to walk with her."

He gave Evelyn's hand a little tug. "Unless you'd like to stay here with Mary instead."

She rolled her eyes. "Da-a-a-addy."

He held up his hands in defeat. "All right. Let's go."

They returned Guy's exuberant waves from the back seat of the automobile as it rolled past, and then they followed the edge of the dirt road, hand in hand. Despite where they were headed, Callum enjoyed walking under the morning sun with his daughter. It raised memories of similar walks with Freida and Evvie when the girl was small enough to be carried. The remembrances were sweet, and an involuntary sigh left his chest.

Evelyn looked up at him. "You really don't want to go, do you?"

For a moment, he thought she meant New York. Then he realized she was talking about church. He gestured to his clothes. "Not really. I'm gonna stick out like a sore thumb in these duds."

She glanced down his length and shrugged. "You look fine to me. Besides, God doesn't care what you're wearing. There's a verse . . . in one of the Samuels . . . when He was showing Samuel which of Jesse's sons were supposed to be the new king. It says men look at our outsides but that God looks at our hearts."

A chuckle scraped past his dry throat. "I'm not sure that's gonna make things much better on my part, Evvie."

"Thank you for going with me, Daddy, even though you don't believe in God anymore." Her face puckered. "But can I tell you something?"

"Of course you can." He answered quickly, but inwardly he wondered what he might hear.

"I stopped believing in God after Mama died and you left Winnie and me at the home."

Her voice was so sad it pierced Callum. He squeezed her hand.

"I blamed Him, and it made me really mad at Him. But I've been thinking about it a lot since I came here."

Callum's feet automatically slowed as he gazed at his little girl's profile—a profile that had lost its chubby cheeks and wide-eyed innocence as maturity etched its beauty into her face.

"I'm still sad that Mama died. A part of me always will be, and I'll always wonder why it happened. But Mama loved God so much. I know she's in heaven with Him now. She isn't mad at Him. She's happier'n she's ever been before. And when I get there"—a smile lifted the corners of her rosy lips—"I think she'll be first in line behind Jesus, ready to give me a big welcome-home hug."

An image of Freida, her smile joyful, flashed in his mind's eye, and his heart fluttered in his chest.

"How can I be mad when I know Mama is safe and happy? Being mad all the time made me ugly. I was hateful to people. Especially to Mother." She stopped and stared straight ahead, her chin quivering. "But she loved me anyway. I finally figured out the reason she could be loving even when I was ugly is because she loves God so much. Her loving Him helped her love me, and it helped me love God again." She squinted up at Callum. "Does that make sense?"

He nodded, thinking of Billy. The man's love for God had spilled over on Callum when they were still strangers. What had Billy asked him that day he'd come to his apartment? He searched his memory, and the man's comment rose from the back of his mind—*"You suffered a loss. Anger's a natural response. But staying there doesn't do you much good, does it?"*

Billy'd been right. Being mad at God wasn't helping him a bit. He saw in his daughter's face a peace beyond her years, and she'd found it by releasing her anger and stepping fully into the light of God's love for her. He needed to follow his little girl's example.

He pulled her snug to his side and kissed the top of her head. "It makes good sense, and I'm glad you told me. But we're gonna be late to church if we don't hurry up."

She grinned and skipped ahead two small steps, reaching for his hand. He caught hold, pausing to take in what she shared and letting it renew his soul. In his heart, he also took hold of the One who'd been waiting for him to look to heaven again. With every forward step, his apprehension about how he'd be received by the members of Hester's church slipped away. What did it matter what men thought when he was once again in right standing with the God of his youth?

At the churchyard, they joined the flow of people entering the building. Folks from young to old offered smiles and hellos of welcome—not a hint of disgust or disapproval on any face. Callum went in, but he doubted that the preacher's sermon, no matter how fiery or inspirational, could top the lesson he'd already been given by his very own daughter.

Chapter Thirty-Nine

Hester

Sitting with Winnie on her lap and Evelyn beside her, Hester battled conflicting emotions throughout the church service. The best word to describe the hour was *bittersweet.* Bitter because after today, she wouldn't have two daughters in her home. Sweet because she and her little family nearly filled a pew from Scotty at one end to Callum at the other—a privilege she'd never thought would be hers.

When the service ended, she lifted Winnie onto her hip even though the child was almost too leggy to carry. But she wanted one more memory of holding the little girl close. They filed out, frequently pausing as people greeted Callum or asked about Scotty's recovery. They finally reached her Model T and she turned to Callum.

"I left a roast and root vegetables in the oven. It's best if we hurry home. Guy or Beckett can sit in the front seat with Scotty and me. If Winnie sits on your lap"—Winnie laid her head on Hester's shoulder—"the rest of you should fit in the back seat. It will be crowded, but it isn't a long drive."

"That's fine." Callum held out his arms to Winnie. "Come with Daddy."

Winnie didn't budge.

Hester bounced her a bit, forcing a soft laugh. "Mama can't drive us home unless you let go." The last time she'd handed Winnie to Callum, the little girl made a terrible fuss. She prayed it wouldn't happen today. The girls would leave with him soon. Winnie had to fully accept her father. "Go to Daddy now, honey."

Winnie sighed out a meek "Okay." Hester handed her to Callum and then hurried around to the driver's seat.

She drove home, frequently glancing in the rearview mirror at Winnie perched on Callum's knee and leaning against his chest. With each peek, her heart lurched. Another bittersweet moment—the child was content, but not with Hester.

As they climbed out of the automobile, Hester gave the reminder she'd given every other Sunday upon their return from church. "Children, please change out of your church clothes while I put dinner on the table."

The boys galloped ahead, Guy whooping. Scotty ambled after them. Callum, still carrying Winnie, trailed on his heels. But Evelyn lagged behind. Hester stopped and waited for her to catch up. "Are you all right, sweetheart?"

Evelyn sighed. "I'm fine. Just feeling a little sad. It was my last time at church. Last times are sort of . . ."

Hester had the perfect word. "Bittersweet?"

"Yes. That's it." She hung her head. "I was hoping to unlock my castle in the sky."

Hester put her finger under Evelyn's chin and lifted her face. "What do you mean?"

A sheepish grin formed on Evelyn's lips. "It's from *Little Women.* Jo says she has the key to her castle in the sky. Mr. Herriott said the castle in the sky represented happiness, and the key meant she had everything she needed to make her dreams come true. I wanted to stay here—at my castle in the sky—but I guess I don't have the key after all."

Hester pulled the girl into a hug. "Honey, you have the key to happiness no matter where you go, because Jesus goes with you. He's the real key to joy and contentment."

Evelyn sniffled and nodded against Hester's shoulder.

Hester put her arm around Evelyn's waist and drew her forward. "Years ago, I read a poem written by a man in Germany. I don't remember all of it, but one part has stayed with me. It was a call not to cry because something was over but to be happy because it once was."

"Don't cry because it's over, but be happy because it once was." A smile slowly brightened Evelyn's face. "I like that, Mother. I'm going to go write it down in my notebook so I always remember it." She ran to the house and let the screen door slam behind her.

Hester reached the back door, and Scotty opened it for her. "Miz Hester, Mary ain't here. Where do you reckon she went?"

Callum strode up from the kitchen. "I think I know."

Hester met his gaze and nodded. Odd how often their thoughts seemed to align. She touched Scotty's arm. "Do you mind feeding the children? I'll go with Callum and find out if our supposition is correct."

"Makes me no never-mind. But there might not be any roast left if you don't hurry. Them boys have hollow legs."

"Thank you, Scotty." Hester accompanied Callum into the yard and across the street. At the Kleins' back door, he checked the knob. It was unlocked. As they stepped inside, Hester called, "Mary? Are you here?"

Very quickly, the girl appeared from the opening to the hallway. She sent a surprised look to both of them. "Is church over already?"

Callum slipped his hands into his pocket. "It sure is. We were worried when you weren't where we left you."

Hester gave a start at his use of the word *we*. When had they become unified in their concern for Mary? The realization was both disconcerting and comforting. She brushed her fingers down Mary's sleeve. "What are you doing over here?"

"The same thing I've been doing for more'n a week already. Trying to find some hidden money." Mary sighed. "I wonder if my grandma made up the story about Uncle Silas hiding money from Aunt Ruby. She never cared much for Aunt Ruby for some reason. But if she made it all up, what'm I gonna do? I can't stay in Millersberg, and I can't leave unless I have money."

Hester slipped her hand through the bend of Mary's arm and drew her toward the back door. "Come with us." *Us.* It felt amazingly good—amazingly right—to use the simple word. "After dinner, we'll sit down and do some praying and thinking." She hugged Mary's arm to her side. "I know you feel helpless and alone right now, but you aren't. God is always with you, and He has a plan for your life that won't be thwarted. We just need to find His pathway."

Mary's eyes flooded. "I can't forget Pa saying I've shamed the whole family. He said God's blistering mad and won't help me."

Hester started to answer, but Callum leaned in and put his hand on Mary's shoulder. "People will fail us, Mary, but God never gives up on us. He gives those who mourn beauty for ashes. You remember that."

Hester gazed at him in amazement. What a perfect thing to tell this hurting young woman. And what a soothing message for her battered heart. They returned to her house and crowded in with the others around the table. To Hester's relief, Mary took a good portion of meat and vegetables. She needed nourishment not only for herself but also for the baby growing in her womb.

When they finished eating, Evelyn turned to Callum. "Do you want me to pack all our stuff now?"

Callum stared at her for a few seconds, his brow furrowing, and then he shook his head. "Not quite yet. I need to talk to your mother."

Hester's heart gave such a leap her entire body jolted. What was he saying? Would he leave the girls with her after all? But she couldn't approach that subject until they'd settled things for Mary. She swallowed twice before she found her voice. "Scotty, will you put Winnie down for her nap?"

"Sure thing. Then I might take one myself."

"Thank you. Evelyn and Beckett, please see to the dishes. And, Guy, with all our seed planting yesterday, we neglected the chickens. Their straw needs raked out and replaced. Please do that, and then come in and wash up. With soap." She skipped her gaze over each of their faces as she spoke. "We'll be across the street having a private chat. I expect you to behave while we're gone. Stay quiet so you don't wake Winnie."

"Yes, ma'am," the boys chorused.

Evelyn sent a confused look at her father. "How long will you be?"

Callum glanced at Hester and shrugged. "As long as it takes." He gestured to the back door. "Let's go, ladies."

No one spoke a word as they crossed the street once again and entered the Klein house. Questions concerning Callum's delay in having Evelyn pack their belongings pressed for release, but Hester held them inside. Whatever his reasoning, tending to Mary took precedence. They settled in the parlor—Callum in one of the wingback chairs, and Hester next to Mary on the sofa.

Hester put her hand on the young woman's knee and gave a gentle squeeze. "Mary, before we discuss you leaving Millersberg, may I ask a very personal question?"

The girl nodded.

"Do you want this baby?"

Mary looked aside. "It's still so new I really don't know. Part of me does. It's my baby. But part of me is scared. I'm eighteen. I don't have a husband. My folks won't help me. Gerry left me to deal with this all by myself." She turned to Hester, agony evident in her expression. "When it's born, what'll I do? Will I even be able to love it when I h-hate its father?"

Callum propped his elbows on his knees, bringing him closer to them. "As you said, it's still new and lots of people are trying to figure out how they feel. The baby won't be here for months. Things can change in that amount of time. It seems to me what you need right now is a safe place to stay until your folks calm down and you decide what to do."

How astute of him. Hester gave him a nod of approval. "Yes, I agree. You're welcome to stay with me." If Evelyn and Winnie were gone, there'd be plenty of room for her. "But I understand if you want to go away from here. Sometimes we need to get away to think clearly and make a fresh start." She'd gotten her fresh start in Millersberg, counties from the family who'd taken her in but never really loved her. She'd met Dale, and her life changed forever. "At your age and in your condition, you shouldn't be alone, though. You need to be with someone who will provide emotional support, see that you receive good care, and be there to help you after the baby is born. Do you have a relative or close friend who would take you in until the baby comes?"

Mary hung her head. "No. No one."

They sat in silence for several minutes, Hester searching her mind for a location that would meet Mary's and the baby's needs. "What about the poor farm in Marion County? I believe they've given shelter to young women in your condition who found themselves alone."

Mary made a face. "I don't wanna sound ungrateful, Mrs. Haak, but I've got kin in Marion, too. My great-grandfather Klein had children with three different wives, and they're scattered hither and yon. There's hardly anyplace I can go in Marion County that somebody won't be my kin or know my kin."

"Well, then, perhaps—"

"William Francis Shelton." Callum half whispered the name.

Hester looked at him. "What did you say?"

He sat up. "William Francis Shelton. He's a really fine Christian man who lives in New York. He helped me get to Millersberg so I could be with my girls again. He might know someone who would give you shelter until the baby comes and you decide what you want to do."

"New York?" Hope glimmered in Mary's tear-wet eyes. "That'd be away from anybody who knows me." Then her expression clouded. "But it'll cost an awful lot for me to travel that far. I . . . I haven't hardly got two nickels to rub together right now."

Callum stood as abruptly as if he'd been fired from a cannon. "I need a telephone. Is there a telephone I could use anywhere besides the post office? This shouldn't wait even another day."

Hester rose as well, his nervous energy making her restless. "The Staffords have one. If it's an emergency, I'm sure they'd let you use it."

"Will you take me there?"

Hester turned to Mary. "Are you all right here by yourself for a little while?"

Mary released a sad laugh. "I don't think I'm gonna be all right until after this baby's born and I can put all this behind me. But there's no place else I know to go."

Hester leaned down and gave her a quick hug, then crossed to Callum. "All right, let's go."

Callum

Callum thrummed his fingers on the windowsill while Hester drove him to the Staffords' house. Was he losing his senses? First he'd told Evelyn to wait on packing. Then he'd gotten the idea concerning how to fix Mary's situation. If Billy said there was a place for Mary in New York, would he really sacrifice the money he'd been given for his own travel? It seemed a foolhardy thing to do, yet he couldn't shake the notion he'd been sent to Millersberg for more than to collect his daughters.

When Hester told Mary that God had a plan for her life that couldn't be thwarted, he felt certain she was talking to him as well. He needed to stop running willy-nilly, forging his own pathway, and seek God's path. It wouldn't be easy. Freida always said he was a bullheaded man—proud and independent. But Evelyn had changed with God's help. Callum now wanted God's help. As he'd told Mary, God wouldn't turn away.

Hester pulled up in front of a bungalow with a big front porch. She held her foot on the Model T's brake and gave him a bashful look. "Do you want me to go in with you?"

"Thank you, but I'll be fine. In fact, I can walk to your place when I'm done. Why don't you go on back and see to Mary? Talk her into going home with you so she's not all by herself." A smile pulled at his lips, and he couldn't resist reaching over and touching her fingers on the steering wheel. "You have a way of putting people at ease. Mary needs that right now."

Her face flooded pink. "All right." He opened the passenger door, and she added, "Good luck."

He paused, one foot out of the vehicle. "Not good luck, Hester. We don't need luck when we've got God on our side." The *our* slipped out as if they'd always been a team. His heart rolled over in his chest. Well, maybe they were a team, destined to share in raising his—*their*—daughters. "Say a prayer, would you, that if this is God's will, it'll all fall into place?"

"Of course I will."

He loved that she agreed without asking for details. She was a rare woman. He gave her a smile, hopped out, and jogged up to the minister's front door.

Chapter Forty

Hester

Fall into place. The phrase became a celebratory anthem ringing through Hester's head that third day of May in 1931. She'd never forget the victory on Callum's face when he stepped into the house less than an hour after being deposited at the Staffords' and announced, "God threw open a door. My friend Billy says Mary can stay with him and his wife until the baby's born." Hester would forever cherish the memory of Callum tenderly taking Mary by the hands and explaining that God had kept him in Millersberg long enough to become aware of her need and had provided the means—"Even before I came here!"—to take her to a place where she could heal.

When Callum pulled the money intended for his and the girls' train tickets from his pocket and placed it in Mary's hands, Evelyn gasped. "Daddy, does this mean . . . we're not going?"

Callum shrugged. "For now. I don't know about later. We'll have to wait and see where God leads."

Together they decided Hester would drive Mary to the train depot in Marion early Monday morning while Scotty and Callum operated the store. Mary, her face blotchy from weeping, thanked them all and then asked Evelyn to help her pack. The two young women went to the Klein house, and Scotty asked Guy and Beckett if they'd like to go fishing. The boys dashed out the door, and Scotty winked at Hester. "We'll be back before supper, hopefully with a string o' fish for fryin'." He sauntered after them.

Hester and Callum were left alone in the living room while

Winnie slept peacefully in her bed a few yards away. Hester gazed across the room at Callum and shook her head, marveling at everything that had happened in such a short time. Things were definitely falling into place for Mary, but what about for Callum? What about for Evelyn and Winnie? So many questions flooded her mind, but only one spilled from her mouth.

"Callum, why?"

He'd been sitting on the edge of the sofa, but he slid backward until his spine met the backrest. He fiddled with a button on his plaid shirt, his unwavering gaze fixed on her face. "Almost a month ago, a man I hardly knew knocked on my apartment door and gave me a fistful of money. He said God had told him how to collect it and it was meant to get me to Millersberg. I didn't understand then how he knew God told him." One side of his lips lifted in a wry grin. "God and me . . . we weren't on speakin' terms, you might say."

A look of wonder crept over his chiseled face. "But on the way to church this morning, my little girl reminded me how much God loves me—still loves me even though I turned my back on Him. The peace I saw in her face made me want it for myself. I thought maybe that's why God had sent me here—to find Him again. And I still think that's true, but there's more."

He cupped his hands over his knees, as if he needed to hold himself in place. "When we were over at the Klein house with Mary after dinner, the name of the man who'd given me train-ticket money came out of my mouth without me even knowing I was gonna say it. And right behind his name, I thought, Mary doesn't need to find money. I've got money." He angled his head slightly, as if trying to hear something from the distance. "Hester, I believe God put Billy's name in my mouth and reminded me about the train-ticket money. When Billy and his wife right away offered to give Mary a safe place to stay, I knew it was right."

Hester pondered his words, amazement rolling through her.

He'd been so determined to leave. This abrupt change must have been orchestrated by God. But . . . She licked her lips and gathered up her thoughts. "It took faith and courage to give that money to Mary. Because you did it without knowing how you'll replace it."

A soft chuckle rumbled. "Yeah, I confess, on our way to the Staffords, I wondered if I'd lost my mind. But I had so much peace about doing it I knew it was right. God brought me here. He kept me here beyond my plans. He prompted me to use that money to send Mary to Billy's house. I guess that means"—his smile of trust and contentment nearly stole Hester's breath—"God will open up a place for me to live and give me a job so I can stay here with my girls. For as long as He wants me here, I'll stay."

On Monday, Hester saw Mary safely off to New York. When Hester got back, Scotty was alone in the store. He said Callum had gone to Ebright's to ask about clerking for him. She wasn't at all surprised when Callum strutted in later and proudly announced he'd gotten the job. That same afternoon, when Dr. Ash came by to check Scotty's incision, Callum tried to return the key to the Klein house to him.

The man shook his head. "In these hard financial times, nobody's going to buy it. At least not for what it's worth. But structures go to rot and ruin if they aren't occupied. If you'll keep up the place, you can stay there until this economic depression lifts."

As the doctor left, Callum held up the key and winked at Hester. "Things're falling into place."

Having him right across the street gave Evelyn and Winnie the freedom to see him every day. He joined the family for evening meals and then stayed and helped tuck the children into bed. Bit by bit, his relationship with Winnie grew closer and Hester found herself growing more and more at ease with him.

Things fell into place not only for Mary and Callum but for

Hester and Beckett as well. A week after Mary's departure, the sheriff's officer who previously visited entered the store and handed Hester the official documents transferring Beckett's custody to her. He also brought a letter from a judge—a written query into her willingness to foster other children in need of care.

She discussed it first with Scotty, then the children, and finally—since his daughters would be affected by the decision—with Callum. They prayed together as a family, and every person from Scotty to Winnie gave approval. So she penned an agreement to open her home to more children. As she sealed the envelope, she laughed. "I guess it's time we put that lumber waiting behind the store to use. Scotty, can you get those rooms built upstairs?"

He rubbed his palms together. "You bet I can! An' I'll git the sidewinder to help me." His teasing grin assured her he no longer held animosity toward Callum. As the men worked together to transform her attic into sleeping rooms, they developed an easy camaraderie that thrilled Hester's heart. When they finished the attic, they took down the sheets and put walls in their place.

In early June, an official from Marion delivered Hester's first foster children—a brown-haired, brown-eyed brother-sister pair named Lee and Delilah. Delilah and Winnie were only weeks apart in age and immediately bonded over their love of dolls and pretend play. Lee fell in age between Guy and Beckett. He was accepted into their close relationship, and before long, Evelyn dubbed the trio of boys the Three Musketeers.

What a glorious summer she enjoyed, living out the things she'd always imagined doing with her children. Picnics on Sunday afternoons, attending music concerts played by the community band on Main Street on Saturday evenings, taking the children swimming in the creek while Scotty and Callum dropped their fishing lines upstream, lying with the children on the grass at dusk and watching stars wink from high in the graying sky . . .

In mid-July, Scotty heard through the local grapevine that the Tipton twins were seeking homes for a litter of pups born to their collie. Although Guy's birthday wasn't until September, Hester drove him to the Tiptons' farm and let him choose a puppy. He picked up the biggest of the litter, a gangly legged, shaggy brown-and-white pup, and held the creature at arm's length. After giving it a thorough inspection, he broke into a smile. "Yep, you're the one. Hi, Frank. I've been waitin' for you my whole life." Then he cradled the dog under his chin. Hester viewed the scene through a veil of tears.

As she and Guy, who held the wriggly pup over his shoulder, headed to the Model T, Amos Tipton called after them, "Before you go, wanna peek at the newest litter of barn cats?"

Guy's face lit, and before Hester knew what she was doing, she agreed to take a brown tiger-striped kitten home to Winnie. The delighted child named the timid little cat Clyde. Frank stayed in the house, but they made Clyde's residence the store, where he could keep mice at bay.

She gathered up memories the way she hid away the little gifts the children brought her—sweetly handwritten notes and pictures, a wilted flower, a pretty rock—in the chest in her bedroom. At times, she grew weary, but not weariness brought on by loneliness. It was a good kind of weariness that let her sleep hard and awake refreshed.

With six children in the house ages four to fourteen, there was more laundry, more food to prepare, more messes to clean and squabbles to settle. Evelyn and Beckett helped with the younger ones, and Scotty and Callum pitched in as well. Even so, there were days she could only define as chaotic. But Hester called it happy chaos. She thanked God every night for the fulfillment of her long-held dreams.

Having Callum across the street proved a blessing in more than his being easily accessible to Evelyn and Winnie and being available to help Scotty with construction projects. Over time, Guy, Beckett, Lee, and Delilah began to view Callum as a father figure. He stepped into the role without a word of complaint, secretly confessing to Hester one evening over coffee that he'd grown up an only child and always hoped for a houseful of youngsters. "God didn't answer the way I thought He would, but He sure answered," he'd told her.

She understood his reasoning. She hadn't borne a child from her womb as she'd hoped, but if she had, would she have opened her home to the children now residing under her roof? Probably not. And now that they were here, she could not imagine being without them. God's plan was best. Her heart overflowed with joy for the blessing and love and challenge each of the children brought to her life. She also thanked God for the easy friendship she enjoyed with Callum. Although some might call it unconventional, she considered him an important member of her family. Each day pushed worry about him departing for New York with Evelyn and Winnie further from her mind.

When fall arrived, Winnie and Delilah trooped off to school with the older children. After a busy, noisy, active summer with children slamming in and out of the store all day long, a hush fell in their absence. Scotty seemed to appreciate the quiet. She took no insult from it. Given his age, having what could feel like a litter of puppies bouncing around his feet might be overwhelming at times, even though she knew he loved each of the children and gloried in his title of Uncle Scotty. But it took Hester back to the days before she drove to Marion and brought Evelyn, Winnie, and Guy home and offered a harbinger of when the children all grew up and departed. Although having an empty house was still years into the future, the thought of it brought an element of melancholy.

September slipped by, and October eased in with its golden leaves and cooler air. The local band returned to practicing in the church basement, and the concerts ended. With the temperatures dropping, Scotty complained of his knees and hips bothering him. Instead of sitting with Hester in the evenings, he retired after supper to his little room, the space heater he'd ordered from the Sears, Roebuck & Company catalog, and Clyde's company.

But Callum stayed, and he and Hester talked. About the children—the funny things they did or said, how school was going, and any concerns they encountered. About the store—repairs that needed to be made or ways to bring in more customers to better meet the needs of her growing family. About expanding the garden next spring and getting a few more chickens and even raising rabbits for a ready meat source. About the preacher's latest sermon and its application to their walks of faith. They talked about everything except their unusual relationship.

Sometimes when remembering the joy of being Dale's wife, Hester considered asking Callum if he viewed her as more than a friend. But afraid of destroying their easy companionship, she held the query inside. What she had with him was special. Why ruin it by expecting more? Callum willingly played a supporting role, a gift in itself. God had blessed her abundantly, so she chose to be content.

Chapter Forty-One

Hester

At closing time on November twenty-third, Hester's thirty-ninth birthday, Scotty stopped her as she was leaving the store. "The children've got a surprise for you, but we need you to hold off a bit. Do you mind?"

With Thanksgiving coming that week, the day had been exceptionally busy. Hester was ready to go in, have dinner, and then perhaps sit with her feet up for a few minutes. But she couldn't spoil whatever the children were planning. She returned to the counter. "Not at all. I haven't had a chance to look at the mail yet. I'll keep myself occupied until you're ready for me."

With a smile and wink, Scotty headed out, and Hester pulled from beneath the counter the mail Guy had brought after school. She held two envelopes, both with New York postmarks—one for Callum from W. Shelton, and one for Hester from Mary. Her heart gave a leap. She tore open the one from Mary and flattened the folded pages on the counter.

Dear Mrs. Haak,

I wanted you to know that I had my baby on November 9. A boy. He was pretty little, only six pounds, but the doctor said he's fine and healthy. I named him William Callum after the two men who helped me so much. (If William had been a girl, he would've been Hester Ruth after you and Mrs. Shelton.)

Remember when you and Mr. Holbrook told me that things were still new and I'd need time to think it all through? I've had all these months here in New York to think. I talked to Mr. and Mrs.

Shelton a lot and to their preacher and his wife. Did a lot of praying, too, with them and by myself, trying to figure out what's best. They all said I shouldn't make any big decisions until after the baby was born and Gerry and my folks knew it was here.

Well, I've called Gerry's folks and my folks. They haven't changed their minds. They don't want me, and they don't want William. It's been a full week now with William sleeping in a little basket beside my bed. Every day, I've prayed for God to tell me what I'm supposed to do. I love him, even though he looks like Gerry with his fuzzy blond hair and navy-blue eyes. But I don't know how I can take care of him unless I have help. The Sheltons are wonderful and said I can stay as long as I want, but they're not young. It isn't fair for them to help me for years on end. And the more I think about raising him on my own, the more I know I'm not ready. He deserves better.

The preacher here said he'd help me find a good family to take William, but I don't want to give him to strangers. Not unless I have to. That's why I'm writing to you. I know it's asking a lot, and if you say no, I won't hold a grudge against you, but I watched you with Evelyn, Winnie, Guy, and Beckett. You didn't give birth to those kids, but you love them. I know you'd love William, too. Maybe even more than I do because you don't have any reason to feel bitter about him. He ought to be really, really loved by his mama.

Mr. Holbrook has the Sheltons' telephone number. You can call me here and let me know what you want to do. Even if you don't want William, I thank you for being so kind to me when I needed it. I hope to hear from you soon.

Love, Mary

Hester set the letter aside, her pulse thrumming a wild beat. A newborn? She crossed her arms against her ribs, a desire to cradle this little baby boy creating a sweet ache. Embers of love were already stirring to life in the center of her heart. But how would she care for a newborn and run the store? Back when she and Dale were trying to have children, they'd planned that Dale would operate the store on his own and let her simply be Mama. She couldn't shift such responsibility on Scotty. And she couldn't close the store until the baby was old enough to spend his days with her the way Winnie had.

"Ma?" Guy burst into the store, his face alight with excitement. "We got your present ready. Come in!"

Hester touched Mary's letter with her fingertips, giving it one more longing look, and then rounded the counter. "I'm coming."

She entered the kitchen on Guy's heels and then stopped and gasped in shock. A new table filled the dining area of the kitchen. Benches lined the sides in place of the chairs and crates they'd used before. Two chairs remained—one at each end. "What . . . How . . . When . . ."

The children beamed at her, the littlest ones nearly dancing in glee. Evelyn crossed to her and gave her a hug. "Happy birthday, Mother! Do you like it?"

Hester laughed and clapped her hands to her cheeks. "I love it! But who did this?"

Scotty scratched his cheek. "The kids, me, an' Callum cooked it up for you. When I went to Marion to fetch your last order, I picked up the table an' benches from the furniture store over there. Callum kept it all hid at the Klein house 'til now."

Evelyn giggled. "But it's kind of for us, too, because we were so cramped around the other one."

Beckett threw his arms wide. "And now if you wanna adopt even more children, there's room for them."

Indeed there was. "It's a beautiful table and benches, children. Thank you." Overcome with emotion, she drew on teasing. "But . . . are we not going to have any dinner?"

Evelyn rolled her eyes, but she grinned. "Dinner's in the oven.

And a cake's coolin' on the windowsill. We'll eat when Daddy gets here." She shooed Hester toward the living room. "Get out of our way so we can set the table and get everything ready."

Hester gladly sat and listened to the sounds of merriment carrying from the kitchen. *Her* children preparing *her* birthday dinner—a joy she'd dreamed of for years and now celebrated in reality. God was so good.

When Callum arrived from work, they all gathered around the table. Callum sat between Evelyn and Winnie on one bench, and the other children scooted onto the second bench. Scotty and Hester took the chairs. Callum offered to say grace, and her heart thrilled in his transformation from a man who ran from God to one who spoke directly to Him. She enjoyed the noodles, canned tuna, and green peas in a mushroom sauce, then partook of a huge piece of chocolate cake, all the while surrounded by happy faces and cheerful chatter. And no one's elbows bumped—a true blessing.

When they were finished eating, the children insisted Hester let them do all the cleanup. She would have protested were it not for the letters in the store. Scotty could supervise. She thanked them, quirked her finger at Callum, and led him outside. "You have a letter waiting from your friend Billy in New York."

"I do? Sure didn't expect that." His pace sped.

She hurried to match it. "I got a letter as well—from Mary. She had her baby."

He came to an abrupt halt and faced her. "Is she okay?"

Regret pinched her chest. She should have remembered how he'd lost his wife and not simply blurted the news. She squeezed his forearm. "Mary's fine. And so is the baby—a little boy named William Callum."

Even in the evening shadows, she saw tears brighten his eyes. He sniffed, and then his lips twitched. "That's a pretty stuffy name for a little fellow. I hope she calls him Willie. Or Billy."

Hester wanted to give a teasing response, but her heart suddenly felt heavy. "She's decided not to keep him. She asked . . ." Her throat went tight. She swallowed. "She asked me to adopt him."

Callum's eyebrows shot high. "You're gonna say yes, aren't you?"

She closed her eyes for a moment, asking God for strength. "I want to. I can't tell you how much I want to. But it isn't practical. I already have six children in my home. I have a store to run. A newborn would keep me up at night and away from the store during the day." She swallowed again, battling regret. "Mary doesn't want to keep him because she doesn't believe she can raise him on her own. She needs help. Well, my situation isn't so different. If I took in a tiny baby, I would need . . . help."

Callum stared at her in silence for what seemed like hours while she stared back, trying to read his thoughts. Then he gave a little start, took hold of her elbow, and escorted her into the store. He punched the button by the door, and light flooded the room. Still lightly holding her arm, he crossed to the counter where Mary's letter lay. He glanced at it, and a sigh left his throat.

"I understand why Mary doesn't think she can raise her baby alone." He leaned against the counter, his expression sad. "I couldn't do it, either. Not without Freida. That's why I put Evvie and Winnie in the orphans' home." Determination suddenly bloomed on his face. "But, Hester, your situation is different. You have help. You have Scotty. Evelyn's a big girl now. She can lend a helping hand. And you have"—he gulped—"me."

Hester moved a few feet away and hugged herself. "Yes, Scotty's a fine help both in the store and with the children. But he's getting older. He needs to be slowing down, not taking full responsibility for the store. And Evelyn is still in school. Her focus should be on her education." She shook her head slowly. "No. I would love the baby—I have no worries about that. But I need to do what's best for him and allow him to be adopted by someone who can give him more attention."

Callum's heels scuffed the floor as he approached. He curled his hands around her upper arms and gazed into her face, his blue eyes fervent. "Would you adopt the baby if you had a husband to operate the store and help you raise him?"

She gently stepped free of his grasp. "Callum . . ."

" 'Callum' what?" He drew close again. "Answer me, please. If you were married, would you take that baby boy into your home and heart?"

Why was he torturing her? She coughed out a strangled half laugh, half sob. "Of course I would, but—"

"Then marry me."

Her mouth fell open. For the count of three heartbeats, she gaped at him, and then she expelled a huff as powerful as any Evelyn had ever produced. "Callum, I can't marry you just so I can take in Mary's baby. Marriage isn't a game to be played. It's a lifelong commitment of love and respect."

"Oh." He turned away and stared across the room, his jaw muscles tense.

She hadn't intended to hurt his feelings. She lightly touched his shoulder blade. "I appreciate the help you've been with the children. You could have taken Evelyn and Winnie across the street into the Klein house and ignored the rest of them, but you didn't. Beckett, Guy, Lee, and Delilah are fortunate to have your influence in their lives."

He angled his head and gave her a puzzled look. "I'm glad to spend time with them. They're all great kids. But I don't come around only for the kids, Hester. I thought you knew that."

She lowered her hand, hope rising in her chest. "What are you saying?"

Callum shifted slightly and fully faced her. "My proposal

wasn't a game. I meant it. You're already my girls' mother. They adore you. How could they not? You're a loving, giving, unselfish, God-honoring woman. I'd be a fool not to fall in love with you." One side of his lips tipped up, a hint of mischief dancing in his eyes. "I might've been a fool before I came here, but I've set my foolishness aside. Is it so hard to believe that I love you?"

Looking into his dear face, she found it possible to believe. But . . . "Why are you telling me this now? You've never said anything like it before. Is it because of the baby?"

"Not because of the baby. And as for why I haven't said it . . ." He shrugged. "I'm not much of a sayer, Hester. I'm more of a doer. I've tried to show you how I felt by taking care of the kids, taking care of things in the house, taking care of you. I hoped you'd see it."

She had seen it. Had appreciated it. But hadn't allowed herself to see it as more than kindnesses from a friend.

He swallowed, his gaze never wavering from hers. "Since I'm talking now, lemme ask you a question. Do you love me?"

Her heart turned a cartwheel in her chest and stole her ability to speak. She slowly bobbed her head, her lips quivering.

A smile of wonder graced his face. He lifted his hand and cupped her cheek. "Since you gave me that nod, I'll say what I said before—marry me." He paused. "Please?"

Hester found her voice. "Yes."

Still cradling her face in his palm, he leaned and delivered a light, sweet, tender kiss on her lips. Then he straightened and drew her into his embrace. She clung, marveling at the turn her life was taking.

"Callum," she said from within the circle of his arms, "shouldn't we go back in with the children?"

His arms tightened briefly, and then he released her with a sigh. "Yes, we should. But let me read Billy's letter first." He strode to the counter and picked up the envelope. He loosened the flap and removed a single piece of paper. His eyes scanned it, and then he burst out laughing.

Curious, Hester moved closer. "What is it?"

He turned the page and held it up.

Callum,

Mary's been talking. My missus and me think you'd be a fool to let this woman go. Marry the girl and live happily ever after.

—Billy

Hester laughed, too, and fell again into Callum's arms. He rocked her to and fro a few times and then pulled back and gazed tenderly into her face. "So, what do you think? Should we get married before or after we bring our little Billy home?"

"After." Perhaps it wasn't conventional, but she wanted all her children to witness her and Callum vowing to love, honor, and cherish each other—and them—for the rest of their lives.

He gave her another quick kiss and then aimed her for the door. "Come on, Mrs. Holbrook-to-be, let's go tell our children."

Readers Guide

1. Hester wanted to be a mother more than anything. Why do you think having a family was so important to her? God granted her desire but not in the way she expected. How, if at all, would her life have been different if she'd given birth to children rather than adopting them?

2. Callum promised to take his daughters with him from the home "the next time he came," and then a full year passed before he fulfilled the promise. Was he wrong to wait so long? Why or why not?

3. Scotty was a self-proclaimed drifter, yet he stayed in Millersberg. What kept him there? Do you think he stayed after Hester married Callum? Explain why you feel that way.

4. Evelyn's rejection of Hester's attempts to mother her caused a lot of pain. Why do you think she persisted in holding herself aloof? If you were Hester, how would you have responded to Evelyn's behavior? How was Hester able to love Evelyn despite the girl's ill-treatment?

5. Mary's situation sent her seeking a means to get away from everyone who knew her. Was her desire understandable? Why or why not? If Mary were alive today, how would her situation differ from 1931?

6. God often puts people in our lives to help guide us in His will. Name the means by which certain people in the story

influenced each of these characters: Hester, Callum, Scotty, and Evelyn. Who has God sent to influence you? Have you ever been used to influence someone else's faith journey?

7. Dr. Ash tells Callum that roadblocks can be God's means of redirection. How have you experienced redirection? How did it bring blessing to your life?

8. Scotty lacked education, but he didn't lack intelligence. In what ways did he prove his wisdom? He called Hester his angel, but how was he Hester's angel, too?

9. Hester, striving to love as God loves, takes in foster children even though she knows they might not always be with her. Have you or someone you know risked loving someone else's children for a period of time? What were the challenges? The blessings?

Acknowledgments

I'll start with a shout-out to my wonderful family—Dad, Don, my kids, and my grandkids—for cheering me on and giving me fodder for stories and characters (whether they realize it or not). They bless my life every day. And even though Mom graduated to heaven, her influence lives on in all of us and always will.

This story is project sixty-three, and I've never acknowledged a pet, but it's time. My kitties, Maizie and Clyde, were my writing "mewses" since 2008, with Maizie on a chair across the room and Clyde in a little bed on the corner of my desk. Within a few weeks in early 2025, I said goodbye to both, and their absence makes me realize just how much I relied on their furry presence in my writing studio. It's true what they say—pets leave pawprints on our hearts.

I've been represented by my amazing agent, Tamela Hancock Murray, since the very beginning of my writing career. I cannot imagine traversing this publishing pathway without her. She's the best.

My talented editorial team from WaterBrook deserves major kudos for helping me make the stories shine. I'm grateful for the suggestions, encouragement, and assistance. I'm truly blessed.

Finally, and most important, I'm so grateful to my Father God. His hand guides my fingers on the computer keyboard and directs every aspect of my life. Not all steps of this God-designed journey have been smooth, but they've all been worth it. May any praise or glory be given to Him.

About the Author

KIM VOGEL SAWYER is a highly acclaimed bestselling author with more than 1.5 million books in print in seven different languages. Her titles have earned numerous accolades, including the ACFW Carol Award, the Inspirational Reader's Choice Award, and the Gayle Wilson Award of Excellence. Kim and her retired military husband, Don, live in central Kansas, where she continues to write gentle stories of hope. She enjoys spending time with her three daughters and her grandchildren.

Also from bestselling, award-winning author

KIM VOGEL SAWYER

Kim Vogel Sawyer offers uplifting and inspiring fiction that is grounded in biblical truth. With meticulous research, vivid storytelling, and themes of hope, redemption, and faith, these stories offer something for every reader.

Learn more about Kim's books at waterbrookmultnomah.com.